D0457797

THE
LOST STORIES
COLLECTION

ALSO BY MICHAEL SCOTT

The Secrets of the Immortal Nicholas Flamel Series

The Alchemyst

The Magician

The Sorceress

The Necromancer

The Warlock

The Enchantress

Magic and Myth

Legends and Lore

Saint Patrick: An Irish Tale

THE
LOST STORIES
COLLECTION

THE SECRETS OF THE IMMORTAL
NICHOLAS FLAMEL

MICHAEL SCOTT

Delacorte Press

"Aoife of the Shadows" and "Scathach the Shadow and the Clan of Eriu"
originally published as "Aoife and Scathach: the Shadow Twins," copyright © 2011
by Michael Scott. "Nicholas Flamel and the Codex" copyright © 2020 by Michael Scott.
"The Death of Joan of Arc" copyright © 2010 by Michael Scott. "Machiavelli: Guardian
of Paris" copyright © 2020 by Michael Scott. "Virginia Dare and the Ratcatcher"
copyright © 2021 by Michael Scott. "Nicholas and the Krampus" copyright © 2021 by
Michael Scott. "Billy the Kid and the Vampyres of Vegas" text copyright © 2011
by Michael Scott.
Jacket art copyright © 2021 by Sam Spratt

Visit us on the Web! GetUnderlined.com

Educators and librarians, for a variety of teaching tools,
visit us at RHTeachersLibrarians.com

Library of Congress Cataloging-in-Publication Data
Names: Scott, Michael, 1959– author.
Title: The lost stories collection / Michael Scott.
Description: New York : Delacorte Press, [2021] | Series: The secrets of the immortal
Nicholas Flamel | Audience: Ages 12+ | Summary: Told through stories featuring series
favorites the Flamels, Machiavelli, the twins Scatty and Aoife, Virginia Dare, and others as
they carry on with fantastical new adventures of myth and legend.
Identifiers: LCCN 2021019612 (print) | LCCN 2021019613 (ebook) |
ISBN 978-0-593-37690-4 (hardcover) | ISBN 978-0-593-37691-1 (ebook)
Subjects: LCSH: Flamel, Nicolas, –1418—Juvenile fiction. | CYAC: Flamel,
Nicolas, –1418—Fiction. | Alchemists—Fiction. | Magic—Fiction. | Fantasy. |
LCGFT: Fantasy fiction. | Short stories.
Classification: LCC PZ7.S42736 Lo 2021 (print) | LCC PZ7.S42736 (ebook) |
DDC [Fic]—dc23

The text of this book is set in 11.5 Sabon MT Pro.

Printed in the United States of America
10 9 8 7 6 5 4 3 2 1
First Edition

Once again, for Beverly and Krista

CONTENTS

Introduction   *ix*

Aoife of the Shadows (500 BCE)   *1*

Scathach the Shadow and the Clan of Eriu (500 BCE)   *69*

Nicholas Flamel and the Codex (1355)   *109*

The Death of Joan of Arc (1431)   *175*

Machiavelli: Guardian of Paris (1793)   *191*

Virginia Dare and the Ratcatcher (1833)   *265*

Nicholas and the Krampus (1945)   *347*

Billy the Kid and the Vampyres of Vegas (2005)   *413*

INTRODUCTION

Dear reader,

The series that eventually became The Secrets of the Immortal Nicholas Flamel grew out of my fascination with folklore, myth, and legend.

I grew up in Ireland, a country with a wonderfully rich mythology and a folklore that is still vibrant and alive. Because Ireland was never invaded by the Greeks or the Romans, its stories, carried down by oral tradition, remained more or less untouched for centuries. I spent many years traveling, researching, collecting, and writing stories set in the world of Irish folklore before moving to European and then eventually world myth, discovering connections, parallels, and similar stories in just about every culture.

Over years an idea formed: to create a series that would tie together elements drawn from the myths, legends, and history from around the world. In time, that became The Secrets of the Immortal Nicholas Flamel. I started with a simple rule: every nonhuman character in the book and all the creatures and monsters had to be drawn from myth and legend, while all the humans were taken from history. And yes, Nicholas and Perenelle Flamel were real; there are streets named in their honor in Paris, and you can visit one of their homes, the Auberge Nicolas Flamel, on the rue de Montmorency. The only two characters in the series that I invented are the twins, Sophie and Josh Newman, but even then I was drawing from a mythological well: every country has stories about legendary twins.

I spent a decade gathering materials and plotting the books and half that time again writing them. When I completed *The Enchantress,* the last book, I believed I was done with that series. However, Mr. Flamel and that vast cast of characters were not quite done with me.

The events in the six-book Secrets of the Immortal Nicholas Flamel series take place over two weeks, but they exist as part of a vast mythological landscape stretching back thousands of years and around the globe. Characters in the books refer to events that happened in the past, or talk about previous adventures. There is a network of connections and relationships that fascinated the readers.

The Secrets of the Immortal Nicholas Flamel series was published in dozens of countries and scores of languages. When the emails and letters (proper letters with stamps) started to arrive, they almost always included questions: When are you going to write about . . . ? What happened to . . . ? Will we see more of . . . ? When is the next book?

It soon became clear that many readers were asking the same questions, or asking me to tell certain tales. Foremost, of course, was the story of how the Flamels acquired the Codex, the book that drives the series. Certain characters have their own fan clubs. Everyone loves Scathach—without a doubt she is the most popular character in the entire series, second only to Virginia Dare and John Dee.

So I returned to the world of *The Alchemyst* and began to fill in a few of the blanks. The first order of business was to reread the series, and out of that rereading came the inspiration for dozens of ideas for stories.

Some of the stories in this collection are referenced in the books, others will be new, but they all slot into that vast web of stories. They all take place before the events in the series that begins with *The Alchemyst*.

Michael Scott

AOIFE
OF THE SHADOWS

500 BCE

I am Marethyu.

And I am Death.

I am called the Destroyer of Worlds.

I have had other names—many other names—and once, when I was still fully human, I was known by a humani name. But that was a long time ago, and no one has called me by that name in millennia.

Look at me now, and it would be hard to put an age on me. My age is no longer measured in decades or even centuries. I have lost count of the number of years I have moved across this earth and through the adjacent Shadowrealms. I have traveled to places where time does not exist or flows according to different rules. In some myths, I am known as the Ancient of Days.

Eons ago, I made a bargain with a monster who had once been beautiful. He gifted me with the ability to move at will along the time streams, though perhaps it is not so much a gift as a curse. But it allowed me to see what was, what is, and what might be. I realized that the future was never fixed; it was constantly in flux, fashioned and shaped by events in the present. I discovered that a single action could change the future of the world.

I have seen things that were never meant for human eyes. I have traveled far into the future, to that time when the sun has grown huge and red and the creatures that walk the earth, though descended from man, are unrecognizable. I have followed the time streams back into the past, to the Time Before Time, when the rulers of the glittering empires which stretched across the globe were serpentine and monstrous and the humani little more than food and slaves to them. I have gone beyond this world and walked the Shadowrealms, those places of myth created by creatures of legend. Every Shadowrealm is different, each one unique, all of them wondrous and terrifying, and while some are paradises, far too many are deadly. And I should know, for I have created my own Shadowrealms, and destroyed them also when I grew bored of them.

And I fought the creatures in the shadows.

The ancient rulers of the earth had been defeated but not destroyed. They lurked in the dark places, and plotted. And because they were ageless, they conceived plans that took generations to come to fruition.

In time I came to understand that my role was to not only protect the humani from these creatures that threatened their very existence, but also to record the stories of those who stood with the humani against the Earthlords, Ancients, Archons, and Dark Elders. Some of their names and adventures have passed into the myths and legends of every nation. Too many of the stories, however, have been forgotten. Now the humani believe that the Isle of Danu Talis, which they call Atlantis, never existed; they believe that the Great Flood, which swept across the world ten thousand and more years ago, never happened and that there were never giants on the earth and thunderbirds in the skies.

But at the heart of every legend, there is a grain of truth.

Traveling through time allowed me to see that history is made and remade in the tiniest of moments, in the most obscure places. And it is true that I sometimes nudged events in certain directions. I ensured that Nicholas and Perenelle Flamel received the Codex at the correct time, that Machiavelli would encounter Eugene Vidocq in Paris during the Terror, and that Sophie and Josh would be in San Francisco that fateful summer to discover the truth about the bookseller and his wife.

I learned to place trusted agents on significant Shadowrealms in the hope—the *belief*—that their very presence would alter the history not only of that realm, but of all the worlds attached to it.

Two of my most trusted agents were the Shadow Twins: Aoife and Scathach. I could fill volumes with their adventures down through time and across the uncountable Shadowrealms. Their names are woven into the legends of a hundred worlds; they are worshiped as goddesses on a dozen more, considered to be the incarnations of destruction on twice as many. Inseparable from birth, they fell out over a boy, and they spent centuries loathing one another. I did my best to ensure that they were never in the same world at the same time, so I would send them off into distant Shadowrealms in search of clues to the lost past and artifacts from our forgotten history. Though they were separate for many years, they were twins, linked by that most mysterious of bonds, one which I knew all too well. I always knew that they were destined to be drawn back together.

From the Codex
The Journal of Marethyu
Translated by Nicholas Flamel, the Alchemyst
On the Shadowrealm Isle of Tir na nOg

1

A flash of light in the gloomy forest below, a blink of silver in the shadows.

It lasted less than a single heartbeat, vanishing in the same moment that the Airgead Sun dipped below the horizon, leaving only the Óir Sun low in the purpling skies.

"Stop!" The slender young woman in the long waxed cloak, scuffed black leather jerkin and trousers raised a clenched fist as she reined in her tall spiral-horned mount.

Behind her, a dozen huge-wheeled ox-drawn carts came to a lumbering, creaking halt. The long-horned oxen steamed and sweated in the chill air, too exhausted to bellow, and the drovers were experienced enough to remain still and quiet. Six mismatched mercenary guards fell into defensive positions, two on either side and two behind the last wagon, bows and crossbows ready.

Standing in the stirrups, the woman pushed back the hood of a heavy wire-lined cloak, revealing short spiky red hair. Shading bright green eyes against the low light of the setting Óir Sun, she looked ahead and to her left, down into the deeply shadowed valley below the narrow trail.

Moments ago, she'd caught a glimpse of something, but it had vanished as quickly as it appeared. It might have been a trick of the fading suns, the warm golden light of the Óir Sun catching a pool of water, a flock of birds, or weaving bats, but her instincts were telling her otherwise, and Aoife of the Shadows had long ago discovered that warriors who ignored their instincts had a very short life span. Though she looked no older than seventeen, Aoife's age was measured in centuries, and she fully intended to live for at least a millennium.

Sinking back into the saddle, eyes wide and unblinking, she slowly moved her head left and right, not looking at anything in particular, nostrils flaring, confident that if there was anything out of place, then her unconscious mind would spot it.

"What is it?" Nels the wagon master demanded, interrupting her. The huge ox drover pushed his way through the steaming teams to stand alongside Aoife. He caught the horn jutting from the forehead of Aoife's mount and held the beast's head away from his face. The aonbheannach were beautiful but ill-tempered, with huge teeth capable of crushing a man's arm. Even though Aoife was sitting on the tall slender animal, the wagon master's bald and deeply scarred skull was almost on a level with hers.

Aoife shook her head. "I'm not sure," she said quietly, still looking. "I saw something in the valley."

"Where is it?"

"Gone now."

"Probably nothing," Nels grunted. "A reflection, maybe." He tugged at the reins of the aonbheannach, urging it forward.

Aoife clamped booted heels against the beast's side; the creature straightened it legs and refused to move.

Nels gave up. Though they were fine-boned and looked delicate and deer-like, the aonbheannach were as strong as his own oxen and only permitted female riders. The big man looked up at the Óir Sun and then back down the wagon train strung out along the narrow track behind them. "We need to move on. We're leaving a trail even a blind snake could follow."

"Most snakes have terrible eyesight but an excellent sense of smell," Aoife remarked, glancing sidelong at the wagon master.

Nels exuded a sour sweat, which, mingling with the rich odor of oxen, enveloped him in an almost tangible miasma. Aoife suspected that there was Boggart or Torc blood in the stinking wagon leader; she had never seen a man so ugly, and it would certainly account for his perpetual ill-humor.

"The light is fading, and I don't want to be out on the mountains after dark."

"Afraid?" Aoife's teeth were sharp white points against her pale, thin lips.

"Yes," Nels said quickly. "And so would you be if you knew what lived in the woods."

"I am Aoife of the Shadows," she snapped. "I fear nothing."

"Not even your sister?" Nels said slyly, but the smile died on his lips as Aoife fixed icy green eyes on him. Color drained from her face, leaving the scattering of freckles across her cheeks and nose looking like spots of bright blood.

"It would be a mistake to mention her name in my presence," she hissed. Her hand fell to the hilt of the coiled metal whip fixed to her saddle.

"I meant no disrespect," Nels mumbled abruptly, realizing that he had overstepped.

"Yes, you did. I will forgive you this time," Aoife answered, "but not a second time. Do not test me. Do I make myself clear?"

Nels stepped away quickly, then turned and stomped back down the wagon train, checking the oxen, grumbling at the drivers. He was experienced enough not to raise his voice: sound would carry far into the gathering night . . . and besides, Aoife might hear him. And though he'd never admit it, there was something about the red-haired girl that frightened him . . . even though he was convinced she was not *the* Aoife of the Shadows.

He knew the legend of Aoife the Gateholder, of course. All of Tir Tairngaire knew the story of the red-haired, green-eyed warrior who'd stood alone at the ancient stone henge and fought the wriggling monsters who'd crawled through the opening. She'd defended that gate for three days and three nights, until the Sheking's army finally arrived. And then, it was said, Aoife led the charge into the henge and carried the fight into the beasts' lair. If she hadn't held the gate, then the monsters would have overrun the island kingdom. Nothing would have survived.

But that had been hundreds of years in the past, and Nels believed that this was just another red-haired green-eyed northern warrior who'd taken the legend's name as her own. Though occasionally, like now, he was not so sure. Sometimes when she looked at him, he caught the same expression he'd seen in the eyes of ox drovers looking at their cattle: they were looking at dumb beasts needing protection. Watching her over the past few days, he'd come to the conclusion that she was not entirely humani. Maybe she was a half-breed and that was what was making him uneasy. She probably had Fir Dearg or Sidhe blood in her. But she was definitely *not* the Aoife of the Shadows.

2

Aoife maneuvered the jet-black aonbheannach to the edge of the trail. Leaning forward, she rested her chin on the beast's bony skull and peered between its upright pointed ears. The valley below was in shadow. There was a creeping chill on the back of her neck that she had come to know and respect. Staring into the gloom, she allowed her gaze to roam over the dense covering of trees, not looking for anything, simply waiting for something to impress itself on her consciousness. Instincts honed on a hundred Shadowrealms and across centuries were telling her that something was there, something old.

There!

Deliberately not turning her head, aware of the object at the very periphery of her vision, she waited. There was a flash of gold-washed silver, indistinct, fragmentary against the gathering gloom. Then it vanished, lost in a swirl of leaves as she heard something ponderous move on the forest floor. Aoife's nostrils flared as she tried to work out what could be prowling through these dark northern forests at this time of year. The air was moist with growth and rot, but she thought it smelled like a Torc Madra, a werewolf, though they usually moved silently. It could be any of the Torc clans: bear, boar, forest lion, or elk. This world had more than its share of monsters. In the days following the destruction of Danu Talis, this Shadowrealm had been created by the Archon Cernunnos, a huge horned creature who had populated his world with all manner of beasts. It was said that he hunted them for sport and then took their heads for his trophy wall. Cernunnos did not distinguish between human or animal either.

The crippled Dwarf known only as Bes rode out from the main body of the caravan, urging a shaggy mountain pony over the muddy path. It whinnied nervously as it drew near to the aonbheannach, breaking Aoife's concentration.

"What is it?" Bes asked, voice rasping and labored. Even though he was wrapped in a heavy oiled traveling cloak, the small man was shivering.

Aoife ran her fingers through her hair. "I saw something in the valley."

"What did you see?" he asked.

"A light where there should be none," Aoife murmured.

"Can you see it now?"

"The light is gone. Something moved through the undergrowth."

"Dangerous?" he asked.

"I'm not sure," she answered. "My instincts are always to err on the side of caution."

"The veil between the worlds is thin within the Wildwoode," Bes said very quietly. "Who knows what creatures have come through from other realms." The Dwarf's single coal-black eye fixed on Aoife, and in that moment, she guessed that he knew her true nature.

Aoife had no idea who—or even *what*—Bes was; he had the copper skin and black eye of an easterner, his manners were elegant and refined, and yet his teeth were filed to points in the style of the cannibal Northsea islanders. She was aware that he spoke the Common Tongue with just the trace of an accent she'd never heard on this world before.

Nels hurried over. "We need to move now. We're losing the light," he said. When he'd seen the Dwarf talking to the woman, he'd tried to creep closer, but both the Dwarf and the woman had deliberately turned to look at him and he stopped. "I'll not delay here simply because this woman has a vague feeling . . . ," he began.

Bes turned his head to face Nels squarely. He was missing his left eye, and the empty cavity was filled with a white marble etched with a swirling triple spiral. His bloodshot right eye fixed on Nels's face. "I hired you to lead this wagon across the mountains," he said, every word a rasping effort, "because you came highly recommended. Aoife I hired as guard because she was as highly regarded."

"I don't know this woman," Nels grumbled. "I heard Aoife—the real Aoife of the Shadows—was killed by a thunderbird in the Westlands. This is probably some army deserter who has taken her name. Who recommended her, anyway? Some rogue—"

"The same rogue who recommended you," Bes snapped.

"Someone I respect, and someone who should not be insulted. Now remember who pays you. Get back to your wagon."

Nels glared at Aoife, who smiled slightly, exposing her pointed incisors. The big man turned away quickly and returned to the first wagon. He took his time checking the two lead oxen, running a calloused hand over the large wooden wheels. Only when he was sure that neither Bes nor Aoife could see him did he spit his disgust into the dirt.

"Something down there troubles me," Aoife said quietly, leaning forward on the pommel of her saddle. Unconsciously, her fingers traced a trio of scars that began just under her left eye and ran down to her jawline.

Bes looked into the shadows. "I can see nothing," he admitted, "but then again, my sight is not as it once was. However, I've lived this long because I've learned to trust the opinions of those I respect."

"I've done nothing to earn your respect," Aoife said, glancing sidelong at him. "I have not worked for you before."

"Oh, I have heard of your exploits, Aoife of the Shadows," Bes said softly. "And unlike our smelly friend, I know you to be the true Aoife. You are held in high esteem by those I respect . . . and that is good enough for me," Bes added, lips moving in what might have passed for a smile.

"Who recommended me for this job?" Aoife asked.

"A woman who might not have been entirely human," he said, a hint of sadness in his voice.

"And you've met nonhumans before," Aoife said, turning the question into a statement.

"I was not always as you see me, half blind and neither as fast nor as sharp as I once was. In my youth I was considered handsome. And I had adventures that took me across this world . . . and others," he added so quietly that she had to strain to hear him.

Aoife nodded. "I suspected that you were not from this place."

"I was not born on this world, but it is home to me now."

"And this woman—the one who might not have been entirely human, who recommended me for this job—did she have a name?" Aoife asked.

"I've heard her called a witch, but when I first encountered her, when we were both a lot younger, I knew her by the name Zephaniah." He paused and added very softly, "No doubt you know her."

Aoife looked back into the valley but did not answer.

"I will take your silence as a yes," Bes said. "She was sometimes in the company of a man with one hand," he added.

Aoife nodded almost imperceptibly. "Zephaniah is my grandmother."

"And the hook-handed man?"

"He has many names. Now he goes mostly by Marethyu."

"Death?"

She nodded. "Death."

"Rather dramatic," Bes murmured.

"But also true. You might know him by other names; he has been called the Destroyer of Worlds."

"Ah." The man nodded in recognition. "My people called

him Inpu." From beneath his cloak he produced a small amulet he wore on a leather cord around his neck. A beautifully ornate sickle, shaped from a single piece of amber. "I often wondered why the symbol for death was a curved blade. I always thought it symbolized cutting down or weeding." He held the amber half circle up to the fading light. "I never thought it simply represented his hook."

"My grandmother," Aoife said, "how did she look?"

"Unchanged, unaged, beautiful. Exactly as I last saw her one hundred and more years ago."

Aoife caught the hint of emotion in his voice, and for an instant, there was the suggestion of moisture in his single eye.

"I presume my grandmother asked you to hire me for a reason?"

"She asked me to pass on a message to you," the Dwarf answered. He sounded almost relieved that they had moved beyond painful memories. "She said the message came from Death himself."

"I wonder why he did not deliver it in person," Aoife pressed.

"I asked her. She said that an old threat has reappeared, and that he had gone in search of an army."

"Usually I—or my sister," she added reluctantly, "are all the army he needs. What was his message?"

"She said I was to tell you that your quest nears its end."

"That's it?" she asked, trying and failing to keep the disappointment out of her voice. "Did she wonder how I was doing or ask after my health?"

"She did not. But she was speaking to me through a scrying mirror," he added quickly. "The connection was not good."

"She is obsessed with glass and mirrors," Aoife muttered.

"She made me repeat the five words and told me I was to deliver them to you when the time was right: your quest nears its end."

Aoife sighed and shook her head. *"Your quest nears its end,"* she repeated. "And how do you know that this is the right time?"

"I suppose I could tell you that I am—obviously—not of the humani tribe and that my race have the Sight. But the truth is far more mundane: we've been on the road for four days and this is the first time you've halted the wagon train. Even when the leshy hunting party were following us two days ago, you simply rode off, took care of the problem, and returned without a word. Yet you did not stop the caravan. You did now, so I knew this must be significant."

"You know, I hate all this mystery nonsense!" Aoife snapped in frustration. "Why didn't she just say 'Give the message four days into the journey: your quest nears its end.'"

"This means something to you?" Bes asked.

"Perhaps if I knew what my quest was in the first place," Aoife answered. "Two hundred years ago, Zephaniah sent me here on a mission for Marethyu. I was to assimilate into the local population and await further instructions."

"And there were no instructions?" he guessed.

Aoife nodded. "Not a word. Worse: the leygate I used to come to this world dissolved into crumbled rocks the moment

I stepped through. I've been unable to find my way off this world for the past two centuries." She glanced quickly at Bes. "Do you know of any active leygates?"

"A few," he said cautiously. "Is that why I was asked to give you the message?" he wondered. "To get you to a leygate?"

Aoife shook her head. "That would be too easy. No. I was sent here for a reason. I just don't know what the reason is. Not yet, anyway." She turned to look back down into the valley again. "I am thinking that the light in the valley may very well be my mission."

Bes nodded. "Are we in any danger?"

"I'm not sure," Aoife answered. "I feel . . . uneasy. Like I have an itch that needs to be scratched."

"What will you do?" he asked.

"Make a secure camp," she decided. "Have the wagon drivers stand watch with the mercenary guards, keep the fires burning all night."

"I will instruct Nels," Bes said, "but what about you? You have a look I recognize—or maybe I should say a look I remember having myself. The look of someone about to do something stupid or dangerous."

"I'll investigate."

"Is that wise?"

"It is always wise to know your fears," Aoife answered.

"And then face them?" Bes pressed.

"No, facing them is not always wise," Aoife said grimly, "but it is often necessary."

3

They made camp for the night in the gutted shell of an ancient stone temple complex.

At some time in the past, fire had raged through the heart of the structure, blackening the walls, coating the ceiling with a thick covering of soot, obscuring the elaborate and beautiful frescoes and patterns incised into the stone. Scores of statues littered the ruins. Most were humani, but there were also Torc Allta and Torc Madra—wereboar and werewolf—among the rubble, though all of the heads had been chopped off and pounded into fragments, and it was only possible to distinguish the humani and nonhuman by their clothes and armor.

Over time, the forest had crept in and claimed the tumbledown building, body-thick vines snaking through windows and gaping doors, cracking walls, uprooting the intricate tile work, ripping apart the carved wooden beams, and crushing ornate spiraling columns. Then, for some unknown reason, the encroaching forest had died back, withered away in an almost circular pattern around the ruins, leaving dead vines, like skeletal fingers, clutching the walls and splayed across the floors.

Although Aoife had no time for the arrogant wagon master, she had to admit that he knew his job. Ignoring the larger buildings, which offered shelter of sorts to both men and oxen but which would have been impossible to defend, Nels had brought the wagons into the central courtyard and had them surround a tiny stone hut that housed nothing more than the shattered remains of a well, now filled to overflowing with red sand.

"You take the well house," Nels said to Bes.

The Dwarf looked at Aoife as she dismounted and raised his eyebrows in a silent question.

She nodded. "One entrance, easily defended, no windows and a solid stone roof. I could not have chosen better myself."

Nels's smile was sour. He didn't need this woman's approval.

"Pull the wagon closer," Bes said. "I will bring my boxes inside with me."

"They'll be safe on the wagon," Nels grunted.

"I will bring them in," Bes repeated.

"Very well," Nels answered. "I can carry them for you."

"It would be better if I carried them myself." The Dwarf smiled humorlessly. "Trust me: you do not want to put your hands on these boxes. Not if you want to keep your hands, that is." He laboriously clambered into the cart, untied the heavy leather waterproof covering, and flipped it back, revealing the contents.

Nels looked over the wooden crates stacked high on the oxcart. Each box was wrapped in chains and ribbons, the locks covered with gaudy, brightly colored mud studded with amulets and beads.

"Do you know what these are?" Bes asked.

"Cursed locks," Nels muttered. "Something you don't want opened."

"Something that shouldn't be opened," Bes corrected him.

"None of my men are thieves," the drover protested. "Everyone knows I'll carry a load without asking any questions."

"No doubt one of the reasons you were recommended to me," Bes said.

"Are these . . ." Nels nodded vaguely toward the boxes. "Are these dangerous?"

"I thought you said you didn't ask questions." Bes smiled.

"When I see an amulet in the shape of a skull, it makes me worried."

"If you don't open them, then you have nothing to fear."

Without a word, Nels turned away.

Bes looked at Aoife. "You have questions?"

"None." She rapped on the nearest box with her knuckles. "Most of these amulets and ribbons are fake, designed to impress and frighten people. But," she added with a smile, "I notice some that are, most decidedly, not fake." She pointed to a small, battered casket, which was wrapped with a rusty chain and a soiled red ribbon. The lock was completely encased in what looked like a blob of gray mud. "That is Golem mud."

Bes nodded. "I am impressed."

"I've fought the mud men before. I know what they look like. So what is this: a tiny mud man who springs into action if the lock is opened?"

Bes made his way through the boxes to find the one Aoife had pointed to. With a grunting effort, he extracted it from the pile. "Nothing so dramatic," he said, carrying the box to the edge of the cart. "If the lock is disturbed, the mud will turn to liquid and slither up the would-be thief's arm into their nose and mouth."

"Hard to run if you can't breathe," she said.

"I've got some wood runes on another lock. Attempt to open it and it will sprout a hundred razor-sharp thorns. Another is washed with phoenix blood."

"That'll leave a nasty burn," Aoife noted.

"It will. Left untreated, it will burn right through to the bone."

"And I am guessing only you have the cure."

"Your guess would be correct," Bes said.

"So you hired six wagons," Aoife said, looking over the back of the cart. "Five of them are filled with ore from your mines. A small fortune, to be sure. But I am guessing that this wagon—and specifically these few boxes mixed amid the dross—is the real treasure."

Bes smiled but said nothing.

"Do you need help getting them inside?" Aoife asked.

"I can manage. But you might check to ensure that we're not being spied upon."

"There's no one around."

"Check anyway," he said.

Aoife faded back into the gathering darkness, guessing that the Dwarf did not want her to see him unload the boxes. And now she couldn't help but wonder if the contents of the crates were also part of her mission.

4

The two Sister Moons were high and full in the sky, turning the night silver bright while etching sharp black shadows on the ground. There was a bitter wind out of the north, and frost was starting to sparkle across the stones. In the moonlight, the ruined temple took on a different aspect. The night's shadows hid much of the destruction, while the stark moonlight hinted at its previous grandeur.

Walking through the devastated buildings, Aoife found herself wondering who—or what—had been worshipped at such an ornate temple in the middle of nowhere. There was also the mystery of the burnt circle of earth. As she'd prowled the perimeter, she'd become aware that there were no living creatures, not even a mouse, within the walls of the temple. It was as if something had sucked out every trace of life and then left a stain upon the place to ensure that nothing would ever live there again.

Her experienced warrior's eye interpreted some of the clues written into the shattered stones and melted walls. A battle had been fought here in ages past. Humani warriors had stood alongside two of the most fearsome Torc clans—wolf and boar—but had ultimately been defeated. Aoife had no idea who they had been fighting—Earthlords, possibly. Even natural enemies banded together to battle the terrible serpent folk. The humani and their allies had been defeated, and the victors had taken the time to deface the statues; that petty destruction was another sign of the Earthlords.

However, later—much later, perhaps a thousand years after the battle, long enough for the forest to have eaten into the place—an incredibly powerful magic had rippled through the temple, creating the circle of destruction. Aoife found herself wondering if a grave robber had disturbed an ancient spell or a cache of wildfire explosives had spontaneously erupted. Either could have caused the devastating fire that had marked the place.

She returned to the center of the complex and was approaching the well house when the small arched door opened and Bes appeared, framed in the doorway. Aoife stopped and allowed herself to be absorbed into the shadows, but the Dwarf turned to look at her, his single white eye ghastly against his dark face, and what passed for a smile twisted his lips. He called her to him with a quick gesture.

"You have inspected this place. It meets with your approval?" he asked.

"There is an interesting history written into the stones. It will not withstand a determined assault by a group of armed men, but it will see us safe against wolves or brigands."

"More, much more, lives in these forests," Bes said softly. "I have seen sights that would freeze your blood." He disappeared into the well house, and Aoife hesitated in the doorway. She waited until the Dwarf turned back and saw her standing on the threshold. "Ah, I forgot, your kind need to be invited. Enter freely and of your own will."

Aoife stepped over the threshold into the small circular room, pressed her back against the wall, and waited, allowing her eyes to adjust. Only a fool rushed from dark to light. "So you know about my kind?" she asked. Bes was moving slowly around the room, lighting fat white candles and setting them into broken stones on the walls, bringing the room to dancing life. The air stank of grease and bubbling fat.

Bes chuckled. "I know what you are: vampire, like your sister. But not a blood drinker, like your modern kin. A vegetarian. You take your sustenance from emotions and feed off the fear and joy of others."

"I do not deny who I am, or what I am," the young woman answered. She lowered her voice, which had risen high enough to draw the attention of the guards though the open door. Only a fool trapped themselves in a room they were not familiar with. Turning her head, she glanced through the opening and saw Nels stepping away from behind one of the wagons. He was watching the well house intently, his head tilted to one side, listening with one misshapen ear. When she saw Aoife looking at him, he shuffled away, busying himself with the oxen.

"It is none of my business who you are, what you are, or what you did." Bes sank slowly, painfully, to the ground, his back against the chill stone wall, and stretched his legs in front of him. He straightened his stiff left leg with both hands. Aoife noticed that his knee was heavily wrapped. He warmed thick-fingered hands over a candle flame. "The guards do not believe you are the real Aoife of legend," he said softly. "You heard Nels; they think you are someone using her name."

Aoife's smile was icy. Folding her arms across her chest, she leaned back against the wall. "Though they are not entirely sure," she noted.

"No, they are not. And because of that, they will not test you."

"It would be their last mistake if they did."

"It would," Bes agreed. "I know that you are the one true Aoife of the Shadows, and I know what you are capable of."

The warrior's head dipped slightly. "And do you know this because the Witch told you, or . . . ?" she asked.

"Even if she had not told me, I would have known. You are not the only traveler I have encountered who was not born on this Shadowrealm," Bes said. "We travelers carry a touch of otherworldliness about us—the leygates leave an alien scent on our auras."

"And yet I can distinguish neither aura color nor scent from you," Aoife said.

"My race do not possess an aura."

"I have never come across that before."

"We are unique. And now we are few," he added. "In fact, I may be the last of my kind. When I was younger, I crossed the Shadowrealms alongside Zephaniah in search of adventure and knowledge."

"And did you find it?" Aoife asked.

"Oh, a bard could fill volumes with our adventures. But as for knowledge . . . well, I think I could fit that into a slender pamphlet."

"But judging from the contents of that cart I saw earlier, you are still seeking knowledge."

"There is nothing especially valuable there," Bes said so quickly that Aoife knew he was lying. "Dangerous, yes, but not valuable."

Aoife dipped her head to peer out into the night. There was no sign of Nels, but she caught a trace of his peculiarly musky odor. So he was either close by or he was so badly in need of a bath that he left his stench on the night air. When she turned back to the room, Bes was watching her closely.

"You remind me of your grandmother," he said. "I can see the resemblance around your eyes and chin."

"You should probably not tell her that," Aoife murmured.

"Did she ever mention my name?" he asked, almost too casually.

"The Witch may be my grandmother, but I can probably count on my fingers the number of conversations we've had. She is closer to my sister. I knew nothing about you until I learned you were offering a huge fee for protecting this wagon train and that you had specifically asked for me. I did a little digging before I accepted, of course."

"Of course. And did you find anything interesting?"

"A mixture of rumor and outright lies wrapped around what might be a tiny kernel of truth," Aoife answered. "You come down from the icy Northlands two or three times a season to buy supplies for an unknown number of miners who work in the ancient and long-abandoned white quartz pits."

"That much is true," Bes said. "Though if digging goes on there, the mines are hardly abandoned."

"No one seems to know exactly what you and your miners are digging. The seams of quartz are long since worked out. However, I did hear a local legend about a vast treasure buried deep in the heart of the earth. The Treasure of the Great Old Ones."

"You don't sound convinced," the Dwarf murmured.

"Every abandoned mine on every Shadowrealm I've visited supposedly contains hidden treasure, a monster, a dragon, and sometimes all three. I've never come across any treasure, though it is true that thunderbirds or wyrms often nest in the lower levels of old mines."

"I've encountered a few in my time," Bes said, and rubbed his wrapped knee.

"The townspeople are wary of you," Aoife went on, "and when I dug a little deeper, they told me some interesting stories." She paused, and then added, "One of which reminded me of something that happened maybe fifty years ago."

Bes continued to rub his knee, but Aoife caught the sudden flare of his eye.

"Fifty years ago, maybe a little more, I took a job as a

sheriff in a small southern town on the slopes of the Mouth of the World," Aoife said. "You know it?"

"A volcano. I know of it," he answered casually.

"Some travelers reported that they'd seen a pile of bodies lying in a field off the highway. I rode out to investigate, a circle of birds in the air pointing the way. The bodies turned out to be the remains of a party of army deserters who had been terrorizing the road for the best part of a season. The five heavily armed men had been killed by something incredibly powerful." Although she kept checking through the open door, Aoife was watching Bes carefully from the corner of her eye. "I made my report and the local judge decided that the outlaws must have been slain by werewolves—never mind that the Torc Madra had not been sighted that far south for centuries."

"Did you ever find out what happened to them?" Bes asked.

"Interesting question. But surely the question you should be asking me is why am I telling you this? That's the question you would be asking if this had nothing to do with you."

The Dwarf smiled, revealing his razor-sharp teeth. "Perhaps I was being polite."

Aoife nodded. "That is a possibility. Or perhaps you wondered how much I knew."

"And what did you discover?"

"It had snowed, and it was easy enough to read the story written into the mud and slush. Two outlaws had stopped a wagon on the road. Then three sets of tracks left the wagon and moved across the field to a stand of ancient trees. The middle footprints were small, like a child's. Or a Dwarf's. There were three more men waiting around the trees, and I could see clearly where the five men had surrounded the smaller figure." She stopped.

After a moment, Bes said, "And then?"

Aoife's smile was grim. "And then something happened. Because suddenly the five outlaws were very dead and the child—or the Dwarf—returned to the wagon. During my investigation," she added, "I discovered that a Dwarf had ridden through the town the day before. I cannot remember his name, which suggests I was never told it, because I have an excellent memory."

"And you think this outlaw killer might be me?"

"Was it?"

"I have traveled the length and breadth of this land," he said, not answering the question. "I've been attacked and mocked, and yes, I have been forced to defend myself." His smile was grim. "I am small, and so sometimes, foolish people think I am a victim."

"That would be their mistake."

"Yes. Often their final mistake." Bes focused on tightening the wrapping around his knee. "You and I," he said suddenly, "are puppets, moved, directed, and placed by your grandmother. And she is as much a puppet as we are: Death manipulates all of us."

"I was told Marethyu can see the threads of time," Aoife

answered. "He moves people now to influence events in the future."

"And who gave him that right?" Bes suddenly demanded. "He has this extraordinary power, and we presume that he is using it for our good. But we simply do not know. Such power is dangerous in the hands of one man. Even if he only has one hand," he added with a wry smile.

"You don't trust him?"

"You're Next Generation, born after the destruction of Danu Talis. But I was there. I watched the battle atop the Pyramid of the Sun. I saw him call down the lightning and ignite the volcanoes, which in turn created the earthquakes, which ripped the island continent asunder. Marethyu destroyed Danu Talis. He tore apart my world. Why should I trust him?"

Aoife nodded slowly. She had heard various accounts of the story over the centuries. "I was told that one world had to die so that another could grow. The races who fled the island founded colonies which established civilization across the primitive world."

"And was it worth it?" Bes asked bitterly. "One of the greatest civilizations the world has ever seen, wiped out so that the humani could rise. Were they worth it? Are they?"

Aoife shrugged. "My sister thinks so. She has always fought for them."

"But you are not your sister. And you know she is under the influence of the hook-handed man."

"If you despise Marethyu so much, then why do his bidding?" Aoife asked.

"I don't. I do this for Zephaniah." Bes drew in a deep, shuddering breath. "Ignore me. I am old, tired, and cold. It makes me cranky."

Aoife nodded. The conversation troubled her, because she too had often wondered if Marethyu was not becoming too powerful. Also, his apparent power over her sister, Scathach, troubled her.

"Have you any idea what you saw in the valley earlier?" Bes asked eventually, deliberately changing the subject. His head was turned so that it appeared he was looking away, though his right eye was fixed on her face.

"No."

"But it disturbed you."

"Yes."

"And now you're going in search of it?"

"I would rest happier."

"It could have been the sunlight sparkling off a pool of water," the Dwarf offered, "the shimmer of silica in an outcropping of rock, the bark of a tree catching the light."

"I know that," Aoife said quickly. "This felt different."

"An excuse," he said eventually, with a ghost of a smile. "Admit it: you are curious."

"It has always been my failing," Aoife agreed, sharp teeth yellow in the firelight. "And I would be failing in my duty to you if I did not investigate."

Bes's smile barely curled his lips. "Your duty is to guard this wagon train."

"Why?" Aoife asked boldly. Crouching on her haunches, she stared hard at the Dwarf. "I am thinking," she said carefully, "that if a person was able to dispatch five heavily armed outlaws, then they would not need someone like me and the mercenaries to guard the wagons."

"That is true," he said, and then added, "I have no need of guards. You grandmother insisted I hire you. So clearly, she wanted you in this place at this time."

"So I could go and see what lies hidden in the forest."

Bes nodded. "The guards are just for show . . . and, well, there's a bridge up ahead, guarded by a particularly ugly half-man goat-headed creature."

"A gabhar. One of the Torc clans."

"The gabhar are very partial to a mercenary or two. Once it feasts off a couple, it'll fall asleep and we can pass."

"You're not a very nice person, are you?" Aoife asked.

"You have no idea who I am. Or what I am," Bes said pleasantly.

5

Nels moved slowly through the ruined and tumbled buildings, gradually edging away from the other drovers. He noted the positions of the mercenary guards as he made his way to the shattered storehouse behind the circular Well House. A glance back over his shoulder, to ensure that no one was watching him; then he ducked into the gutted building. With infinite care he lifted a brick from the wall and pressed his face against the gritty stones, peering in through the tiny opening. He could make out flickering shadows, and faintly, he could hear the thin sound of Aoife's and Bes's low voices on the other side of the wall. The drover's thick lips drew back from stained, misshapen teeth. He'd been little more than a boy when his father, a notorious brigand, had shown him this place and demonstrated the acoustic qualities of the walls. Noise bounced off the curved interior of the well house and was funneled through this opening. Later, when Nels became a drover, leading ox-carts across the mountains, he realized he could put the place to good use. He always timed his trips to include an overnight stay in the ruined temple and insisted that his employer take the warm and dry safety of the well house.

Nels had grown wealthy by simply listening to some of his passengers talking. He'd learned the whispered locations of buried wealth, the muttered revelations of military and trade secrets, and clues that lead to wills hidden under floors or treasure maps tucked behind pictures. Nels passed the information on to his network of thieves, brigands, and pirates, and as payment he took a share of the treasure without ever having to place himself in any danger.

Even before he'd seen the amulet-protected boxes in the cart, he'd known he was going to bring the Dwarf to this place. He knew that Bes had never used guards before, so he was certain that there was treasure in the wagons.

And he wanted it.

A few miles up the road, a particularly ill-tempered gabhar had laid claim to a bridge. The creature demanded a tribute before allowing anyone to cross what he now considered to be *his* bridge. The gabhar took his tribute in meat, cheese, and beer. Like most of the gabhar and Allta clans, the creature loved honey, and Nels always brought a fresh honeycomb when it was in season or a jar of rich southern clover honey as a treat for the monster.

The gabhar owed Nels a favor or two.

The wagon master wondered how Aoife would fare against the ancient forest creature. It would be a shame if anything were to happen to her and the other mercenary guards.

Nels pressed his face against the dry, dusty stones, closed his eyes, and listened intently. It was at times like this that he wished he could write, so he could make notes.

6

"You are aware that the earth has shifted recently?" The Dwarf's voice was a low whisper rasping off the stones.

"I've heard about the earthquakes and upheavals in the high mountains and valleys. The Airgead and Óir suns are aligning, as they do once every thousand years." Aoife's voice sounded flat and disinterested.

"In places whole mountains have split," Bes answered. "Gullies have appeared like wounds through the ancient stone; valleys have disappeared, entire communities vanished, wiped away as if they never existed."

"I don't see what that has to do with me—" Aoife's voice was harsh, arrogant. Nels decided that he would be there when the gabhar killed her. And he'd make sure she saw him so she'd know who had betrayed her.

"New creatures haunt the Highlands," the Dwarf interrupted Aoife. "Some resemble beasts of legend and history, but others . . . well, who knows what has awakened and crept from the heart of the shattered mountains? It is said that the Lord Cernunnos himself rides with the Wild Hunt seeking new trophies for his walls."

"I have heard those stories, and I am not sure I believe them," Aoife said. "Not that it matters: Cernunnos does not frighten me. I know him for what he is . . . and he knows me. He would not dare lay a finger on me."

"Cernunnos should terrify even you. He is an Archon, one of those who ruled the One World in the Time Before Time, before the creation of the Shadowrealms. He is dangerous beyond belief. And it is said that he is now mad. You know how dangerous mad gods can be?"

Nels heard Aoife laugh, a harsh ugly sound. "Cernunnos is not a god. He is a creature of breath and blood. He can be killed."

"You have killed gods before, Aoife?" Bes asked.

"Only those who deserved it."

A long silence followed. Nels waited patiently, knowing that if he moved, the noise might alert either Bes or Aoife. Had he had learned anything of value? The Dwarf certainly believed the woman was the real Aoife of the Shadows, and that information had some value, though he wasn't entirely sure who he could sell it to.

A sudden thought struck him, and his lips twisted in an ugly smile. Although Aoife had dismissed Cernunnos and claimed that he was afraid of her, the drover wondered if he dared bring the information to the green-robed priests of the Horned God.

Hmm. Perhaps it would be more profitable not to betray her to the gabhar, but to sell her out to the priests. He could tell them about the woman who'd stolen Aoife the

Gatekeeper's name and then blasphemed the Horned God. The priests allowed no one to mock their god; they would certainly kill her. He nodded. Watching the gabhar tear her limb from limb would give him immense pleasure but would earn him no coin. The priests would pay handsomely, and she would be just as dead when they were done with her.

Cloth rasped, and Nels heard Bes wheeze and sigh as if he was settling down for the night. When the Dwarf spoke again, his tone had shifted, becoming sly and conspiratorial. "The recent earthquakes have brought forth more than just new creatures from the bowels of the earth."

Aoife remained silent. Nels closed his eyes, his forehead and cheek pressed against the stones, focusing intently.

"I have also heard stories of the earth splitting apart to reveal ancient, long-forgotten secrets and artifacts. . . ."

"What sort of artifacts?" Aoife asked quickly.

"All manner of treasures," Bes answered. "Why, not a month ago, a sheep farmer just to the north of here found a sword as tall as himself in a recently torn gash in the ground. The sword was made of a stone he'd never seen before—and this man had previously worked as a miner and had some experience with stones."

"I have seen stone swords aplenty," Aoife said.

"As have I. But hidden beneath the sword was a suit of armor cast from solid silver, etched in gold and inlaid with jade."

"To fit a man or a woman?" Aoife asked, almost too casually.

"A woman, I believe." Bes paused, then asked, "Why, have you heard of this armor before?"

There was a long silence, and just when Nels was beginning to think she was not going to answer, Aoife spoke. "Once, a long time ago, I watched a blond-haired girl wearing similar armor ride into battle at the head of an army of monsters."

"Which side were you on?" Bes asked.

"The losing side. What did you do with the sword and the armor?" she asked.

"The sword is stone and worthless. A curiosity, nothing more. But the armor is priceless. It is in one of the boxes on the wagons."

On the other side of the wall, Nels flashed a quick smile and his lips formed the word *priceless*. He liked that.

"I will buy it from you," Aoife said.

"It is not for sale."

"I was not asking," Aoife said. "I will exchange it for the fee you owe me."

"It is worth more than that," Bes answered.

"It is worth exactly what I am prepared to pay for it," Aoife snapped.

"I am not sure it is your size."

"I do not want it for myself. I want to return it to the fair-haired warrior." Nels heard something in the woman's voice he'd not heard before: respect. He wondered who the fair-haired warrior was.

"But you've no idea where she is."

"The hook-handed man will know. He will tell me," she said with enough confidence that Nels began to wonder if she was indeed the real Aoife.

"Can I ask why you want to return it to her?"

"She saved my life; I am in her debt."

"But I thought you were on opposite sides."

"We were."

"Ah, a debt of honor," Bes said. "I understand that. If we are without honor, we have nothing. Complete your quest in the forest and I will gift you with the suit of silver armor. But I will not be paying your fee," he added quickly.

"Then it is not a gift," Aoife reminded him.

"Well, perhaps there might be room for negotiation," Bes said finally. "I am wondering if what you glimpsed in the forest earlier might be related to these earthquakes and up-heavals." The Dwarf's voice had grown thick and sleepy. "I've traveled this road most of my adult life, and I've never heard of anything silver in the forest. There are beasts aplenty; they are all hair and hide, fangs and horns. None of them are silver, as far as I know."

"This was silver," Aoife said confidently. "Metallic or crystal."

Nels heard something change in the young woman's voice even as she was speaking, a hint of what might have been excitement. "My grandmother sent me to this place in search of ancient artifacts."

"When I traveled the worlds with your grandmother, she

collected all the ancient remnants of the old world," Bes said. "Perhaps she wants to add this to her collection."

Aoife's laugh echoed off the stone walls, turning bitter and harsh. "The Witch will destroy it. She is determined that all the knowledge of the old world be wiped away."

"There is much we can learn from the past," Bes murmured.

"And not all of it good."

The Dwarf's only response was a gentle snore.

7

Aoife blackened her face and hands with wet soot before she crept from the camp. She had elected to go on foot; riding across unfamiliar ground at any time was dangerous, but riding through a forest at night almost guaranteed a broken leg for the horse or rider, or both.

She waited until the smaller moon had disappeared below the horizon and the three Ugly Children rose in the east to chase after their mother, the Silver Lady. They cast confusing shadows through the trees and onto the irregular ground.

Her route was relatively easy. Twice she stopped: once when something that smelled suspiciously like a Torc Allta—but sounded bigger than any boar she'd ever encountered—lumbered through the undergrowth to her left, and again when a huge, faintly luminescent nightsnake as thick as her body slithered lazily across the path. It raised its flattened head to stare at her with yellow eyes before curling away, allowing Aoife to see the distinct outline of a tree fox lodged in its throat. The warrior slid her knife into its sheath and pressed on.

It was close to midnight when she spotted the first glitter of light through the trees directly ahead.

Aoife stepped into the shadow of a long-dead stump and dropped to her haunches to stare in the direction of the milk-white light. It did not pulse or ripple like moonlight on water, nor did it flicker like firelight. Turning to look back into the trees, she shifted her head slightly, so that she was seeing the image almost from the corner of her eyes. It was an old hunter's trick used for revealing details often hidden by looking at something straight on. She began to get a shape of the item: tall, slender, and, she was convinced, crystalline. She guessed that it was in a hollow, so she was only seeing the topmost portion. Aoife loosened the short sword and whip on her belt and checked the knives strapped to her forearms, then moved silently toward the light. She tested each step before pressing down; she did not want to risk snapping a fallen twig or crunching through leaves. Although her vision was exceptional in the dark, like all great warriors, she knew the value of her other senses—especially her sense of smell, which had always been acute. She breathed deeply, identifying the beasts and birds that had moved through this place. She smelled Torc Allta—wereboar—spoor first, the odor rank and cloying. A few steps farther on, she caught the unmistakable stench of a Torc Arzh Gell, a werebear—and then the bittersweet perfume of a female centaur.

Aoife shivered, and not from the chill night air. Something was wrong here. Boar, bear, and centaur were never found together.

Mixed among the scents of the living, there were other, less familiar odors: the foul scent of headless Dullahans and

43

the once-smelled-never-forgotten stench of the rotting fear ghorta. What had drawn the walking dead from their graves, she wondered.

She stopped, crouched, and ran her hand across the shadowed ground; it was pocked with prints from hooves, paws, and feet . . . and all of them were heading in one direction, toward the light. None returned.

This close to the ground, she suddenly felt the electric trickle of ancient power trembling just beneath the forest floor. She was suddenly aware that her heart was thundering, her stomach cramping, and it felt as if ants were crawling through her hair and spiders cocooning her flesh with silk. It took Aoife a moment to recognize the emotion she was experiencing. This was fear: the deep, primal terror etched into the consciousness of every living being, the recognition that they were in the presence of something alien to all life.

Aoife couldn't remember the last time she'd felt an emotion so strongly, and it had been a long time since she'd experienced anything even approaching fear. Closing her eyes, she threw back her head and breathed deeply. She was vampire: emotions were her sustenance. If all the other creatures drawn toward the light had experienced the same terrors that were shivering through her skin, she should have been able to feast off that raw emotion.

But there was nothing on the air.

No rich soup of sensations, not even the raw stink of fear.

Wiping damp palms on the legs of her trousers, she moved

forward, slipping from shadow to shadow, almost completely invisible.

The light was clearer now, brighter than the Lady and the three smaller moons in the sky. The source had dipped below a black-edged rise directly ahead. Aoife watched as steam curled out of the hollow ahead, tendrils of yellow-white light snaking through the trees, coiling across the roots like a nest of serpents.

It was bright enough to see clearly now, and Aoife crouched to examine the earth again. Impressed into the muddy mass were tracks from beasts alien not only to the forest but to this part of the Northlands, and from some that she'd never encountered on this Shadowrealm before.

Loosening her metal whip, she dropped to the ground and crawled through the icy mud toward the edge of the rise and the light.

8

Tracking the woman was relatively easy.

On the few occasions he lost the trail, Nels simply continued in the general direction of the point of light, crossing and recrossing the path until he picked up the woman's tracks again. Like most drovers, Nels could identify animals and beasts by their tracks; the depth and crispness of the edges allowed him to estimate how much time had passed since the tracks had been made. Aoife wore distinctive square-heeled riding boots, which left a clear impression in the earth.

Nels stopped when he encountered other prints. Animals, beasts, and were-creatures had all traveled down this narrow path. Most of the prints were days old, though some of the Torc Allta tracks were fresher, certainly made within the last day. Nels straightened and raised a studded club as he slowly examined the tracks. He didn't want to meet with any of the creatures that had preceded him here. Individually they were dangerous; together they were deadly. He had survived because he'd always been cautious—some would have said cowardly, but those who'd said that were all dead. Aoife's tracks overlaid the beasts' marks, so she was following them.

He straightened and took a step back. Maybe it would be better to let the beasts in the forest feast off the woman. He could return in the morning, take her weapons and boots . . .

He was turning away when he caught a brilliant flash of white light. Before it faded, it turned yellow, like polished gold.

Nels hesitated for a single heartbeat . . . and then greed drew him on.

9

Keeping close to the ground, Aoife crept closer to the light blazing out of the hollow. As she drew nearer to the ancient artifact, she realized that despite the number of animal tracks on the ground, she could hear nothing: no panting, snorting, stamping, or even rustling. They were probably sitting and standing silently before the light, entranced by its power. Though why could she not smell them?

She popped her head over the lip of the hollow, only to discover there were no beasts, not even a bone or a shred of fur or feather. Where had they gone? There was, however, a stone.

It was as tall as Aoife, as thick around as her torso and capped with a golden pyramid, a white crystal stone jutted from the earth in the middle of a circular clearing. Mud ran in long streaks along the length of the crystal. The ground around the artifact was cracked and broken, the earth shattered and split, and the tip of the stone was crusted with earth. It had obviously been pushed from the ground by the recent earthquakes and upheavals.

The crystal was the color of chalk, shot through with

tendrils of green and gold, silver, black, and red. It throbbed and pulsed with a soft white heartbeat of light, and occasionally a shimmering strand of brighter light washed through it, curling from the golden cap to flow down the length of the column. The fluid light was mesmerizing as it drifted downward—yellow-white, the shimmer of gold, then ice-white, the color of pearls—before it finally flowed off the crystal and washed over the ground, melding with the mist, until it seemed as if the light itself was rolling along the forest floor.

From top to bottom, the stone was etched with symbols and twisting lines reminiscent of the ancient Ogham texts Aoife had seen on the oldest Shadowrealms. When she tried to focus on the marks, they shifted and spiraled beneath her gaze, forming new patterns and words. A dozen languages curled into existence, then faded to form a dozen more. Some she recognized; others were completely alien.

The warrior felt the power radiating from the stone flow across her skin like marching insects. It sizzled through her short hair, making it stand up straight, while sparks crackled from her belt buckle, buzzed across the metal whip she carried coiled on her shoulder, and fizzed around the steel toe caps of her boots. Then the sparks danced blue-white along her flesh to reveal, in stark shadow, the bones beneath.

She had seen stones like this before, but they had always been finger-length shards of clear crystal and, occasionally, larger, head-sized globes carved into the infamous crystal skulls. She had never encountered anything so large.

This was a remnant from the Time Before Time, an artifact from the age of the Earthlords.

The tiny pieces she had encountered previously had been imbued with incredible power and dangerous knowledge. She'd handled a crystal ring once worn by an Archon and was instantly conscious of the slither of bizarre thoughts and the hum of discordant music in her head. She'd lifted a crystal pendant from an Earthlord mummy, and the instant it brushed her skin, she'd felt such a crushing fear that it had forced her to her knees. She went blind and deaf momentarily, and when her sight and hearing returned, she'd found herself speaking in a language that had not been used for millennia. In the days that followed, her red hair turned snow white before falling away, leaving her bald, and her green eyes turned an unnatural black. It took a decade before her hair grew back and her eyes returned to their original color.

Once, she'd held a crystal skull and felt the knowledge of ages past flow into her, threatening to swamp her consciousness. In the instant it had taken for the cool crystal to become flesh-warm, she'd known *everything:* the past, present, and myriad futures were laid out in a fractal kaleidoscope. It was overwhelming. She'd felt the walls of her sanity begin to crumble beneath the overload, and right at the very edge of her perception, she had realized that a sentience lurked within the skull, something indescribably alien. Luckily, Scathach had been there and had knocked the skull from her hands with her nunchaku—breaking two of Aoife's fingers in the process. Aoife thought she'd escaped lightly; if she'd held that skull a moment longer, she knew that her own awareness would have been wiped clean, allowing the creature in the skull to take control. For months afterward she'd spoken with a curious accent and her dreams had been bizarre beyond belief.

And if those small slivers of crystal were that dangerous, then what could this enormous shard do? What wealth of arcane and forbidden knowledge did it contain?

Eons ago, her grandmother Zephaniah had discovered the dangerous knowledge encoded in the crystals.

She had sent both Aoife and her sister, Scathach, across the Shadowrealms in search of the crystal artifacts. "Destroy them," the Witch had said. "Destroy them, before they destroy us all."

But Marethyu's demands had been contradictory: he wanted the crystals and skulls whole and intact. Aoife knew he'd sent her sister on incredibly risky missions in search of the ancient treasures. No one knew what he did with them, but on one occasion he suggested that the ancient knowledge they contained was essential for the survival of the human race.

Aoife knew why Zephaniah had sent her to this place: she'd want the crystal column destroyed. But what about Marethyu? The hook-handed man would want this treasure. Sometimes she agreed with her grandmother—there were some things best left dead and buried. She'd lived long enough to realize that knowledge itself was neutral. It could be used for good or ill. Yet at the back of her mind were the bitter memories of the few times she'd touched ancient crystal pieces. Something lived within them, and it was most certainly not neutral.

Slowly, carefully, Aoife uncoiled the metal whip and rose to her feet. Shivering tendrils of ashen sparks ran along the length of the whip. Here was power, indescribable, incredible power. She could feel the raw energies buffeting her like a strong wind, pulsing out like a solid heartbeat. With artifacts like these, the Archons and Earthlords had created the Shadowrealms. But even they had only had tiny fragments of crystals, usually worked into rings, bracelets, or necklaces or set into the tips of wands. A huge crystal like this could create . . . She stopped. She had no idea what it was capable of.

Almost unwillingly, Aoife took a step forward.

She knew what to do with the smaller shards and even the crystal skulls. Years ago Zephaniah had given her and Scathach a dozen tubes filled with a coarse black power that melted crystal, making it run like melted wax. She wondered if she had enough to destroy this.

The stone suddenly pulsed green and the mist flowing off it turned emerald, the same color as her eyes. It rolled out in a long, sinuous wave and washed over her feet, splashing up against her thighs. Instantly she felt the dull muscle aches and the tightness from old wounds fade. Even the sting from the blisters on her heels disappeared.

Aoife took a step forward, the whip now hanging limp by her side, trailing on the ground, sparking and fizzing like a firecracker.

The stone throbbed blue, and now soothing sapphire mist washed over her feet and legs. It was like stepping into warm bathwater. Pins and needles crawled up her body, setting her legs tingling and cramping. The whip slipped from nerveless fingers, and she dropped to all fours in the blue mist. Dipping her hands into the shifting cloud, she brought her damp fingers up to rub her face, bathing in it. The scarred skin on her left cheek burned and itched, but when she touched it again, the flesh was smooth and the deep grooves were gone. And when she looked at her hands, she discovered that her chewed fingernails were strong and unbroken.

Then, on hands and knees, she crawled toward the stone.

Aoife blinked tears from her eyes; they rolled down her cheeks and fell onto the churned earth before her like tiny globular sapphires. When she looked toward the stone again, she discovered that the night had become even clearer, the stone assuming shape and definition, each wriggling pictogram and shivering line of text now sharp and precise.

She knew what was happening: the stone was healing her, soothing old aches and wounds, wiping away scars. The ache in her lower back was gone, the ingrown toenail no longer pinched, and she could actually feel a new tooth pushing through her gum to replace the one a domovoi had knocked out.

She felt amazing. Alive. Young. Whole. But somewhere at the back of her mind a tiny voice was crying out in warning: there was something wrong here . . . something terribly wrong . . .

The stone pulsed cool silver light and the air was suffused with the scent of salt and the scent of the sea. Aoife continued to crawl toward the stone.

And then a studded club took her between the shoulders, snapping bones, cracking her skull as it drove her face-first into the mud.

Grinning hugely, Nels stepped over the woman's body.

10

The Lia Fáil.

Nels recognized it immediately: the Stone of Destiny. At the heart of every legend was a grain of truth, and Nels had just discovered the truth about Tir Tairngaire.

Every child in Tir Tairngaire learned how Cernunnos had stood with his hand upon this crystal and created the world. It was one of those stories told and retold around the camps, but Nels had always dismissed it, relegating it to tales of lost cities, vanished islands, and mysterious otherworlds where the skies were filled with silver discs. Yet if the Lia Fáil was real, that meant that every other legend—the gods and monsters, the lost worlds, and magical gateways—must also have some truth to it.

The Lia Fáil pulsed crimson and black, and a thick bloodred smoke curled across the ground toward him.

Nels stepped into the mist, sending it coiling around him. The drover could feel the ancient power flow across his skin, easing the ache of knotted muscles and wrenched shoulders. His skull itched abominably. Running his hand over it, he felt the rasping fuzz of hair he had lost in his youth.

Stepping closer to the stone, he could feel the flesh on his face tightening, muscles rippling beneath the skin, and when he touched his forehead and cheeks, the deep wrinkles and grooves around his eyes and mouth were missing. He spat out a rotten tooth and discovered that the space was already filled with a new one. His hands cramped as missing fingernails appeared, and the deep scars across his palms, caused by decades of gripping leather reins, were turning pink with new flesh.

Nels knew what was happening: the stone was healing him, rejuvenating him, making him younger, stronger.

The Lia Fáil.

Like everyone on Tir Tairngaire, he had grown up hearing the legends of the stone and the stories of the generations of adventurers and mystics who had sought the crystal. Some of the temples to Cernunnos had tiny crystal relics, chips supposedly taken from the stone, each of them capable of working miracles. Priests of the Horned God paid handsomely for these crystal artifacts from the Time Before Time.

The big man put his hands on his hips and tilted his head to one side, looking at the stone with suddenly clear eyes. His vision was crisp, the hints of cataracts at the corners of his eyes now gone.

The Stone of Destiny. Here was his fortune. But he would not sell it. He had no need to. There were a hundred ways he could use this stone. A thousand ways. A stone like this could make a man wealthy. . . . No . . . a stone like this could make a man a god.

Why, with the power of the Lia Fáil, he could challenge Cernunnos himself for the world. And not just this world: with the power of the Lia Fáil he could create his own world or any number of worlds. Here was his destiny.

Nels dropped the club to the ground and stepped up to the Lia Fáil, arms wide. . . .

11

There should be pain.

Aoife had been wounded before. She knew the sickening agony of injury, the burning snap of broken bones, the piercing heat of torn flesh. Even as she'd been falling, she'd known what had happened: she'd been so distracted and confused by the stone that she'd allowed Nels to creep up behind her. He'd struck her down with his club. She knew her skull was cracked—she had heard the pop of bone—and there was a tingling in her legs that made her suspect her spine was damaged.

Yet there was no pain.

Was this what death—the true death—was like? No pain, merely a gentle warmth that flowed across her skin and settled into her muscles with a soothing heat.

Green and blue mist curled and eddied over her, individual colored droplets standing out on her skin like tiny jewels before sinking into her dirty flesh, lending it an almost metallic appearance.

When she'd fallen, she'd sliced her palm on the edge of her metal whip, a long, ragged cut. Lying on the ground, her hand curled before her face, blood pooling in her hand, she watched the skin pull together and knit itself in a long red line that almost instantly faded to white, then vanished.

There was no pain . . . and she knew why.

It was the stone. The stone was healing her.

But if Aoife had learned anything over her centuries of life, it was that everything had a price. What was the price of this healing? she wondered.

Taking a deep breath, she raised her head, broken bones and torn muscles knitting and snapping together, stronger than before. She saw the wagon master standing before the stone, arms wide. And she knew she was going to be too late to stop him.

12

If just the mist rolling off the Lia Fáil was able to make him young and whole again, then what would happen if he touched the stone itself? The legends whispered of the dark lore at the heart of the stones. If he touched it, would he absorb some of that knowledge? Would he know what the gods knew? And if knowledge was power, would that make him as powerful as Cernunnos?

Nels shivered with excitement. The Lia Fáil would give him everything he had ever wanted: wealth beyond imagining and unimaginable power. The knowledge of the Earthlords and the Archons would be his. No one would ever laugh at him again. No one would ever look down on him because he was a simple drover. He would rule this world. He would remake it. Conquer it.

Nels stood before the stone, mesmerized by the swirling red and black smoke within the dark crystal, and then he reached out and placed both hands flat against it.

The Lia Fáil instantly turned bloodred, shades of crimson pulsing like a heartbeat.

Power—icy, raw power—flowed into his body, shocking

him rigid, and then the chill turned warm, comforting, absorbed into his flesh. It flowed through muscles and settled deep in his core, nestling in his stomach.

The weight of his four and forty years dropped off him, and suddenly he was young again, young and strong and vital. A thick mat of hair crawled across his skull; muscles swelled his chest and his arms; his spine straightened in a series of cracking pops, allowing him to stand tall.

Nels pulled his palms off the stone, leaving bloody imprints on its surface, raised his arms to the skies, and howled in triumph.

13

Aoife climbed shakily to her feet as Nels reached out to embrace the stone. He saw her from the corner of his eye and turned his head to smile savagely at her. Then he pressed both palms against the stone, holding it close, arms almost completely encircling the crystal.

The throb of color that flooded the Lia Fáil was the color of old blood, brown and ugly.

Aoife watched the bronze and black energies flicker and flow into the man's body, pulse through his flesh to highlight the skeleton beneath. She watched his muscles fill and swell, hair coil serpent-like down his head, tufts of coarse black fur sprout on his chest. The man twisted his head and spat, his old, discolored, chipped teeth spinning onto the ground, and when he raised his head to snarl at her, she saw that his mouth was filled with perfect white teeth.

The stone had made him young again.

"Fear me!" Nels thundered, voice powerful and commanding, lifting his hands off the stone to stretch his arms wide.

She watched how the bloody imprints of his hands on the glass were absorbed into the crystal.

"Fear me!" Nels yelled again, and he gripped the stone, leaned forward, and pressed his lips to it. He breathed in its very essence. "Today I will become a god."

The stone made him young.

Only, he was still changing. Still becoming younger.

From middle age to prime of life had taken moments, from prime to youth took even less time, and from youth to child and child to babe took only a handful of heartbeats again. It happened almost too fast to see, the man becoming a teen, a youth, a boy, a toddler, a newborn.

Aoife squeezed her eyes shut, and when she opened them again, Nels was gone. She knew then why she'd found no beast or animal tracks returning from the stone: it had taken them all, absorbed their very essence into its crystalline core. This close to the artifact, standing in the swirling multicolored smoke leaking from the crystal, she could hear countless voices—human and animal—whispering in her skull. Faintly, very faintly, she thought she even heard Nels's lost screams. She learned its name then: the Lia Fáil, the Stone of Destiny.

Fragments of images danced before her eyes: images of incredible beauty and unimaginable terror. Standing still, eyes closed, she could feel the promises of power and knowledge pulsing from the Lia Fáil, battering her consciousness like waves on the shore. The stone was—like all the ancient crystals—vaguely alive, but it was a foul, vampiric half-life. It needed energies to live, and it sucked the life from the living, drawing their essence deep into its crystalline heart.

There were thousands—no, tens of thousands, hundreds of thousands—of lives, humani and nonhuman, beasts and monsters, even some Earthlords and Elders, Archon and Ancients—caught within the stone, mingled together, not quite dead but not fully alive. All seeking to escape.

The stone whispered, promised, wheedled, cajoled. . . .

All she had to do was to reach out and touch the Lia Fáil. Then she could rule not only this Shadowrealm but all the Shadowrealms. She could become the Empress of the Universe.

Aoife managed to take a step back.

When the stone realized she had no interest in wealth or power, it reached into her mind and tore through her memories, unearthing desires and old fears. The Lia Fáil could give her everything she ever wanted and help her destroy what she most feared.

Unconsciously, Aoife took a ragged step forward, closer to the stone.

The stone dug deeper, finally unearthing her deepest, darkest secrets and fears. The whispers became a shout, the sound echoing within her skull: the Lia Fáil could help her kill her twin sister, Scathach.

Images—terrifying images—battered her. Suddenly, Aoife saw Scathach—red-haired and green-eyed, the very image of herself—lying broken at her feet.

The voices in her head grew triumphant, whispering in a hundred languages . . .

That is what you want.

"No." The word puffed out of her mouth in a hint of blue mist.

Yes. That is what you have always wanted.

"No."

Yes. You hate her. You fear her. You want her dead.

"I never wanted her dead."

Yes.

"No."

You have not spoken to her in centuries.

"We had an argument. A stupid argument. Over a boy." Even as she was saying it, she knew how ridiculous it sounded. She had to struggle to remember the boy's name: Cuchulain. That was it: Culain's Hound.

She hates you.

"She does not."

You hate her.

"I do not." She breathed in blue smoke, and in that moment, she truly believed it.

Kill her. We have made you strong again, all your old ailments wiped away. Now you will be able to overcome her.

The images flooded back, and Aoife abruptly saw herself fighting her twin, whip and sword against nunchaku and sword. And Scathach falling beneath a flurry of blows. The sudden horror shocked her, leaving her shivering and sick to her stomach.

"No, I will not."

She did not fear her sister. She did not hate her. She missed her.

"No," she said again, and then she threw back her head and screamed aloud her defiance. "No. I will not."

The Lia Fáil's countless voices dissolved into a mindless, howling static. Aoife staggered back from the stone. She could feel the Lia Fáil pushing against her, probing her mind, even as the colored smoke washed over her skin. She stumbled and fell backward, and her hand curled around the hilt of her metal whip.

We can give you everything.

"I have everything I want."

As she rolled to her feet, she lashed out with the whip. Static crawled along the metal as it snaked through the air, and there was a solid crack of lightning as it struck the crystal.

The Lia Fáil screamed.

The sound drove Aoife back.

A million voices cried out in agony. And perhaps a million more roared their rage.

Aoife's whip snapped fire and lightning on the pillar again and again. She could feel its confusion now; in all the millennia of its existence, it had never been attacked. She stepped closer, the whip leaving curling patterns in the smoky air, cutting black lines in the crystal. When she was close enough to touch it, she reached into the pouch her grandmother had given her centuries ago. As her fingers closed around the finger-length metal tube of special salts designed to melt crystal, Aoife recalled that Zephaniah had given Scathach an identical pouch and tube. She wondered if her twin had ever used it. She'd make sure to ask the next time she saw her.

14

"What did you find in the forest?" Bes asked as they broke camp the following morning.

"Nothing," Aoife said shortly.

"More than nothing, surely." The Dwarf looked openly at her unscarred forehead, the bloom of youth on her cheeks, the bright sparkle in her eyes.

"Nothing I could not handle." Aoife smiled. A sound moaned out of the valley below, and they both turned to watch a whirlwind of silver dust spiraling up in the morning air.

"I wonder what happened to our wagon master," Bes said quietly. "He went missing in the night."

"So I heard."

"For a moment, I was fearful he had gone after you," Bes said.

"We met in the forest," Aoife admitted.

"Did you kill him?"

"No," she said truthfully.

"But he will not be back, will he?"

Aoife shook her head. "No, he's gone."

"Where will you go when we are done?" Bes asked.

"Home." Aoife looked across the treetops. "You said you could find me a leygate to take me back to the Earth Shadow-realm."

"You have family there?"

"I have a sister," Aoife answered. "We have much to talk about."

SCATHACH THE SHADOW AND THE CLAN OF ERIU

500 BCE

Dearest Joan,

The Druid here claims that he can take my words, convert them to a cloud of water vapor, and send them through the leygates, where (because we are linked by blood) they will find you. Apparently, the words will appear as if written in moisture on windows and mirrors around you. Startling the first time, I'm sure, and you'll have to read quickly before they dribble away. He's still struggling to find a name for the process—"water-vapor messages" hasn't quite got a ring to it. He is either a genius or the greatest con man I have ever encountered. I have told him that if I discover you have not received these messages, then I will hunt him down and introduce him to an ice-cold lake. Preferably one with a peist in it.

I am afraid that I went against your advice and took a job Marethyu offered me. I know, I know! Of course, my problem is that I am simply too accommodating. I should have said no to Marethyu, but if I am being honest with myself, the truth is that I was bored. It was supposed to be a quick reconnaissance on Tír fo Thuinn, a backwater Shadowrealm. I'd fit right in, he told me. This was an old world with Celtic roots, possibly created by Balor or even Lugh himself. Marethyu had heard rumors of an Archon library, and he wanted me to check it out.

Of course, I should have realized there'd be a catch. There always is with the Hook-Handed Man. It turns out he wanted me here to try to prevent a war. It seems as though some of the creatures on this world will play a significant role in a huge upcoming battle. He was quite mysterious about it, but you know Marethyu: he can be so dramatic.

From Scathach,
on the Tír fo Thuinn Shadowrealm,
via water-vapor message
to Joan of Arc, my sister-in-blood.

1

A flash of light in the gloomy forest below, a blink of silver in the shadows, lasting less than a single heartbeat.

The redheaded rider was already falling, instinct, intuition, and experience driving her down behind the skittish stag before she heard the sounds. A chunk of metal exploded against the cliff face to her right, less than a hand span above the stag's head. The startled beast reared, metal-shod hooves pawing the air, and Scathach slid out of the saddle and rolled to one side to avoid being trampled.

A second shot rang out, and she recognized the distinctive ping of a tonbogiri, an ornate long-barreled rifle that should not exist on this world. A third shot bit into the ground between the stag's feet and it reared again, eyes wide, mouth frothing, prancing dangerously close to the edge of the narrow track.

Instinctively, Scathach had begun counting from the moment she'd seen the flash of light and then heard the snap of gunfire. From the direction of the shot, the angle they'd struck at, and the slightly different sounds, she worked out that there were at least two shooters in the valley below and to her left.

A third shot sizzled close enough to the stag's rump to draw a thin line of blood, and the creature bucked widely. The saddle shifted, and Scathach realized that one of the straps had loosened. Feeling the weight move on its back, the stag arched its back and kicked out. The strap broke with a sharp snap, and when the stag pranced again, it threw off the saddle and saddlebags. Its rear hooves struck the ground hard, shattering the edge of the track, which sheared off and tumbled into the darkness. The stag bellowed once, a deep grunting sound, almost human in intensity, forelegs scrabbling for purchase, before it slid over the edge.

The red-haired young woman rolled to the verge and looked down, expecting to see the broken body of the creature on the ground below. But the stag had dug in its hind legs and stretched out its forelegs and was sliding down the loose shale and scree into the shadows. She caught a flicker of its antlers moving through the forest as it bounded to freedom.

A quick smile curled Scathach's thin lips, revealing her pointed vampire teeth. The stag had been nothing but trouble—temperamental, with a nasty habit of snapping whenever she went too close—but she would have hated to see it fall to its death.

Two more shots rang out almost simultaneously, and she smiled again. Definitely two ambushers, and she caught the faintest hint of burnt powder on the chill air. She realized that these were antique single-shot tonbogiri . . . which was probably the reason she was still alive. The early models were barely accurate to a hundred paces and took minutes to load. However, this was an Anpu weapon, and she wondered how the technology of the jackal-headed people had ended up on this world.

Another shot screamed off the cliff face above her head, showering her with tiny flecks of red-hot metal, but Scathach didn't move. Moments later a pair of shots dug into the ground to her right and left and she smiled again, knowing her attackers were unsure that they—or the hooves of the prancing stag—had gotten her. They were firing blindly, hoping to force her to move. Which was a mistake. It revealed their locations, and if immortality had taught her nothing else, it had taught her patience. Scathach squinted toward the heavens; the sun was low in the sky and the first of the five tiny moons—the Ducklings—had risen. Storm clouds were gathering in the north, and the air was already touched with the promise of icy rain. It would be dark soon and then she could slip away.

"I wonder who you are," she murmured. "Brigands or assassins?"

Road thieves were commonplace, and she'd been long enough on this world to have made a few enemies—the price on her head brought out assassins with all manner of skills. The tonbogiri rifles made her wonder if some new players had entered the game, or had some old enemies tracked her down?

Rolling over onto her stomach, resting her chin on her

folded arms, the young woman absently traced a route down the hillside, picking out a pathway that would bring her in and behind the ambushers. Once—when she had been called Scathach the Pitiless—she would have taught her ambushers a fatal lesson. But that had been a long time ago. Over the centuries she had seen too much death and destruction, fought in too many wars on too many Shadowrealms. She had mellowed as she aged, and she'd grown weary of the endless cycle of death and destruction. She had made a promise to herself that she would not kill unless her own life, or the lives of those she loved, was in danger. She'd more or less managed to keep to the promise on this Shadowrealm.

"Who are you?" she wondered aloud. Somehow she doubted it was the Anpu. The jackal-headed warriors were excellent shots and would have been using the modern repeating tonbogiri rifles. The Torc Clans on this world had no access to tonbogiri and she doubted they'd used them; the were-clans preferred to fight hand to hand. So that left the humani.

Scathach had fought with and against the humani. They were among the most extraordinary of the many races she had encountered: brilliant, creative, imaginative, and passionate. But all too often that same brilliance and creativity, the same imagination and passion that allowed them to produce wonders, had taken them down dark roads: into making weapons, waging wars and finding ever more inventive ways to kill one another. It was a waste. They lived such brief lives, but were prepared to squander them needlessly. Not all of them, it was true. She had seen what they were capable of if the shadow of war was removed from their lives.

Her sister, Aoife, on the other hand, did not agree with her: Aoife always believed that the greatest acts of humani invention and creativity came during times of war. Scathach didn't know; she'd ask Marethyu the next time she saw him. He'd know; the hook-handed man knew everything.

Cradling her head in her forearms, she settled down to wait, idly wondering who was attacking her. The Iron Mountains and the Great Northern Forest were occupied by scattered bands of humani who lived in uneasy coexistence with creatures straight from the darkest of legends. Feuds and clan wars were commonplace, and strangers were not welcome. But it was unlike them to shoot at a single traveler. She wondered if those shots had been designed to scare her away or to kill. Perhaps the really important question was, were they waiting just for her?

Scathach looked longingly at her leather pack still attached to the saddle, lying in the middle of the track. She could see the outline of a Fomor blowpipe in the nearest bag. If she could only reach it and the selection of darts in their wooden cases, she could send her attackers a little stinging present. She had darts tipped with lethal poison, others with numbing agents or sleeping potions, and a handful coated with the secretions of a tree toad that brought on the most terrifying visions. She had no doubt she could hit the attackers below. But the bag, for the moment, was out of reach. If she made a move for it, she would reveal her location, and while she didn't think the shooters were good enough to hit her, they might get lucky. Immortality was no guard against death. She could be injured and killed, and though she looked no older than seventeen, her age was measured in centuries and she fully intended to live for at least a millennium. She would not die here.

Scathach's hands moved absently to the leather pouch cinched tight around her throat. At least she hadn't lost that. The bag was the reason she was on this road. She occasionally took employment as a courier, specializing in discreetly delivering high-value merchandise. Her reputation was impeccable, and she'd never lost a package. She wondered if someone had learned that she was heading north with a package of immense value. Was this an ambush?

Possible, but unlikely. There were a dozen places on the road better suited to an ambush, and given her reputation, they'd hardly have attempted it with just two attackers. The last time someone had tried to steal a package from her, they'd brought twenty-two heavily armed men. She hadn't actually killed any of them, but every one had ended up with the local healer. While only some would limp for the rest of their lives, all of them would carry the scars of fighting the Shadow.

Centuries ago she'd learned that the simplest way to grow your legend was to let your enemies live. No one wanted to admit that they'd been defeated by a girl. So the losers boasted that they had been bested by an ancient warrior, a goddess, a warrior queen. Of course, in her case, most of that was true. Even the goddess title. There were worlds on which she—and her sister, Aoife—were worshipped as The Shadow Twins. On those Shadowrealms, twins—especially twin girls—were considered holy and gifts from the gods.

Scathach squinted toward the heavens; the sun was low in the sky, and the second of the five moons had risen. She could see storm clouds growing angrier in the north, pulsing white with unheard thunder. It would be dark soon, and she would be able to retrieve her bag. Then she could slip away. But even as she was formulating the thought, she knew—deep in her heart and soul—that she was going to go down to see who or what had attacked her.

Easing her double-edged knife out of her right boot, she quickly mapped out her options.

They were depressingly few.

She was without a mount in the high country, at least two days' ride from the nearest settlement. This far north the weather was unpredictable, and a storm could whip down from the Ice Lands without warning. Creatures that were little more than legend in the rest of the country roamed freely here, surviving in the hidden valleys and isolated caves. There were few human settlements left; the Road Fever that had swept along the length of the Bothar Ri, the King's Road, in previous generations had devastated many of the towns and villages, leaving them nothing but tumbled ruins.

Scathach was not humani, had no need to eat or drink and rarely slept. And although she was more or less immune to extreme weather, if it got cold enough, she could fall into a coma so deep it would seem that she was dead. Mythology was littered with characters who had fallen asleep and awoken centuries later; they were usually Next Generation, like her.

The first fat droplets of icy rain spattered into the ground about her.

Scathach hated the rain. It was the one abiding memory of her childhood in the Celtic lands on the Earth Shadowrealm. She'd spent far too many years cold, wet, and thoroughly miserable. When she'd finally discovered that there were countries where it seldom rained, she'd left her damp homeland, and she rarely went back. One of these days she was going to retire to a nice warm desert town.

Rain sleeted in again, peppering the ground with speckles of hail.

That settled it; she hated rain, but she really detested hail. She wasn't going to hang around here a moment longer and get drenched. Time to change tactics. Squinting through the gathering clouds, she peered down into the valley again. Her attackers probably had mounts of some sort—horses, oxen, or deer. And she needed a mount. So she'd head down into the valley and ask them for a mount to replace the one they'd scared away. No doubt they'd refuse, but she'd take one anyway. Or maybe two.

Scathach spotted movement on the far side of the valley, across the ravine, hunched and twisted shapes scuttling through the undergrowth, heading toward the shooters. Reinforcements. She squinted again, trying to make sense of what she was seeing. They were well camouflaged, but from the way they moved, she knew they were not humani. They were unlikely to be were-folk, and she got the impression that these might be one of the Fir races: Fir Mhor, Fir Dearg, or even the dreaded Fir Bolg, a creature more beast than man. They often hunted in packs. A knife would prove little protection against the armored hide of a Fir Bolg, and she was thinking she might have to break her promise not to kill anyone.

She heard a crack, and then a fist-sized green ball came sailing up out of the valley to spatter against the wall almost directly above her head. Scathach jerked back instinctively as thin green slime dripped off the rock. The stench was overwhelming: foul, bitter, a noxious mixture of rotten eggs, sour milk, and rancid food.

She recognized the stink immediately. It was a moor pod.

She knew then that she was in real trouble. Only the Fir Bolg and Fir Dearg, the hairy stunted dwarves, used the moor pods in their slingshots, and this far north, they were rumored to eat humani flesh. She idly wondered if Next Generation flesh tasted different from humani. She didn't think the Fir Dearg would be too fussy.

Another pod burst on the narrow path almost directly in front of her, sticky green pustules spattering across her jerkin. Ducking her head, Scathach gulped air, jumped to her feet, and darted out onto the track. Putting as much space as she could between herself and the stinking fumes of the moor pod was more important than avoiding the chance of being hit by the tongobiri. She snatched her pack off the ground and darted down the track, the edge of the path crumbling beneath her left boot. But even as she took her first staggering steps, she knew she had inhaled some of the moor pod gas. The world was shifting, rainbow colors bleeding at the very edge of her vision turning the world vivid and startling. Speckles of light danced before her streaming eyes, and the muted colors of the northern landscape became brighter, sharper, cleaner.

She should have done this from the beginning, she thought. Instead of lying on the ground and allowing them to plan a new strategy, she should have waited until they had fired, then leapt to her feet, grabbed her bag, and run.

The sky turned bright yellow, and all the colors were smeared in long streaks as if they were flowing past her face. The ground beneath her looked so very far away, and she felt as if she were running in slow motion.

She heard a buzz, and suddenly a stone chipped flakes of rock from the cliff face alongside her head; another struck her a glancing blow on the shoulder, numbing her entire arm, and then a puffy green ball exploded directly in front of her. Unable to stop her forward momentum, Scathach raced directly into its billowing cloud . . . and instantly the world lit up in a kaleidoscope of fractal colors. She stopped as abruptly as if she had run into a stone wall, and stood swaying. Then, slowly, she dropped to her knees and fell forward. She knew she was falling, and it seemed to take a long time before she finally hit the earth. The sudden shock and the sting of gravel on her hands and knees brought her briefly back to consciousness.

With the last of her strength, she attempted to pull herself toward the ravine. If she could throw herself over the edge, she might be able to mimic the deer and slide into the dark valley below, where she could disappear into the forest. Sure, she'd get scraped up and maybe break a bone or two, but at least she would not be eaten alive. . . .

2

The face was hideous.

A hairless head covered in leathery skin, the nose flat and piglike, eyes yellow, speckled with broken veins, and a ragged mouth filled with two upward jutting tusks. "I know what you're thinking. And you should know that I am considered beautiful among my people." The voice of the creature was a shocking contrast to its appearance. It sounded like that of a young woman, high and pure without a trace of an accent, and all the more disconcerting because it issued from the creature's mouth.

Scathach struggled to sit up, grateful that the creature—neither Fir Bolg nor Fir Dearg, though obviously kin to both tribes—made no effort to help. She had a crushing headache and felt sick to her stomach, and her right arm was aching from shoulder to elbow. Drawing her knees up to her head, she pressed both hands to her throbbing temples while surreptitiously taking stock of her surroundings. She was in a reed hut, circular in the Bolg fashion, but decorated with woven beads and spectacularly beautiful knitted tapestries on the walls and floor, which were completely alien to Bolg culture. Beyond the walls, she could hear children's voices and laughter over the gurgling backdrop of a nearby stream.

Finally, she looked back at the creature waiting patiently at the side of her bed. Scathach had traveled the length and breadth of Tír fo Thuinn, had seen most of the myriad beasts that inhabited the land, but she had never encountered anything quite like this creature.

By the voice, Scathach assumed she was female. From her thick armored hide, it was clear that there was Fir Bolg blood in her, but the deep ocher hue of her skin and the shape of her skull suggested that she might also be related to the Fir Dearg. Her decorated tusks were Torc Allta, and yet her voice had all the pure tones of a trained De Danann myth singer. She was wearing a long robe stitched and worked with countless thousands of beads, shells, and polished pebbles, similar to that a De Danann priestess might wear.

The creature proffered a beautifully carved stone goblet. "Drink. It will clear your head and ease your stomach." She smiled at Scathach's hesitation, showing terrifying tusks and a thick black tongue. "If we had wished to harm you, we could have done so before now," she said reasonably.

"That is true." Scathach nodded, dipping her head to hide her smile, well aware that some cultures took the baring of teeth as a threat. She sipped the green liquid. It was bitter, with a slightly chalky aftertaste.

"We make it from the root of the moor pods. It is only the fruits and pods that are poisonous; the leaves and roots have many medicinal uses."

"I feel better already," Scathach admitted. The headache had lifted almost immediately, and she could actually feel the liquid move through her body. Her stomach rumbled. She pushed herself upright, then sat back on the bed, pressing her spine against the wall of the hut. She was surprised to find her pack on the ground beside the straw pallet. It looked untouched.

The creature caught her gaze. "It is as you left it. We are not thieves."

Scathach finished the last of the liquid and handed over the goblet. She noticed that each of the woman's six short, blunt nails were painted a rainbow of striped colors. "How long have I slept?"

"Though the night. The sun has just risen."

The Shadow groaned. "I need to get back on the road. I have an appointment I must keep." Then she added, "Forgive my rudeness. I am Scathach."

"And I am Moriath. I am of the Clan of Eriu."

"I've not heard of your clan before," Scathach answered.

"Few have," Moriath said in her quiet, musical voice. "We are a solitary people. We keep to ourselves and have little commerce with the rest of the world. Do you have a clan?"

"Not anymore," Scathach said cautiously. She wasn't sure how the creature would react if she learned she was a vampire. Nearly every Shadowrealm had some version of her race, but most of those were monsters and all were blood drinkers. Many killed the blood drinkers on sight.

"It must be lonely without a clan," Moriath said.

"I am not entirely alone," Scathach answered frankly. "Although my birth clan is long gone, I found as I got older that I'd built another clan around me, a clan of choice rather than one of blood."

"Family is everything," Moriath agreed.

"What happened on the mountain?" Scathach asked, leaning forward to drag her pack toward her. The woman made no effort to stop her. She'd been shot at, drugged, and kidnapped, but she didn't feel she was in any real danger. "I was attacked for no reason."

"I'm afraid some of our young men got a little overenthusiastic," Moriath answered without a trace of apology in her voice.

The Shadow bit back a snap of anger. "Do your young men usually attack lone travelers in the mountains?"

"Not usually," Moriath said. "But these are not usual times."

Something was terribly wrong here. Scathach wondered if she still had some of the drug in her system, because things weren't making sense. The woman had just admitted that theirs was a solitary community, virtually unknown to the outside world, and yet they had brought her here, into their village. She found herself idly wondering again if she was on the menu. Scathach opened her pack and pulled out a small stone jar of sweet-smelling salve. She rubbed it on her grazed and scratched hands, wincing as it stung her flesh. But she had seen too many warriors lose fingers and even limbs because they hadn't cleaned even the simplest of wounds.

Carefully peeling off her scuffed leather jacket, she examined the bruise on her shoulder.

"I suppose I should be grateful that it wasn't a tonbogiri bullet. Why did they change back to catapults and stones?"

"I would imagine they were probably shooting at the stag. Stones have little effect against their thick hides." She smiled quickly. "And bullets are too expensive to waste on humani. A stone will do." She stretched out her hand. "If you will allow me?"

Scathach handed over the jar.

Moriath brought it to her nose and breathed deeply. "Lambsbane, beeswax, mint, and bruiseworth."

"You are a healer?"

"I am many things," Moriath said. "You sound surprised."

"By your costume, I thought you might be a myth singer."

"I am many things," Moriath repeated, continuing to examine the paste. She rolled the thick salve between her fingers and then carefully applied it in slow circular motions to the dark bruise on Scathach's shoulder. "This ointment is a little thick," she murmured. "There should be more oil."

"I make it from a recipe my sister taught me when we were children," Scathach answered.

"Ah, you do have family, then."

"We have not spoken recently. We had an argument."

Moriath concentrated on easing the salve into Scathach's bruise. "Hmm, it is fading beneath my fingers. You have excellent healing skin." She paused, and then asked, "Was this argument a long time ago?"

"Too long."

"And would you argue today over the same subject?"

"We fought over a boy, and no, we would not!" Scathach grinned. "I have no idea why I am telling you this. It must be some of the moor pod in my system, making me talkative."

"Perhaps you are not telling me. Perhaps you are admitting it to yourself. Does your sister have a name?"

"Aoife. Are you a witch, Moriath, as well as a healer? A Truthfinder, perhaps? I have heard they are common in the Eastern courts," Scathach said quickly, desperately trying to change the subject. She was surprised she'd even mentioned Aoife's name; she never spoke to anyone about her twin.

"I am many things," Moriath said again. She leaned forward to examine Scathach's arm. "Remarkable. The bruise is almost entirely gone. This must be a miraculous salve. Though I do think you should add a little more oil to make it easier to spread." She took the warrior's hands in hers and turned them over to examine the scratches and scrapes. They were completely healed. "You are not humani," she said softly, stepping back to look Scathach up and down.

"I am not," the Shadow admitted. She opened her mouth, revealing her pointed incisors. "I am vampire. Not a blood drinker," she added. Unable to read the other woman's expression, she asked, "Is this going to be a problem?"

"Not here," Moriath said simply. She held out her hand and Scathach took it and rose slowly to her feet, swaying as the room shifted and spun around her. Moriath caught her wrist, holding her up with an iron grip, until everything settled. "You do not flinch from our appearance," she remarked, "and yet I understand we are hideous to you."

"As I must be to you."

Moriath's smile was savage. "You are not pretty," she agreed. "Though the red hair is common among my people."

"I spent two seasons sailing with the Island Bolg. I never found them hideous. They loved my hair. They would cut locks of it to make into amulets. I had a Bolg . . . *companion* for a while," she said, choosing her words carefully. "More than a companion, Rua was my friend. Bravest warrior I ever fought alongside."

"You speak of him in the past tense."

"Oh, he is still alive, I hope. He sailed into the Western Seas in search of the mythical homeland of the Fir clans."

"My people are kin to the Fir Bolg and the Fir Dearg," Moriath said, turning away. "You did not accompany him?"

"I wanted to . . . but I was in search of a different legend. We parted as friends and made a promise that we would look for one another when we had found our myth or given up on the attempt." Scathach followed Moriath to the door.

"You might want to close your eyes for a moment," Moriath advised. "Your pupils are still dilated from the drug."

Scathach squeezed her eyes shut, but even through the lids, she felt the blast of light, red and pink, against her flesh. Her eyes watered, and tears ran down her cheeks. She brushed them away quickly. Even though she was not a blood drinker, all the vampire clan shed crimson tears, and they could be alarming for others to see.

Standing in the doorway of the hut, Scathach opened her eyes and looked out across a neat village of twenty huts straddling either side of the fast-flowing stream, the stream she had heard earlier. The village was enclosed behind a palisade of spiked furze. Children's squeals made her turn toward the water. Four children were splashing on the bank. Two were almost pure Fir Bolg, with armored skin and snaking tails; another was hunched like one of the underground Dwarves; and the fourth had the flaming red hair, bright green eyes, and copper-colored skin of the Dearg tribe. The red-haired boy spotted the two women and came running up, moving around to stand behind Moriath, clutching her gown, peering at Scathach.

The warrior crouched and looked into the boy's bright green eyes. They were almost the same color as hers. She smiled, keeping her mouth closed. "Hello. My name is Scathach."

"Mountain lady," the boy said, pointing to her, and ran off.

Scathach straightened. "A fine boy."

"My son," Moriath said.

Scathach was unable to keep the look of surprise off her face. Moriath was related to the Fir Bolg, and the red-haired boy's father must be Fir Dearg. Scathach had never known the tribes to mix. The Fir Dearg had never forgiven the Bolg betrayal at the Second Battle of the Bridge, even though it had taken place a thousand years ago.

"Look around." Moriath walked away from the hut,

forcing Scathach to follow her. "What do you see? You may be honest with me."

The warrior turned in a slow circle. "I see a dozen races, creatures who should not live easily together, were-boars and were-dogs, representatives of all the Fir clans, mixtures the like of which I've never seen before," she answered honestly.

"We are . . ." Moriath hesitated, ragged tusks biting her lip as she sought for the proper word. "Well, you might say that we are experiments."

Scathach felt a chill settle along the length of her spine. Such experiments had been outlawed since the time of the Beast Wars.

"We are not freaks," Moriath said. "Well, perhaps we are," she added with a grin. "But think: in a generation, or two or three, if we can prove that the myriad native and magical races of the Tír fo Thuinn can mix and live together, then much of the cause for conflict will have been removed."

Scathach's laugh was a harsh bark.

Moriath rounded on her, then abruptly stepped back, gaze fixed over the woman's left shoulder.

Scathach turned smoothly, hand falling to the knife in her belt. A figure had appeared behind her. He was tall and thin, with a heavily muscled, deeply tanned human body, but with the head of a jackal. A mane of snow-white hair flowed down his back. He was wearing an alligator breastplate, studded alligator-skin trousers, and a battered kopesh, a sickle sword hung from his belt.

"Anpu," Scathach breathed. She had fought the jackal-headed warriors across a dozen Shadowrealms, and on more than one occasion, she had come close to losing her immortal life.

"Our guest is a warrior," the Anpu said quietly, his accent almost identical to Moriath's. "She is experienced in the ways of death and men. She knows that outsiders will find it difficult to accept our way of life. They will use it as an excuse to kill us."

"In my experience, people need little excuse for killing," Scathach said.

"True. But here"—he spread his arms wide—"here we are trying to give them one less reason. Living in scattered clans makes us fearful. Here we can see that many races, clans, even individuals and their offspring can live in peace together."

"Attacking travelers is not very peaceful," Scathach remarked.

"Aaah yes. There is a reason, but that does not excuse the action. I apologize. I am Ophois."

Scathach brought both hands together, thumbs to lips, forefingers touching the center of her forehead.

Ophois's smile was brilliant, revealing a mouthful of savage fangs. "You know my race and customs."

"I spent four summers as bodyguard to the Boy King."

Ophois's smile hardened. He stepped closer to examine her scarred leather armor inset with metal rings and plates designed to turn a blade. Moving to one side, he looked at the triple-spiral tattoo high on the warrior's right arm and nodded slightly. "I know of you: you are Scathach the Piti-less." It was a statement, not a question.

"Once." The warrior answered, staring into the creature's golden eyes. "No more. Now I am just Scathach, sometimes called the Shadow."

Ophois nodded almost imperceptibly. "We all change. And how fares the Boy King?"

"He was assassinated three days after I left his employ."

"Aaah." There was a world of pain in the single word. "He had such promise."

Scathach nodded sadly. "He did. But those who usurped his throne did not live long enough to enjoy it," she said, and turned away. "What brings an Anpu warrior to this place?"

"I am Anpu, but I am not a bloodthirsty warrior like the rest of my race—just as you are not a bloodthirsty vampire."

Scathach turned to look around. "Tell me what is happening here?" she asked.

"As Moriath said. This is a place where all the races can live in harmony. It used to be that way, you know. Before Danu Talis fell, in the Time Before Time, the One World was a paradise."

"I've heard the story. But I am not sure I believe it."

"I do. And I have done my best over the centuries to make this place in the image of the world as it was in the olden days."

"How long have you had this village?"

"This is one of a hundred similar villages scattered throughout the Northlands. We've existed in secret for five hundred years. Few know of our existence. A nearby humani settlement considers us forest myths, but there is a Fir Dearg mining village we sometimes trade with. They know about us, though they do not approve. They consider us abominations."

"A hundred villages!" Scathach exclaimed. "Five hundred years is a long time to keep a secret of that magnitude. . . ."

"A secret not for much longer." He reached for Scathach's arm, but his hand fell away when he saw the expression on her face. "My people are dying," he said simply.

Ophois led her to a hut set apart from the others. He stopped before a white line etched into the ground and pulled a cloth from a bucket of pale white liquid. Pressing the square of cloth to his face, he stepped across the line. Scathach hesitated a moment before lifting a second cloth from the bucket, covering her nose and mouth and following him.

The Anpu stopped outside the hut and stooped to peer inside. Scathach looked over his shoulder. There were six bodies in the hut. At first she thought they were lifeless; then she realized that the blankets were moving slightly. She saw fingers twitching, veins throbbing. Ophois stepped inside and knelt by the first body, carefully lifting the blanket off a young man. The medicinal square pressed to Scathach's lips suddenly tasted sour: the man's stunted Dearg body was covered in weeping sores.

"It started about ten days ago," Ophois said quietly, gently wiping the sores with a cloth. The man moaned in his fevered sleep. "The elderly went first. From this village alone, we lost twenty-four in one day. Then we lost five children in two days. So far the total is thirty-eight, and though the rate of infection seems to have slowed, we still lose one or two a day." He tilted his head to look up at the warrior. "The young men on the mountain weren't trying to attack you. They were trying to scare you off. When they didn't see you running away, they were afraid you would come to investigate. That's why they used the pods on you." The Anpu's smile turned bitter. "Because, you see, now that you are here, it means that you too might be infected. And I'm afraid that that means you can never leave this place."

3

Scathach had always believed she would die in battle. She had been little more than a girl—twelve, maybe thirteen summers—when she had had her palm read by a wild-haired crone on the eve of the battle that would be remembered by history as Bloody Lake. "I see you as an old woman, white-haired, withered, with a sword in your hand and a mound of dead at your feet." There had been other rubbish about a husband and sons and daughters and riches aplenty, but Scathach had believed none of that; she had wanted to believe that she would die an old woman.

Now she wasn't so sure.

She was more or less a prisoner in the village, free to wander it but not free to leave. Thirty-eight of the villagers were dead, six were dying, and another eight or ten were obviously ill. The healthy remained in the village not only to care for the sick, but also to prevent the disease from spreading. Scathach recognized the look in their eyes, one she had seen in so many faces: they felt trapped, besieged, doomed. The villagers were simply waiting for death, and from what she'd been told, the situation was repeated in the hidden villages along the length of the river.

After parting from Ophois, Scathach walked along the river-bank with Moriath. The sun was low over the horizon, touching the distant mountains with purple, and the air was chill enough for the women's breaths to smoke and plume about their heads. Frost sparkled in the deepest shadows.

"You are a healer; have you ever encountered a disease like this before?" Scathach asked the other woman.

"Never." Moriath shook her bald head. "The clan are remarkably healthy. Disease is relatively unknown here. We grow our own vegetables and drink only from the stream. If I knew the cause, I might be able to formulate a cure." She lowered her voice and glanced over her shoulder. "Some of the people believe that we have been cursed, spell cast, by the Fir Dearg. The young men are recommending a sudden raid against the Dearg, taking hostages and forcing them to lift the spell."

"Do you believe that?"

"I know enough about Fir Dearg medicine and magic to know that this is not a Dearg curse."

"Do you know if the disease has struck the Dearg settlement?"

"No, it has not, which is why my people think it comes from there."

"I've traveled the length and breadth of this land, and I've never seen anything like it," Scathach admitted. "And I most definitely do not want to die from it," she added.

"It is unfortunate that you were on the road."

"I am older than I look," Scathach said, "and I have come to believe that we are usually exactly where we need to be."

The two women continued along the stream, Scathach's sharp eyes darting left and right, reading animal tracks as they approached and left the water's edge.

"What put you on the road?" Moriath asked.

"Three days ago, a merchant paid me double my usual fee to bring a small package to a one-eyed Dwarf in a village to the north of here. Timing was tight, because the Dwarf uses a lunar-powered leygate to come through to this realm from another world, and would only be in Tír fo Thuinn for two days while the gate recharged. If he missed the two-day window, then it would be another month before he could head back to his own Shadowrealm, and that would make him angry. And apparently, this was not someone you wanted to anger. The day I've spent here is a day lost."

"You do not strike me as someone who would be fearful of a Dwarf's anger," Moriath said with a smile.

"The only reason I took the commission was because the merchant paid me—in advance—with a fragment of a map. I've been promised another piece of the map when I deliver the package to the Dwarf."

"Nor do you strike me as someone who puts much credence in a treasure map," Moriath said.

"I don't," Scathach answered. "Every abandoned mine on

every Shadowrealm I've visited supposedly contains hidden treasure, a monster, or a dragon, and sometimes all three. I've never come across any treasure. This is different, though. The map is reputed to show the location of an ancient Archon library, a place piled high with crystals of all shapes and sizes, including some crystal skulls."

Moriath's face twisted in disgust. "Foul things. I would not have taken you for a collector of such abominations."

"Oh, I don't collect them," Scathach added quickly. "I destroy them. Forty years ago—yes, I am older than I look—I came across the first rumors of a complete Archon library, a relic of the Time Before Time. The library was supposed to exist in a cave system in the heart of the Great Chasm in the far west."

"There was once a great city there," Moriath said. "Destroyed when the sky rained fire. And then the very earth itself ripped apart into what became known as the Great Chasm."

Scathach nodded. "Well, over the centuries, ancient artifacts have been found in the warren of caves that riddle the sides of the chasm. And one of these caves was reputed to hold the Archon library. But it's a vast cave system, which is why I need the map."

"Odd that your search for the crystal-filled Archon library should have led you here."

"Everything has a reason," Scathach said quietly.

"Even the bad things?"

"Especially the bad things."

Scathach knelt by the water's edge, brushing the long

grass with her fingertips. She idly ran her fingers through the water, then rubbed her hand dry against her legs. "I would not go up against the Fir Dearg," she said absently. "They are a formidable foe. And even if you were victorious, they have long memories. Sooner or later—probably later—they would take their revenge." She straightened, and looked up and down the river. "The people who first fell ill, where did they live?"

Moriath crouched beside the Shadow and drew a waving line in the mud. "This is the river." She added pebbles to either side of the line. "And here are the villages. . . ."

"Where are we?" Scathach asked.

Moriath dropped a sprig of wildflower onto the mud. "Just here. . . ."

4

Ophois was in the center of a group of heavily armed villagers when Scathach strode into their midst. One, a squat male with classic Bolg features, attempted to stand in her way; Scathach knocked him down without even breaking stride.

"I say we burn them out," someone shouted.

"Knock them out with marsh pods, then kill them all," another villager said.

"No!" Ophois's voice was a harsh bark, but Scathach could hear the desperation in it. "We have no evidence that the Fir Dearg are behind this. None!"

"Only they know of our existence. It has to be them. Who knows what foul poisons they cook up in their deep mines. They have brought down this curse of pestilence on us," a huge Torc Arzh Gell were-bear shouted.

"None of them are sick."

"I say we burn them, burn them out."

"Burn them!"

"Burn them!"

"No!" Ophois shouted. "You either stand with us or you're siding with the Fir Dearg—"

Scathach knew that Ophois was losing control of the mob. At any moment, they would simply ignore him and march off to attack the Fir Dearg settlement.

"The Dearg are not your enemy." Scathach used her battlefield voice, projecting it so that her words could be heard all across the village.

"No one asked you!" The speaker was a thickset Torc Allta holding a studded metal club.

Without hesitation, Scathach kicked him in the soft flesh beneath his chin, dropping him to the ground writhing in agony. Another were-boar reached for her, and the sound of his snapping arm shocked the mob into silence. The sudden agony sent the boar flickering between his human and animal forms. Scathach calmly stepped over him. "If the Dearg wanted to destroy you, they could have done so at any time. And if you go up against them, then they will obliterate you."

A huge Bolg warrior carrying a war hammer almost as tall as himself took a step toward Scathach.

"Know me. I am Scathach the Shadow. The Daemon Slayer and the King Maker. One more step and I will take that hammer and beat you over the head with it," she promised.

"I don't believe you," he growled.

"Ask your boar friend about his arm, then." She smiled, deliberately showing her fangs.

For a moment he looked as if he was about to risk it, but he took a step back, retreating into the crowd.

Scathach stood alongside Ophois and faced the mob. She looked at each member in turn, staring until they had backed down or looked away. "If you come with me, I will show you what has brought pestilence to your village."

Pushing through the crowd, she strode out of the village, not once looking back. Ophois hesitated a moment before he ran after her. The rest of the villagers followed more slowly.

Scathach led the villagers into the gathering gloom along the banks of the stream, refusing to answer any of the Anpu's urgent questions, simply because she had no answers.

If she'd had the time, she would have investigated her suspicions, but the mob had gathered too quickly, forcing her to act. She was aware that if she was wrong, then the mob would turn on her and she'd be forced to fight them all—which would certainly brighten up her evening—or they would race off to attack the Fir Dearg.

"Where are you taking us?" Ophois asked a little breathlessly. "They'll not follow for much longer."

Just as the hum of discontent was beginning to rise from the mob behind her, and at the precise moment when she thought that she might have been mistaken, she caught the faintest hint of foulness on the evening air. She knew, in that instant, that her supposition had been correct.

"Smell that?" she said.

She saw Ophois's nostrils flare. His golden eyes widened, and she knew that he too had caught the odor.

And then they rounded a bend in the stream.

Into a scene of primal horror.

5

The entire village gathered in a circle on both sides of the stream.

In the middle of the circle, in the center of the river, were the rotting remains of two monsters.

"A Caorthannach wyrm," Scathach said, using her nunchaku to point to an enormous lizard-like creature whose flat head was encircled by a fleshy frill. Spikes—many of them broken—ran the length of its spine. "I've never seen one so far north. And, I should note, this is a small one," she added.

"I thought they were legend," Moriath said, loud enough for everyone to hear.

"At the heart of every legend, there is a grain of truth." Scathach moved to the second creature, which resembled a huge brutish horse. "This is a full-grown Dullahan."

"Where's its head?" someone asked.

"They don't have any," Scathach said. "Once, a long time ago, they were the preferred mounts of the Epiphagi, the headless men."

"Headless men on headless horses." Ophois nodded. "Part of the Legion of the Damned."

"Ten days ago, by my reckoning, judging from the decomposition, the two creatures met and fought here. Neither survived. I'm surprised you didn't hear the sounds of the battle. It would have echoed through the forest."

"Ten days ago, a ferocious storm rolled down from the mountains," Ophois said. "The thunder was so fierce and so close that it rattled some of the huts apart, and there were hundreds of lightning strikes. Luckily, the torrential rain doused the fires."

The Shadow nodded. "That's probably why you did not hear them fight. And who knows, maybe the storm itself precipitated the battle. Both creatures are incredibly sensitive to noise."

Scathach walked to the edge of the river and prodded an ivory horn with the tip of her boot. Bones made brittle and soft by the rushing water gave way, dipping the Caorthannach's rotting head beneath the surface. Pale fluids swirled in an oily pattern before they dispersed.

"There is your pestilence," Scathach snapped. "No Dearg poison, no magical disease, just nature." She looked at the villagers. "You would have gone to war—and been wiped out—over a pair of rotting carcasses." Shaking her head, she walked away. "You owe me a mount," she called back, "and supplies and water. Though not from the stream," she added.

6

Ophois led a tall, prancing Aonbheannach to Scathach. The creature stabbed at her with its single horn, and its slablike teeth snapped close to her fingers.

She rapped it between the eyes with her knuckles. "Behave."

"Our gift to you," the Anpu said. "Food and water—though not from the stream—enough to last you ten days. He watched her sling her saddlebags across the Aonbheannach's back and cinch the straps. "You prevented a lot of bloodshed, Shadow. My people would have raided the Fir Dearg mines; the Dwarfs would have retaliated. Within the month, the entire Northlands would have been ablaze. By year's end, the entire continent would have been at war. And this"—he spread his arms and looked around—"our little experiment would have been forgotten."

"Our world is very fragile," she said quietly. "Easy to break, hard to mend. A long time ago, I learned the dangers of rushing to judgment."

"How did you know the water was poisoned?" Ophois asked.

"I looked at the pattern of sickness and death. Villages farther up the river, closer to where the monsters had battled, were hardest hit. Those farther south, less so. This village was almost right in the middle, so the water still carried enough of the Caorthannach and Dullahan blood to poison the villagers. I noticed bird and animal tracks approach the water's edge but turn away before they got to it. When I smelled the water, I caught the faintest hint of foulness from it."

"Moriath has been working through the night on a remedy. Once she knew the cause, she was able to formulate a potion. She's brewing it now." Ophois stretched out his right hand.

Without hesitation, Scathach grasped it, gripping his wrist as he caught hers.

"There will always be a place for you here," Ophois said. "A place to rest, to recuperate. A place to hide if you need it."

"I will remember that," she said.

"Take care of yourself, Shadow." He turned and strode away, nodding to Moriath, who was hurrying toward Scathach.

"You will come and see us on your return journey?" she asked a little breathlessly.

"If I can, I will," Scathach said. "Though my life is sometimes adventurous, and often unexpected roads and byways open up."

"We will be here. Thanks to you." She reached beneath her cloak and produced an ornately carved amber bowl. "I made you some salve. With one or two ingredients of my own. And some extra oil," she added. She handed over a tight curl of parchment. "I wrote out the recipe for you. I thought you might share it with your sister."

Scathach smiled. "What makes you think I will see her again?"

"I think you will. You have much to talk about," Moriath said gently. She turned away quickly, but not before Scathach had seen her eyes brighten and sparkle with liquid. "Come back to us someday, Shadow; you are now, and will forever be, a member of the Clan of Eriu. Bring your sister."

"I will do that," Scathach promised. When she rubbed her cheeks, she discovered that her fingers were red with tears.

NICHOLAS FLAMEL
AND THE CODEX

1355

I am old now, so very, very old.

I was born in the year of Our Lord 1330. The world was very different then: dark, dangerous, indescribably smelly, a time of superstition and fear. People believed that demons wandered the earth. They feared the monsters in the forests and the creatures under the bridges. They prayed to countless saints but left offerings to forest sprites. They kept holy the church holidays but also honored the ancient festivals of Midsummer and Midwinter. The supernatural, the other-world, was very close indeed.

I had no idea just how close. I believed myself a scientist, and had little regard for superstition. I did not realize that at the heart of every legend, there is a grain of truth.

It was a time when life was short and even the simplest ailment—a toothache, a splinter, a burst appendix—could be fatal. But I was lucky. I always enjoyed a robust constitution, and I have all my original teeth, except for the one the Yeti knocked out in 1700. I grew up in an age of simple food: fruits and vegetables, cheese, eggs, wine, and newly baked bread. We drank wine because it was safer than drinking the water. We rarely had meat, and after I became immortal, I lost the taste for it entirely. These habits continue to the present day and have no doubt contributed to my overall good health.

Well, those habits and the formula for immortality that I brew afresh every month. The recipe is in the Codex, the Book of Abraham the Mage, that most extraordinary collection of knowledge, the most dangerous book in the world.

The *Ancients* believed that over the course of one's life, there were a few—a very few—life-changing instances. Some Western cultures believe that these number no more than five, while the Eastern sages maintain that there are seven. These are the moments when the direction of one's life shifts in an entirely new direction. Looking back over my own years, I find it easy to pinpoint some of those life-changing incidents. Meeting Perenelle, the woman who would become my wife, changed my existence immeasurably. Discovering the Twins of Legend was another.

But if there is one event that not only altered the direction of my life but also transformed the history of the world, it was the moment when I bought a slender metal-bound book from a mysterious one-handed man.

From the Day Booke of Nicholas Flamel, Alchemyst

1

The river stank.

The winter of 1354 had been particularly hard, and the Seine, clotted and sluggish with filth and refuse, froze solid in early December, a thick skin of ice growing from the east and west banks. As the year turned, only a narrow channel in the middle of the river remained open, and the ice on either bank was said to be as thick as a child was tall. But an unexpectedly mild spring brought on a rapid thaw, and suddenly the Parisian air was foul with a hundred noxious odors that had been locked in the ice.

The smells—of rot and decay, of bloated fish and other, less identifiable carcasses, of stinking mud and human waste—tainted everything. Bakers discovered that it polluted the flour, butchers grumbled that it was impossible to remove from their meats, fish were inedible, and the flower sellers around the newly completed Notre-Dame cathedral complained that even the sweetest-smelling rose reeked of the Seine.

This year it was so bad that the king himself, John the Good, threatened to leave the capital and establish his court elsewhere.

But in the back room of a tiny shop off the Rue du Montmorency, one man was delighted. Nicholas Flamel—tall, thin, beardless, hair unfashionably short and eyes sunk deep in an unhealthily pale face—was passing out small cloth-wrapped bundles to ten barefoot urchins standing before him. The air in the tiny room was heavy with the rich scents of roses, herbs, and a suggestion of spices from faraway lands.

"Now, repeat after me. . . ." Flamel's accent betrayed just a hint of his country upbringing, but he was working hard to mimic the more cultured Parisian intonation. "This nosegay is a concoction of the finest herbs and spices from the mysterious lands of Cathay."

"This nosegay is the finest . . ."

"This concoction . . ."

"What's a nosegay?"

"What's a Cathay?"

Nicholas sighed. The urchins—six boys and four girls— were the latest recruits to sell the small perfumed bags, each with the letters *NF* burned into the cloth. At the moment he had thirty children, ranging in age from six to twelve, on the streets, hawking the bags to Parisians. Business, especially close to the river and outside the alehouses and theaters, was brisk. On a good day, his troupe could sell around two hundred bags. The crisp, cleansing scent lasted about forty-eight hours before it faded, and most of the customers came back for more.

"You do not have to know what it means. You just have to remember and repeat it. Now, let's try again." He held up a sachet. "Each of you will have one of these. This is your special bag. It's a little bit bigger than the ones you will sell, and it has this sign burned into the cloth." Tilting the pouch, he revealed a large X. "You do *not* sell this bag. You wave it under your customer's nose and you say, 'Smell this.'" Flamel brought the bag to his own nose and the ten children mimicked him. The mixture of peppermint, licorice, spices, and rose petals was almost overpowering. Two of the children sneezed. "Then you say, 'This nosegay is a concoction of the finest herbs and spices from the mysterious lands of Cathay, blended here in Paris, by the most wonderful apothecary Nicholas Flamel.'"

"By who?"

"Apoca-what?"

"By me. I am Nicholas Flamel." He sighed again. "Let us take a moment. Go into the kitchen. Madame Perenelle has some hot soup and bread for you. Perhaps the food will improve your memory. In the meantime, I will prepare more sachets."

Flamel descended the steps to the basement in total darkness. There were candles set into niches in the wall, but he was reluctant to light them: candles were expensive, and the last time he'd lit one, he'd almost set his sleeve on fire.

The square room at the bottom of the stairs was bathed in the dull red glow from a low fire in the center of the room. Balanced over the fire on a tripod was a fat-bellied pot. The lid was rattling precariously, leaking a sweet citrus odor into the air.

"Just in time," Flamel muttered, wrapping a cloth around his hand and raising the lid. He was immediately engulfed in scented smoke, which made his eyes water uncontrollably. "This was not how I saw my life." He coughed as he poured the perfumed water into a series of smaller pots. He was twenty-five now, and in the past few years he'd struggled to make a living in Paris. He'd found work as a scrivener, writing letters for people, and copying manuscripts and books. Shortly after he married, and with Perenelle's encouragement, he'd begun the study of alchemy, a mixture of several sciences along with a dash of superstition. Alchemy was the science of the future, the science of invention and discovery, and it was said to hold the answers to two great mysteries: how to turn ordinary metal into gold, and how to attain eternal life. While eternal life sounded good, right now Nicholas would be satisfied with just being able to turn metal into gold. Or silver. Even copper would do. For the past couple of years, they had been living off Perenelle's money, but that would not last forever.

He'd not yet turned fifteen when he'd run away from home in search of adventure. He had such dreams: he was going to be rich and famous, travel the world and discover its secrets, become an advisor to kings and princes. He spent nearly five years wandering across Europe, but the lure of home was too strong and he'd eventually returned to his hometown of Pontoise. But there was nothing there for him.

Both his parents were dead, his sisters married with families of their own, and his brothers had divided the small family farm between them. He stayed two nights, paid his respects at his parents' grave, and struck out for Paris, seeking his fortune, still following his dreams.

Which had led him to a back street brewing cheap perfume.

Growing up, he never thought he would marry, but he'd been wrong about that too. And for that he was truly grateful. He was the first to admit that Perenelle Delamere had changed his life for the better. On the surface, it appeared that they had little in common: ten years his senior, she was wealthy and a widow, and came from a family who could trace their history back to the first Norse Viking invaders. Flamel had no idea where his family came from. His father and grandfather were farmers; they never spoke of the past, though his father's mother had the dark olive skin and raven hair of those from southern Spain. He'd fallen in love with Perenelle Delamere the first time he'd seen her. He would never forget that moment. He was renting a little stall huddled between the columns of the Cathedral of Saint-Jacques de la Boucherie. There, he wrote letters for those who could not write, copied pages from manuscripts and books, and went hungry every day, and still barely made enough to pay his rent.

Four years ago, on a bitterly cold Christmas Eve, he had looked up and watched a tall, slender, raven-haired women sweep across the courtyard, heading toward the church.

Almost as if she felt his gaze on her, she'd stopped, turned, and looked at him. Through the gloom and fading light he was conscious of her startlingly green eyes. She strode across the courtyard toward him and stopped before the stall.

"I am the seventh daughter of a seventh daughter," she said, her eyes fixed on his, holding them. "Do you know what that means?"

He nodded, though he was unsure how to answer.

"My touch can heal—not always, but often. I can see the shades of the dead and talk to them. Sometimes they answer. When I was six years old, my grandmother, who also possessed the Sight, took me to see the Hooded Man, who lived in a crystal-studded cave on the shores of the Bay of Douarnenez, close to my home. He told me that I would marry and become a widow. He told me that my life would be filled with books and writing. And that I would know my true love the moment I set eyes on him. My name is Perenelle Delamere."

"I am Nicholas Flamel."

They married six months later, on the eighteenth day of August.

Theirs was not a conventional relationship. She supported his studies, paid the rent on the Montmorency house, bought him books, and encouraged his research into alchemy. Perenelle had even suggested the nosegay, found the herbs and spices, and brewed the first batch from a recipe she remembered from her childhood. Right now, the cotton bags, stitched by Perenelle and filled with dried paste, were bringing in more money than they'd earned in the past year.

Nicholas knew that the market would not last forever. The Seine was still frozen in many places, but once it was flowing swiftly, it would carry all the floating filth and the accompanying stench out to sea. There were perhaps another ten days of sales left before the air cleared. The money they'd earned from the sachets would last them a month, maybe five weeks, and he had no idea what they were going to do then. He pushed the thought from his mind; he'd learned a long time ago that a lot of the things he worried about never actually came to pass. And right now he needed to focus without distraction. The last time he'd gotten distracted, he'd allowed a batch of herbs to burn and cost them an entire day's takings.

He wrapped a leather apron around his waist, pulled a cotton mask over his mouth and nose, and then set about distilling and decanting the bubbling water. When this was all over, he promised himself, he was never going to wear perfume again, and if he was ever wealthy enough to have a garden, he'd make sure there were no roses. He sneezed. And no peppermint either!

The church bells were tolling eight o'clock when Flamel finally climbed out of the cellar. The perfume had given him a pounding headache, and his clothes and hair stank of peppermint and rose.

Perenelle was waiting at the top of the stairs, a single candle held high above her head, illuminating her sharp features and silver-streaked black hair. "I was just coming down to get you." She pressed her knuckle under her nose and blinked away a sneeze. "You stink."

"You should smell it from here." His voice was hoarse, throat raw from the cloying smells. "I brewed up another batch. I added more rose petals, as you suggested. You were right," he added with a smile. "As usual."

"I told you: licorice and citrus are masculine; women prefer florals, and more women buy scent. Now, I have left some hot water in your room. Go and wash, change into your best clothes. There is someone waiting for you in the shop. A man."

"At this hour?"

"He came late because he wanted to speak to you in private."

"I can see him now. . . ."

Perenelle shook her head firmly. "Wash, change. There is something about this person . . . something odd. I think this is someone we treat with respect."

"A nobleman?"

"No . . . neither noble nor merchant. But powerful."

Nicholas reached out and caught his wife's hand. "Is that fear I hear in your voice?"

Perenelle stiffened. "Not fear. Excitement. You know I possess a little foresight. But strangely, Nicholas, I can tell nothing about this visitor." She paused and drew in a deep breath. "Nor can I see a future for us beyond this night."

Nicholas licked suddenly dry lips, rose and peppermint sour on his tongue. In the past four years, he'd seen countless examples of his wife's extraordinary gifts. And he'd never known her to be wrong. "No future? What does that mean?"

"It means that whatever decision we make tonight changes the entire direction of our lives. But that decision is as yet unmade, and so our future is undecided."

"And you believe it is connected to this mysterious man?"

"I do."

Thirty minutes later, Nicholas stepped into the small front room. Perenelle had drawn the heavy black curtains, and the only illumination came from a thick beeswax candle set on a polished metal plate in the center of the table. In the gloomy, shadow-thick room, it took Nicholas a few moments to distinguish the figure standing against the far wall. The man was wearing a hooded black cloak, and the oily material seemed to absorb the wan light.

"I do apologize . . . ," Flamel began.

The figure half turned, and candlelight washed over deeply tanned skin and a pair of bright blue eyes beneath the hood. In the flickering light, it was hard to make out his features, but while his skin was smooth and unlined, with no trace of a beard, Flamel immediately knew that this was not a young man.

"Please do not trouble yourself," the man said. "I was admiring your library."

"Why, thank you. It's one of the larger collections in private hands," Nicholas admitted proudly, nodding toward the thirty-six books of various shapes and sizes on the shelves behind the hooded man. "You are a collector?"

"Of sorts." The stranger stepped forward and pushed back his hood, revealing a shock of blond hair. "I have an ever-growing library, and am always looking for something interesting."

"Ah, then let me recommend the Chrétien de Troyes on the top shelf," Flamel began, "a masterful tale of Perceval, a knight at the court of the English king Arthur."

"I looked at it. I'm afraid that it is a forgery," the stranger said with a wry smile, revealing astonishingly white teeth.

"Oh, surely not . . ."

"Chrétien de Troyes died before completing this work."

"Oh . . . I did not know that." Nicholas shook his head slightly. "I bought it from a nobleman from an excellent family—a duke. He said the book had been personally given to his ancestor by de Troyes and handed down through his family for generations. I paid far too much for it," he muttered.

"And besides," the stranger added, in peculiarly accented French, "I have everything Chrétien de Troyes wrote. Including some works he personally inscribed to me."

"Personally inscribed?" Flamel muttered disbelievingly. "This is the same Chrétien de Troyes who died over one hundred and fifty years ago?"

"One hundred and sixty-four," the blond-haired man said. "And yes, the same Chrétien de Troyes, author of *Lancelot, the Knight of the Cart* and, of course, the unfinished *Perceval, the Story of the Grail*."

"With the greatest respect," Flamel said carefully, "you do not look that old."

"And how old do I look?"

"At first glance . . . eighteen?" Nicholas suggested.

"And at second glance?"

"There is something about your eyes, the way you carry yourself, that suggests you are older."

"How much older?"

"Five and twenty summers, perhaps?"

"Oh, I am a lot older than I look," the stranger said enigmatically. "Older than you can imagine."

Flamel moved around the room, maneuvering to place the table between himself and the stranger. The hooded man might be telling the truth, or . . .

"You are frightened of me?" the man asked.

"Cautious," Flamel admitted. "You come here late at night and tell me that you knew a writer who died over one hundred and fifty years ago—"

"One hundred and sixty-four."

"—and that you are older than I can imagine."

"Much older."

"So if you are lying to me, then I have to wonder why. Are you an agent of the Crown, or the Church? Or perhaps you've been sent by one of my rivals to discredit me."

"I am none of those," the man said. "But tell me, Nicholas Flamel: what if I am telling the truth? What if I am indeed an Ancient of Days?"

Flamel licked dry lips with a tongue that suddenly felt far

too big for his mouth. "Then that would make you a remarkable man." In his research into alchemy, he'd read stories of men and women who lived far beyond their allotted span of years, of ancient kings who had ruled for centuries and mysterious wanderers doomed to roam the earth for eternity.

The door opened and Perenelle appeared. She was carrying a small woven tray, holding a bottle and three wooden goblets. Without saying a word, she arranged the three goblets on the table and poured a clear, faintly scented liquid into each.

"Boiled water. With lemons from the Côte d'Azur. Sit. Drink."

Nicholas folded his arms, allowing his right hand to rest on the hilt of the small knife tucked in his belt. "This gentleman claims to be over one hundred years old."

The blond man pulled out one of the carved wooden chairs and sank into it. "I never *claimed* to be over one hundred years," he said mildly. "I claimed to be much older than that." Then, shaking loose his cloak, he raised his left arm and rested it on the table. Although Perenelle's face remained unmoving, Nicholas gasped. A wickedly curved metal hook took the place of the man's left hand. The flickering candlelight shimmered wetly on the metal, highlighting arcane symbols etched into it.

Perenelle folded her arms and looked into his blue eyes. "When I was a child, I was taken to see a hooded man who told me a little of my future." She frowned, chasing the childhood memory. "I believe he had a hook similar to yours."

The blond-haired young man sipped the lemon water and did not answer.

Perenelle's long, elegant finger traced the outline of the man's face and the curl of the hook in the air. "I seem to remember that the man I was met was older. You perhaps, but with age written more deeply upon your face. I remember the hook, though." Even as she was speaking, the symbols cut into the metal winked with reflected light. "The hook was identical."

"I have no memory of meeting you, Mistress Perenelle." He raised his left arm, the hood reflecting rainbowing light around the room. "But that is not to say you are mistaken. This hook is unique. Perhaps that event, which lies in your past, awaits me in my future."

"I grew up in Quimper with stories of the groagez."

"I am not one of the fairy folk." He smiled. "Too tall."

"But we all know that the world is filled with mysteries and wonders," she said, eyes fixed on the hook, "and that at the heart of every myth, there is a grain of truth." She looked into the young man's bright blue eyes. "Are you human?" she asked sharply.

Nicholas turned to his wife, startled. "You think this is a demon?" He looked the stranger up and down. "He doesn't look like a demon."

The young man smiled. "And when was the last time you saw a demon, Nicholas Flamel?"

"Never. Though I have seen the gargoyles carved onto the new cathedral. They look like demons."

"They look nothing like real demons," the hooded man said.

"You say that as if you've seen the monsters," Perenelle said carefully.

"Many times. They are not always ugly. The most dangerous ones are handsome indeed."

Perenelle pulled out a chair and sat opposite the hook-handed man, staring intently at him. Was this the man she'd met as a child? But even as she grasped the memory, it fragmented and slid away until she was unsure if it was a real memory or a dream. She moved her goblet around in her hand, releasing the sharp lemon scent, breathing it in, trying to clear her head. "You know who we are, sir; you know our names, but we have no idea who you are."

"I have many names," the hooded man said, "but you may call me Fearnua."

"*Far-new-a*," Nicholas said, rolling the name around in his mouth. "An odd name; German? Russian, perhaps?"

"It reminds me a little of the Breton I spoke in my youth," Perenelle said.

Fearnua nodded. "It has Celtic roots." He looked up at Nicholas, who was standing behind his wife. "Are you going to continue lurking there with your hand on your knife, or will you sit?"

"Sit, Nicholas," Perenelle said quietly. "I believe if this gentleman wishes us ill, there is little we can do to prevent it."

"You are wise, Mistress Flamel." The cloaked man moved his left arm and the hook sent shivering crescent reflections around the room. "I wish you no harm." He suddenly raised his head and closed his eyes, and his nostrils flared. "But we must hurry."

Even as he was speaking, Nicholas and Perenelle felt the subtle change in the atmosphere. The temperature had dipped, and a faint odor, something sickly sweet, like rotting meat, tainted the flower-scented air.

"Something's coming," Perenelle said quietly. Her thin nostrils flared. "Something wicked."

"You are being pursued?" Nicholas said to the blond man.

"I may have picked up a tail on my journey."

"And you've led them here?" the alchemyst snapped.

"They are not here yet . . . and when they arrive I will not be here. Nor will you."

"We're going nowhere," Nicholas said defiantly.

"Who are you?" Perenelle pressed. "I asked you before. I will not ask again."

"I am . . . a traveler," Fearnua said carefully. "And a collector." As he was speaking, he reached under his cloak with his right hand to produce a slender rectangular package wrapped in thick oiled leather, secured by a thin knotted strap. "My travels bring me into contact with many strange and interesting objects." He pushed the package into the center of the table, then placed the metal hook on its oiled leather. Suddenly the symbols etched into the metal began to glow. A rainbow slick of iridescent light ran down the hook, and it steamed a warm amber mist. The small room was suffused with the scent of oranges. "And when I come across something particularly interesting, I like to make sure it finds a good home," the man finished.

Nicholas and Perenelle stared at the leather-wrapped object beneath the glowing hook. "It looks like it might be a book," Nicholas said.

"And how did you deduce that?" the man asked.

"The size, the shape, and the fact that when I first saw you, you were examining my library."

"It is a book," Fearnua said, slipping the edge of his hook under the leather strap and easing it open.

"Not an ordinary book," Perenelle said.

"Far from it."

"It is dangerous?" she asked.

"Yes," Fearnua said simply. "This is the most dangerous book in the world."

"And you want to sell it to us?" Nicholas said.

"No. I want to give it to you."

Nicholas leaned forward to examine the parcel, but Perenelle sat back, pushing away from the table. She laid a hand on her husband's arm, stopping him. "Everything has a cost," she said quietly. "Even gifts."

Fearnua nodded again. "Especially gifts."

"And what will this gift cost us?" she asked.

Fearnua shrugged. "Everything."

"Doesn't sound like much of a gift, does it?" Nicholas said.

Perenelle smiled. "I think the better question is: What will this book bring us?"

"Everything," Fearnua repeated.

"A book of riddles," Flamel said.

The hooded man shook his head. "A book of answers."

Nicholas and Perenelle stared at the leather-wrapped book. For a single moment, Nicholas imagined he saw the leather pulse, beating like a heart.

"You now have a decision to make," Fearnua continued. "If you accept this gift, then I will open this binding. Unfortunately, that will release a wash of power that will alert my pursuers to my location. Refuse this gift, and I will not open the book but will be on my way. Your lives will continue as they were, undisturbed and unremarkable."

"And the book?" Nicholas asked.

"I will not leave the book behind. You would not survive the night."

"This is a rare tome?"

"There is nothing like this in any of the known worlds. It is unique in ways that you cannot even imagine."

"It is a grimoire," Nicholas said. "A spell book."

"There are spells within in its pages," Fearnua said carefully, "but this is not a witch's grimoire." He tapped the leather with his hook again, and the room blossomed with the acidic tang of oranges. "All human and inhuman knowledge lies within. The known and unknown history of this and the many Shadowrealms is writ upon these pages."

"Shadowrealms?" Nicholas asked.

"This world does not exist in isolation. It is linked to countless others: the secret places, the veiled worlds. The myths and legends of every race tell of hidden lands, lost islands, secret valleys, fairy mounds filled with all manner of wonders."

Perenelle nodded. "Only recently a traveler from Saxony told us a story of a piper who lured all the children in the town into a magical cave. None of the children were ever seen again." She saw something shift behind Fearnua's eyes. "That's wasn't you, was it?"

"No," he said. "I regret not being there to save the children. Yes, they were lured into a cave that was the entrance to a Shadowrealm. One day I will find them or, at the very least, avenge them." He tapped the book again. "Shadowrealm lore from a hundred worlds and countless times is contained in these pages."

"It seems very slender to contain such a vast wealth of knowledge," Perenelle said carefully.

"The text is ever changing," the man explained. "It moves, shifts, and rearranges itself according to the rotation of the planets, the cycles of the moon, and the wishes and needs of the reader. Ask it a question, and it will answer."

Nicholas pulled in a deep breath. "It must be old."

"Older than the pyramids, older than Babylon or Thebes. Think of the oldest civilization you know, and then add ten thousand years and more. And even then you will still not have come close to the age of this book."

"But if it is that old, then we will not be able to decipher the script," Nicholas said. He waved vaguely toward his shelf of books. "My Latin is good, but the older Greek sometimes defeats me."

Fearnua's lips curled in a smile. He tapped the leather parcel with his hook. "The text will rearrange itself into the language you are most comfortable with." Suddenly, the candle on the table flickered and danced in an unfelt breeze. "Quickly now. Make your decision."

"I need to talk to Perenelle about this," Nicholas said, glancing at his wife.

The hooded man nodded. "Let me step outside for a moment, then. But before I do that," he added, "you should know that the two great secrets of alchemy, how to turn base metal into gold and how to become immortal, are contained in this book." He nodded to Nicholas and bowed more deeply to Perenelle; then he stepped outside and pulled the door closed. The moment he left, the light from the flickering candle bloomed a little brighter.

Nicholas and Perenelle stood and, almost unconsciously, began to circle the small table, eyes fixed on the leather-wrapped parcel.

"You want the book," Perenelle said simply.

"If what the hooded man is saying is true—that it contains all the knowledge in the world —then yes, of course. For generations, alchemists have sought the secret of immortality and worked to turn metal into gold."

"And you believe this hook-handed man?"

Nicholas stopped and looked across the table at his wife.

"Yes. Yes, I do. Even the Ancients knew that the world is far older and stranger than we could ever imagine. For centuries alchemists and scholars have written about the mysteries at the heart of the world. This . . . this book and this stranger have just confirmed what we suspected. And Fearnua himself . . . is he entirely human? I think not."

"I agree," Perenelle said. "Once, perhaps, but no longer."

"And you've seen the hook. It pulses and glows with arcane energies."

"Magicians and witches have their wands and brooms. Perhaps it is his wand," she suggested.

"But I am often a poor judge of people," Nicholas admitted. "You have said that yourself. *You* have the gift: what do *you* think?"

Perenelle leaned over and put her face directly over the small package. Closing her eyes, she breathed deeply. "Oranges, and something else, something older, much older. I can almost taste the power steaming off the book." And then she stiffened.

Memories flickered. . . .

Images . . .

A crystal tower lashed by a storm.

A creature, both human and inhuman, more metal than flesh, standing atop the tower, bathed in terrifying cracking energies. The figure turned to look at her, a single gray eye in a golden mask holding her gaze. His ruined mouth shaped words.

Take it.

Massive waves crashed around the tower, battering it. A huge chunk of iridescent crystal broke away, and the platform tilted precariously.

Take it.

Perenelle staggered back and Nicholas caught her. "You saw something?" he asked.

"Something ancient," she said, exhaling sharply. "A golden creature, metal and flesh combined. It stretched out a hand and gave this book to . . ." She hesitated. "It was almost as if it handed it to me." She shook her head quickly. "And there was someone else there, someone I did not see. A woman, I think. She took the book from the monster."

"The woman was Tsagaglalal, She Who Watches," Fearnua said, suddenly reappearing at their side, "and the creature you call a monster was Abraham the Mage, one of the most powerful beings ever to walk this earth. All of humanity owes him a debt." Neither Nicholas nor Perenelle had seen or heard the hooded man reenter the room. He looked at Perenelle, blue eyes bright and searching, and for a moment, the woman wondered if he was related to the creature she had seen in her vision.

"You have the Sight," Fearnua said. It was a statement rather than a question. "What you saw happened ten thousand and more years ago. You caught a glimpse of the night when the old world fell and this world—the Time of the Humani—truly began."

In the silence that followed, a sound shivered in the air, a faint, high-pitched howling that echoed across the rooftops of Paris.

"Ah, your glimpse of the past has revealed our location," Fearnua said sadly. "No doubt your aura flared and my pursuer latched onto it."

"You believe this book is meant for us?" Perenelle asked.

"I do," Fearnua answered simply. "This is your destiny."

"We will accept it," Perenelle said carefully. She turned to look at Nicholas and waited for him to nod before continuing. "But on one condition."

Fearnua's thin lips curled in a smile. "I've never heard of anyone putting conditions on a gift."

"We will not accept this as a gift," Perenelle continued. "We will pay you for it."

The hooded man nodded. "Ah, so you know something about the nature of magical gifts."

Nicholas looked confused.

"Gifts come with obligations," Perenelle explained, her eyes fixed on the hooded man's face. "Obligations that might have to be repaid someday. Whereas if we pay now, then we have already discharged our debt."

Fearnua bowed. "I can assure you that there are no strings attached to this gift, but if it eases your mind, then reach into your purse, Nicholas, and give me the first coin that comes into your hand."

Flamel tugged open the purse at his belt and reached inside. "I don't have much . . . ," he began.

"The first coin," Fearnua repeated.

Looking vaguely embarrassed, Nicholas handed over a single battered and slightly misshapen denier. "That's the only coin."

Fearnua tossed the coin into the air and neatly caught it. "A penny. It is enough."

Silently, Perenelle reached out and took her husband's hand. Turning it palm up, supporting it, she stretched both their hands across the table.

Fearnua dropped the leather parcel into the center of Nicholas's palm. "This is the Codex, the Book of Abraham the Mage," he said slowly. He slipped the point of his hook under the leather strap at its center and eased it open. "This night your world changes forever."

2

Two cloak-wrapped figures stood on the roof of Notre-Dame. One was no longer entirely human, and the other had never been born. An icy mist rose off the river far below, covering the lead roof tiles in a thin layer of frost. One of the figures moved, almost lost its footing, and only managed to right itself in a windmill of flailing arms and screeching metal.

"This city will be the death of me." The voice was a peculiar rasp, a clicking rattle of gears and whirring cogs. The hooded cloak fell away to reveal a body composed of lengths of rusting wire and metal wrapped in red-and-yellow cord and draped in chain mail. Shivering washes of sparks ran across the mail like a pulsing heartbeat. The head looked as if it had once belonged to an antique suit of armor. Gossamer wisps of stinking sulfurous smoke leaked from every joint and crack in the helmet.

"You know that there are times I regret making you, but mostly, Talos, I regret giving you a voice box." The second speaker was English, his voice cultured and educated.

"You wanted someone as clever as you to talk to," the metallic man continued.

"There is no one as clever as me."

Talos's mouth opened, let out a belch of smoke, and closed again.

The Englishman known as Roger Bacon and Dr. Mirabilis had reputedly died sixty-three years previously. All of England had mourned the passing of one of the great scholars of his age. The king, Edward Longshanks, had even sent an emissary to Oxford for the funeral. Bacon, in disguise at the back of the crowd, had been vaguely disappointed that the king himself had not come.

"Did you know I became immortal in this city seventy-five years ago?" Bacon said quietly.

"I did not. I remember everything you have told me," Talos said. "There are some significant gaps in your history. I can only assume you have kept things hidden from me for a reason."

"I am protecting you. The Church has always looked askance at my work. You know that there are some rumors of your existence. If you were taken from me and interrogated, you would not be able to answer any questions because you simply do not know."

Talos leaked smoke in intricate spirals while he considered the statement. "I believe the appropriate response is 'Thank you,'" he said.

Bacon raised a long-fingered hand and pointed across the

shimmering, ice-creaking river toward a sparkle of lights on the other side of the Seine. "I was a friar in the Franciscan monastery just there, spending my days doing repetitive menial tasks, with no access to my beloved books and letters. On the feast day of John the Hermit—"

"The twenty-seventh day of March," Talos offered, each word accompanied by a puff of smoke.

"—I was visited by two creatures who made me an extraordinary offer."

"Were they angels?"

"I thought so at the time."

"Demons, then. Though I have to add that the evidence for angels and demons does not stand up to scientific scrutiny."

"You are a talking metal head," Bacon snapped, "kept alive by a science that is equal parts sorcery and ancient magic. Do not be so quick to dismiss either angels or demons. Magic is just science we do not comprehend yet; perhaps the angelic and the demonic are visitors from unknown lands. The Ancients write of Shadowrealms, worlds that link to ours—"

"The two creatures who visited you?" Talos interrupted, reminding him to continue.

"Ah yes. Male and female, but alike enough to be twins. Their clothing and jewelry had the look of the Land of Aegypt about them, and indeed, they called themselves Isis and Osiris, after the old gods of the same name. In time, I came to believe that they were the original bearers of those names."

"Which would make them over three thousand years old," Talos stated.

"Older," Bacon said, shaking his head, ice glinting in his mane of fine white hair. "Much, much older. They offered me two gifts and made a request." The old man paused, waiting for Talos to ask about the gifts or the request, then turned away from the river to look at the sparkling metal figure. "What: no smart suggestion?"

"I do not have enough data with which to formulate a response. However, you have stated that you become immortal in this city; then you spoke of the visitation by the two Aegyptian figures. It is not unreasonable to suggest that they made you immortal. Therefore, I have no question to ask or statement to make."

"If you were human," Bacon snapped, "you would be very irritating."

"I am created in your image," Talos muttered. "What did Isis and Osiris offer you?"

"They offered me immortality. What human could refuse such a gift?"

Talos's metal head was wreathed in smoke as he processed the idea. "I can list several reasons for refusing it."

"Well, yes, yes, so can I, now. But at the time I did not. I had not anticipated that I would have to fake my own death, and have to continue to do so every fifty or sixty years for the rest of my very long life. It seems almost ridiculous. However, they were insistent that I not reveal the secret of my immortality."

"Why do you keep me hidden?" Talos asked suddenly.

"Because the humans would fear you," Bacon answered. "And, in their fear, destroy you."

"And why would they fear me?"

"Because you are different," Bacon said.

Sparks shifted in a wavy pattern along Talos's chain-mail covering. "The humans may have respected you, Dr. Mirabilis, but you know that respect was tempered with fear. If they discovered that you were unaging, that you were different, they would have killed you."

Bacon sighed. "You are correct, of course." The white-haired old man reached beneath his cloak and unsheathed a short sword. Wan starlight ran like liquid on its blue-black stone blade. "This was their second gift to me."

"An unprepossessing weapon in the style of a Roman gladius," Talos answered. "The stone is unusual, however."

"I believe it is actually made of ice." Bacon held the sword up to the black Parisian night. Tendrils of chill white mist curled off the blade, and when he moved it, the air parted with a high-pitched musical whine. "This is the sword Caledfwlch."

"Excalibur!" Talos breathed a surprised puff of yellow smoke. He reached for the sword with a three-fingered metal gauntlet.

Bacon yanked the sword away. "Best not to touch it. Who knows what it would do to your metal workings."

Talos snatched his fingers back. "So, Excalibur is not a myth."

"At the heart of every myth," Bacon said, "there is a grain of truth."

"But if Excalibur is real, then so too is Arthur, and the Round Table."

"Just so," Bacon said. He moved the sword through the air again, the night parting with the faintest of whistles. "Two gifts: immortality and the sword."

"And you said these gifts came with a request attached?" Talos asked.

"They wanted me to retrieve a book that had been stolen from them."

"That seems simple enough," Talos concluded.

"If creatures who are almost ten thousand years old, who possess one of the legendary Swords of Power and can gift immortality, cannot recover their own book, then there must be a problem," Bacon said. "It is clearly no ordinary book. And no ordinary thief either."

Talos turned to look out over Paris, glowing yellow eyes peering through the smog of ten thousand chimneys. "And you are sure it is here?"

Roger Bacon picked his way carefully over the roof of Notre-Dame, tapping the carved gargoyles with the flat of the black-bladed sword. The sword flared silver and black with each touch, white smoke seeping off it, soaking into the stone statues, leaving them covered in sparkling frost. "Oh, I am quite sure," he said. "Ten days ago, the mysterious Isis and Osiris spoke to me from a mirror and told me that the book would arrive in Paris this very night."

"The book that is too dangerous for them to acquire themselves?" Talos asked. "I presume it must be protected by an army."

"I asked the same question," Bacon said. He touched the gargoyles again with the point of the sword, scraping a triangular symbol into the stone. The chill night air was broken by the sound of rock grinding off stone. "They told me it would be in the possession of one man. Immortal like me, powerful, but not invulnerable."

"A man? Just *one* man?"

"Just one," Bacon said. "I thought it odd myself."

Talos leaked stinking smoke across the roof. "Can I suggest that if Isis and Osiris were afraid to face this man, then we should be terrified? Or rather, you should be terrified. I am incapable of fear."

Rock crunched and pebbles rattled off the lead tiles. Talos turned as three of Notre-Dame's huge carved gargoyles came to shuddering life. Stone eyes blinked a dull gray light, and dirty smoke dripped between stone fangs. One appeared to be a cross between a dragon and a lizard; the second looked like a squat, incredibly muscular man with long pointed ears and an almost human face. A horn jutted from its forehead. The largest of the gargoyles was a three-headed dog with an unnaturally long body so thin that ribs showed through the stone flesh. Instead of paws, it had lion's claws. The metal man turned away from the animated stone statues. He'd seen Bacon bring statues to life before. It was little more than a useless trick. "Does this mysterious man have a name?"

"They told me he was called Marethyu. I do not know if that is a name or a title."

"Both," Talos answered. "Marethyu is one of the many names for Death."

And then, like distant thunder, something ancient and elemental pulsed across the city in a long slow wave. The night, which had been punctuated by barking dogs, grew silent, and from their vantage point high over the city, Bacon and Talos could see the lights from fires and candles blink out in ever-expanding concentric circles, plunging the entire city into darkness.

"There." Bacon raised the black-bladed sword and pointed toward the center of the circle. The trio of stone gargoyles, freed from their frozen forms, scrambled down the side of the cathedral, claws tearing holes in the soft stone. Moments later, they reached the ground in a clatter of rocks and raced off into the deserted streets.

"You will have time enough to read it later." Perenelle snatched the book from her husband's hands and shoved it into one of the two leather satchels on the bed.

Nicholas stood in the center of the tiny bedroom and turned around. The usually neat room was in chaos, and the carved wooden box at the end of their bed gaped open, clothes spilling out onto the bed. "We can't just leave," he said.

"We are leaving," Perenelle answered firmly. "Something

is coming, and we do not want to be here when it arrives." She looked at two pairs of shoes, then shoved one pair into a leather satchel and tossed the others aside. "We have space for one pair of trousers," she said. "Do you want the black ones with the hole in the knee or the brown ones with the torn pocket?"

"Black," he muttered. "I'll need the pockets."

Perenelle strapped up the worn leather bag and shoved it toward her husband. "Empty the lockbox. Take the money and any papers you think might be useful."

"What sorts of papers?"

"The important ones. Deeds to the house. Wills. Also, the letters you wrote me when we were courting."

"You're talking as if we might not be back."

Perenelle continued to pack the second bag. "And while you're downstairs, make sure the fire in the basement is out. We don't want it flaring up in the middle of the night and burning the street down. Go. Quickly now. I'll finish up here." She heard Nicholas clomp down the wooden stairs, and then, moments later, there was a metallic rapping on the bedroom door. "It's open," she called.

Fearnua pushed the door open but did not step into the room. In the light of the single candle, only his eyes and the metal hook at his wrist were visible. "We don't have much time," he said quietly.

"I know that." Perenelle lifted her head, eyes closed, and turned toward the river. "I can feel something unnatural . . . a disturbance."

"You are sensitive to the elemental magics. Something inanimate has been animated." Perenelle turned back to face Fearnua and saw the liquid flash of his tongue moving across his lips. "It has the taste of stone about it. A statue, no doubt," he said.

"And you can tell that by the taste in the air?"

"In time, Mistress Perenelle, you too will share these gifts."

Perenelle shoved the last of her clothes into the bag, strapped it tightly, and slung it over her shoulder. She turned to look at Fearnua. "I do not believe you are lying to me."

"I am not."

"And even if you were, then I know there is nothing I can do about it." She glanced toward the river again. "You've led something dark and dangerous to my home."

"It only became a danger when you accepted the book."

"Had you any doubts?"

"No. I knew you would take it."

"Did we have a choice?"

"There is always free will," Fearnua said.

Perenelle stepped closer, cold green eyes fixed on Fearnua's face. "If anything happens to my husband tonight, I will burn your precious book to cinders."

"Mistress Perenelle, you do know that the book is as much yours as it is your husband's. There are pages that only you will be able to decipher, spells only you can cast."

"The only reason I encouraged Nicholas to accept the book is that I cannot see a future for us beyond this night."

He nodded. "The future was awaiting your decision. Now

that you have made the decision, your future will begin to unroll."

"But I have always known that our future is not in this house."

"Is that why you seem willing to leave all this with less regret than your husband?" Fearnua asked.

"All that is important to me I carry here"—Perenelle tapped her head—"and here." She rested her hand over her heart. "Everything else can be replaced. If the book is as you say it is, then we will soon have more money than we know what to do with. I can buy new clothes, shoes, and jewelry."

"The book is all that I say it is," the man answered. "Within its pages you will find how to turn base metal into gold, and on the last two pages you will find a recipe—a unique concoction of herbs and spices, a mixture of salts and metals—that you must only brew and drink every month upon the full of the moon. It is the second great secret of alchemy: it will extend your lives indefinitely. Choose carefully the moment when you first activate it. You will never age beyond that day. But while you will become immortal, you will not be invulnerable. You can be killed. And from tonight, you will be forever hunted by creatures both natural and unnatural." He nodded toward the satchel dangling from her shoulder. "The book—the Codex—exudes an essence, a stink of ancient power. When I unwrapped it this evening, that power pulsed over the city and highlighted our position. In time, you will learn how to block and disguise the book's power. But be aware, Mistress Perenelle, that no matter where you go in this world, there will be those who will want this book: humans, inhumans, immortals, creatures of myth, monsters from legend, those you would call gods, and others who wear the guises of daemons. When you and your husband accepted the book, you took on the duty of guarding it for the rest of your lives."

"Guarding it?" Perenelle asked. "Why do I think we are merely holding it for someone else?"

"In time, you will be able to translate the book. In time, your destinies will be revealed and you will know exactly what you must do. But yes, you are now the guardians of the Codex. There will come a time, and this will be many years hence, when you will know what to do with the book."

Perenelle nodded. She glanced over her shoulder at the tossed bed and scattered clothing.

"This is the first night of the rest of your lives," Fearnua said.

Footsteps suddenly pounded up the stairs. Nicholas's face appeared out of the gloom, his eyes wide and dark with terror. "There's something outside. It's scratching at the door."

"This night might also be the last," Perenelle added softly.

Roger Bacon stopped at the top of the narrow street and peered down. Behind him, Talos stood so close that his rotten-egg odor completely engulfed Bacon. "I am never going to get your stink out of these clothes," the old man grumbled.

"You should have used something other than sulfur to

power me," Talos said, gears clicking softly as he attempted to whisper. "I cannot smell it myself, but I understand it is quite noxious."

"You stink of sour milk, unwashed feet, and rotten eggs," Bacon muttered.

"I presume you are equally fragrant."

"I had a bath last Christmas Eve," Bacon said, indignant. "Excessive washing removes the essential oils from a man's skin."

"History would suggest that that is a complete fallacy. Both the Greeks and the Romans bathed every day . . ."

Bacon raised a hand and Talos fell silent.

In the middle of the street, the three huge stone gargoyles had stopped outside a small, slightly squalid building. The largest of the gargoyles, the three-headed dog, reached out and almost delicately scratched at the wooden door. Its lion's paws shaved thick curls of wood off the door, leaving long white scars on the dark panels.

Bacon shook his head, confused. "I was convinced our chase would lead us to someplace more . . ." He paused, hunting for the correct word.

"Grand?" Talos suggested.

"Yes. More grand. This is a shabby house, in a shabby part of town. Hardly the sort of place in which to find a magical book."

"Or the perfect place," Talos said. "The last place you would think of looking."

"There is that," Bacon agreed.

One of the gargoyles, the squat, muscular creature that most resembled a man, turned to look at Bacon, awaiting direction.

Bacon pointed at the door with his sword. Immediately, the beast charged straight toward the narrow doorway, stone claws spattering mud and half-frozen filth in every direction.

The door opened, light flooding out, throwing the long shadow of a hooded man through the doorway.

The gargoyle lowered its head, aiming its wickedly pointed stone horn at the figure's chest.

There was a flash of metal, a half circle of orange light, and the gargoyle exploded into a thick cloud of crystalline dust. The icy Parisian night was abruptly heavy with the scent of oranges.

"This must be Marethyu." Talos's attempt at a whisper echoed down the street.

The figure standing in the doorway raised his head. Blue eyes blazed in the shadow of his face, and both Bacon and Talos clearly heard him speak. "Ah, the legendary Dr. Mirabilis and his mechanical man." There was a distinct note of disappointment in his voice. "I thought the Dark Elders would send someone more interesting." Then he slammed the door shut.

"I think Death has just insulted us," Talos muttered.

"Is there a rear entrance?" Fearnua demanded.

Perenelle turned and led the way down a narrow corridor

to the kitchen. She was about to pull open the back door when the hooded man placed his hook against the handle.

"Where does this open onto?"

"The backyard," Nicholas said, "and there is a gate there that leads to a lane."

"Will there be someone—something—there?" Perenelle asked.

Fearnua shook his head. "I am sensing nothing."

"What was out there?" Nicholas demanded. "I saw . . . something. A man, a demon, with a horn in the center of its forehead. It charged at you, and then you hit it. I watched it explode into dust. There were two more behind it. Monsters."

"Gargoyles," Fearnua said, "or, to be precise, chimera. Gargoyles are the water spouts."

"From Notre-Dame," Flamel guessed.

"I would imagine so. Our adversaries have a taste for the dramatic. However, the two figures at the end of the street are far more dangerous," Fearnua said. "The legendary Dr. Mirabilis, Roger Bacon, has come to claim the book, and he has brought his mechanical man with him."

"Roger Bacon is dead," Nicholas said.

Fearnua's bright blue eyes crinkled in amusement. "Death is not always the end, nor it is always permanent. Right now, the doctor is striding down the street, carrying . . ." He paused, throwing his head back, nostrils flaring. ". . . carrying a weapon older than most civilizations." He turned to Nicholas and Perenelle. "When I open the door, I want you to run. Stop for nothing. Make your way to the Tour de Nesle. A carriage and driver are waiting there. They will carry you south and protect you if . . ." He paused.

"If what?" Nicholas asked.

"If Fearnua fails here tonight," Perenelle said.

Fearnua nodded. "Stop for nothing," he said. "Go now."

"Will we ever see you again?" Nicholas asked.

"If we three survive this night, then yes, our paths will cross through the centuries. I have viewed the twisting strands of time, and our destinies are woven with the Codex. Guard it well. In time to come, we will need it to destroy and create the world."

The hook-handed man gently eased the door open and ushered Nicholas and Perenelle out into the frigid night. As Nicholas passed, Fearnua leaned forward and put his mouth close to his ear. "Promise me this: you will destroy the Codex before it falls into the hands of Bacon and his like. They would use it to return the world to Chaos and Old Night. And in that new world, humans are little more than slaves or food."

"D-destroy it!" Nicholas stammered. "But—"

"Destroy it, or it will destroy the world. The choice is yours."

3

Talos knew he was unique.

Oh, there had been other metal and mechanical men before him, going back to the time of the Greeks. His own namesake, Talos the metal statue, appeared in the tales of Jason and the Argonauts and down through the centuries; Bacon's predecessors had used the ancient Arabic manuscripts to fashion talking metal heads.

But Talos was different.

Perhaps the formula Bacon had used to animate him was flawed: a missing mineral or too much of an essential salt, an incorrect incantation, a mispronounced word. Shortly after Talos had been brought to flicking life, he'd realized just how extraordinary he was. While Bacon thought he was nothing more than a scientific curiosity, able to calculate formulas, predict the weather, and speak in a dozen languages, he had no idea that Talos had developed not only a self-awareness but that uniquely human skill: he had discovered how to lie.

And Talos had ambitions.

As Bacon and Talos moved cautiously down the narrow street, the mechanical man suddenly pointed to a narrow laneway, almost invisible in the night. "There is a high degree of probability that this lane leads to an alley at the back the house."

Bacon nodded. "Well spotted."

"I will find that alley and secure it. If Marethyu was bringing this magical book to Paris, then he undoubtedly intended to give it to someone."

"The owners of the house." Bacon nodded in agreement.

"If we try to attack through the front door again, I predict that Marethyu will challenge you and attempt to delay while this person or persons makes good their escape through the rear entrance," Talos said. "I will ensure that they flee directly into my arms."

"That is an excellent plan. Do you want to take one of the gargoyles with you?"

"My appearance should be enough to frighten them into submission. Also, there is little they can do to harm me, is there?"

"Nothing," Bacon answered. "You are practically invincible."

"Given how quickly Marethyu dispatched the gargoyle, I think you should concentrate your forces," Talos continued. "I am confident that nothing can stand against you, Excalibur, and two animated gargoyles. Though, to be precise, they are chimeras," he added.

"Find the alley," Bacon directed. "Let nothing escape. If they have the book, bring it to me."

"Do you not want them alive?"

Bacon shook his head. "My masters just want the book."

Trailing the scent of rotten eggs, Talos slipped into the alleyway. The walls were so narrow that his jutting metal shoulders scraped sparks off the stones. He had no idea what was in the book. But if the creatures who called themselves after ancient Aegyptian Gods, and who had the power to grant immortality, wanted it, then the tome must be valuable. Maybe he would find what he was looking for in the book, or he might be able to trade with the Aegyptians. They had made Roger Bacon immortal; perhaps they would be able to make him human.

Marethyu carefully gathered Flamel's precious few books, stacked them in the corner, and then moved the table to cover them. He took a last look around before blowing out the candle, plunging the room into darkness. Not that it made much difference to him; his enhanced senses allowed him to see wavelengths of light invisible to humans.

Marethyu knew that Roger Bacon was a dangerous adversary: cunning, intelligent, ambitious, a man whose search for knowledge and learning had brought him down some very dark paths. Over the long years of his life, Marethyu had come to realize that knowledge was the ultimate power. The wisdom of the Ancients could be used for good or ill. Knowledge was impartial, but humans were not. Bacon had come to believe that his knowledge made him superior to ordinary men, and that arrogance colored all his actions. Everything he did now was simply to advance his own knowledge, rather than to benefit his fellow man. He could have focused his vast intellect on eradicating diseases or famine; instead, he had copied the Chinese formula for gunpowder.

And now, accompanied by his fabled metal man, alongside two animated stone statues, he was also in possession of Excalibur, which he thought made him unbeatable.

Almost unconsciously, Marethyu traced the curl of metal that took the place of his left hand. A lattice of runes etched into the flat metal flickered to life. In the Once and Future Time, the boy who would become Marethyu would hold not only Excalibur, the Sword of Ice, but the other swords of power: Clarent, Joyeuse, and Durendal. In that moment, he had learned the secret at the heart of the four swords of power: they were only as powerful as the intent of the user. And that made Bacon, one of the most intelligent and learned men of the time, an incredibly dangerous enemy.

Marethyu had been planning his visit with Nicholas and Perenelle Flamel for centuries. Working closely with Chronos, the infinitely dangerous and increasingly insane Master of Time, he had picked through the endless time streams to choose the most promising. The real problem was that this moment was a crux. This was a point in time when the entire history of the world had the potential to change. Thousands of time lines flowed to this moment—the moment where he offered the Flamels the Codex—and ten times that number flowed out. And every single one was different, and not all of them were pleasant.

In many time lines, Nicholas and Perenelle refused the Codex. They died a few years later, impoverished and forgotten, in the slums of Paris.

In others, they took it, but were hunted down the very next day by Bacon's creatures.

Or they took it, studied the ever-changing pages and used it for themselves, becoming corrupted by its dark knowledge. Together, the Flamels—now a Warlock and an Enchantress—ruled a vast Alchemycal Empire that stretched from the Baltic to the Mediterranean.

There were time streams in which the Flamels, lost and starving in southern Spain, sold the book for the price of a loaf of bread. . . .

Marethyu had watched the Flamels drown when one of the Spanish Armada ships, the *San Marcos,* sank off the Irish coast. . . .

He saw the Codex burn in the Great Fire which engulfed London. . . .

He watched the Flamels, pursued by dragons, fall into the gaping mouth of the volcano, Krakatoa, taking the book with them, sacrificing themselves to protect it. . . .

Saw it destroyed in the earthquake that ripped San Francisco apart. . . .

He saw the book, abandoned and forlorn on a forgotten library shelf, nibbled apart by a nest of rats . . . then watched those same rats mutate and morph into sentient monsters who gathered the black and brown rats into an army numbering in the billions and unleashed them across Europe. Within a decade, all life—animal and human—had been wiped out. Then the Kingdom of the Rats began its expansion into Asia and down through Africa.

There were ten thousand and more alternative futures from this night, and Marethyu had lived every one.

But there were some—a very few—in which the Flamels escaped Paris with the Codex; traveled south to Spain, where they began the task of translating the book; and brewed the immortality potion.

In this time line, Marethyu watched as they experimented with one of the great secrets of alchemy and turned a lump of iron into an ingot of gold. He saw them return to Paris and use their extraordinary wealth to found churches, hospitals, and schools.

He followed them across continents, down through the centuries, as they gradually unraveled the secrets of the Codex and finally began the hunt for the twins who were spoken about in the myths and legends of every race. He was there the day Nicholas and Perenelle finally found the twins in a city on the edge of the world, half a millennium and more into the future.

That was the time line Marethyu needed the Flamels to follow. He was hoping he'd chosen the correct one.

His enhanced senses caught the sound of sticky footsteps, and then the entire front of the Flamels' house folded in as two stone gargoyles—dragon and three-headed dog—

crashed into it. Behind them, Bacon's sword came to blue glowing life.

"I have come for the book," the man bellowed.

Hand in hand, the Flamels moved as quickly as they could. But it was slow going. The alley behind the house was in almost total darkness and littered with all manner of waste. The ground was frozen solid, but their footsteps broke the thin sheen of ice, releasing the stink of rotting food, rancid fish, and other, less pleasant odors. Either side of the alley was piled high with filth, and some of the cloth-wrapped bundles in the shadows wore human shapes. They stirred as the Flamels hurried past.

"Will he be all right?" Nicholas asked.

"Who?"

"Fearnua," Nicholas said.

"You saw him destroy the gargoyle," Perenelle reminded him. "He is not human. Well, not entirely human. Human once, but now, more than human. I think he can take care of himself. I've just realized what his name means," she said, her voice puffing the words into white clouds. "It's Celtic . . . Fearnua . . . *fear nua*. New man. His name is Newman."

"Is that a name or a title?"

"Both, possibly."

"When I awoke this morning, I never thought I'd end the day running from my own house," Nicholas grumbled.

"Perhaps we should have taken a little more time to think it through. Everything happened so fast."

"I believe that from the moment we decided to take the book, events started to run away from us," Perenelle said. She hopped over a puddle. Nicholas walked right through it, sinking up to his ankles in filth.

"I hope we've not made a terrible mistake," he muttered, lifting the hems of his trousers and jiggling his feet, trying to shake off the clots of gooey liquid on his shoes. "Tell me you packed a spare pair of shoes? I'm going to have to burn these." He sniffed cautiously. "They smell of . . ." He sniffed again. "Rotten eggs."

And then the alley blossomed in a sickly yellow light as a terrifying metal man stepped out of a side lane. It looked as if scraps of a suit of armor had been animated. The Flamels shrank back, horrified, as the monster stretched out a three-fingered metal gauntlet and a wave of glittering sparks ran over the chain mail that was both covering and skin. Deep in the metal helmet, yellow eyes bled foul smoke, and there was the sound of gears clicking and settling into place. The voice was a peculiar rasp, a rattle, echoing and magnified from within the helmet.

"I have come for the book."

"You are too late, Dr. Mirabilis," Marethyu said. "I do not have it."

The three-headed dog and the dragon gargoyle stepped

into the shattered room, fixing their stony gaze on the hook-handed man.

Bacon pushed through the rubble, brushing dust off his shoulders. "Where is it? Tell me now. I have never been known for my patience."

"I was unaware that your hearing was failing."

"What?"

Marethyu raised his voice. "I said that I was—"

Bacon raised the blue-bladed sword. "Enough. Where is the book?" He stopped, suddenly aware of the wispy blue smoke curling off the sword.

Marethyu raised his hook, and it too trailed the same sapphire-colored mist. "Interesting," he said. "Never seen it do that before."

"Have you any idea who I am?" Bacon demanded.

"Of course," Marethyu answered. "It is an honor to meet you, Dr. Mirabilis. "I have read everything you've written, and there is a very fine copy of your *Opus Majus* in my personal library."

"So you are a learned man . . . or are you even a man?" Bacon asked. He used Excalibur to point toward the hook. A crackling blue spark snapped between the two metals.

Marethyu jerked his hook back and held it to his face, bright blue eyes reflecting the shivering coils of light that twisted around the metal. Tiny pictographs and runes etched into the flat hook shifted, forming new patterns. "Yes, I am human," he said absently. "Perhaps a little bit less than I used to be." He dropped his left arm and looked at Bacon.

"I believe it would be a mistake to bring Excalibur close to my hook."

"Why?" Bacon demanded.

"The sudden release of energies would probably flatten this entire street and punch a hole through to a Shadowrealm," Marethyu predicted. "Who knows what might crawl through."

Bacon lifted the sword. "This is Excalibur, the greatest of the swords of power—"

"No, not the greatest, and not even the most powerful," Marethyu interrupted. "Clarent, the twin blade, is arguably far more powerful."

Bacon stopped, clearly surprised. "Oh, I did not know there was a twin blade."

"Carried by Arthur himself alongside Excalibur. I watched the king stride into battle wielding one in each hand. It was a sight to behold."

"You saw Arthur?" There was no disbelief, only envy in Bacon's voice.

"Many times. And I was there when Mordred used Clarent to kill his father, Arthur."

"A twin blade. Why have I not heard of this before?" Bacon sounded almost irritated.

Marethyu raised his left arm. "I have held it in this hand . . . well, I did when I still had a hand. Tell me, Doctor, who are your masters now?"

"Masters?" Bacon asked. "I have no masters."

"You traded your human existence for an immortal life,"

Marethyu noted. "Your immortality was not a gift, but part of a bargain. Who controls you now?"

"No one." Bacon took a step toward the hooded man and the two gargoyles shuffled after him.

"Then who sent you out tonight to find me and the book?"

The Englishman hesitated before answering. "I suppose it matters little if you know their names. You will not survive this night."

"You have no idea how many men and monsters have said that to me, and yet, here I am, and they are no more," Marethyu replied.

"They call themselves Isis and Osiris, after the Aegyptian gods," Bacon admitted.

Marethyu smiled. "I have met with all the Aegyptian Gods. And this pair are no more Aegyptian than you or I. In fact, they are not even human. We use the term *monster* very loosely, Dr. Mirabilis, but let me tell you, that pair are both monsters and monstrous."

"There is nothing you can say to me to convince me to leave here without that book," Bacon snapped. "I know what you are doing. You are trying to delay me to allow whomever you gave the book to escape. But you are wasting your time. I have set a trap for them."

The gargoyle dog suddenly lunged forward, all three heads snapping at Marethyu's face. He carved a figure eight with his hook before him, trailing blue, then yellow light, and the room suddenly smelled of oranges. The gargoyle dissolved into an enormous pile of sand. A tiny whirlwind danced across the top of the dust, scattering it around the room.

"Oh, your infamous mechanical man," Marethyu answered. "You believe he will simply bring the Codex back to you like an obedient hound? I am afraid, Dr. Mirabilis, that you lost control of your metal creation a long time ago. He has his own agenda now."

Nicholas and Perenelle stepped away from the metal man. He moved forward in a squeak of gears, his outstretched hand unwavering. "The book."

"Who are you?" Nicholas asked.

"*What* are you?" Perenelle said.

Talos looked at the humans curiously. "Ah, such an interesting response," he said. "Usually, humans run screaming from me."

"This has already been a night of wonders," Nicholas said. "You are just one among many, and it tends to dull the senses."

"My name is Talos, and I am a creation of Dr. Mirabilis," Talos recited. "I have been instructed to retrieve the book from you."

"We were instructed not to part with it," Perenelle answered. She stepped behind her husband, put her hand on his shoulder, and tugged him backward.

Talos inched toward them. "You will not be able to outrun me. Once my master has dispatched the hook-handed man, he will loose the gargoyles. Chimeras, actually. You'll not escape the three-headed dog or the dragon."

Perenelle's fingers tightened on her husband's shoulder, pulling him back another step.

Talos's three-fingered hand squeaked open and closed. "Give me the book, and I will allow you to make your escape. My master wants only the book; he has no use for you." The mechanical man suddenly stopped, and his helmet plumed fetid yellow smoke. "Why you?" he abruptly asked. "Why did the hook-handed man give you the book?"

"He did not give it," Perenelle said. "We bought it."

"Such a valuable tome must have cost a fortune, and yet"—Talos's metal head whined left and right, taking in the surroundings—"and yet you do not seem wealthy enough."

"It cost a denier," Perenelle answered.

"So little?"

"Actually, that's all I had," Nicholas admitted.

"So why did he give it—sell it—to you? What makes you so special?"

Nicholas shook his head. "I have no idea."

"You are a magician, a necromancer, a warlock, and you, madame, must be a sorceress or an enchantress?"

"We are none of those things," Nicholas answered, feeling the tug on his shoulder as his wife urged him backward. "I am a scrivener, a bookseller, and an apprentice alchemyst."

"There is a mystery here," Talos said. The outstretched hand rasped open and closed again. "The book. Give it to me and you can turn and run. Resist me . . . well, I am metal and you are but flesh."

"No, we're not going to do that," Perenelle said. "But we are going to turn and run." Catching Nicholas's hand, she deliberately turned her back on the monster and darted down the alley, practically dragging her husband behind her.

In a rancid explosion of steam, Talos strode after them . . . and plunged his left foot ankle-deep into the stinking puddle Nicholas had trod in earlier. Heavy metal legs sank deep into the muck and splashing ice sent waves of fizzing sparks dancing up the length of the chain mail covering. Talos's weight drove him deeper into the hole. He scrabbled on the ground, three-fingered claws attempting to find a grip on the slippery earth, but all he managed to do was to accumulate handfuls of foul mud. Dialing his volume up to full, he shouted, "You cannot escape me. I will find you. I want my book!"

Suddenly, the entire alleyway vibrated and Nicholas, Perenelle, and Talos turned to look toward the rear of their house. In the flickering yellow light they could see that something had struck the wall hard enough to send a spiderweb of cracks from top to bottom.

On the other side of the wall, Marethyu and Bacon heard Talos's shout.

"Looks like things are not going so well back there. And

you will note that he said *his* book," Marethyu said. "I do wonder what he wants it for?"

"He speaks for me," Bacon said, but there was a touch of uncertainty in his voice.

"*I will find . . . I want.* Has he always spoken of himself in the first person?" Marethyu smiled. "Why, it is not a stretch to say that he has developed a consciousness."

"Impossible," Bacon spat.

"You created him. That should be impossible. You animated stone statues this night. That should be impossible also. I think, once you set your mind to things, nothing is impossible. Why, sometimes, I've done six impossible things before breakfast," Marethyu said.

He was focused on the dragon gargoyle. The muscles in its short, stunted legs were flexing, and he knew it was preparing to jump. Suddenly, Bacon moved, the tip of Excalibur describing an arcane circular symbol in the air. A ball of glittering blue light sped across the room and exploded in the center of Marethyu's chest. The force of the blow drove him back against the wall. He cracked his head against the stone and the room spun to blackness as he momentarily lost consciousness. Blinking away the spots of color dancing before his eyes, while trying not to throw up, he was aware that the blue ball was still buzzing against his skin, melting down his body, encasing him in frigid ice.

And then the stone dragon advanced.

"You may think yourself clever, Marethyu, but I am

Dr. Mirabilis," Bacon shouted. "I am over one hundred and forty years old, and my long life has taught me much."

Marethyu pushed himself up against the wall. His legs felt like rubber. "My age is not measured in centuries, Doctor, but in tens of millennia, and it's clear that I have learned nothing." Catching the side of the glittering ball with the edge of his hook, he spun it across the room, where it shattered like glass. The ice coating his body steamed and was absorbed into his leather cloak.

Bacon grinned. "It is clear that you are not invulnerable."

"Immortal only, but nothing and no one is truly invulnerable."

"So do you think you are quick enough to defeat the gargoyle and me?"

Marethyu slowly sank to one knee and pressed his hand against the back of his head. It came away sticky with blood. He looked at it in something like amazement. "Do you know how long it's been since I last saw my own blood?"

"Prepare to see a lot more of it," Bacon said, gripping Excalibur in both hands and striding forward. The dragon opened its stone jaws and then launched itself into the air.

The Flamels raced down the alleyway and out into the street. It took them a moment to get their bearings. Fearnua had told them to go to the Tour de Nesle, which was on the south bank of the Seine.

"Wait, wait, wait a moment." Nicholas staggered to a halt and bent double, trying to catch his breath. "Do you think he'll be able to get out of that hole?" he asked.

"My experience with metal men is limited," Perenelle said with a smile. "But I would imagine he is strong. He'll pull himself out."

"He has no way of tracking us, has he?" Nicholas took in a deep, shuddering breath. "I cannot run another step."

Perenelle caught her husband's face and turned it to look up. Standing on a nearby roof, head wreathed in swirling yellow smoke, Talos slowly scanned the streets below.

"If we don't move, he cannot see us," Nicholas breathed.

The metal head stopped, then spun to look directly in their direction. Eyes blazed and a metal claw, still dripping black filth, pointed at them.

"Can you still not run another step?" Perenelle asked.

Nicholas heaved a sigh and stood up and they ran, twisting and turning down the narrow Parisian streets. Nicholas led Perenelle through the oldest part of the city, where the houses on either side were so close together their first floors practically touched, and the sky overhead was little more than a starry strip.

They crouched in doorways as the monster leapt from roof to roof, dislodging slates, smashing through chimneys and raining bricks into the street below.

"My book . . . my book . . ."

The words, howled across the city, sounded like the call of a wild animal, and those few Parisians brave enough to crawl from beneath their beds and peer into the night swore they saw a huge ape leaping from building to building.

Finally, Nicholas and Perenelle reached the Seine. The river was a shimmering curl of solid dirty-gray ice. The thin black line in the middle was the narrow channel of running water. On the opposite side, they could clearly see the white stones of the imposing Tour de Nesle. Perenelle squinted. "I don't see any driver."

"Now what?" Nicholas's words were warm against Perenelle's ear. "Nearest bridge is the Pont au Changeurs. But even if we reach it, there's no place to hide and we'll be exposed. How do we get across?"

"He's gone very quiet," Perenelle said. "I wonder where he is?"

The silence was even eerier than the endless wailing. Initially every dog in Paris had howled in response to the monster's shouts, but then, one by one, the animals had fallen silent, as if sensing that this was something unnatural.

"Maybe he's gone back to his master?" Nicholas suggested.

There was a click and whir and the sudden waft of rotten eggs. "And maybe he is standing behind you," Talos snarled.

Catching Perenelle's hand, Nicholas pulled her out of hiding and raced toward the riverbank. They slithered down the crumbling sides and out onto the frozen river. Clinging to one another, slipping and sliding, they moved farther out onto the ice.

Talos clambered down the riverbank and stomped onto

the frozen river. Ice creaked and spiderwebbed beneath his weight, but it held. As he dragged his feet, the metal cut grooves in the surface and gave him purchase, allowing him to stride forward, claws outstretched. "You should have given me the book when you had a chance. You could have walked away, made new lives for yourselves, and pretended this night never happened. Now I will simply take the book from your corpses."

"You talk too much," Perenelle snapped. She dragged Nicholas forward, moving farther away from the bank, out toward the center of the frozen river.

"The ice is thinner toward the middle," Nicholas said, realizing what she was trying to do. "It might not support his weight."

"There's a narrow channel of water in the middle," Perenelle said. "Maybe we'll be able to leap across it. If he tries to, he'll punch straight through the ice."

"And if he catches up with us?" Nicholas asked.

"Then we toss the book into the river."

Still kneeling on the floor, Marethyu looked up and smiled. "I did mention that Excalibur was not the most powerful of the swords. And not even the most interesting."

He abruptly flattened himself as the dragon gargoyle leapt forward and sailed overhead, ragged claws extended and close enough to ruffle his hair. The dragon hit the floor, stone claws sliding, tearing up the wood as it slithered toward the wall. Just as it was about to hit the stone, Marethyu's left arm shot out, his hook blazing red and blue, white and green, as he plunged it into the stone. The wall turned to almost transparent dirty gray smoke. The gargoyle slid into the smoke, and then Marethyu pulled his hand away. The wall coalesced back into stone, leaving the dragon stuck like a bizarre sculpture, its back legs trapped in the room while the head, shoulders, and claws looked out over the alley.

Bacon gripped Excalibur in both hands, raised it high over his head . . .

Marethyu tapped the floor with the flat of the hook. The floorboards turned to sawdust, and Bacon plunged into the basement below. He fell onto a fat-bellied pot, dousing himself in rose-scented water. Scrambling to his feet, he grabbed Excalibur and pointed toward the gaping hole in the ceiling. But before he could bring the sword to life, Marethyu tapped the floor again, and thick white clouds boiled up in the cellar. Thunder rumbled, and a flicker of lightning worked its way across the ceiling. When the rain came, it was torrential, blinding Bacon, filling his open mouth. He coughed and waved Excalibur about. It sparkled and fizzled, and suddenly the rain turned to snow.

Marethyu sat cross-legged over the ragged opening in the floor and looked down. Through the swirling clouds, he could see snow and ice beginning to pile up in the corner. Bacon was almost completely covered in snow, and his thin lips were starting to turn blue.

"Using the sword of ice in the middle of a rainstorm was

not a good idea," Marethyu said. Abruptly the clouds disappeared, leaving the Flamels' basement covered in inches of thick white powder. A man-shaped snowdrift moved, and Bacon's head appeared.

"Would you like me to continue?" Marethyu asked.

Bacon was shaking so hard he could not hold his sword. It fell from frozen fingers and disappeared, instantly freezing the snow around it into a solid ball of ice.

"It was not really a fair fight," Marethyu offered. "You were using one element, whereas I have access to all of them."

"What happens now?" Bacon asked through chattering teeth.

Marethyu stood up and dusted off his cloak before carefully touching the back of his head. "You've given me a headache," he said. "I'm going to leave you to explain to your masters how you've lost the Codex. I can guarantee you that they'll not be pleased." He indicated the shattered room and the gargoyle still stuck in the wall. "This sort of thing attracts attention, and the Dark Elders do not like that."

"I suppose you're going after the Codex and Talos?" Bacon asked.

"No. The Codex is in new hands now. And Talos . . . well, he has no idea what he's up against."

He turned to the back door and pulled it open. He tapped the gargoyle's hindquarters. "Remember," he called, "you owe Notre-Dame three gargoyles."

"Ch-ch-ch-ch-chimeras," Bacon said.

"Here's what we'll do," Nicholas said. He looked toward the narrow band of running water, then back to where Talos was quickly gaining on them. He knew they were never going to reach the center of the river in time. "You take the book and get it to the water. I'll stay here and see if I can slow this monster down."

"I'm not going to leave you," Perenelle answered simply.

"We have to protect the Codex at all costs."

"I'm not leaving you. We'll fight it together. Maybe if the three of us fight on the one spot, the ice will crack and pull us through. We might even have a chance then; he'll go straight down."

"And probably drag us with him," Nicholas muttered. "I don't suppose you packed any weapons?"

"Clothes and shoes."

"Give me the shoes. I can use the wooden soles as a club."

Talos slid closer. The smoke leaking from his helmet had turned even more rancid, while the patterns of sparks on the chain mail was agitated and irregular, unlike the previous smooth washes of lights.

"I think we've irritated him," Nicholas muttered.

"If he feels emotions, perhaps he can be reasoned with," Perenelle said.

"I am not deaf," Talos snapped. "I am possessed of excellent hearing. And I cannot be reasoned with."

"So you are irritated," Perenelle pointed out.

"You have needlessly extended an encounter which should have ended in the alley behind your home," Talos called. "You should have given me the book."

"Why do you want it?" Nicholas asked.

"That is, as you humans are wont to say, none of your business."

"We are humans, and humans are first and foremost curious," Perenelle said. Reaching into the satchel, she pulled out the cloth-wrapped book. "I think we know why Bacon wanted the book, but you?" She held it up. "What use is this to you?"

Talos's smoking eyes followed the book. "Look at me," he said finally. "I am a hideous thing of rusting metal and broken chain mail." His three-fingered claw pointed. "That . . . that could make me human." He lunged for the book, but Perenelle turned away, slipping on the ice and flinging the book as hard as she could toward the center of the river. It hit the ice and slid toward the water's edge.

Talos charged forward, metal arms and legs striking Nicholas, driving him to the ice. A pointed shoulder caught Perenelle on the side of the head and she fell onto her husband. They watched, helplessly, as Talos raced toward the Codex, ice splintering underfoot. He reached the Codex and snatched it up, inches from the edge of the water, before holding it aloft and howling aloud in stinking triumphant smoke.

Talos stomped back to the Flamels, now huddled together on the creaking ice. There was a trickle of blood running down Perenelle's face from a scalp wound, and Nicholas was sure he'd broken a couple of ribs.

"I am unsure whether to kill you now to tidy up any loose ends, or leave you here to die upon the ice," Talos began. "You have inconvenienced me—" He stopped, suddenly realizing that the man and woman were looking beyond him. "Oh, am I supposed to think there's someone behind me?"

"Oh, there is definitely someone behind you." The voice was female and spoke French with a strong Irish lilt.

Talos spun around. He was facing a slender, pale-skinned young woman with a shock of spiky red hair. Despite the bitter chill, she was bare armed, wearing a black leather jerkin, black leather trousers, and knee-high black boots. The hilts of two swords were visible over each shoulder. "And who are you?"

"The coach driver." The young woman looked past Talos at the Flamels. "I grew tired of waiting."

"I will have to kill you also," Talos said. "This is becoming tedious. I will kill the three of you and drop your bodies in the river." Talos's claw closed into a fist as he stepped toward the girl.

There was the high-pitched whistle of swinging metal . . . and then Talos's head leapt into the air, trailing a plume of yellow smoke, and toppled from his body. The girl sheathed the two swords no one had seen her draw and stepped forward to pluck the Codex from the creature's lifeless fingers before the body crashed to the ice in a clang of metal. The severed head hit the ice and bounced alongside it.

The red-haired young woman handed the book to the Flamels. "This is yours, I believe. Now we need to get out of here. Tonight's adventure will have attracted all sorts of attention." She kicked the metal head at her feet and the yellow eyes blazed alight.

"How dare you! Look what you've done," the helmet shrieked.

The young woman helped the Flamels to their feet. "When the hook-handed man contacts you in the middle of the night and asks you to do him a favor, my advice is to make an excuse or just say no." She kicked the head again, and it bounced and skidded across the ice before dropping into the black water in a hiss of bubbling steam.

"You must be Nicholas and Perenelle Flamel. I am Scathach the Shadow. Call me Scatty."

THE DEATH
OF JOAN OF ARC

1431

I am convinced this physician is killing me.

Certainly his treatments are much worse than what ails me. He comes each morning with his poultices and potions and pronounces me a little better every day. It gives my children comfort—except perhaps for my eldest son, Richard, who begrudges paying the physician to keep me alive. Richard imagines that when I leave this earth he will inherit everything, but he is wrong. My fortune will go to my youngest, William, who followed me into the army and fought valiantly for England in the wars against France.

In truth, there is little wrong with me, except the seventy years which lie heavily upon my bones and some old wounds which trouble me in damp weather. And seventy—or it might be seventy-one, or seventy-two, my mother was always vague about the year—is a goodly age in this, the Year of Our Lord 1481.

I have a few regrets. There was a girl I should have married, a war in which I should never have fought, a loaf of bread I should have shared, a lie to which I should never have listened. And there is a story I should have told.

It is time to tell it while I still can.

No doubt you will have been told the tale of the death of the Maid of Orléans. I have heard accounts told by people who were not there, who were either too young or too cowardly to have fought in that terrible war. I have listened to their boasts and their lies and never once have I been tempted to question them, to call them liars.

Perhaps I should have.

I know what happened on that day, the last day of May, in the Year of Our Lord 1431 in Rouen. I was there.

from the Last Will and Testament of William of York,
This day, the 13th day of October 1481

1

William of York heard the crowd moan behind him, then a huge indrawn breath, and knew that the prisoner must have been brought up from the cells. He didn't turn to look. He had been fighting for most of his adult life and he had no wish to see another condemned prisoner—especially not this one.

"Eyes front," he snapped at the two guards on the gate. They glowered at him but obediently turned back to watch the long straight road that led into the French town of Rouen. "If there's to be an attack, it will be now," he added, "when the prisoner is in the open air."

"There will be no attack," one of the guards, a sullen Dutchman, said in his accented English. "The French want rid of her almost as much as we do."

"Some, maybe," William agreed, "but not all. I was there at Orléans, where she claimed her first great victory. I saw her fight at Jargeau and I was one of the few archers to escape from Patay. The French—the real French, the true French—worship her." Pulling his heavy leather cloak tighter around his shoulders, William wandered out from beneath the shelter of the gate and stood in the center of the track. Despite his words, he doubted there would be any rescue attempt for the young woman the people were calling the Maid of Orléans. Any attack would be suicide. Rouen was a fortress. The guards had been doubled and then redoubled as the date of her execution grew nearer. English archers guarded the walls, alongside German and Austrian mercenaries, and roving bands of savage Scots patrolled the fields.

Another rousing cheer went up inside the fortress and William turned to look back at the guards on the gate. The sound had distracted them and they were looking into the town square, where the huge pyre had been built.

"Eyes front," William bellowed again.

"But they're going to burn the witch," Thomas, the younger guard, said excitedly.

"She's no witch, she's a nineteen-year-old girl," William snapped, and immediately regretted his words. He would be reported to his commanders and marked down as either a potential heretic or a French sympathizer. Or both. The English bowman turned back to the road. William's sister, Anne, was nineteen years old, and every time he thought of the condemned girl, he was reminded of her.

In the distance, close to the edge of the forest, birds fluttered up into the morning sky, circled and then disappeared south.

William stared straight ahead, remaining perfectly still. Every archer knew that peripheral vision often revealed things that were otherwise missed. Something had startled the birds, something unusual—otherwise they would have settled back into the trees.

The big man turned his face slowly. The wind from the south was warm, scented with the rich growth of the forest, the hint of exotic flowers, the suggestion of vines. Closing his mouth and his eyes, he breathed in. If there were men massed under the distant trees, he should be able to smell their rank odor: a mixture of sweat, stinking clothes, rusting armor, and horseflesh. There was nothing.

William relaxed his shoulders. If there was anyone there— and he was beginning to doubt it now—then it was a small force or a few individuals. They were no threat. He rubbed his hands down the length of his longbow. He had been an archer all his life and he could fire between ten and twelve shots in a minute and hit everything he aimed at. There were thirty arrows in the quiver on his hip and at least a dozen archers on the wall behind him. They could lay down a withering rain of arrows. Nothing would survive.

Behind him he heard the crowd start to chant. "Witch . . . witch . . . witch . . ."

William shivered. Dying in battle was a hazard every soldier faced, and this young woman, this Joan, had fought gallantly. She deserved to die a soldier's death, not to meet this terrible end she'd been condemned to suffer.

From the corner of his eye, William caught the flicker of motion. In one fluid movement, he drew an arrow and nocked it to the bowstring. "Someone's coming!" he shouted. Behind him, he heard the two guards scramble into position.

"I don't see anyone . . . ," the Dutch guard began.

"There!" Thomas said.

"I see it," another guard, high on the wall, shouted. "A single rider, moving fast . . ."

William's eyesight had always been excellent. He could see the most distant objects with absolute clarity, though his close vision was often blurry. He turned to look at the shape. It was a single rider wearing unusual black-and-white armor that had gone out of fashion decades ago. The lone rider, who looked slender even beneath the metal and leather armor, was sitting astride a huge black horse. Metal plates, the same color as the knight's armor, protected the horse, so that it was difficult to distinguish between the rider and the animal.

"How many?" he called up to the guard on the wall.

"One. Just one."

"No one follows?"

"No one."

"Any banners or flags?"

"None."

William raised his bow and drew back the bowstring and waited for the rider to draw a little closer. He would loose the arrow in an arc that would direct it right into the center of the knight's chest. The arrow's heavy metal bodkin tip was designed to punch through a knight's metal armor.

"Is it an attack?" the Dutchman asked, coming out from the gate to stand beside the English archer. "It cannot be an attack. There is just one," he said, answering his own question. Then he leaned forward and shaded his eyes with his hands. "Is that a girl?"

"It is a girl," William whispered. He had just come to the same conclusion. Initially, he'd thought it might be a cape or a scarf, but now that the rider had drawn closer, he saw the mane of fiery red hair that streamed out behind her. Squinting against the light, he saw that she was not carrying a shield, nor was she holding the reins. She was clutching a long, slightly curved sword in each hand.

William raised his bow, drew the string back to his chin, and loosed the arrow in one elegant movement. He didn't care who the rider was—but she was galloping toward him on a heavily armored horse, so she certainly wasn't a friend. He watched the arrow arc high into the air and drop, and knew his shot had been true. The force of the blow should be enough to unseat the rider. Then, before she could clamber to her feet, he and the other guards would rush in and . . .

The rider's right hand moved; the sword flashed . . . and sliced the arrow in two.

"Impossible," Thomas said in a ragged whisper.

William fired again, twice in quick succession. He heard the twang-hiss of arrows shot from the battlements above his head, and suddenly there were six arrows raining down on the rider.

Sitting tall in the saddle, she moved her left and right hands, the swords blurs of metal as they sliced the arrows to slivers of wood.

"Demon!" The Dutchman turned and ran. The rider was

close enough to see clearly now. It *was* a young woman, with pale skin and shockingly green eyes beneath the mane of bright red hair. And then William saw her lips curl and realized that the woman was smiling.

And that frightened William even more.

He fired again, this time aiming to take down the horse, but the unnaturally fast woman chopped the hissing arrow out of the air. He distinctly heard the whistle of the blade and the snap as the heavy arrow was sliced in two. Then he turned to run. "Close the gates, close the gates!" He heard wood scrape as the huge gates slowly started to close, but he knew the rider would be upon them before the gates sealed shut. They would have to stop her before she got into the town. The Dutchman suddenly appeared in front of William, a long, hook-headed pike in his hands. He planted the end of the pike in the ground and positioned it so that the horse would run onto the spike. The young archer, Thomas, stood behind him and fired arrow after arrow at the approaching creature. Wood pinged and cracked as the rider cut arrow after arrow out of the air.

William reached the Dutch mercenary, grabbed hold of the thick shaft of the pike, then turned to face the rider, confident that she would not be able to stop her headlong plunge.

Arrows whistled over their heads as Thomas continued to fire at the rapidly approaching rider. "Who is she?" he shouted, his voice high with terror.

"*What* is she?" William muttered. Unlike most others, he was not a superstitious man, but he had seen enough in his years fighting in the Scottish Highlands and the wilds of Ireland to realize that creatures who were more—and less—than human walked the shadows of this world. The rider was so close now that he could see the speckling of freckles across her nose, and he realized that she was around the same age as the condemned Frenchwoman. Her eyes, a brilliant grass green, were mesmerizing.

Only his reflexes saved him.

At the very last moment, just as the huge black mount reached the razor-sharp tip of the pike, the rider leaned low over the beast's neck and the great horse leapt into the air. It sailed over the wooden pike. William and the Dutchman ducked. An iron-shod hoof punched into the mercenary's breastplate, leaving a perfect semicircle in the metal. William saw the silver arc of a sword flashing toward him and threw up his bow to protect himself. The blade sliced through the thick yew, the force of the blow driving him back onto the muddy ground. The horse landed neatly and surged ahead. Thomas threw himself to one side to avoid being trampled, and then the red-haired rider was through the half-closed gates and racing toward the square.

"After her!" William shouted. The Dutch mercenary and the English bowman looked at him as if he was mad. Then they turned and ran in the opposite direction.

William grabbed Thomas's abandoned bow and raced after the rider. Maybe this Joan *was* a witch, and maybe the rider was a demon come to rescue her . . . but he'd never heard of a demon with freckles before. And why would a demon need to ride into the town—why not just materialize in the square? He was sure the red-haired girl was human. She was fast, but every archer knew stories of men who could catch arrows, and she rode the huge horse easily and without reins, but he'd watched mounted knights gallop into battle with a sword in one hand and a mace in the other, guiding their horses with their knees. And why would she bother swatting the arrows out of the air if they were no threat to her?

William followed a trail of devastation through the narrow, filthy streets. Scores of English foot soldiers and archers lay on the ground. A knight in armor had been flattened into the muddy road, the steel plate dented with the impression of the horse's hooves. Another knight in chain mail lay crumpled in an awkward heap against a broken door, the metal links sliced apart, torn like cloth. A huge German mercenary sat in a dirty pool of water, his face the color of parchment. He was holding the stump of a shattered sword in both hands; the remaining chunk of metal lay half buried in the mud between his feet.

William rounded a corner and suddenly found himself in the town square.

Hundreds of people had crowded into the Vieux-Marché in Rouen earlier that day to watch the execution. Guards armed with staves and sticks had kept them away from the huge funeral pyre, while more soldiers patrolled the mob, looking for troublemakers. There were archers on the roofs of the surrounding buildings and mounted knights in the side streets. And despite the terrible event that was about to take place, there had been a carnival atmosphere, with jugglers and minstrels, food vendors and poets moving through the crowd.

Now it was chaos.

Up to that moment, William had wanted to believe that the girl on the black horse was human. Now he knew she was not.

The armored horse carved a path through the mob, right up to the tall pillar in the center of the square. Joan was tied to the pillar, and stood, eyes closed, face turned to the sky as Geoffroy Therage, the executioner, piled tall bundles of tinder-dry wood around her. The fire had been lit, and crackling flames and twisting black smoke were curling around the girl. Her clothes had started to smolder. The red-haired warrior leapt off the horse and sliced her way through the soldiers, her curved swords blurring so fast that they reflected the morning light until it seemed as if they blazed.

William saw the Frenchwoman open her eyes and look down. And then her face lit up with a brilliant smile. He saw her lips move and form a single word, a name. Later, much, much later, Geoffroy Therage told him she had said the word "Scathach."

William watched the executioner scream and throw himself on his knees in front of the red-haired girl. She swatted him away as if he was a fly, and the sword in her left hand darted out, cutting away the burning wood. Then, standing back, the warrior chopped at the manacles around Joan's wrists. Metal sang off metal and the chains fell away.

Scathach tossed one sword to Joan. William heard the red-haired warrior laugh, a sound of pure delight, as she turned and attacked the gathering knights. He watched, both awed and horrified, as the two women fought their way through the square. Nothing could stand against them. Even though she was weak from months in prison, Joan of Arc drove back the waves of English knights, while Scathach chopped arrows out of the air, and slashed and cut at anyone who came too close. William watched in amazement as she fought with fists and feet, her metal-gloved hands as deadly and dangerous as her sword. The two women were now standing back-to-back, working as a team, fighting their way to the black horse, which was surrounded by knights and soldiers attempting to catch it. The huge armored beast reared and kicked, cracking shields and shattering armor.

Ducking back into the side street, William tried to nock an arrow to his bow, but his hands were shaking too badly. He had never believed Joan was a witch, but the evidence was overwhelming. He didn't think the red-haired girl was a demon, but she certainly wasn't human. She was . . . He tried to find the right word. She was unnatural.

He pressed back against the wall as four heavily armored knights wielding broadswords, spears, and axes rushed past him and attacked the two women. Joan ducked under a flailing ax and chopped its wooden handle in two. Scathach neatly dodged the spear thrust at her, then grabbed the shaft and tugged, pulling the knight toward her. Off balance, he fell to the ground, bringing two of his companions with him in a heaped pile of metal and flesh. Scathach leapt onto the back of the fallen knights. She caught Joan's arm, hauled the smaller woman up and then flung her into the air. For a moment, the ragged warrior hung suspended in midair, and the image momentarily silenced the uproar in the square. Then Joan dropped onto the back of the black horse.

Scathach screamed, a long, terrifying, triumphant war cry that drove the men around her to the ground, holding their ears. Dancing lightly across the squirming bodies, she somersaulted onto the back of the black horse and dug in her heels. The armored beast surged forward, crashing through everything in its path. Arrows rained down from the roof, but the red-haired warrior knocked them out of the air as she and her companion raced toward the gate.

William realized with horror that they were escaping: one woman had defeated an entire army to rescue Joan of Arc. He pressed himself back against the alley wall as the horse bore down on him. Now that it was close, he could see that, like its mistress, it was not entirely natural. Beneath the spiked metal sheath that covered its head, its eyes blazed bloodred.

William could not allow the prisoner to escape. The moment the horse thundered past him, he stepped out of the shadows and fired after them.

The heavy metal-tipped arrow bit deeply into Joan's shoulder. She shuddered and slumped forward and would have fallen from the horse if Scathach had not caught her. The red-haired girl screamed again, but this time it was a sound of pure anguish. Then she turned to look back at William, and he saw her face undergo a terrible transformation, mouth opening to reveal a maw of needle-sharp teeth. She pointed her sword at him, and although she did not speak, he clearly heard her words in his head: *You will pay for this injury. I swear it.* Then she pulled the arrow out of her friend's shoulder and flung it back at William. It hit him with tremendous force, striking him high on the arm, breaking bone and tearing muscle, and in that instant, William of York knew he would never pull a bow again.

In the last moments before unconsciousness claimed him, he watched Joan of Arc and the red-haired warrior escape on the black horse.

2

Joan of Arc escaped—but that is the story you have never heard.

History records that Joan of Arc, the Maid of Orléans, died in Rouen on that last day of May in the Year of Our Lord 1431.

A girl died that day, but it was not Joan.

Sick with pain, I watched as a girl who bore but the slightest resemblance to the Maid of Orléans was dragged out of the dungeons and hauled to the place of execution. Knights moved through the crowd, warning the people that if they spoke about what had just happened, they would be condemned as heretics and suffer the same fate.

I could not bear to stand and watch an innocent girl die. I walked away from Rouen, abandoning everything I owned, and began the long journey back to England. After that day I never fought in another war. My left arm withered and I was never able to hold a bow again.

I have often wondered what happened to the Maid of Orléans and Scathach, the red-haired, green-eyed warrior who rescued her. Where had they gone? Had Joan survived the wound I gave her? I hoped she had. And what of Scathach? Did she still live? I was guessing she did: I imagined that killing her would be almost impossible.

from the Last Will and Testament of William of York,
This day, the 13th day of October 1481

MACHIAVELLI: GUARDIAN OF PARIS

1793

===

ENCRYPTED EMAIL—512-BIT ENCRYPTION
From: Niccolò Machiavelli <theprince@███████.com>
To: Billy the Kid <whbonney@███████.com>
Subject: More memories

Dear William,

I trust you are healing well. Remember, we are immortal, not invulnerable, and while I know you have been friends with Black Hawk for many decades, maybe you will pause and reconsider if he ever asks you again to go up against an army of Little People, especially Leprechauns. Next time you might not be so lucky. When you see Scathach, ask her what happened when she fought them. If I've learned anything in my long life, it is that you don't mess with the Little People!

I want to circle back to something we touched upon in your last email. I was surprised to discover that you have kept no record of your remarkable life. I would like to encourage you to begin a diary. The process of faithful documentation will certainly spark memories, and the longer you live, the more valuable you will find those memories.

It should come as no surprise to you that over the course of my long life I have kept a daily journal. Long before I became immortal in the sixteenth century, I was in the habit of recording my life in a series of day bookes which I encoded using a cypher given to me by Leonardo da Vinci. (We were never really friends; he was a genius, but he smelled!) At first, they were just a way to note everything that occurred on a daily basis. Later, when I became ageless, the diaries became more important. They allowed me to keep track of the world. When days and weeks and then months blended into one another, when I could recall the years only by the great holidays, events, and seasons, my letters and diaries were essential. They gave the years and then the centuries a shape that would otherwise have been lost.

And of course, one of the great gifts of immortality is the ability to put in place plans that take decades to come to fruition. While my memory is excellent, even I was unable to track everything without committing it to paper. Now, although I have access to the most sophisticated bit-locked computers and encrypted journals, I still handwrite my diaries every night. The process helps shape my day.

But even without my diaries, there are certain events that have seared themselves into my memory.

I remember the night I accepted the gift—or was it the curse?—of immortality.

I remember the first time I met Dagon, the millennia-old creature who would become my companion and friend for centuries. (I always regret that you never got to meet: you would have liked him and he would have loathed you.)

I know to the precise hour, the moment I met that dangerous human monster, John Dee.

I can recall with absolute clarity the time Perenelle Flamel and I fought on the slopes of Mount Etna.

As I am writing this to you, what has just struck me is that these memories are of those times I came close to losing my immortal life.

Perhaps that is why I will never forget the time Black Annis came to Paris.

It was 1793: the year of the Terror.

It came to be called that because of a wretched man, whom I disliked intensely, called Bertrand Barère. Billy, you would have despised Barère on the spot. He had what you would call a very punchable face.

Barère liked to call himself a revolutionary; in truth he was nothing more than an amateur politician, who came to a decision only once he saw which way the wind was blowing. He was one of those who voted for the king's execution, and rounded out his pretty speech by saying "the tree of liberty grows only when watered by the blood of tyrants." And if that sounds familiar to you, it was because he'd stolen the phrase from your third American president, Thomas Jefferson, who'd used it six years previously. No doubt Barère didn't think anyone would notice, but I did.

He was a journalist and clearly spent a long time crafting his speeches. In one infamous address, he declared, "Let us make terror the order of the day."

And that is what they did.

Billy, I have lived through some of Europe's worst excesses. I grew up in the time of the Borgias and the Medici; I watched the Witch Hunts sweep across nations; I was in Seville during the terrible days of the Great Plague and in France when we lost two million people to the famine. I have seen some truly awful things: the worst of what humanity had to offer. But the Reign of Terror was shocking beyond belief. France was in the midst of the Revolution. There was upheaval everywhere; law and order were breaking down; there were mobs protesting in the streets. So the government of the day decided that the only way to control the country was by terror tactics. They called it "a speedy, severe, and inflexible justice."

It was not justice. In the months following Barère's pretty speech, thousands would die, disappear, or end up imprisoned on false charges.

And sometimes, just sometimes, I wonder if the Terror was orchestrated by the Dark Elders and their followers. Certainly, it allowed creatures like Black Annis to operate undiscovered, their crimes hidden and lost amid the chaos.

I added Barère's name to my little black book the moment I heard his plagiarized speech. Those whose names go into my book sooner or later have unfortunate accidents.

There are some immortal humans who choose not to take an active role in politics or public life. They live quietly and try not to leave a mark on the world. I have come to the conclusion that this is a waste of their immortality. Before I became immortal I believed that my work, my writings, would make a difference. After I "died" I was determined that *I* would make a difference.

In Florence, where I lived for most of my life, I learned the value of working behind the scenes. Billy, there is an old saying that comes from the country of your Irish ancestors: "Happy is the man who remains unknown to the law." In Paris, in 1793, I was the law. Never officially, of course; operating in the shadows, I effectively commanded the various police forces, and my vast fortune ensured that the newly elected politicians did what I told them. Piece by piece, I dismantled the Terror and ensured that those who orchestrated it paid for their crimes. It is true that I saved some lives; I wish I could have saved more.

I thought that humans were the worst part of the Terror.

I was wrong.

I have scanned these pages from my diaries, converted them into text and rendered them into English for you. Perhaps they will encourage you to keep your own diaries and record your adventures.

(As an aside, Billy, you must learn a few more languages. English and Spanish will take you far, but may I also suggest French? And Italian, of course. And if you have Mandarin, Arabic, and Hindi, you can travel the world. Don't tell me you don't have the time! Time is something we immortals have aplenty.)

When you are fit enough to travel, do come and visit me in Paris. I have an apartment you can stay in on the Rue de Montmorency, almost directly opposite Flamel's old house. Paris is a city of wonders; I could show you the catacombs beneath the city; the hidden rooms in the Louvre; Notre-Dame, where Dee, with a little help from me, brought the gargoyles to life and the leygate in Sacré-Coeur that carried Nicholas and the Twins to this city and my attention.

And you did say you wanted to visit Disneyland Paris.

Give my regards to Black Hawk, of course.

And, Billy, try to stay out of trouble.

Your friend

Niccolò Machiavelli

(P.S. Now go and learn those languages!)

1

Thursday, 5th Day of September, the First Year of the Revolutionary Calendar of the French Republic (1793 of the Julian Calendar.) New Moon.

There were mobs in the streets again today. It was not unexpected: it was sunny and warm after weeks of rain. I have noticed that no one likes rioting in wet weather.

All morning I received reports of scattered outbreaks of violence from across the city. One by one, ragged men and women, children too, would rap on the window of the little house on the Rue du Montmorency I used as my headquarters. A few came to the front door; most preferred the rear, where they could slink down the alleyway and collect their coin without being spotted. In every city I've lived in, I have maintained a shadow army of ordinary men, women, and children—especially children, for they are invisible. I call them my Irregular Army. My spies know I will pay well for information. They also know that my bodyguard will punish them if they lie or make up stories for me.

Dagon stood guard at the door. He was dressed head to

foot in the slightly shabby blue-and-white uniform of the old royal army. His shape was further disguised by a heavy gray frock coat with the collar turned up, and a large bicorn hat on his head. Purple-lensed glasses hid his peculiar eyes, and stuffed leather gloves made it appear that he had the correct number of fingers. No amount of human clothing could disguise the rancid fishy odor that enveloped him, but even without that, my visitors instinctively knew that there was something amiss. They would stand in the door and whisper their secrets to him and he would note them down with a metal stylus on a wax tablet; I have tried to get him to modernize, but he is very firmly stuck in the past. He is fond of telling me that he recorded the original epic of Gilgamesh on wax and in clay, and if it was good enough for Gilgamesh, then it should be good enough for me. Wax, unfortunately, attracts flies.

As my spies hurried past my window, I heard them whisper about Dagon, wondering about his appearance: guessing he was a descendant of the Mongol army, an African, a Turk, and a Viking—one even suggested a Golem—but they could not have been further from the truth. I wondered how they would react if they knew he had once been worshiped as a god.

Around noon, Dagon drew a black shade across the front and back windows. This was the signal that I was either not at home or not to be disturbed. Sometimes, the foolhardy ignored the sign. But they only did it once. Dagon has many fine gifts; humor is not one of them.

We sat across the scarred wooden table from one another and had lunch. While my bread was fresh, the cheese was as hard as an old boot, and my wine was probably a week away from becoming vinegar. Dagon delicately picked apart a freshly caught river trout and sucked out the innards with a long black tongue that came with a spike at its tip.

I nodded at the pile of wax tablets and brushed away a cloud of flies. "What do you make of this morning's reports?" I spoke in Dagon's hissing tongue, a language not used on earth for millennia. Although I was confident that we were alone, I had survived a long time by being cautious.

"The entire city is in upheaval," he said, opening his mouth to reveal far too many needle-pointed teeth. His voice was a sticky bubble of sounds. "Food is scarce. People are upset. Some riot in search of attention and answers, others riot simply to be noticed, and others do it because they are bored."

I divided his wax tablets into two piles. The left-hand stack was little more than gossip and could be discounted, but the four tablets on the right told a very similar story. "See here: Rue de Reuilly, a riot because the police did not investigate the disappearance of a child. And here, just off Rue du Temple, there is unrest because an entire family of children has gone missing and remains uninvestigated. Here, in Rue Reaumur, a brother went in search of a missing sister and then he too disappeared. The police show no interest. Rue Saint-Jean, twins disappeared in the middle of the day."

Dagon shrugged, an odd movement of his broad shoulders. He had left his watery kingdom a long time ago and had lived on land for countless millennia, but he still found it impossible to mimic certain human movements. "Children go missing all the time. They either turn up, or they do not."

"You have a heart of gold."

"I do not," he answered. "I have a two-chambered heart below my gills. It is muscle, not metal."

"It is a saying," I explained.

Dagon dissected the fish with his hooklike claws. "And is this expression a compliment?" he asked.

Deciding that explaining sarcasm to a three-thousand-year old Babylonian fish god was more trouble than it was worth, I tapped the wax tablets again. "There is something going on here. Four reports, all to do with the disappearance of children."

Dagon stopped chewing.

"And all in the same area," I reminded him. "The poorest slums in Paris."

"A child hunter?" he asked.

"You are far older than I am. You must have encountered beings who collected children."

"I know of creatures who would take a lost child, like a fox taking a chicken. Trolls, were-beasts . . ." He paused, his lips sticky with bubbles. "But they are individuals, taking single children. You are suggesting something else, something more organized."

"These are not isolated cases. There are at least eight children that we know of. And what about the others, whose parents are dead or missing, lost to war and revolution? Who counts them? In your vast experience, who would steal children?"

Dagon suddenly stood and began to stride around the room, his mouth slowly opening and closing. "Fairy folk, perhaps. They have colonies in just about every country in the world. Many names: Sidhe, fairies, elves, xana, Tomtra, Jogah, Menehune . . . but they are more or less the same race. Their ancestors came from Danu Talis—the island you know as Atlantis—and were among the first to flee when it was destroyed by the Twins of Legend. They will swap their own children for humans."

"Changelings."

Dagon nodded. "They have a plan that one day, when they have enough Changelings in places of power, they will rise up and proclaim themselves the rulers of this world." He made a quick dismissive motion. "It will not happen."

"I cannot see them taking children from the slums. They would take the children of people in positions of power. Besides, don't the fairy folk always replace the child they take? There are no replacement children being left now."

Dagon stopped pacing. "You are correct, of course. So they would not be missed."

"Do you know whatever happened to the Rattenfänger? Just over five hundred years ago, he took one hundred and thirty children from the town of Hamelin."

"Disappeared from this realm completely. A host of immortals led by Aoife of the Shadows chased him through countless Shadowrealms. But they never caught him."

"And the children were never recovered?"

"No."

"Could he have returned to this world?"

He shook his head with that peculiar movement of shoulders that turned his entire body. "I heard the Witch of Endor did something to the scent of his aura, marked him so that he'd leave a trail wherever he went. As soon as he stepped out of hiding, every Awakened Humani or immortal being within fifty miles would become aware of his presence."

"Well, something is here! It must be. Perhaps drawn by the Terror, or using the Terror to disguise its activities."

"Perhaps it is the most cunning and dangerous of all villains," Dagon said quietly. "A humani."

The thought had crossed my mind. In the long years of my immortality, I had met Ancients and Elders, Next Generation and immortal humans, but in my experience the most dangerous monsters were human.

"So, the only certainty is that someone . . ."

"Or something . . . ," he reminded me.

"Or something, is kidnapping children. Human, inhuman, monster, or legend; something evil has come to Paris."

Dagon swept the fish carcass onto the floor and picked up the wax tablets.

"Rue de Reuilly . . . ," he muttered, slipping from his own tongue into French, butchering the sound. His mouth was not shaped for any human language. "Reaumur . . . du Temple . . . Rue Saint-Jean." He arranged the tablets on the table, according to their locations north, south, west, and east in a cross shape, with a square opening in the middle. A black claw tapped the empty space. "What is here?"

"La Cour des Miracles," I answered.

Dagon looked at me, huge wet eyes wide and unblinking. "The Court of Miracles," he repeated.

"Yes," I said. "And you remember what happened the last time we sent police into the court."

"None came out."

2

Paris has always been one of the finest cities in Europe: rich, elegant, sophisticated, a place of culture and learning. But there is not a single city in the world that does not have a dark stain on its map.

And in Paris, that stain was the Court of Miracles.

Like every modern city, Paris has beggars aplenty. Throughout history beggars have always been with us, and there is no shame in begging. I was brought up to believe that to give charity to a beggar, to give a little to those who have less, is the right thing to do, and I am not alone in my thinking. The concept of giving is enshrined in all the great religions. Indeed, the legendary alchemyst Nicholas Flamel himself used some of his vast wealth to establish churches, hospitals, and schools in this very city.

But while there were those genuinely in need, there were others who abused the role of the beggar. Some even considered it a career. And these professional beggars quickly discovered that those with an affliction—missing a limb or their sight, or speckled with skin diseases—earned more than those who were whole in body and mind. So the streets and bridges of Paris were filled with those who appeared to be disabled or blind. One-legged soldiers hobbled alongside mothers with leprous children, while one-armed jugglers performed alongside legless fire-eaters. Kindhearted—and though it pains me to say it, gullible—Parisians gave what they could. And sometimes they were giving to those who did not deserve their charity. Also, I noted that those who had the least always gave the most.

As each Parisian day drew to a close, the streets teemed with limping, hobbling, faltering vagrants heading home to the slums. But the moment some stepped off the main thoroughfares and slipped into the warren of side streets, arms and legs appeared where there had been none before, rubbed and stretched out to relieve cramps and pins and needles from being bound up all day. The blind could see, the deaf could hear, and a jug of none-too-clean water washed away all manner of skin diseases.

No wonder the area was called the Court of Miracles.

3

"How do I look?"

Dagon inspected me up and down. Although his fishlike face was incapable of human expression, I had known him long enough to recognize the disappointment and—shall I say it—the fear in his eyes.

I was wearing overlong blue pantaloons, a striped shirt with mismatched buttons, and a short coat with one sleeve missing. A brown overcoat that reached my ankles completed my costume.

"You look like you belong in the Court of Miracles," he said finally. "Except for one thing . . ." Turning to the chimney, he ran his finger across the stones and then looked back at me. "Open wide."

Obediently, I opened my mouth.

"You do not have the mouth of a beggar." Dagon wiped the soot across my teeth and then carefully blacked out one of my incisors. It was an actor's trick. "Better," he said. "I bought the clothes this morning off the washerwoman on the corner. Although they are ragged, they are clean and lice free."

I had wondered about that. The last time I'd gone in

disguise into the Court of Miracles, I'd brought home such an infestation of fleas that I'd had to burn my second-best bed, my couch, and all my pillows. I'd itched for a month.

Dagon held up a pair of wooden shoes. "You really should wear the sabots," he said. "However, if you have to run, they will be a problem." He lifted a battered and down-at-heel pair of army boots. "These will not seem out of place. You'll look like an old soldier fallen on hard times."

I pushed my feet into the boots. Naturally, they fit me perfectly. Dagon had a wonderful fish eye for detail.

Finally I settled a floppy red liberty cap—a bonnet rouge—on my head and arranged it so that the top draped over my left ear.

"Better." Dagon nodded approvingly. "And finally," he added, handing me a battered T-shaped wooden crutch. "Now you are an old soldier with a limp." He turned the crutch over and showed me two wooden pins. "Pull these out and the crutch will come apart, leaving you with two batons. I drilled a hole in the section that goes under your arm and filled it with liquid lead. It should be hard by now." He pressed one of the pins and the crutch split in half, leaving me with two sticks—one with a heavy T-shaped head, like a hammer, the other a straight length of wood.

Dagon lifted a piece of unburnt firewood and held it out at chest height in both hands. "Try it."

I swung the lead-filled hammer at the wood. The force of the blow almost dislocated my shoulder, but the wood dissolved into black and white splinters.

"At least you will not be unarmed," Dagon said, tossing the broken wood onto the fire.

I matched the two halves of the crutch together and slotted in the pins. "What would I do without you?" I asked.

"You would be dead already." There was no humor in his voice.

We locked up my rooms and slipped out into the alley that ran along the back of the house. There was no moon, and the alleyway was in gloomy darkness. My enhanced senses allowed me to see more or less clearly at night, and Dagon could see lights and colors invisible to the human eyes. We had determined a long time ago, however, that he could not see the color red. It appeared as shades of gray to him.

"Let me tell you plainly," Dagon said in the ancient language of his species. "I am unhappy with you going into the Court of Miracles on your own."

"If we send in police or troops, or even undercover officers, word will spread through the tenements in minutes," I answered. "We'll probably end up with a riot on our hands, and whoever or whatever is in there will be left to fade into the night. Besides, I will not be on my own. You've arranged a guide, yes?"

"One of my best agents, the Wild Boar, will meet you."

"How will I recognize him?" I asked.

"I've given him your description. He will find you."

"Is he to be trusted?"

"He is, first and foremost, a thief. And like all thieves, he can be bought. But I trust him." Dagon pressed a surprisingly heavy bag into my hand. "Give him this. He gets the other half when you return safely."

Two shapes suddenly stepped out of a small side alley, big men with long knives in their hands and scarves wrapped around their faces. Before they could even make their demands, Dagon reached under his long coat and produced a short metal pole. He snapped it, and the pole extended with a click, doubling in size. He shook it again and it sprouted three wickedly hooked spikes at the tip. The two would-be thieves looked at the trident and then retreated without a word. We heard their wooden sabots tapping on the stones and squelching in the mud as they raced away.

Dagon folded up the trident, sliding the blades into the pole and then pushing the two lengths together until they slotted into place.

"Did you get a good look at them?" I asked.

Dagon nodded. "I saw enough to recognize them. I doubt they have a change of clothing, and their gaits are distinctive. I will find them."

"Good. Pick them up in the morning," I told him. "I don't want people like that on my streets."

"*Your* streets? Since when did Paris become yours?" he asked.

"The moment I moved here."

"You have become sentimental," he said.

"I have become careful," I corrected him.

"You were always careful."

We walked in silence for a while. I knew by the slow

opening and closing of his fingers that he was mulling over a thought, and I knew from experience that it was better not to interrupt him.

"I read your book," Dagon said finally.

"Which one?"

"*De Principatibus. The Prince.* There is no sentimentality in it."

I shook my head, unsure what he was getting at. Sometimes I forgot that he was older than the city itself, hailing from a time completely alien to me. And he was a fish god.

"You say in your book that it is much safer to be feared than to be loved."

"I said it was best to be both," I replied.

"Those are not the words of a sentimental man," he continued.

"I was not immortal when I wrote those words," I reminded him.

"Do you still believe it?" he asked.

"Those two ruffians in the alley earlier. Why did they run?" I pressed.

"Because they were frightened of us."

"If we had spoken soft words to them, would they have left us alone?"

"I doubt it," he answered. "Bullies feed off weakness. Soft words would have encouraged them."

"So they ran because they were fearful," I said, proving my point. "They knew we are capable of protecting ourselves. Or at least you are."

"That is true. I am not sure what that has to do with your theory."

"From the moment I came to this city, I claimed it as my own," I explained. "I determined to protect it, to look after it and keep it as safe as possible. In doing so, of course, I am looking after myself, keeping myself—and you—safe. I did not know that there were immortals in Rome, Florence, or Venice when I lived in those places. Here, I know every immortal in the city, and they know me. They know they can stay here so long as they do not cause trouble for our kind. Do you remember when John Dee came to Paris?"

"I was in Egypt at the time, looking for that emerald tablet you wanted. The Black Knight nearly took my head," he reminded me unnecessarily.

"Dee was spying for the English Queen. And while he spied on us, we watched him. We were not alone: the Spanish, the Portuguese, the Dutch, half a dozen German states, and Rome were spying on him. Although Dee was here on the Queen's business, he was also in search of Nicholas Flamel's Codex for himself. He was meeting many people—not all of whom were human. It was only a matter of time before someone saw something odd or unusual, and then . . . well, you know what happens."

Dagon nodded. He'd spent millennia drifting from place to place, keeping to the shadows, always moving on when someone discovered that the shepherd on the mountains, or the old man who lived in the caves, or the hermit on the island, or the wild man in the depths of the woods, never aged. "Mobs and pitchforks. Always pitchforks. And flaming torches. The humani do like their flaming torches."

"My race likes drama," I admitted.

"I prefer nonfiction," Dagon noted. "Truth is strange enough."

I had to agree with him. Humans believe that the myths and legends are fictions to entertain, that fairy tales are little more than stories used to educate and frighten children. I used to think that also. But that was before I met mythological gods and legendary goddesses and was hunted by hungry creatures from fairy tales.

"What happened to Dee?" Dagon asked.

"I had my men pick him up, and he spent three days in the Bastille. And not in the nice rooms either. Then we blindfolded him, put him on a wagon, and drove him to Calais. I accompanied him every step of the way. I'd used one of the Utukki limnûti spells you taught me to render him mute so he could not cast any spells or cantrips. I sailed with him to Dover before setting him free."

"You should have thrown him overboard."

"I should have. But I fear he has powerful masters, and I do not want to incur their wrath. I just wanted him out of my city before his behavior shined a . . . a flaming torch—"

"Always with the flaming torches," Dagon muttered.

"—on us, the immortals and the inhumans," I continued. "We survive because the humani do not know of our existence."

"And the humani survive because they do not know about

us," Dagon added. "If it ever came to open warfare, the humani would not fare well. We have the advantage that they are already fearful of the monsters in the dark."

"Humans kill what they fear," I reminded him.

We stopped in the shadow of an alleyway and looked across a muddy street toward a stinking lane that led down to the Rue du Caire. What looked like two vagabonds were slumped against the greasy wall, but Dagon and I both knew they served as guards and lookouts.

"There are those amongst the inhuman races who believe that it is their right to rule the world," Dagon whispered suddenly, his voice leaving sticky bubbles against my ear. "There was a time when the humani were little more than slaves and food, servants and soldiers. Some wish to return to that Golden Age."

"And what better way to start a war with the humans than to kidnap their children," I said.

"It is certainly possible; the Elders, Ancients, and Earthlords always used humani armies, led by inhuman officers. They started training their armies when they were still children," he added.

Struck by the same thought, we both looked toward the alleyway again: Was someone—some ancient thing—gathering an army of human children from the slums of Paris?

Dagon's claws bit hard enough into my shoulders to leave bruises. "Tell the Wild Boar that if you are not out by sunrise, I'll be coming to find you," he said.

I was unsure if it was a promise or a threat.

4

The two guards did not even glance at the old soldier limping across the road. As I slipped into the alleyway, I glanced back over my shoulder. For an instant I thought I saw Dagon's outline in the shadows across the street, his arm raised in farewell, but that was probably my imagination. He'd never raise his arm; that would show sentimentality.

The smell hit me as soon as I stepped into the soot-covered darkness.

Paris, though beautiful, was never especially fragrant. Like most great European cities, it had its own particular odor. The air in Rome was always tinged with wax and incense, the scent of Venice was the ever-present mustiness of rot from the canals, and for some reason the air of Florence always smelled of money and fear. Paris smelled of the Seine. And that stench permeated everything. After a while you got used to it, and the other countless noxious aromas that filled the air, so for a scent to be noticeable, it had to be incredibly strong. The stink in that narrow alley was an almost physical thing, made of rotten wood and crumbling stone, mold and rancid food. But there was one odor that dominated: the stench of too many unwashed humans crammed together. Swallowing hard, trying not to breathe through my nose, I pushed through the dark alley and out into the blazing heart of the Court of Miracles.

Fire and light were everywhere. Fire burned in barrels, blazed from tar-wrapped sticks; sparks spiraled upward from a dozen bonfires. I blinked away sudden tears and coughed with the bite of smoke in my throat. As my eyes cleared, I remembered how this place had once looked, a long time ago, not long after I had first come to Paris. It had been beautiful. A broad square surrounded a tall fountain. On all four sides, elegant buildings looked over the square, and I recalled the stalls of fresh fruit and flowers.

Now, although everything remained—the square, the fountain, the buildings—nothing was the same. The buildings were crumbling ruins, with gaping holes where there had once been windows and doors, and most of the roof tiles missing to expose the rafters beneath. If there had been a statue on the fountain, it was long gone; only a stump remained, pocked with holes suggesting it had been used for target practice. The ground was a mixture of ankle-deep, squelching mud and rancid filth, scattered with straw.

Although it was close to midnight, the square was teeming with people. Citizens from what looked like every country in Europe and most of North Africa milled about. Costumes ranged from the outrageous to the ragged. The music of as many nations competed in a not entirely unpleasant cacophony. There were food stalls everywhere; none of the fruits or vegetables looked fresh, and the meat and fish were nearly unrecognizable. Barefoot urchins moved through the crowd, carrying trays of bread, scraps of meat on a stick—I suspect it was the two staple meats of the tenements, either pigeon or rat—or selling wine served in stone cups, lest the liquid burn a hole in a metal goblet.

I stayed away from the crowd as much as possible, leaning back on a gritty, crumbling wall, watching the shifting waves of people. I had been here before and was always struck by the energy in the air. This was not a happy place—I am not one of those who believe there is a joy in hardship, and terrible poverty and hunger were evident everywhere you looked. But I was also conscious that no one here had given up. They went about their lives and in many small ways—not all of them legal—tried to make them better. It was that spirit, that perseverance, that would ensure that the humani prevailed. The Earthlords, Ancients, and Archons who had come before Dagon would never understand this. Perhaps Dagon himself did not understand it. Those ancient inhuman beings had once ruled the world, but then they had been defeated and had given up. But humans . . . humans were different. I had seen it many times in my travels across Europe, and I saw it here tonight, in the Court of Miracles. Humans could lose everything, they could be knocked down, but they would never give up.

I propped myself up with the crutch. I was reluctant to move too far from the entrance because I was sure Dagon's agent, the Wild Boar, would be watching for me.

I waved away two children, one selling meat, another what

looked like bread and cheese. A wild-haired woman sidled over and asked if I was interested in selling my coat. I shook my head and grunted a no, but I was aware that her eyes were watching me carefully, appraising me from head to foot.

"Will you sell me the boots?"

"Only boots I have."

"I'll give you a good price," she said.

"Few francs would be nice, but I'd be barefoot."

"Them boots—taken you far, have they?"

"Far enough." I tried to keep my answers short. My French was excellent, though I occasionally used words that had gone out of fashion fifty years previously.

I watched her move to a stall where another woman, who looked like her mother or perhaps her older sister, was stirring a pot. They both turned to stare at me.

Had they seen through my disguise so quickly? I wondered what had given me away.

I glanced back toward the alleyway. A small crowd was coming through, mostly professional beggars, laughing and joking as they revealed strapped-up arms and legs or pulled off eye patches to expose the perfectly good eye beneath. When I looked back, the woman was standing before me again, a bowl of stew cupped in her hands.

I shook my head. "Much as I would like it . . . I cannot pay. And I'll not swap my boots for it either."

"Take it. No charge. Gift for an old soldier," she said, pushing the bowl into my hands and turning away. "But if you do change your mind about the boots . . ." Her voice trailed off.

I looked into the bowl of oily gray liquid. It was filled with vaguely recognizable vegetables—onion, carrot—and an assortment of lumps that looked like nothing I'd ever seen before.

"If you have any respect for your stomach, you'll not touch it. Might have *le vautrin* in it."

Le Vautrin. Wild Boar.

Standing before me was a slender, shaggy-haired young man. It was impossible to assign an age to him: he could have been anywhere from fourteen to eighteen, with a mop of curly back hair shoved under a knitted hat that was more holes than wool. None of his clothes fit—his pantaloons were too short and had clearly been made for a man twice his girth; his shirt was too long and missing every button—but I noticed that he wore a fine pair of army boots not dissimilar to mine. His eyes were an astonishingly bright blue, and his nose crooked slightly to one side, as if it had been broken and badly set.

"You have something for me?" he said, settling back against the wall. I glanced sidelong at him; although his body was still, I noticed his eyes were constantly moving.

"I think you have me confused with someone else," I said cautiously.

"We both know a man who stinks of fish and yet is not a fisherman. This is the same man who bought me these fine boots, probably in the same place he got yours. Told me I'd not be able to run in sabots." There was a touch of the country in his voice.

Satisfied, I slipped him the heavy purse Dagon had given me.

"Feels light."

"Half now, half when you get me out at sunrise," I told him.

"And if I don't get you out?" he asked.

"Our fishy friend said he'd come and find me . . . and you too."

"He doesn't frighten me," he said a little too forcefully, as if trying to convince himself.

"Oh, he should," I said.

"Where's he from?"

"A place that no longer exists," I said. "What do I call you? Wild Boar seems a little dramatic."

He grinned, showing a mouthful of irregular teeth. "I was always in trouble when I was younger, getting into fights, stealing. My father said I was like a wild boar tearing through the town. The name stuck. I became le Vautrin."

"It's a fine name, though not entirely practical if I have to call out to you in the middle of a crowd. That's the sort of name people remember."

He tilted his head, considering my point, before nodding. "Never thought of that. My name is Eugène François Vidocq, but everyone calls me Vidocq."

"Then I will call you Eugène, because I am not everyone."

"What do I call you?"

"Call me Nick," I told him.

5

I followed Eugène through the crowd, taking care to use my crutch, just in case someone was watching us. He seemed to know everyone there, and he provided a running commentary on the characters we met.

". . . you have to be careful of Tiny Tim; carries a snake in his sleeve.

". . . And that's Mary-Mary the herbalist. She can cure a headache or kill you stone dead with the same potion.

". . . We call him English Tony, though I don't think he's ever been to England. Speaks eight languages.

". . . In the corner, sitting behind the barrel, that's One-Franc. He'll buy anything you have to sell, but he'll only give you one franc.

"And just around the corner is his twin sister; she sells everything on her barrel for two francs."

"I suppose you call her Two-Francs?"

"No, most people call her Cosette."

Eugène's powers of observation were remarkable. I could see why Dagon had chosen him, and if he survived a few more years, I was sure I'd be able to find a role for him in my organization.

"Where are you taking me?"

We'd been moving deeper and deeper into the tenements, leaving the lighted square behind. The buildings had become even more dilapidated, and only individual candles burned behind scraps of cloth covering windows.

Though we were alone on the narrow street, Eugène dropped his voice to a whisper. "Our fishy friend said you are looking into the missing children."

"I am."

"The police aren't. So why are you?"

"I don't like the idea of someone taking children," I answered.

"Even from a place like this? Sure, who'd miss them?"

I heard the ice in his voice and guessed that he was testing me.

"From any place. And children should always be missed."

"You've children of your own?" he asked.

"None alive," I said, surprised by the bitterness of my tone. The true cost of immortality is to watch everyone you know and love grow old and die.

We walked on in silence for a while, and then he said, "Even before the fish-man reached out to me, I was looking into the disappearances, following leads, talking to the witnesses."

"You sound like a policeman."

He shook his head quickly. "I'm better."

"What makes you better?"

"I'm one of what you'd call the criminal class. I can ask questions no outsider would ever get to ask. Do you know who'd make the best police?" he asked, a touch of excitement in his voice. Without waiting for an answer, he jerked his thumb over his shoulder, back toward the square. "That lot. Any one of them. They know every trick in the book. Set a thief to catch a thief."

"Not that simple . . . ," I began.

"Why not?" he demanded. "Thieves catching thieves, forgers chasing down forgers—and no one knows how to defeat a burglar better than another burglar."

Set a thief to catch a thief. I had to agree, it made some sense. But it would never work; who would want to employ thieves, forgers, and burglars?

6

We climbed three flights of increasingly rickety stairs. At one point every second step was missing, and I could see right through to the floor below.

"During the winter, everything that can be burnt—doors, window frames, floors, ceilings, stairs—will be put to the fire," Vicocq explained. "It's either that or freeze to death."

We came out onto a narrow landing. There were six doorways, but only two still had a wooden door in the frame. The rest were covered with sheets of billowing cloth. "Stay here." He pushed me back into the shadows.

Eugène went to the first wooden door and rapped gently. It was opened almost immediately by a tall, surprisingly well-dressed woman. Her clothes fit her perfectly, which suggested that these were not some stall-bought secondhand rags. Here was someone displaced by the Revolution, now fallen on hard times. I watched how she grabbed at his hands, and even without being told, I knew this was the mother of some of the missing children.

Eugène waved me forward. As I got close to the woman, I

realized that she was blind, white cataracts stark against the shadows on her skin.

"This is Madame Bougon," Vidocq said gently, taking the woman's hands in his and leading her into the small bare room. "Madame, this is Monsieur Nick; he has come to help me look for your children."

The room was a simple square, with a bed against one wall and a table and chair pushed against another. Children's clothes were draped across the end of the bed. A second chair was set before the open window. Vicocq helped Madame Bougon into it, and she turned toward the opening. I knew she was listening for her children.

"Tell Monsieur Nick what you told me," he urged the woman.

She turned to me. Her iron-gray hair was pulled back, emphasizing her cheekbones, giving her face a slightly skull-like appearance.

"Do you know what took my children?" she asked.

I noticed that she said "what" rather than "who."

"I do not," I answered. "I know that at least eight children have gone missing."

Eugène shook his head. "Three times that number at least. Probably closer to thirty. Maybe more," he added.

Resting my crutch against the wall, I crouched before Madame Bougon and gently took her hands in mine. Her flesh was cool and felt like paper. "Tell me about your children."

"Marius and Simplice," she said so quietly I had to strain

to hear her. "Twins. Thirteen years old. They were never any trouble. My husband is a sailor and away for months at a time. Since I lost my sight, the children look after me, keep our room clean. We have a little money. Marius sells bread, and Simplice flowers. It brings in a few francs. We are not wealthy, monsieur, but we want for nothing."

"Tell me what happened?" I asked.

"A week ago . . ." She stopped and turned toward Vidocq. "Was it a week, do you think?"

"It was a week," he agreed.

"I first smelled it on them a week ago," she said. "When you live here, Monsieur Nick, you learn to ignore the usual odors. It is the unusual ones that stand out." She leaned forward and sniffed the air before me. "I can tell you are not one of us," she murmured. "Your clothes are freshly washed, and you have bathed with lavender soap within the past few days."

"You are very perceptive, Madame Bougon," I told her, impressed.

She tilted her head slightly. "What does he look like, Vidocq?" she asked.

"Like an old soldier."

She caught my hand and turned it over, running her fingers over my flesh. "This is not the hand of a soldier."

"Tell me what you smelled a week ago," I urged her gently.

"When the children came home, I smelled something sweet and spicy in the air. They had brought me a slice of freshly baked gingerbread."

I glanced at Vidocq and he shook his head.

"They'd met someone—Marius said she was a baker, but Simplice said she made sugar candy—and this person had given them the treats. They'd brought the gingerbread back to me but admitted that they'd eaten the candy."

"No one in the Court of Miracles bakes gingerbread. No candy makers either," Vidocq said.

"The following day when they came home, the smell of sugar and spices was even stronger," Madame Bougon said. "And when Simplice kissed me good night, I could feel sticky honey on her lips."

"Not a lot of honey in the Court of Miracles," Vidocq added.

"The third day they did not return." Madame Bougon buried her face in her hands and wept. Over the course of my long life, too often have I heard the sound of a mother weeping for her children. There is nothing more heartbreaking.

"I found Madame Bougon wandering the streets, calling out for the twins," Eugène said. "I brought her home. I told her that if Marius and Simplice were lost—and it is easy to get lost in the maze of streets and alleyways—they would come back here once they found their bearings."

Madame Bougon clasped my hands again. I could feel her tears against my skin. "Will you find my children, monsieur?"

"I will do my utmost," I promised her. I looked up at Eugène and he nodded toward the door. "Let me go and look for them, madame, and I assure you that I will return before the dawn with some news."

She squeezed my hands a final time and then released me. "Find my children, monsieur."

I stopped at the door and looked back, seeing her outlined against the window, listening intently for her missing children.

7

"Follow me."

Without a word, Vidocq led me up a series of increasingly narrow stairs and onto the roof. The building was a little taller than most nearby, allowing me to see across the Court of Miracles. The glow from the square was clearly visible, but as my eye moved farther away from it, lights became fewer and fewer and huge swaths of the slums were in darkness. Above the stink of rot and mold, the air was a little clearer, and I drew in a deep breath, filling my lungs.

I was standing at the edge of a low brick wall that enclosed the roof. Vidocq hopped up onto the bricks and started to balance his way along them, ignoring the six-story fall to the street. Perhaps he expected me to tell him to get down; if so, he was going to be disappointed. I have always believed that people should be free to make their own mistakes.

"You brought me to Madame Bougon for a reason," I said, more a statement than a question.

"And what do you think the reason is?" he asked.

"Has to be the candy. I presume it links to the other missing children."

"You're smart. I can see why the fish-man likes you. I've talked to all the families who have lost children," he said. He turned at the corner and started walking back toward me. "In four cases, there was some evidence that they had been given candy or cake." He stopped before me. "Also, the sister of a missing girl had this in her pocket." He produced what looked like an irregular orange stone, speckled with hair and threads. He carefully pulled the threads away before handing it to me, then automatically licked his fingers.

I recognized the half-melted lump as a piece of candy.

"These are street-smart children," I said, bringing the candy to my nose and breathing in carefully. "They are not going to be lured by a piece of candy." I held the nugget up to the night sky and squinted at it. "Maybe something has been added to the sugar. . . ." I glanced at Vidocq. "Might be wise not to lick your fingers after you handle this."

He hopped off the low wall and rubbed his hands on his dirty trousers. "A poison?"

"Unlikely, but perhaps something to draw the children back to the source."

"Like a magical spell?"

"Perhaps."

"And you believe in that stuff?" He was clearly trying to sound as if he didn't, but I could hear the touch of fear and wonder in his voice.

"I believe that we don't know everything about the world. There are wonders being discovered every day. In fact, I am of the opinion that we knew much more in the ancient past than we do now." I brought the orange candy to my nose again and breathed deeply. The scent of citrus was strong, but there were other, less easily identifiable odors: mint certainly, licorice, and something else, something damp and earthy and vaguely foul. I'd certainly be able to recognize it again.

"There was another reason you brought me to this house," I said. "You had several families to choose from. Why this one?"

Vidocq picked up a broken slate and pulled out a battered, blunt-tipped pocketknife. "We are here," he said, marking an X on the slate. "Children have gone missing from here . . . here . . . here. . . . and here." He drew a series of dots. They were all relatively close to the X. Then he drew two circles, one within the other, linking the dots. "These children," he said, pointing to the inner circle, "disappeared first. These"—he tapped the dots in the outer circle—"were the next to go."

I tapped the center of the smaller circle. "What's in here?"

The young man led me to the opposite side of the roof and pointed. Across a series of dilapidated rooftops, I could make out a steepled roof. "What is that?" I asked.

"Once, maybe fifty years ago, it was a church."

I was now able to make sense of the white and gray slabs that completely encircled the building, jutting from the dark earth like broken teeth. They were gravestones.

"It hasn't been used as a church for as long as anyone can remember; it was deconsecrated a long time ago," Vidocq said.

"Who lives there now?"

"Would you be surprised if I told you no one?" His arm swept wide to encompass all of the Court of Miracles. "Every building here is teeming with families. Upward of a hundred people can live in a single tenement. But no one lives there. No one, not even the bravest ruffian, will steal a length of wood from the door or a piece of lead off the roof."

"Why is that?" I asked, although I already had a very good idea.

"Because people who go into the church do not come out again. It is said to be haunted by the ghost of Joan of Arc."

"I doubt that very much," I said.

"Why, do you not believe in ghosts?" Vidocq demanded.

"Of course I believe in ghosts. But I saw Joan about ten years ago, and she was very much alive. So whatever is haunting the church, it's not the ghost of the Maid of Orléans."

I turned back toward the stairs before he could ask the question on his lips. "Let's have a closer look at the church everyone is afraid to go into."

"You're going into it, aren't you?" he asked.

"I'm thinking I might just have to," I answered. "You don't have to come, of course. It will be dangerous. In fact, perhaps you should go and find the fish-man. Tell him where I am or, better still, bring him here."

Vidocq shook his head firmly. "I'm not letting you do this on your own. You'll go in there, rescue the children, and claim all the praise."

"I promise you, no matter what happens tonight, no one will ever hear of it. Try to stay invisible, Monsieur Vidocq. There is an old Irish saying you might take to heart: Happy is the man who remains unknown to the law."

8

We stood in an alleyway, looking toward the church. The small wooden building was dilapidated and run-down, but it was still in better repair than most of the houses around it. It had obviously once been a small country church and had simply been swallowed by the city, then enclosed within the Court of Miracles.

"You were joking when you said you'd seen Joan of Arc," Vidocq said. In that moment he sounded very young indeed. "She died . . ." He struggled to remember the date. "Fourteen something . . ."

"It was 1431. Over three hundred and sixty years ago."

"So when you said you saw her . . . you saw a relative, a descendant of hers?" he said hopefully. "Someone who looked like her. Perhaps you saw her in a dream."

"No, it was Joan herself in the flesh. She was rescued from her English executioners by Scathach the Shadow—someone you definitely do not wish to meet—and made immortal. Luckily, she did not see me. Last time we met, we did not part on the best of terms."

The young man looked at me as if I'd gone mad.

"What would you say if I told you I am just a little younger than Joan? That I was born in the year 1469, which makes me three hundred and twenty-four years old?"

Vidocq's mouth opened and closed as he tried to find words. "And I suppose you're going to tell me that the fish-smelling man is hundreds of years old also."

"No. I'll not tell you that. What I will tell you is that he is thousands of years old and is not even human. He is Dagon, and in the ancient past he was worshiped as a god." I gripped Eugène's shoulder and squeezed tightly, focusing his attention. "And I am telling you this so that you will know that there are creatures other than humankind in this world, and that monsters are real."

"Monsters are real," he repeated.

"So that when we go into the church, you will be prepared for whatever we might find there. I don't want you freezing in terror."

Vidocq looked from me to the church and then back to me. "What do you think is in there?" he asked in a ragged whisper.

"I don't know." I closed my eyes and, tilting back my head, breathed in the night air. All the smells of the Court of Miracles came rushing in. I identified them one by one and then dismissed them . . . which left me with the faintest hints of orange, mint, and licorice drifting from the church. Suddenly I recognized the previously unidentifiable scent: it was the smell of wet earth, an odor I always associated with an open grave.

"I think I know where the children are." I looked at Vidocq. "Last chance: you could go and find Dagon."

Without a word, the young man drew a long dagger from beneath his coat.

I lifted my crutch and pressed the hidden buttons, snapping it in two, leaving me with two batons.

"I knew you didn't really need the crutch," Vidocq said. "Sometimes you forget to limp."

9

I pressed my hand flat against the church's wooden door. Time had worn it smooth, and I noticed that the iron studs that usually dotted these types of doors were missing, the holes stuffed with moss and mud to prevent the wood from rotting.

Vidocq watched me pick away the moss filling one of the holes. "The studs are gone. Maybe I was wrong. Maybe someone was brave enough to steal a little scrap metal."

I shook my head. "The studs were not stolen; they were deliberately removed. Some of the nonhuman races cannot stand to be around iron. It is poisonous to them."

Vidocq swallowed. He looked at the knife in his hand. "Should have brought a bigger knife," he muttered.

I tapped the knife with one of my batons. "An iron blade: you brought the perfect weapon."

I pushed open the door, expecting it to squeal and groan, but it opened smoothly without a sound, and we slipped inside.

"Hinges have been oiled," Vidocq said. "Thieves will sometimes do that when they're going to break in so no one hears the door opening or closing. Or so I've been told," he added quickly.

The interior of the building was bare. Where there should have been rows of pews facing an altar, there was nothing but dust, scraps of wood, a scattering of feathers, and a few ancient bones. The main altar and all the other signs of religion—the statues, the side altars, even the stained glass—were missing.

Vidocq lit a candle stub and held it up, throwing yellow light around the space. Then he tapped my arm and pointed down.

Barely visible beneath a thick covering of dust, the floor was a patchwork of black and white tiles. Marble, and no doubt worth a fortune; that they had not been stolen was a testament to the locals' fear of this place. A path, worn clear by many feet, wound its way through the dust. All the footprints were child sized.

The young man traced the route with the blade of his knife. "Goes around there, back where the altar would have been," he whispered. "The footprints are heading in one direction."

"And none return," I noted.

"Maybe they go out the back door," he suggested. He caught my look and shrugged. "Just a thought."

We set off along the track cleared by countless children's feet.

The smell of sugar and honey grew stronger the deeper we moved into the church. I dropped to my knees, pressing my face close to the floor.

Eugene knelt beside me. "What do you smell?" he asked.

I tapped the floor.

Holding the candle away from his face, he drew in a deep breath. "Burnt sugar. It's stronger down here." He looked up, eyes wide. "The smell is rising. Do you think there are crypts under the church?"

"I'm sure of it. Limestone—*le calcaire lutécien*—has been mined from the ground beneath us since the time of the Romans. Much of the city was built with it, and there are miles of old uncharted tunnels below us."

Behind where the altar would have once stood, the trail of footsteps disappeared.

Vidocq moved the candle around. Standing the stub upright on the stones, he took the point of his knife and slid it into the join between two marble tiles. Then he pried gently . . . and a section of the flooring shifted. I quickly slipped one of my batons into the opening, and then, together, we lifted the slab. It was lighter than I expected. A square of wood had been painted black and white to look like the marble tiles. The flickering candle revealed stone steps disappearing into the darkness below.

And while the stink of burnt sugar was strong, the stench of opened graves was even stronger.

"Crypts," Vidocq whispered. "I hate crypts. Full of dead people."

"I don't mind them so long as the dead stay dead." I looked at the young man. There was no doubting his courage, but it was a bravery born of ignorance. He had no idea what he was up against, and although I had told him my age, the better to prepare him for what we might encounter, I knew he didn't believe me. "Perhaps you would like to get Dagon now," I offered again.

For a moment, it looked as if he might agree, but then we both heard a sound echoing up from below: the thin, heart-breaking sobbing of a child.

Without a word, the young man snatched the candle and disappeared down the steps. I made a vow as I followed him: no matter what happened, if we survived this night, I would ensure that Eugène François Vidocq would want for nothing ever again. And in years to come, when the time was right, I knew an ancient Egyptian king who could make him immortal. I'd make sure Eugène knew the true cost of immortality before he made any decision.

10

I reached over, took the candle from the young man's fingers, and blew it out.

"I can't see," he whispered.

"But I can: a side effect of my immortality. And this candle will blaze like a beacon, warning whatever lies at the other end of this tunnel."

"Where are we?" he asked.

I looked around. "A crypt, as we suspected. There are coffins set into the walls. Mostly stone, but some wood. Most of the stone coffins have cracked, and the wooden ones have rotted through."

"Can you see bodies?" he asked, horrified.

"Why would I be looking at . . ." I stopped. "No," I said finally. "All the tombs and coffins are empty."

With Vidocq tightly gripping my sleeve, I moved as quickly as possible down the narrow tunnel. My enhanced vision allowed me to see the imprint of children's footprints on the ground. But there were other prints too—skeletal feet, and something like the claw of a huge bird: a trio of spikes, with the middle toe twice the length of the others. It was on top of the other prints, which suggested that the creature was following the children. I wished Dagon were with me now; my experience with inhumans was limited, whereas he had met all of them at one time or another. He'd immediately recognize the owner of the claw marks.

"We're going deeper," I whispered to Vidocq, aware that he could not see. "We are in the ancient mining tunnels."

"Are there still tracks?" he asked.

"Yes. Still children's. And—you need to know this—there are skeletal footprints as well."

"You're telling me we might come across skeletons?" His voice was dry and raspy with fear.

"I think we'll be lucky if we only encounter skeletons. If you must fight one, try to twist its head around backward. That confuses them."

"I'll try to remember that."

"Oh, and don't let them bite you or stab you with their finger bones."

"Why?" he asked. "Will that turn me into a skeleton?"

"No. It will just really hurt," I said. Then I stopped so suddenly he ran into me.

"Is it skeletons?" he whispered.

I moved aside so he could see down the tunnel. There were lights in the distance.

"What's that sound?" he asked.

I tilted my head and concentrated. Faintly, very faintly, I could make out a metallic plinking sound. "Metal on metal?" I suggested.

"Chains?"

I nodded. It certainly sounded like chains. I could imagine the kidnapped children chained together.

We moved deeper into the tunnels, heading toward a flickering light. The odor of burnt sugar and honey was eye watering, but it was mingled with other odors now: the cloying scent of too many unwashed humans and the heavy earthiness of freshly turned soil.

The tunnel grew even brighter; Vidocq no longer had to hold on to me. Noises were clearer now. The plinking sound was clearly metal hammering metal or stone, and was accompanied by a rasping shuffle and the click-clack of what could only be bone on stone. We dropped to the ground and crawled the last few feet to the tunnel's entrance.

I peered over the edge of the opening, then ducked again. Even as Vidocq was raising his head to look, I clapped a hand over his mouth to stifle his horrified scream and dragged him back, out of sight.

"Now do you believe me?" I asked him.

His eyes were wide circles. Finally, he blinked, swallowed, and hiccupped. "Did I just see . . . ?"

"Yes."

"I think I'm going to throw up."

11

"Stay here." I pushed Eugène down, crawled back to the edge of the tunnel, and peered out over a scene straight from a nightmare. "There is good news and bad news," I whispered back to him.

"I saw some of the bad news," he muttered. He was taking great heaving breaths, clearly trying to settle a churning stomach.

"We've found the missing children," I said.

The tunnel opened into a huge circular chamber. Hundreds of candles were stuck to every niche and crevice in the walls, shedding a thick wax that coated the stones like a lizard's skin, turning the ceiling soot black. At least a dozen smaller tunnels radiated in every direction. Children were streaming in and out of the small narrow tunnels. They were all carrying small hammers, picks, and shovels and dragging cloth bags. They emptied the bags, dumping out stones and freshly turned earth at one end of the chamber, then trudged back into a tunnel. What were they mining in the tunnels? I wondered.

And there were skeletons guarding them.

Vidocq crawled up beside me and peered into the chamber. "Skeletons."

I nodded. "That's the bad news. All from different periods of history. Look at their clothing, armor, and weapons." Some of the creatures still had flesh, though it was weathered to deep wrinkled leather, while others were nothing but shining bone. They all carried swords and spears.

"Skeletons," he repeated. "Hundreds of them."

"Dozens," I corrected him, but still, I had never seen so many animated skeletons in one place.

"Where are they coming from?"

"There's your answer." I pointed to one of the side tunnels. We watched as a trio of children—they could not have been more than twelve or thirteen—dragged a rotting wooden coffin out of the narrow opening. A fourth child, a girl, used a small hand ax to chop open the coffin lid and peel back the wood with her bare hands.

"They're digging them up . . . ," Vidocq breathed, horrified.

The children scattered as an enormous skeleton, all dried leather skin and poking yellow bones, dragged itself toward them. He was huge, nearly seven feet tall, still wearing the ragged chain mail and rotting white robe of a Crusader knight. Reaching into the coffin, he hauled out another skeletal figure, slung it over his shoulder, and turned back to the center of the chamber, where an enormous black pot sat on a bed of white-hot coals. It was bubbling furiously, spitting a thick orange-black liquid into the air. The pot was the source of the stinking sugar-and-honey odor. The Crusader dropped the skeleton to the ground, with its head facing the pot. Laid out around the cauldron, in an ever-growing circle, were hundreds of skeletal figures. Many of them had weapons by their sides or in their bony hands.

We watched as another group of children dragged an ancient-looking stone coffin from a narrow tunnel. Four of them tried to open the lid, but it refused to move, sealed by time and dirt. The huge Crusader stomped over, lifted a battle-ax, and brought it crashing down on the stone, which shattered into dust. The skeletal knight peered inside the coffin, then turned away without lifting out the contents.

"Why?" Vidocq wondered, and then answered his own question. "Too decomposed."

"Exactly," I said. "You'll note all the corpses he's chosen are in relatively good condition."

"Someone is building an army," he whispered.

"Exactly. I came here thinking the children were going to be the soldiers. But they are just laborers, chosen because they can get in and out of small tunnels."

"And will not be missed," Vidocq added. "But who is gathering this dead army?"

"*What* is the better question," I answered.

12

A bell rang, its chime high and pure, sounding completely out of place in the underground chamber. Children began to stagger from the tunnels, obviously drawn by the sound. They were all filthy and ragged, and there were far more than I'd thought.

"There must be a hundred," Vidocq breathed.

This time I could not correct him.

Vidocq tapped my arm and pointed to two children at the end of one line. "Simplice and Marius, Madame Bougon's children. They look to be in slightly better condition than some of the others."

"Because they were taken recently," I noted.

He nodded. "How long has this been going on?"

"Too long."

We watched as the children formed a long line in front of the bubbling pot. No one spoke, but we could see that some were crying, while others kept looking about.

"So they are alert?" I said. "I thought they might be under a spell."

"Maybe they can't dig if they are ensorcelled."

"Good point. And why waste a good spell if keeping them in terror will do?" I said. "Think how you felt when you saw the skeletons. Now imagine being down there amongst them, forced to dig bodies out of the ground."

"I'd be terrified out of my mind," Vidocq admitted.

The bell rang again.

The skeletal guards lined up on either side of a tunnel that was taller and wider than the rest.

"Prepare yourself," I whispered. I wasn't sure if I was speaking to Vidocq or myself.

At first glance, the figure who stepped out of the tunnel looked like a hunchbacked old woman, wrapped in filthy rags. One by one, the skeletons knelt—or attempted to kneel—as she passed between them. None of the children even looked at her; their eyes were fixed firmly on the ground beneath their feet.

"She walks funny . . . ," Vidocq breathed.

The old woman walked with a peculiar staccato motion, her head and body leaning forward.

"Like a chicken," the young man added.

And suddenly I knew who the three-clawed prints belonged to. "Look at her feet," I whispered in Vidocq's ear.

He squinted, eyes watering with the candle smoke, and his breath caught. "She has chicken's feet. But bigger, much bigger."

The old woman stepped up to the black pot and threw back the shawl covering her head. She was incredibly ancient, her skin lined and etched with creases so deep they looked like scars. Her skin was a deep blue, the ugly shade of oil on water. And where her nose and mouth should have been, she had what looked like an owl's beak. Although I'd not met many inhumans, there weren't that many blue-faced chicken-toed hags.

"Black Annis," I said.

I pushed myself away from the tunnel entrance and dragged Vidocq with me.

"She has an owl's beak for a mouth . . . ," he said in horror.

"Yes, and her fingernails and toenails are iron-hard talons."

"What is she?" he asked

"A creature older than humankind. "She's one of those Elder gods who consider humans little better than cattle or food."

"What are we going to do?"

"If I ask you to go back and get help, will you do it?"

"I'm not leaving you here," Vidocq said defiantly. "I'm not leaving the children."

"I didn't think so."

Below, Black Annis was crouched over the bubbling cauldron, stirring the thick orange-black syrup. Clawlike hands added leaves and what looked like flower petals to the mixture. Then, from beneath her ragged clothing, she lifted a round object and held it aloft in both hands.

"What is that?" Vidocq asked. "It looks like a . . . glass skull?"

"Crystal," I whispered. "Dagon told me that one of the

very oldest races, the Archons, stored all their forbidden knowledge in a vast cache of crystal skulls. I've never seen one myself."

"It doesn't look human."

The flickering candlelight turned the crystal the color of old butter, highlighting the deep-set eye sockets and tiny blunt teeth. I noticed that there *was* something odd about the skull's shape: it seemed to sweep to a point at the back. "They are so dangerous that one of the Elders who still walk this earth, an incredibly powerful witch called Zephaniah, travels the globe looking for them."

"What does she do with them?" Vidocq asked.

"She destroys them," I answered.

Ignoring the bubbling liquid, which must have been scalding, Black Annis dipped the skull into the thick fluid. Once. Twice. After she raised it a third time, it was thickly coated in the liquid, making it look as if its flesh was melting.

"Why is she called Black Annis if her skin is blue?" Vidocq asked.

"I think it refers to the color of her heart," I said.

We watched the creature dip a ladle into the liquid and then come around the cauldron on her birdlike feet and pour the sticky mess into the open mouth of the closest skeleton, a warrior in the remains of a medieval suit of armor. The liquid steamed and bubbled, hissing as it frothed around the skeleton's mouth.

"But it's got no stomach," Vidocq protested. "And no tongue, so it can't taste or swallow."

The skeleton suddenly started to tremble, bones rattling. Its entire body shivered. Then, in a screech of armor, the medieval knight sat upright.

"Never apply logic to magic," I reminded Vidocq.

Black Annis moved to the next skeleton, the almost perfectly preserved body of a young man wearing the white coat and red stockings of a *fusilier du roi,* now ragged and soiled. He had probably been dead for only a hundred years. She poured more of the sticky liquid between his lips. He came alive almost immediately, sitting upright and rising to stand to attention.

Black Annis returned to the cauldron and scooped up another ladle of the thick liquid. The Crusader knight shuffled over. I noticed that one of his feet was twisted at an ugly angle. He was carrying a battered metal shield, holding it upside down, so it resembled a shallow bowl.

Black Annis poured a ladle of the sticky liquid into the shield. It steamed and hissed and immediately started to harden and crack into orange chunks.

Vidocq reached into his pocket, pulled out the orange candy, and tossed it aside. "I am never eating candy again," he muttered.

"Told you not to lick your fingers."

We watched as the children filed up in front of the Crusader knight, who stood alongside Black Annis. With clumsy fingers, he presented each child with a piece of candy from the shield. When they took it, they stepped out of line and headed back to the tunnels. Most started sucking on the sweets immediately, but I saw Marius give his to Simplice.

"That's what keeping them going," I realized. "Probably the only food they get."

"We have to do something," Vidocq said desperately.

"I have an idea," I told him. "But I'm not sure you'll like it."

13

I watched Eugène creep down into the chamber. We both agreed that my plan was terrible, but it was the only one we had.

Black Annis continued to move around the skeletons, feeding them the sticky liquid. Each ladle held enough syrup to bring two dead bodies to shuddering life. Some resurrections were more successful than others. I saw one skeleton attempt to sit up, and then watched as its arms fell off and its head rolled away from its body. So the formula was not foolproof. It animated the bones, but if the skeleton was too decomposed, all it succeeded in doing was shaking the body apart. What I wouldn't have given for a sample of that solution—though I was sure Dr. Mirabilis, Nicholas Flamel, or John Dee would be able to replicate it.

The formula obviously had no effect on the living. I watched the children suck on the candy; the combination of sugar and honey gave them the energy to continue digging up corpses for Black Annis to reanimate.

Vidocq was deep in the chamber now. Judging his moment perfectly—when everyone was concentrating on a skeleton in full medieval armor jerking noisily back to life—he joined the end of a line of children and began the slow shuffle toward Black Annis.

Scrabbling on the ground, I found the piece of candy Vidocq had thrown away. It had picked up more fluff and lint and now resembled a hairy caterpillar. Pulling a thread from my heavy coat, I quickly wrapped it around the candy, then tore a strip from my shirt and tied it to the candy bundle with more thread.

Vidocq was close to Black Annis now, but he had to bide his time; she'd filled her ladle and gone to awaken two more skeletons.

I laid the cloth-wrapped candy on the ground before me, took out my small circular tinderbox, and unscrewed the lid. Inside were a flint, a firesteel, and hemp threads.

Black Annis had returned to the cauldron and was ladling the sticky mess into the shield again.

I draped the hemp threads over the cloth-wrapped candy, then took the flint in one hand and the firesteel in the other. I would get only one chance.

The girl in front of Vidocq stepped forward to accept her candy. Then it was his turn. Neither Black Annis nor the Crusader knight even glanced at him—yet he was clearly taller and in better physical condition than the rest of the children. The Crusader handed him a chunk of candy.

I raised the flint . . .

And Vidocq dropped the candy. He fell to his knees immediately, grabbing for the piece. I saw his hand rise, and I slammed the flint onto the firesteel just as his hand fell.

I'd been worrying unnecessarily: no one was going to hear the noise of flint on steel over Black Annis's agonized high-pitched screeching.

Sparks flew onto the hemp threads. They ignited, and then the cloth beneath popped alight. Catching hold of the length of cloth I'd wrapped around the candy, I spun it in the air, bringing it to blazing life, and then I launched it toward a pile of shattered wooden coffins. The tiny meteor fell into the wood and disappeared. Without waiting to see what happened, I grabbed my two batons and raced into the chamber, toward Black Annis, the Crusader, and Eugène.

A skeleton reared up in front of me. Dagon's lead-filled baton made contact with its skull and turned it to fine white powder.

Another stabbed at me with a rusty sword. I easily parried with one stick, and a long swinging blow from the second shattered the skeleton's spine.

What Vidocq had done was risky and dangerous, and to his credit, he hadn't hesitated when I'd discussed it with him. We needed to take Black Annis out of the fight; she was the most dangerous one. When Vidocq had "accidentally" dropped his candy before the inhuman, he'd taken the opportunity to drive his iron-bladed knife through the creature's foot, pinning her to the ground. The iron was poison to her; she wouldn't be able to touch it.

What I hadn't told him to do was to push the Crusader

knight, who was already off balance, into the black cauldron, but he'd done it anyway. The heavy pot tipped and the sticky liquid splashed into the fire, bringing the coals to sparking life; then the liquid itself caught fire. The cauldron rolled across the floor, spewing a thick blazing fluid in every direction.

On the other side of the chamber, wood snapped and crackled and then popped alight. The tinder-dry coffins were starting to burn.

"Vidocq! Eugène!" I yelled. He'd picked up the Crusader knight's battle-ax and was flailing wildly with it, hitting skeletons more by chance than skill. "The children! Get the children out of here!" He heard me and spun away, disappearing in billowing smoke.

A pair of skeletons wearing rusty chain mail loomed before me. They were both carrying long spiked halberds, and they moved as if they knew how to use them. For a moment I thought I was in trouble, but even as one was jabbing at me, the metal head of the halberd snapped off, and when I deflected the other, the pole dissolved into splinters. The weapons were rotten with age. Two blows shattered the skeletons.

And all the while, Black Annis was still screeching.

The sound set my teeth on edge and made the hair on the back of my neck stand on end. This was the sound of ancient evil.

I glanced over my shoulder. The chamber was filling with fumes, but I could see Vidocq herding the children toward the tunnel. Madame Bougon's children were leading them. Through billowing smoke, I saw Vidocq dart into all the smaller tunnels and call out. Finally, satisfied that we'd left no one behind, he ran back to the tunnel entrance and took up a position there, holding the battle-ax in both hands, protecting the fleeing children.

Suddenly, Black Annis stopped screaming. Smoke shifted, and when I turned, I realized she was looking directly at me. Her eyes were orange-and-black circles. The owl beak snapped, and when she finally found words, they were so mangled I had difficulty understanding them.

"No normal humani are you."

I bowed slightly. "I am Niccolò Machiavelli," I said, "guardian of Paris."

I beat away a skeleton who came at me with a pair of short knives.

"An immortal. And your aura: it reeks of serpent. Who is your master?" she demanded.

"None of your business." I had no intention of telling her who had made me immortal. There was every possibility that my master was related to this foul creature.

She stretched out her hand. The tiny crystal skull was balanced in her palm, making it seem as if its empty eye sockets glared at me from between her filthy claws. For a single heartbeat, I imagined that the eye sockets pulsed red.

And suddenly my aura came alive: a dirty gray-white mist leaking from my flesh like smoke. It curled across the floor, twisting and slithering, touching the sugar-scented air with the tang of my serpent odor. And, like a serpent, I watched it rise off the floor in a thick semitransparent band and sway before Black Annis. Then it suddenly shot into the mouth of the small crystal skull.

I staggered, abruptly pulled forward.

Black Annis cackled. "Have you ever seen a humani drained of its aura?"

Another twist of my aura disappeared into the crystal skull, and I felt a wave of exhaustion wash over me.

All I knew about auras was that every human had one. Each was a unique combination of color and smell. An experienced magician or warlock could draw upon the power of their aura to work what could best be described as magic.

The blue-skinned hag dipped a claw into the gray-white smoke of my aura and brought it to her mouth. "I can use this skull to drain your energy, humani. I can suck you dry and leave you a withered husk, with every one of your measly three hundred years etched into your body. You will still be alive, you will still be immortal, but you will be trapped within a rotting shell." She held up the skull. "And every morning, I will sip a little of your aura and dine on your memories."

My aura had now thickened to a rope of white smoke, connecting the center of my chest to the mouth of the crystal skull. I could feel my heart hammering in my chest. I was terrified, but most of all I was angry at myself: my arrogance and stupidity had put me in this position. And now Black Annis was going to drain every ounce of energy from my body and leave me nothing more than a husk.

"You've sided with the humani. You've chosen the wrong side."

"I have, more often than not, allied with my Master and the Elders, but tonight, I chose to stand with the humani against a monster. It was the right decision; only a fool blindly chooses a side and stays there even when they know they are in the wrong."

Black Annis cackled. "In a few days, these humani children will have dug out another thousand corpses. I will bring them to life and then loose them into the city. Your precious humani will not be able to stand against them. Within the week, I will control Paris. Within a month, all the surviving Elders and Next Generation scattered across the globe will flock here. I will establish this city as the capital of the new Dark Empire. Within six months, I will rule this world."

"You underestimate the humani," I said through gritted teeth as I was jerked closer and ever closer to Black Annis and the crystal skull. I barely had enough strength to lift my feet.

"Humani are a failed experiment. Nothing more than slaves and food," she spat.

"And yet, look at what one humani—and a mere boy, at that—has done here tonight," I said.

Black Annis stretched out her hand holding the crystal skull, bringing it close to my face. Now I could see that the eye sockets were glowing the same slate gray color as mine, and its crystal interior was swirling with a thick gray cloud that matched the color of my aura.

"You've lived a long time for a humani," Black Annis said. "I will ensure that your dying takes an equally long time. You should have chosen a better side."

And then I saw her eyes flicker to one side. Reflected in the crystal skull, I saw an enormous battle-ax swoop in, and Vidocq's determined face, distorted in the glass behind it.

The hag attempted to jerk back, but she was still impaled to the floor, and she twisted awkwardly. Desperately, she snatched her hand away. The edge of the ax screamed off her black fingernails, leaving sparks, before Vidocq's battle-ax turned the crystal skull in her hand to powder.

The force of my returning aura hit me, driving me to my knees. I was aware that Vidocq was by my side, dragging me away. "We need to get out of here now!" he shouted. "The roof's going to collapse!"

Black Annis started screaming again, a primal sound of rage and hatred.

I paused in the mouth of the tunnel. "We have everyone?" I gasped.

"I'm sure of it . . . ," Vidocq began. Suddenly, an enormous skeletal shape reared out of the smoke. It was the Crusader knight with a sword in one hand, a spear in the other. He came directly for the young man. With a grunting effort, Vidocq spun the battle-ax in a short arc and neatly separated the skeleton's head from his shoulders. It hung suspended in midair for a moment, and I used the T-shaped baton like a racquet to send it sailing across the chamber toward Black Annis. We heard it hit something solid and she stopped screaming.

"Did I tell you I played tennis with William Shakespeare?" I called.

"You didn't," Vidocq said. "And I have no idea who that is."

14

"It's Vidocq." Dagon pronounced the name as a series of popping bubbles.

"Bring him in," I instructed.

It was a week after the events in the Court of Miracles. I'd not seen Vidocq since we'd escaped the tunnels and raced out of the abandoned church moments before the floor collapsed into the crypts below.

The event went practically unnoticed. There were often fires in the Court of Miracles, and unfortunately, building collapses were not uncommon either. The fire seemed to have removed the locals' fear of the place. Within a couple of days, the roof tiles and the remaining wooden window and doorframes disappeared. The marble floor was destroyed in the fire, but even the scraps were valuable, and they vanished also. I doubted anything would remain of the building by the end of the month.

Vidocq was dressed more or less as I had last seen him, though I knew his clothes must be new—or newish—since they did not stink of smoke. I'd had to burn everything I'd worn that night. He looked around the small bare room.

"I thought it would be fancier," he said at last.

"This is where I work, not where I live."

"I still can't discover exactly what sort of work you do," he said, pulling out a seat and sitting down uninvited.

"I keep the peace," I answered.

Without a word, Dagon dropped a heavy purse on the table. Coins clinked.

"Triple what you are owed," I said. I reached down beside my chair and placed a leather-wrapped bundle on the table between us.

Vidocq unwrapped it. It was a long-bladed hunting knife with an ornate Damascus steel blade and polished walnut handle.

"To make up for the one you lost," I said.

"It is magnificent."

"You deserve it. It was a gift to me from Caesar Borgia himself. He was once my employer, and an absolute villain. I think you would have liked him. Now, tell me: How are the children?"

"Most of them seem to think they got lost in the tunnels and hallucinated because of lack of food and water."

"Most of them?"

"Some—like Marius—are suspicious and confused. But who does he tell?" Eugene shrugged. "And what does he say? 'I was digging corpses out of the underground crypts so that a blue-skinned chicken-legged woman could bring them back to life and attack the city'? 'Oh, and I was guarded by skeletons'?"

"And Madame Bougon?"

"She thanks you, said she will be eternally grateful to you. Said you are a man of your word. I think that's a compliment."

"As time goes by, the children's memories will fade. Eventually, they will not know if it really happened or if it was a dream."

Vidocq poked the bag of coins with his dirty fingers. "I'm already starting to wonder myself. It really did happen, didn't it?"

I glanced up at Dagon. If I was going to lie to the boy, this would be the time. "Yes," I answered, "it really happened."

"And there really was a blue-faced chicken-legged old woman . . ."

"Black Annis," Dagon said, managing to pronounce the name with a layer of disgust.

Vidocq swiveled in his chair. "Were you really worshiped as a god?"

"I still am," he said.

"Do you ever answer prayers?" he asked cheekily.

"I'm not that sort of god."

The young man turned back to me. "What happened to Black Annis? She was still pinned to the floor when we left."

"You can rest assured: she's gone. Everything in that chamber was burnt to a crisp."

He grinned, and I could see that a weight had lifted off his shoulders. "I keep thinking she's down there, stuck to the floor, just waiting for the knife to rust through so she can come and find me."

"You're safe," I said. "Safer than you have ever been, Monsieur Vidocq, because now you are under my protection. I will be watching out for you in the years to come. And when the time is right, I am thinking you might make a fine chief of police in this city."

Vidocq started to laugh, then stopped. "Oh, you're not joking."

"I am making you a promise," I told him with a smile.

Dagon saw Vidocq to the door and locked it behind him. When he returned, he was carrying a length of stained cloth. "What do you want me to do with this?" he asked, unrolling the cloth.

It was Black Annis's foot, still with Vidocq's knife embedded in it, complete with the chunk of limestone it was impaled in.

"I searched every inch of the tunnels for her," he said. "This"—he tapped the foot—"was the only evidence that she'd ever been there."

"She'll grow another?" I asked.

"Those Elders are practically indestructible. She's probably limping around on a tiny chicken's foot right now."

"So she'll be back?"

"Not here. Too many bad memories. She'll find a new

nest, in a new country. And if we're still around in a couple of hundred years, she might try again."

"Will we still be here?" I wondered.

"Not sure about you," Dagon answered, "but I will. I have unfinished business with Scathach the Shadow."

VIRGINIA DARE AND THE RATCATCHER

1833

To my most esteemed colleague, friend, and mentor, Dr. Dee,

I am in receipt of your most recent letter and funds. Your comments on my latest writing, which I have decided to call *The Narrative of Arthur Gordon Pym,* are insightful, and I will endeavor to incorporate your suggestions into the final manuscript. The work was inspired, as you are no doubt aware, by recent events. As I attempted to make sense of all that occurred and all that I saw, I realized I should create a narrative for myself, and for you, inasmuch as it intimately involves that most mysterious of women, Virginia Dare, whom I know you hold in high regard.

My narrative begins in the month of

November, in the year of Our Lord 1833, in
Boston.

I had just won the most extraordinary sum
of fifty dollars for my short story "MS Found in
a Bottle," which was published by the Baltimore
weekly the Saturday Visiter. (You will recall that
you were generous in your praise of the work; I
have taken the liberty of posting a copy to your
London address.) My success brought me to the
attention of some people of note, and there is the
chance of employment on a quality newspaper or
magazine in the near future.

One of the unexpected consequences of my
newfound fame is that people who heretofore
ignored me now seek me out. They are happy
to ply me with food and drink as they regale me
with their own stories. Everyone, it seems, wishes
to become an author, though few wish to write
themselves and prefer others do the tedious work
for them.

In a rather low-class drinking house on the
Boston docks, I was first told the story which
served as the catalyst for all that was to come. . . .

Edgar Allan Poe
Boston
December 1833

1

The only light in the uncomfortably cool room came from the low, dying fire. Coals were dusted white with ash, and logs were little more than hollowed-out shells, suggesting that the fire had been unattended for a very long time.

The small, wild-haired man standing at the hearth noted the unusual way the logs had been set: in a half circle pointing upward, almost like a campfire. It took an enormous effort of will not to pull a scrap of paper from his pocket and record a note of the placement. It would make an interesting detail in a story. And something else to note was that the clock on the mantel had stopped, both hands settling on the twelve. A stopped clock is correct at least twice every day; he'd read that once. Maybe he could do a story about a stopped clock.

He turned his back to the fire and looked around the shadow-wrapped room. He had been here twice before, and on each occasion it had been subtly different. Furniture was almost, but not quite, where it had been previously, and pictures he'd remembered on one wall were now on another. And although this was a substantial property in the best part of Boston, he'd only ever encountered one servant. He thought—though he could not be entirely sure—that it was the same man. English, perhaps, but with a hint of the Gael to his accent, a suggestion of red in his gray hair. Only now he realized that the man he'd seen today seemed much younger, his hair a bright copper, and Poe momentarily assumed he was the elder servant's son . . . except both men had an identical tattoo on the back of their wrists, and the merest hint of a scar along their jawline.

As his eyes adjusted to the gloom he became aware with a start that he was not alone in the room. There was a figure in the high-backed chair to the left of the fire.

Or was it a shadow?

Squeezing his eyes shut, he looked away from the silhouette before opening them again. Lately, he'd been plagued by shapes glimpsed from the corner of his eyes, speckles which sometimes took the form of skulls floating across his vision. He was terrified he was going to lose his sight, or worse: go mad.

No, there was definitely a figure in the chair. He could see the outline of a head, the hint of a face, the suggestion of arms and black-gloved hands.

Someone asleep? A dead body? It was not beyond the bounds of possibility; the last time he'd visited this house, a delivery of mummies had just arrived from Egypt. They were lined up in the dining room like guests at a banquet.

He tried a polite cough. "I do apologize. You must forgive my rudeness. I did not see you there."

The figure did not move.

Suddenly the fire behind him exploded into spiraling sparks. When he spun back, there was a second figure crouched before the grate, adding logs to the flames. Even before she turned to face him, he recognized the cascading sheen of jet-black hair.

"Miss Dare . . ." His heart was thumping so hard it was difficult to form the words. "I did not hear you come in. . . . I was unaware that you were here. . . . I thought . . ."

He turned back to the chair. The blazing firelight revealed that it was empty.

When he looked at the fire again, Virginia Dare was standing before it, tall, stern, hands clasped behind her back. Shockingly, she was wearing a man's black suit, and a white shirt with a black cravat. Her boots were so highly polished they reflected the firelight.

"Miss Dare . . . ," he said again.

"Mr. Poe."

"Miss Dare . . ."

"For a man who purports to make a living from his writing, you seem to be in possession of remarkably few words this evening." Virginia spoke English with the hint of a Boston accent, but touched by something else, some indecipherable twang. "Thus far, all we have determined is that you remember my name."

"You must forgive me. I was sure . . ." He checked the chair behind him again. "I was sure you were sitting in that chair. So finding you behind me gave me a start." He rubbed his hands together and smiled in embarrassment. "I saw a shadow."

"I wonder who it was." Dare sounded unsurprised. She stepped past him and lowered herself into the seat. "Every old house has its share of secrets. Especially this one." Virginia leaned forward and firelight ran across her face, catching on high cheekbones, turning her gray eyes amber. "If you listen closely enough, you can hear its heartbeat." She indicated a chair opposite her. "Sit, Mr. Poe."

Edgar Allan Poe sank into the sighing leather chair and attempted to compose himself. He knew very little about the woman facing him beyond the fact that Virginia Dare was either unmarried or a widow and was obviously extraordinarily wealthy. They had been introduced by the English doctor John Dee at a literary function some years previously, and it was clear that Dee held her in high regard. There was something odd and wild about Dee, and Poe thought he noticed some of the same characteristics in Dare. Perhaps they were related somehow.

"You return here as a published author, Mr. Poe. I must congratulate you on your success."

Poe felt warmth in his cheeks, a mixture of embarrassment and pride. "You are most kind."

The woman smiled without showing her teeth. "Did I detect some hints of our last adventure in your story?"

"I drew some inspiration from it," he admitted. "I hope you are not offended."

"Not in the slightest. For the writing to live, the writer

has to live also. I think I might have been more offended if you had *not* used those experiences in a story. So tell me, Mr. Poe, what brings you here?"

Poe stared into the fire. He automatically reached for the glass on the small side table. On each of the previous occasions he had visited, it had been there, in exactly the same position, and no matter how much he drank from it, it never emptied. Yet he'd never seen anyone fill it. The glass brimmed with water, which, in normal circumstances, he would not touch, but this was crystal clear, flavored with a hint of unidentifiable spices.

"You recall when we first met," he said when he had gathered his thoughts.

"I have an excellent memory," Dare replied.

Poe glanced over. Dare had sunk back into the chair, only her extended legs and the highly polished toes of her boots visible. It appeared as if little flames were dancing at the ends of her feet.

"Dr. Dee introduced you as Virginia Dare and I commented that it was a remarkable name."

"You recognized my name. I doubt if there was anyone else at that rather tedious party who knew as much about the first English settlers to land in the Americas."

"Virginia Dare, the first European to be born on American soil. And then, along with the rest of the Roanoke Colony, to disappear. A mystery. A tragedy. What writer would not be attracted to that tale?"

"Only a writer with your peculiar interests, Mr. Poe."

"You will be unsurprised to learn that I attempted to research your past. And Dr. Dee's also," he added.

"I would have expected no less."

"I can trace a series of Virginia Dares weaving in and out of the fringes of American history, appearing and disappearing through the generations. Unfortunately, critical records are missing. Deeds are nonexistent. Wills have vanished."

"Most unfortunate," she answered. "However, I have little interest in genealogy. I prefer to live in the present."

"Similarly with Dr. Dee. His most famous ancestor and namesake served with honor at the court of Queen Elizabeth. His accomplishments were remarkable."

Virginia Dare laughed. "Dr. John Dee: scholar, spy, geographer, alchemist, magician, necromancer, charlatan. Take your pick. The historical Dee has been called many things, Mr. Poe."

"Like your own esteemed ancestors, Miss Dare, his also weave in and out of the records. There are hints and suggestions of a Dee at some of the most pivotal times in human history."

Virginia Dare leaned forward, the firelight turning her face to a mask. "I presume there is a reason for this history lesson?"

"When we first met, you said you were intrigued by what you called my low connections."

"As a newspaperman, a journalist, a writer, an ex-soldier, you get to hear stories which might not be reported in the press."

"You specifically said you had an interest in the unusual, the bizarre, the oddities."

"I did," Dare replied. "I also said that I would pay handsomely for the stories."

"You did."

"And I have."

Poe nodded quickly. He thought he detected a note of irritation in the woman's voice.

"At first I believed you were collecting material for a book of folktales," he continued. "On three separate occasions, I have brought to your attention stories which might be considered unusual, even bizarre. A sighting of a Golem in New York; a loup-garou, a werewolf, running wild in the forest of the Green Mountains outside Albany. I have no idea if you ever investigated those tales." He paused, expecting an answer, but the woman did not fill the silence.

"The last story I related to you was the haunted ship sailing out of Bativa. You asked if I was interested in accompanying you on that investigation."

"I did. I knew your connections in the bars on the wharves would be invaluable. And they were," she added.

"I . . . I am not entirely sure what happened when we boarded the haunted ship. I think . . . I am sure I saw things. But I might have been hallucinating."

Virginia Dare said nothing.

"However, as you noted, I did use those experiences for my short story."

"A prizewinning story," she added.

"Just so, Miss Dare."

"One does not need to be a genius to ascertain that you have come here tonight with something new and strange to tell me. Are you perhaps looking to be paid a larger finder's fee?"

Poe managed to look shocked. "On the contrary. The idea never crossed my mind," he lied. He had briefly thought about looking for an increase in the fee he was paid for each story he found. But the success of his last story had suggested an alternative.

"So what do you want, Mr. Poe?"

"This very day, I came into possession of some interesting information. The sort of tale which well might interest you. If you choose to investigate the circumstances surrounding this story, then I would very much like to accompany you as your assistant." He finished in a rush. "Just as I did with the Bativa story."

Virginia Dare sank back into the chair, but not before Poe had caught the merest hint of a smile. "And you turned our Bativa adventure into a prizewinning story. You are in search of new material, perhaps hoping for lightning to strike twice?"

"Ideas are my stock-in-trade. I am coming to the understanding that the public has an appetite for the bizarre, the unusual."

"It was ever thus, Mr. Poe. Tales of mystery and imagination have always struck a chord with humanity. Perhaps, at some deep and primitive level, they are reminded of the times they crouched in caves and were fearful of the monsters in the shadows."

"There are no monsters in the shadows," he said uneasily.

"Oh, Mr. Poe, there are always monsters lurking in the shadows. But those are not the ones you have to be careful of; the ones who step into the light are the most dangerous."

Poe opened his mouth, then closed it, unsure if the woman was mocking him. He sipped from the glass, finding his mouth abruptly dry. "So you would allow me to accompany you once again?"

"It would depend, of course, on the story. What have you found, Mr. Poe, that would tempt me to leave my warm home in the middle of November?"

Poe took another sip of water to steady his nerves. Although he had practiced this story a dozen times, the woman's presence and his surroundings unsettled him. "It is another ship story," he began, almost apologetically.

"Hardly surprising, Mr. Poe. Boston is one of the gateways to America. I would imagine all sorts of wonders and terrors come through these ports."

"This very night, there is a boat at dock in the harbor with a cargo of thirteen dirt-filled coffins. A white-faced German who calls himself the captain, but who has clearly never captained a ship before, is looking to hire a wagon to carry the coffins into the countryside, no questions asked."

As he was speaking, Virginia moved out of the shadow of the chair and into the light. Huge slate-gray eyes fixed on Poe's face. "Coffins? You are sure of this?"

"Listed as wooden crates on the manifest, but I have been assured that they are coffins."

"I take it you have not seen these boxes yourself?"

"I have not seen them myself, but my informant is certain, and he is particularly observant."

"And how does your informant know that they are filled with earth?"

"The deck beneath each is apparently speckled with dirt which has leaked through."

"And are there any bodies in the coffins?" Dare asked.

Poe blinked. That had been the first thing he'd thought of, but he was surprised that a lady of breeding and refinement like Miss Dare would even entertain such a horrifying idea. "Why would someone ship out empty coffins?"

Virginia waved a hand dismissively. "Many immigrants put a value on the soil from their homeland. We need to know if there are bodies in the coffins."

"I could find out," he said quickly. "The informant, a boatswain, is a good friend of mine. A few dollars will get us all the answers you require. He brought this story to my attention, and he is convinced that the man who calls himself the captain had never commanded a ship before."

"And the name of this captain?"

"Pfeifer. A German name, I believe. I am unsure of the translation."

"It means Piper," Virginia Dare said very softly.

2

Two hours later, Virginia Dare and Edgar Allan Poe stood on a rotting wharf in Boston Harbor, looking at a ship rocking at anchor. Virginia was completely enveloped in a high-collared, ankle-length riding coat. Poe had no overcoat, and Dare had thrown him a horse blanket to wrap around his shoulders as they'd climbed out of the coach which had taken them to the docks. The sea air was frigid, stinking of fish and salt, rot and waste. Somewhere in the night, a ship's bell tolled mournfully.

"The *Grampus*," Poe said through chattering teeth. "A coal ship. Reinforced hull and keel. Registered out of Hamburg in Germany." His breath plumed whitely before his face as he spoke.

The woman scanned the decks with a long, slender telescope. "Plenty of coal hereabouts. Why would you need to import any?"

"It's not carrying coal. The manifest shows it is loaded with semi-finished iron goods."

Virginia glanced sidelong at Poe. "Which are?"

"Ingots of metal, probably; wire, nails, that sort of thing.

The manifest also lists copper, lead, and a small consignment of linen among the cargo."

"But no mention of caskets or coffins?"

"None." He produced a stained page ripped from a note-book. "I copied this directly from the manifest."

Virginia scanned it quickly. Poe noted she was reading it in almost complete darkness. "Just another unremarkable ship working the trade route between Europe and the Americas," she said. "What first brought it to the attention of your contact?"

Poe grinned, revealing discolored misshapen teeth. "The crew."

Virginia scanned the deck again. "I don't see any crew."

"Exactly," Poe said. "No one saw it sail into harbor. Came in overnight and was found at this berth here. The harbor-master was not expecting it."

"That is curious."

"I also checked into some of the drinking houses and eateries on the wharves. None of them had any crew in from the *Grampus*."

Virginia folded the telescope and slipped it into one of her voluminous pockets. "That is curious," she repeated.

Poe watched as the woman threw back her head and inhaled deeply. For a moment he wondered why she was breathing in the stinking harbor air, but then he realized she was seeking a scent like a bloodhound, and though the night was chill, he felt a shiver of icy fear trickle down his spine. He'd often wondered who Virginia Dare was; he was beginning to think he should have been wondering *what* she was. "What do you . . . *sense?*" he asked.

Virginia turned to look at him, her face pale and ghastly in the light.

"Nothing," she said. "And that is very curious indeed."

3

Virginia sat with her back to the wall in the wharfside tavern.

Even though it was after midnight, the low-ceilinged rectangular room was busy with people, and from where she was sitting she could distinguish eight different languages being spoken. Stale air curled with a dozen odors, none of them pleasant: unwashed humani, brine, rotting fish, and the thick oiliness from the coal on the fire, all of it overlain with the sharp tang of cheap liquor and the stench of various tobaccos.

Poe slid into the seat opposite her and set three frothing mugs onto the scarred tabletop. "I know you won't drink," he said, "but I had to get something for you so as not to arouse suspicion. I'll drink it," he added.

Virginia nodded. "I'm impressed you remembered that I do not drink."

He shrugged. "I have a memory for trivial details."

"Just what every writer needs: details, Mr. Poe. People rarely remember all the details from the completed work, but they do recall phrases or incidents. You must ensure that your work has plenty of incidents. Memorable incidents and phrases."

"That is good advice."

Virginia glanced up. A slender, dark-skinned man was moving through the crowd, heading toward the table. "The gentleman we are meeting, this friend of yours . . ."

"The boatswain?"

"An African gentleman? Graceful, elegantly dressed?"

"That's him." Poe twisted in the chair and raised a hand. "Originally from Loango in Lower Guinea."

The boatswain raised a hand in response, slipped into the seat beside Poe, then lifted and emptied the mug in one long swallow.

Without a word, Virginia pushed across the drink in front of her.

"This is—" Poe began.

"Jupiter Dupin Tempest," the boatswain said with the trace of a French accent. "Most people call me Tempest." He pulled off his cap to reveal a completely hairless head.

"Dare," Virginia said, and stretched out her hand.

The boatswain blinked in surprise, wiped his palm on the front of his woolen jacket, and took her hand. Before he released it, he turned it over and ran a blunt thumb over the creases and ridges on her fingertips and across her knuckles.

"The hand of a worker, the dress of a man, but the eyes of a woman." Tempest grinned, showing teeth badly stained by chewing tobacco. "Poe collects the oddest of people."

"Including you." Poe nudged him in the ribs.

"None of us is *ever* quite what we seem," Virginia said. "How did you know I was a woman?"

Tempest sipped some of the beer she had given him. "I've been on the seas for most of my life. Sailed around the world three full times. Speak six languages fluently and can get by in six more. Stopped in just about every country with a port. And what has kept me alive, with all my limbs and most of my teeth intact, is that I am observant. When you spend a long time at sea, you learn to notice even the smallest details. Because it is the trivial which might just keep you alive: a fraying rope, a splintering board, a white cloud on a gray sky, seabirds where there should be none."

Virginia glanced at Poe. "I believe Monsieur Jupiter Dupin Tempest would make an interesting character for one of your stories."

"I have already started taking notes," Poe admitted.

"I do believe I quite like that idea," the boatswain said.

Virginia pushed back into the shadows. "So, tell me what you saw when you looked at me."

Tempest finished his second drink and dropped the empty mug to the table with a clang. Almost immediately, a boy who looked to be no more than ten years old appeared and swept up the two empty mugs. "Bring us four more," Tempest said. A pair of coins flashed silver against his dark flesh as he dropped them in an empty mug. "That should be enough. Keep what's left for yourself. Understand?"

The boy nodded, eyes widening in surprise.

"And don't let anyone know you have it."

The potboy nodded again.

Tempest turned back to Virginia. "I watched you come in with Poe. You stepped into the room and immediately put your back to the door, waiting until your eyes adjusted."

Virginia nodded. "Only someone who does the same would know that."

"I learned the hard way." Tempest touched the dark line of a scar over his right ear.

Poe pulled out a scrap of paper and the stub of a pencil and started to make notes.

"I watched how you progressed through the crowd. Your head didn't shift, but your eyes were swiveling from side to side, watching everything. I've seen hunters move like that. They know that any movement, even a turn of their head, might alert their prey. And I saw how you managed not to even brush up against anyone as you crossed the floor. That takes skill. You moved like a dancer, a warrior. You chose the darkest end of the room, tucked yourself into a corner with your back to the wall so no one could come at you from behind. I've seen outlaws and wanted men in a dozen countries do the same."

"You are very observant, Monsieur Tempest."

"Tempest. Just Tempest."

"You still haven't told me how you knew I am a woman."

"What shall I say? That I knew by your feet, which are small, by your posture, which is elegant, by your slender neck, which is without an Adam's apple, by your smooth beardless face, even though we are after midnight and a man would have some stubble visible?" Suddenly, he grinned hugely. "Or that Poe told me my story might be of interest to a woman he knew and there might be money in it for me?"

Virginia smiled. "I am guessing that even if Mr. Poe had not told you, you would have known."

"I would."

The young potboy returned, struggling with four mugs which looked huge against his slender frame. Tempest slid out of the seat and took them from him and Virginia saw him slip another coin into the boy's hands.

"Tempest, when this is over, you must come and see me. Mr. Poe has the address. I might have some work for a man with your skills." She looked at Poe. "You are in search of stories, and yet here beside you is a fascinating character who deserves a host of stories. Lots of people look but do not see. Perhaps you should create a character who observes."

"An inquirer, a questioner," Tempest added.

"An investigator," Virginia said. She leaned forward out of the shadows. "There is a gentleman in Paris, Eugène François Vidocq. Like Monsieur Tempest, he goes by a single name: Vidocq. By a particularly interesting set of circumstances, he established a secret security force within the French police called the Brigade de la Sûreté. He has only recently retired and sent me a copy of his memoir. His methods are not dissimilar to Monsieur Tempest's. You will find it interesting." She stopped. "Ah, it is in French. Will that be a problem?"

"I studied French and Latin at the University of Virginia," Poe said.

"You must borrow it. I will ask you to take special care of the book; it is inscribed to me." Even as Poe was opening his mouth to ask a question, Virginia turned to the boatswain. "Now tell me, Tempest, what did you find aboard the *Grampus*?"

The smile faded from the man's face. He took a long moment to drain one of the mugs before him, and when he finally looked at Dare, his eyes were wide with fear.

"I found monsters."

4

The testimony of Jupiter Dupin Tempest, transcribed by Edgar Allan Poe

I have spent my entire life at sea. I have crewed and indeed captained my own vessel, but it is as a boatswain where I find myself the happiest. I have none of the responsibilities of a captain, nor am I a lowly crew member. It is a career which has allowed me to travel the world, and I have seen both wonders and terrors.

My travels have taught me that the world is not as most perceive it. I believe that this world is far older than the 5,837 years the Church teaches. The past is still with us. It lurks in the secret places and hidden valleys, on top of the highest mountain peaks and in the heart of the densest forests. Creatures of legend, long believed dead, and monsters from the edges of myth still walk the earth. This I know to be true because I have seen them with my own eyes.

We live in a new age of science and marvelous discoveries. I find myself wondering if we are not discovering but merely rediscovering skills and technologies from our distant past.

I have seen men and women—what the educated would call primitives—perform feats of wonder, using skills handed down to them through the generations. In the heart of Africa, I watched a sangoma—a healer—raise a man from the dead, and I know he was dead because I killed him myself. In Greenland, I saw an Inuuk shaman perform an identical ritual and bring a child who had fallen through the ice back to life. In England, I watched an old man find water buried deep beneath the ground by holding two sticks in his hands. The rods—he called them dowsing rods—twisted and curled of their own accord when they were above water. On the other side of the world, in the wild Australian desert, a native woman, a kadji, pointed without hesitation to a spot where she said a pool of fresh water lay beneath solid trackless ground. It took an hour of digging to reach it, but none of her tribe doubted for a moment that it was there. And it was. How is it that these ancient skills are identical across the world? The African sangoma and the Inuuk shaman, the English dowser and the Australian kadji will never meet, but they are all drawing upon skills and talents passed down through the generations.

I have spent more than half my life at sea. It taught me that there are creatures in the depths unimagined by modern man. I have seen the ruins of ancient civilizations in places which exist on no maps. There is a string of artificial islands in the heart of the Pacific called Nan Madol where the natives worship a creature known as the Old Spider. This is not a graven idol, however; the Old Spider, which they call

Aerop-Enap, actually exists. It is as big as a carriage, and I alone survived when my entire crew was tossed into the sacrificial pit.

I stood on the lip of that great rip in the earth, the Grand Canyon, and watched a trio of what the native peoples call thunderbirds rise from the depths of the earth and spiral in the air. Tribes across the Americas believe in the existence of these birds, so why should we doubt them? The Maya worshiped Quetzalcoatl, the feathered serpent. I have often wondered if the feathered serpent and the thunderbird are one and the same creature. And in every country I have visited there are tales of dragons. I no longer believe these to be myths or bedtime stories: I think they are memories.

I say all this to you so that you know that I am comfortable with mysteries and so that you know I am not easily impressed.

Because I have seen wonders, I have also experienced terrors. I was chased by an albino man-ape in northern India; pursued by a hopping, snarling monstrosity in China; and serenaded on a beach on Ireland's west coast by an ashen-faced beauty with holes where her eyes should have been. I know the smell of evil; I can taste it on my tongue. That rancid smell, that foul taste has kept me alive.

I smelled it last night. I have tasted it on the air throughout this very day.

It did not take me long to discover the source of that loathsome miasma: a mysterious boat—unannounced and expected—had docked overnight. The *Grampus* out of

Germany. A few inquiries revealed that no crew were seen disembarking, there were no new faces in the bars and eateries, and none had taken a bed in the doss-houses.

I spent the day watching the boat. I found several menial jobs on the waterfront which gave me reason to be there. And although I spent hours in sight of the craft, I saw no crew in the rigging, none swabbing the decks, none tending to the countless minor jobs which keep a craft seaworthy.

The harbormaster told me the captain was a man called Pfeifer, a German or Pole. And yet, the previous time the *Grampus* had come into harbor, it had been under the command of Augustus Barnard, who sailed out of Nantucket.

Around noon, I watched Pfeifer disembark. It was immediately obvious that he did not have a mariner's rolling gait, that peculiar walk common to men who have spent many months at sea. He took short, hesitant steps and clutched at rails and rigging to keep himself upright. He was a big man, made all the larger by the greatcoat he wore, and the broad-brimmed hat and thick scarf wrapped around his face made it almost impossible to distinguish his features. I caught a glimpse of the flesh around his eyes and forehead—it was pale, clearly never having been exposed to the elements. Even a few hours at sea will turn skin red and peeling, and then later, deeply tanned and traced with lines. He wore gloves with the fingers cut away, and though it might have been a trick of the light, his fingernails seemed unnaturally long.

When he came ashore, he was leaning on one of those black, silver-topped canes which, in my experience, conceal a sword blade, and once on dry land, he carried himself with a military air, straight backed and stiff legged.

Pfeifer hailed a cab at the end of the pier and I heard him give the address of the new newspaper, the *Boston Post,* on Milk Street, so I knew he would be gone awhile.

I waited until the cab had disappeared and then counted to one thousand before borrowing a little skiff and rowing out to the *Grampus.*

I am not by nature a fearful man. I believe the length of our lives is predetermined, and no matter what we do, we are allotted a certain amount of days. Once we have used those up, we die. As I rowed out to the *Grampus,* as the stench of evil grew ever thicker around me, I began to think that perhaps my time on this earth was drawing to a close.

The ship was dead. I knew that the moment I touched it. Every sailor will tell you that a ship is a living, breathing thing. The wood creaks and groans; the rigging whispers and sighs. The wood trembles with the footsteps of the crew, and the movement of bodies aboard the ship vibrates through stays and sails. I knew the moment my hand touched the wood that there was nothing living aboard the *Grampus.*

When I climbed onto the deck, it was plain to see that the *Grampus* was in poor repair. Decks had not been sanded; ropes lay uncoiled and scattered about. Nothing was tied down. It looked derelict and deserted.

But the smell, that smell of evil, was strong.

I followed my nose belowdecks, through unlocked doors

and along passageways stained with salt and streaked with seaweed.

And I found them in the hold.

Thirteen rectangular boxes arranged in two rows of six, with one set apart from the others, each twenty-four inches across and perhaps eighty inches long. And although they were not adorned with brass handles or etched with ornate scrollwork or incised patterns, I knew immediately that they were coffins. Closer examination revealed a scattering of earth and soil on the deck beneath and around each coffin. I knew that it must have leaked from the joints.

Did I open the boxes?

No, I did not, because although I have often been foolish, I am not stupid.

And let me add this one final thing to my recounting: as I crept through that hold, passing between the coffins, I heard movements within. Do not try to tell me that I was hearing rats. I've heard rats aplenty; I know the sounds of their clicking claws and swishing tails. No, these sounds came from within the coffins.

And I swear that they sounded like fingernails on wood.

5

"I got myself ashore as quickly as possible," Tempest finished. He reached into his coat and produced a copy of the *Boston Post*. Turning to the back page, he folded the paper in half and spread it across the table. The edges of the coarse paper sprouted damp circles from the beer mugs. "It didn't take me long to discover why Pfeifer had gone to the newspaper." A blunt, ragged nail picked out a rectangle of print at the bottom of the page.

Poe leaned forward, squinting at the tiny font, then shook his head. "I need a candle. . . ."

Virginia moved out of the shadows, and for a single instant her slate-gray eyes shimmered and glowed. "Wanted," she read. "Drover/wagon driver to transport thirteen boxes a max distance thirty miles. Excellent pay. Discretion expected. References required. Apply in person to the captain of the *Grampus*, currently docked in the harbor."

"You have exceptional eyesight, Miss Dare," Tempest murmured. "I can scarce make out the words, even though I've read them a dozen times."

"Thirty miles," she said thoughtfully. "Where does that take us?"

"Thirty miles east takes us out over the sea, so we can discount that," Tempest said.

"North takes us up toward Salem," Poe added. "A place with plenty of interesting associations."

"How far is Salem?" Virginia asked.

Poe looked at Tempest. "Twenty-five, thirty miles?"

"About that," he agreed.

"And westward?" Dare wondered.

"Newton? Watertown," Tempest said. "Nothing interesting or untoward comes to mind."

"And south?"

Poe suddenly sat upright, knocking against the drink on the table, splashing the newspaper with beer. "Of course . . ." He looked from Dare to Tempest and then back to the woman in excitement. "South! I know a place of dark mysteries and foul legends. I thought to use it in a story."

"Of course." Tempest nodded. "I think Mr. Poe has it."

"And is either of you going to tell me?" Virginia wondered.

"Hockomock Swamp," Poe and Tempest said in unison.

"I am sure you are pausing for dramatic effect," Dare said, unable to keep the curl of a smile off her lips. "But I'm a stranger in a strange land, and I've never heard of this place."

"Once a Wampanoag fortress, now it is a cursed place," Tempest said. "The Native People believed that the souls of the dead congregated there. The early English settlers called it the Devil's Swamp."

"Sounds fascinating," Virginia murmured.

"Monsters have been sighted in the swamplands," Poe said breathlessly. "Thunderbirds, giant snakes, monstrous dogs. There are local legends about a tribe of hairy men who live in the depths of the place. You can hear them howling and hooting through the night."

"And there are lights," Tempest added. "Dancing globes of fire and streamers of burning smoke which twist and curl through the trees."

Virginia nodded. "I cannot believe I've been here so long and never visited."

"These stories do not frighten you?" the boatswain asked.

"I believe that there is little which frightens Mistress Dare," Poe said.

The woman smiled. "On the contrary, Mr. Poe. Many things distress me, some frighten me, and one or two genuinely terrify me. But nothing you have described here give me cause for alarm. An isolated swampland, touched by old legends. Why, every forest, swamp, cave, and island on this continent is attached to a story of a mysterious past. And in my experience, there are usually monsters—described but never captured, glimpsed but never seen, heard but never trapped."

"And the lights?" Tempest asked.

She shrugged. "Swamp gas perhaps. Fireflies."

"So you do not believe us?" Poe asked, sounding disappointed.

"On the contrary, I do believe you. Because if this Pfeifer is looking to transport thirteen dirt-filled coffins there, then there must be something at the heart of his swampland. I will need to consult some charts, but I wonder if this place is at the nexus of some ley lines."

Poe and Tempest looked at her blankly.

"Invisible lines of occult power which curl around the globe. Every ancient site, every archaeological wonder in every country is situated on these lines. When several lines cross, they create an area of extraordinary power: a leygate. An opening to another . . . realm, a Shadowrealm," she said before they could ask the next question. "Tempest is correct: this world is older than you can imagine. But it is not the only world. There are countless others linked to this one, accessible through these gates."

"You . . . you say all this with such confidence," Poe said, "almost as if you believe it to be true."

Virginia looked at Tempest. "Tell him."

"What Miss Dare has just told us makes perfect sense to me. The myths and legends of a dozen countries include similar tales." He tried to find Virginia's face, but she had moved back into the deep shadows. "Yet I believe Miss Dare may be speaking about these gates out of some personal experience."

There was a flash of white teeth in the shadows. "Gates, as we know, work both ways, so sometimes creatures from these other dimensions step through into our world."

"What sort of creatures?" Poe whispered.

"Thunderbirds, giant snakes, monstrous dogs." She smiled and leaned forward to look at the newspaper again. "So here is what we shall do," she began. Then she stopped and glanced at the two men facing her. "Ah, it was presumptuous of me to include you in this adventure. I would, however, be grateful for your assistance. If I am correct in my assumptions, there is certain to be danger. If we all survive, I can guarantee you both a fine payday. And for you, Mr. Poe, I foresee enough material for at least a dozen stories."

"Why do you feel you need to follow these coffins to their destination?" Poe asked. "They have nothing to do with you."

"And if I do not?" she asked. "What then?"

Poe looked at her blankly.

"Mr. Tempest believes that there is evil aboard that ship."

"I do," Tempest agreed.

"So should we just ignore it?" she asked. "Should we stand back and allow Pfeifer to bring these boxes ashore and scatter them across the country?"

"No, no, of course not," Poe answered. "We could take the story to the authorities, though."

"And tell them what exactly?" she snapped.

"Miss Dare is correct," Tempest said. "We have a story built upon some odd circumstances, my fears, and, I should add, Miss Dare's understanding of the dark history of this world. I am unsure the authorities would pay any attention to our report. Also, you, Poe, are a writer, I am a foreigner, and Miss Dare is a woman. None of us has any credibility with the law."

"I could not have said it better myself," Virginia Dare said. "Also, Mr. Poe, this is what I do: I investigate the mysterious and the arcane. And when the occasion demands it, I act."

"And you believe tonight is one of those occasions?" Poe asked.

"I do."

"Then I would be honored to be of assistance," he said.

"As would I," Tempest added. "I believe you suspect—no, I think you are certain—what lies in the boat's hold."

"I have an idea," Dare answered.

"Would you care to share that idea with us?" Virginia Dare drew back into the shadows and the boatswain pressed on. "Miss Dare, I have already admitted to you that I have seen both the best and worst of what this world has to offer. And Mr. Poe is a student of the macabre. I am sure nothing you say now is going to startle us."

Virginia moved into the light. "You deserve an answer. It is not an enormous stretch of the imagination to conclude that there are bodies in the coffins."

The two men nodded.

"Have either of you heard of vampires, the undead blood drinkers?"

"Vampires," Tempest said with a shudder. "I've heard the stories all across the world. Different names, but they all drink the blood of the living."

Poe looked confused. "I have read 'The Vampyre' by Dr. Polidori. But it is a fiction, is it not?"

"A fiction based on terrible facts," Virginia said. "Polidori

297

was Lord Byron's personal physician. Seventeen years ago, the pair traveled through Europe in search of adventure. Those adventures often led them down dark and dangerous roads. I believe one of those adventures was the inspiration for Polidori's novel."

"So you are saying that vampires are real," Poe asked.

"I think you will find that at the heart of every myth there is a grain of truth."

"But . . . vampires," Poe said cautiously.

"Previously you have brought me tales of Golems and werewolves."

Poe nodded. "Did you hunt them?"

"I did."

"And when you found them?"

"I destroyed them."

"And will you destroy these vampires—if that is what they are?" Poe asked.

"I will, if I can."

"Is this what you do, Miss Dare? Do you hunt monsters?"

Tempest laid his hand on Poe's arm. "I do not think Miss Dare is a hunter," he said with a smile. "I think she is a protector."

"You are very observant," she said. "So, gentlemen, are you with me? Normally I prefer to work alone, but the peculiar nature of this task will require assistance and assistants." She looked at Poe. "Earlier, you asked if you could accompany me because you were in search of inspiration. Well, here you have all the elements of a Gothic tale: a mysterious boat, an unlikely captain, thirteen earth-filled boxes occupied by undying vampires, and a haunted swamp."

"You are missing a piece or two." The boatswain smiled. He jerked a thumb at Poe. "The writer in search of inspiration . . . and a woman who is more, much more than she seems."

Virginia bowed her head slightly.

"What do you need, Mistress Dare?" Tempest asked.

Virginia tapped the sodden newspaper, smearing black ink on her fingertips. "Do you know where we can hire a horse and cart?"

6

Hidden in the shadow of an alleyway, Virginia Dare pressed the telescope to her eye and squinted through the early-morning mist. Dawn had broken, but the November sun had not yet risen over Massachusetts Bay, and the air was bitterly cold, a low cloud of gray fog lying over the water. Wrapped in a horse blanket, Poe huddled by her side, shivering with the chill, arms wrapped around his body, hands tucked deep in his armpits.

"Do you not feel the cold, Miss Dare?"

"I spent my childhood in a cold, damp climate. This is positively balmy for me." She moved the telescope, focusing on the small rowing boat approaching the *Grampus*. "Ah, the captain is now on deck. He's spotted Tempest approaching," she reported.

In the air, the suggestion of voices echoed across the waters.

"German," Virginia said. "But an old accent, one I have not heard in a very long time." She tilted her head to one side, listening. "Tempest is climbing aboard the *Grampus*," she reported. "He is holding up the newspaper and handing

Pfeifer the reference I wrote. The captain is reading it. Tempest is pointing back toward the quay. Pfeifer's nodding; he's handing over a purse. I think we may have a deal."

Poe heard something change in Dare's voice and pushed away from the wall he was leaning against. "What's wrong?"

Virginia adjusted focus on the telescope. "This captain, this Pfeifer . . . there is something about him. Something familiar."

"You've seen him before?"

"Not him personally. But something like him."

"You said 'thing' rather than 'one.' Some*thing*, not some-*one*."

Virginia closed the telescope with a snap. "Yes, I did."

Dare and Poe watched as the captain turned away and disappeared belowdecks. Tempest climbed down into the small boat and began to row back toward the quayside.

"I have a question," Poe said finally.

"Only one?"

"You believe there is something dangerous aboard the ship. These vampires."

"I do."

"So why are we risking bringing them ashore? Why not just burn the ship in the harbor?"

"I did consider it," Virginia admitted, surprising him. "I have discovered that boats, by their very nature, are notoriously hard to burn."

Poe attempted a laugh. "Why, Miss Dare, you make it sound as if you'd burned boats before."

"More than one. Also, as soon as the fire started, every boat—large and small—would race to its aid. A fire would in all probability awaken whatever sleeps in the coffins. All we would have done is delivered a mass of humanity. Brought dinner to them, as it were."

A figure moved in the alleyway behind them. Poe whirled around, a huge .69-caliber, single-shot percussion pistol appearing in his hand. "Show yourself."

"You are full of surprises, Mr. Poe," Tempest said, stepping out of the shadows. "I didn't know you carried a gun."

"Normally I do not, but I thought it might be useful today. I only have lead shot; I've no idea where to find silver bullets."

"Silver bullets are only effective against the Torc Madra, the werewolves," Virginia said. She turned to Tempest. "Pfeifer employed you?"

"He did. I believe your reference swayed him. He asked me several questions about your glowing letter and about you."

"Me?"

"He was quite specific. Wanted to know how long I'd known you, if you were a native of Boston, your age, your marital status."

"And what did you tell him?"

"I lied. I told him you'd lived here all your life, that you were a widow of around eighty years, and that I'd been working odd jobs for your family for most of my adult life when I'd not been at sea. He seemed satisfied with that, said he knew some of the Dare family and wondered if you were related."

"You did well, Tempest."

"What happens now?" Poe asked.

Tempest produced a leather purse, which clinked as he hefted it. "Captain Pfeifer gave me some money for expenses. I'll have to hire some dockers to help me, then find a skiff or a larger vessel to take the containers off the boat. He wants a guard on the quay to watch over them. I was thinking you could do that."

Poe nodded.

"Then, when all thirteen have been unloaded, we can load the wagon. Only then will Pfeifer reveal our destination."

Virginia turned to scan the boat again with the telescope. "How long will it take you to unload?"

"We'll have to lug each container up from the hold, carefully load it into the smaller boat, and then row back over here and unload onto the quayside. Then we'll row back out to the *Grampus* and begin the process all over again. That's at least forty-five minutes per container. Longer, as the day goes on and we get tired. Eight, maybe ten hours total. Bringing us into the late afternoon or early evening. Then I have to hire the wagon and horses. I'll need a four- or six-horse team to haul the weight of the thirteen boxes. By the time we're finished loading the wagon, it will be full night." He looked at Virginia. "Will he want to take to the roads, then, do you think?"

"Unlikely. If we start out at night, we'll arrive close to dawn. If we're correct in our supposition and he's heading south to Hockomock Swamp, I'm guessing he'll want to arrive there as night is falling." She straightened and smoothed down her rumpled coat. "How long will it take to get to the swamp from here?"

"I'll not push the horses, because once we deliver the load, I think we should turn around and head straight back. I'll keep the horses to a walk, so we'll cover say five miles an hour. That's at least six hours on the road."

Virginia nodded. "Tempest, you have your work cut out for you today. Poe, get a couple of hours' sleep—you look exhausted—and then return here so you can 'guard' the boxes as Tempest brings them ashore. Bring your pistol and plenty of shot for it. I will return to the house and change into some traveling clothes in anticipation of an early start in the morning. If there is any alteration in the plan, Edgar, you will come and inform me. If I do not hear from you, I will assume we're starting at dawn, or by sunrise at the very latest. You'll not see me, but I will be with you every step of the way."

7

Poe spent the day standing on the quayside, guarding the slowly growing pile of boxes. He had intended to make notes about each box as it arrived, but he stopped by the time Tempest had brought the third box ashore. All the boxes were identical, anonymously ordinary rectangles of plain, untreated wood leaking sap in sticky wounds, and spiky with splinters. When the boatswain and his workers heaved them ashore, they shed crumbs of black earth. Unwilling to touch the debris, Poe had lowered himself to the ground to smell it. Surprisingly, he thought he could discern a distinctly floral odor, strong enough to cut through the usual dockside stinks.

And every time Tempest brought a box ashore, he left Poe with the same instruction: "Don't be tempted to peer inside."

"Why not?"

"You never know: something might peer out at you," the boatswain said with a wink.

Pfeifer accompanied the fifth box over.

This man is diseased was Poe's first thought as the captain climbed out of the boat onto the quayside. He was tall, wrapped in too many layers of clothing, with the military bearing and the black sword cane exactly as Tempest had described but, close up, Poe observed that while the man's clothing had once been of the highest quality, it was now dirty, fraying at the collars and cuffs. His shoes were unpolished, and the hems of his trousers were stained with rust-colored mud. Or at least what Poe hoped was mud. With a hat pulled down low on his forehead and a thick scarf wrapped around his nose and mouth, only a thin strip of flesh across his eyes was visible. He noted the white skin and wondered if the man was albino, but Pfeifer's eyes did not have the pink tinge of one suffering from albinism. His eyes were in fact so dark they looked black, and the whites were threaded with countless burst blood vessels. The semicircles of visible skin beneath his eyes were puffy and dark.

Pfeifer inspected the boxes and then turned to look Poe up and down. "You are the guard here?" His English was precise, with the same intonation Poe had heard from the native German speakers scattered throughout Massachusetts.

On a sudden impulse, Poe executed a sharp salute. "Yes, sir."

"Ah, a military man?"

"Yes, sir. United States Army, Sergeant Major, Artillery. I recognize an officer when I see one."

"You too have the bearing of an officer," Pfeifer said.

"West Point did their best to make me into officer material. I fear they failed."

"It must be an odd set of circumstances that a man of your breeding and intelligence should end up here, working security on the docks."

"I'm afraid I did not complete my training in West Point. I was court-martialed," Poe said, a hint of pride in his voice.

Pfeifer took a step back. "Court-martialed. That is serious business. Were there crimes?" he snapped. "I cannot have a criminal in my employ."

"My only crimes were that I did not attend classes, or church."

"Hardly seems like a court-martial offense," the man said.

"West Point's rules are quite strict," Poe replied. "Is it not the same in your country? You are clearly an officer and a gentleman."

Pfeifer shook his head. "A man's faith is his own affair. I never knew the religion of the men under my command. Nor did I care." He gestured at the boxes behind him with his cane. "You understand that while these boxes are of no commercial value, they are precious to me. No harm must come to them. No one must interfere with them."

"I understand, sir. Mr. Tempest's instructions were very clear."

"Good. You are armed?"

From beneath his coat Poe produced the big single-shot pistol.

"A French officer's percussion pistol." As Pfeifer leaned forward, a miasma of floral essence wafted around Poe, setting his eyes watering. It was identical to the scent from the black soil. Poe also caught the merest hint of another odor: the tincture of rot and decay. "It looks well cared for."

"Cleaned and oiled every day," Poe lied.

"The sign of a good soldier." Pfeifer turned awkwardly to look at Tempest, who was maneuvering a casket off the boat. "You are to be congratulated, boatswain. You chose wisely with this one."

"I followed your instructions to the letter," Tempest said. "Only the best."

Pfeifer looked back at Poe. "You will accompany Boatswain Tempest tomorrow?"

Poe nodded. "He asked me to guard the boxes to their final destination. Whatever that is," he added. "Mr. Tempest did not tell me where we were going."

"Because I did not tell him," Pfeifer said crisply.

"Perfectly understandable. That is the military way," Poe said. "Less chance of our destination leaking to curious ears."

"Precisely."

"If you will forgive the impudence of a direct question, do you intend to stay around Boston?" Poe asked.

"Why do you ask?" Pfeifer barked.

"As one military man to another, perhaps you might find employment for a man with my particular skill set and training."

"I'm afraid my business will conclude tomorrow night. I doubt I will return to Boston," the captain said shortly.

"Well, if your plans change . . ."

"My plans never change," Pfeifer said quickly, and turned away. He stomped across the quayside, the iron tip of his cane tapping on the stones, and climbed back into the boat.

Tempest sidled up to Poe. "You've irritated the captain," he said with a smile.

"I was trying to wheedle some information out of him. All I got was that his business will conclude tomorrow night and that he will not be returning to Boston."

"So whatever he's up to, tomorrow night is key."

8

Letter from Virginia Dare to Dr. John Dee, encoded in the Angelic script.

> *11th day of November 1833*
>
> *John,* .
>
> *I shall dispense with the usual formalities, inasmuch as time is now of the essence.*
>
> *I am about to embark on what may very well be my final adventure. You have my Last Will and Testament in your possession; I would like to add a few lines to it.*
>
> *A note of explanation might be in order: in the morning I am off in pursuit of what I am convinced is a nest of vampires. These are not the modern, much-debased American vampires; I believe these to be native European Nosferatu. It is a full nest of thirteen, so a master or mistress and twelve acolytes. These do not overly concern me. It is their human—or inhuman—servant who*

*troubles me. Immortal, probably. He is using
the name Pfeifer, which, of course you know,
means piper. As soon as I laid eyes on him, I felt
a connection, the merest hint of recognition. You
should know that one of the men in my employ
informed me that Pfeifer was asking pointed
questions once he learned my name. You have
always taught me that like calls to like.*

*I will be accompanied on my adventure by
Edgar Allan Poe and an experienced seaman
from Africa, Jupiter Dupin Tempest. If I do
not survive, I ask that you make sure they are
properly recompensed. If either of them is also
slain, then seek out their families and ensure that
they want for nothing.*

*I will do my utmost to destroy the vampire
nest and the piper. But if I fail, then I know I can
count on you to avenge me. You want to rule this
world, John. If the vampires or the piper escape
out across America, then within a generation
there will be nothing left for you to rule.*

*If I survive, I will write you again tomorrow
night with a full accounting of my adventure.*

*Your friend,
Virginia Dare*

9

The road out of Boston was little more than a rutted lane lined on either side by winter-stripped trees.

Wrapped in blankets, Poe and Tempest sat side by side on the wagon. Behind them, beneath a waterproof tarp, the thirteen coffins were neatly stacked one on top of the other. Six huge dray horses pulled the wagon at a slow and steady pace, while ahead of them, Pfeifer rode a prancing stallion.

Tempest let the reins hang loose in his hands. The horses were an experienced team and kept to the road without any urging. "Something got into Pfeifer's mount," he said. "I don't understand it. I've ridden that horse myself and he's as docile as they come."

"Maybe he doesn't like Pfeifer."

"I can understand that." The boatswain shuddered. "There is something about him."

Poe nodded. He was scribbling furiously in his stained notebook, keeping a record of everything they passed on the road. He had a small compass open on the page and was watching the twitching needle.

"Are we still heading south toward Hockomock?" Tempest asked.

"This is the road to Quincy." Poe looked at the scrap of map folded into his notebook. "We continue south, through Braintree, then Abingtron, and on toward Bridgewater. I think we're into the swamplands then. I'm not sure, though; I've never been here before." He twisted on the seat to look behind him. "No sign of Miss Dare."

"She did say we wouldn't see her," Tempest reminded him.

"How is that even possible? This is the only road. If she's on horseback, we'd have seen her, and any carriage would be either in front of or behind us. It's not humanly possible to pass us . . ."

"Edgar, I think the mistake you're making is assuming Miss Dare is human."

Poe turned in the seat to look at him.

Tempest stared straight ahead. "I've come across others like her on my travels. People who are more and sometimes less than human. Some, like Miss Dare, choose to fight alongside humanity and make this world a better place, but there are others who use and abuse their powers. I think there is a war going on in the shadows, fought by beings and creatures older than time."

Poe licked suddenly dry lips. "You're suggesting that all we see is but a dream within a dream?"

"I think most of humanity moves through the world

half asleep. People like Miss Dare are the ones who are fully awake."

"Maybe that is why I never could find out anything about her family." He sat upright. "So . . . so, do you think she might be the real, the original Virginia Dare?"

"I have no idea who the original Virginia Dare is or was," Tempest said.

"The first English child born in the Americas, on August 18, 1587. Some weeks later, the entire colony simply disappeared. All that remained was the word 'Croatan' caved into a wooden post. None were ever heard from again. It is one of the great mysteries."

"Doesn't sound like much of a mystery to me. Had these English colonists any experience with the Americans before choosing to settle here?" the boatswain asked.

"I do not think so."

"Where they equipped for life in the new land?"

"I do not believe so."

"Suddenly, the disappearance does not seem like such a great mystery, does it?"

"Oh, leave me my little mysteries and fantasies."

"A writer with your imagination will never be short of mysteries and fantasies," Tempest said. "Wait. Pfeifer is coming back."

The captain reined in the prancing, sweating horse alongside the wagon. "I cannot control this beast," he snapped, anger thickening his accent.

The sweet-sour stink rolling off him was strong, and both men knew what had probably spooked the horse.

"I will ride in the back of the cart," Pfeifer announced. "Also, it will be easier for me to give you directions."

"Of course, sir. You're in command." Tempest slowly pulled the wagon to the side of the road. "We can take a moment to water the horses."

"Can't you make them go any faster?" the captain demanded.

"We're shedding soil from the boxes," Poe said quickly. "If we move any faster, we'll lose even more or even risk rattling a box open."

Tempest reined in the horses and the wagon rolled to a halt. Pfeifer hitched his horse to the back and hauled himself inside. He examined the boxes carefully, muttering in archaic German as he gathered up some of the perfumed black soil and slipped it into his pockets.

Tempest attended to the horses, feeding and watering them in turn, while Poe leaned against the side of the wagon and watched birds spin in the air above a nearby copse.

"Ravens," Pfeifer said, leaning over and following the direction of Poe's gaze.

"No, there are no more ravens in Massachusetts. They were once common, but the early settlers considered them vermin and all but exterminated them. Ravens preferred dense forests, so when they were cleared for farming, it removed their breeding grounds and sanctuaries. The ravens moved on. What you are looking at are crows, and the smaller birds are grackles. It is a shame too; ravens are stately birds."

Pfeifer slapped the wooden sides with the metal end of his walking stick. The sound was like a gunshot. "We need to move. I want to get to the . . . to our destination before it gets too dark."

As Poe was climbing into the front of the cart alongside Tempest, a flicker of movement in the tall grasses on the opposite side of the road caught his attention. He turned. It was nothing—waving grasses shifting in a morning breeze. And then the pattern altered and quivered and Virginia Dare coalesced out of the background. She was dressed in Native American fringed buckskins, which rendered her almost invisible against the waving grass. Her mane of jet-black hair now flowed down her back in two thick ponytails. She saw Poe looking at her, nodded once, stepped back into the grasses, and disappeared.

When Poe turned to Tempest, he found the boatswain looking in the same direction. Tempest gave the merest hint of a nod. He'd also seen her.

"I think it is time I tell you our ultimate destination," Pfeifer said from the wagon.

Both men turned to look at him. He was sitting on top of the largest box, drinking from a metal traveling flask. He'd pulled his scarf low on his chin, revealing the rest of his ghastly pale face. His lips were thin blue lines, and the few teeth in his mouth were rotted black stumps. "We'll follow this road south for much of the day; then we'll be turning westwards. We're going to the Hockomock Swamp." He stopped, perhaps expecting a reaction, and seemed almost disappointed when there was none.

"We'd best be on our way, then," Tempest said, turning back to the horses and flicking the reins.

10

Late in the afternoon, Pfeifer directed them off the main road and deep into the Hockomock Swamp, reading off directions from a scrap of what looked like old tanned leather. The road quickly became a muddy track, barely wide enough to accommodate the wagon. Thick brush rose on either side, scraping at the wooden sides of the cart like fingers on a chalkboard, slapping at the horses, irritating them.

"Is it much farther?" Tempest asked. He gestured to where the horses' hooves were sinking into the mud and the big wagon wheels were churning up thick wet clods. "We're about to run out of road, and if we get stuck, we have no way of turning back."

"We're not turning back," Pfeifer snapped. He pointed with his cane to the twisted stump of a tree directly ahead. "At the rotten lightning-struck oak, we turn left. The track will widen, slope upward, and be firmer underfoot. We will follow that track for a couple of miles. At the end of the trail we will find the remains of an abandoned Wampanoag village. That is our final destination. Once you unload the wagon, you can head back."

Poe glanced up to the heavens. The sun was dipping in the west and the shadows were starting to lengthen. "It's going to be early evening before we're done, and there's no moon. I don't think we should be out on the swamp at night."

Tempest nodded in agreement. "Easy to stray from the trail and get lost."

"It would be hard enough to find our way out during daylight; at night, with no light, it would be well-nigh impossible." Poe twisted on the seat to look back at the captain. "Do I take it that you will not be accompanying us? You said 'you can head back' and not 'we can head back.'"

"I will not be accompanying you; my journey ends here," Pfeifer said. "And if I were you, I would go as soon as you can. You are correct that you do not want to be on the swamp at night. It has an evil reputation."

"But we cannot just leave you here . . . ," Poe began.

"You will unload the boxes, climb back into the wagon, and ride away," Pfeifer snapped. "This is not a suggestion. It is an order."

Poe opened his mouth to respond, but the boatswain spoke first. "Let us make that decision when we've reached our destination and the boxes are unloaded," Tempest said reasonably. "We'll see how much light is left."

"This is not open to discussion," the captain said.

"No, it is not," Tempest agreed. He cracked the reins and the horses lurched forward, the wagon's wheels spinning in the wet earth and sending sticky streams into the back of the cart, spattering Pfeifer with mud. "Did you say we turn left at the oak?" Tempest asked with a smile.

The track was slightly wider than the wagon, a raised isthmus of dry land over turgid swamp water.

"I can see why the Wampanoag liked this place," Poe said. "Easy to defend. A single warrior, two at most, could hold this strip of land against a much larger force."

Tempest nodded. He raised his chin. "Listen."

"I cannot hear anything."

"Exactly. Birdsong disappeared shortly after we started down this track. This is swampland. It should be alive with sounds."

"No insects either," Poe added.

"Well, that is something to be grateful for."

Poe was the first to notice the irregular oval stones set in the ground on either side of the track. Most were lost in the tall grasses and weeds, but a few jutted up, and although they were coated with moss and lichen, it was clear there were glyphs carved into the ancient rocks. He sketched a quick impression of the markings in his notebook and tilted the page toward Tempest. The boatswain glanced at it and then at Poe, who deliberately turned his head toward the nearest stone. Tempest followed his gaze and gave a brief nod.

"Captain Pfeifer, this place we're going to," Poe called, not looking back. "You've been here before?"

"Never. How could I? This is the first time I have visited the Americas," Pfeifer said gruffly.

"But you seem to know this place. You knew about the swamp, knew to turn at the lightning-struck tree, knew this secret path also."

"I am in possession of a chart. I know where I am going. You've seen the stones," he said suddenly.

"Which stones?" Poe asked innocently.

"The ones you sketched and showed to Tempest."

"Oh, those stones. Aren't they interesting? They looked like they are carved with runes. Are they old?"

"Older than you can imagine. They were ancient when the native peoples first walked this land." Pfeifer stopped abruptly, almost as if he realized he was talking too much. But both Poe and Tempest heard, for the first time, a hint of excitement in the man's voice.

"They're growing taller," Poe observed.

The rocks jutting out of the ground on either side of the track were clearly visible now. Irregular slabs of stone, speckled with crystal and mica, etched with wavy lines and curled tracings, a cross between a script and pictograms.

"I've traveled the word, and while I've seen similar, I've never seen writing quite like that," Tempest said.

"It is the script of a lost world," Pfeifer said.

The track wound on for another hour. The deeper they moved into the swamp, the taller the stones became. The script was clearer now, with new symbols appearing on every standing stone. Some were completely bare, while others were carved from top to bottom in markings. Poe covered pages of his notebook with drawings. He tapped a page with his three-inch pencil. "These two designs have the appearance of Egypt about them. And this looks like a Greek tau."

Tempest pointed to one: a single vertical cut with a horizontal line slashed across it, where the ends of the bar dipped down. It looked like a bird in flight. "I've seen symbols not dissimilar to these on stones in Hawaii."

"This is the script from which all languages flowed," Pfeifer said, surprising them. His accent was very strong now. "Once, when the world was very young, there was a vast continent in the middle of the Atlantic. All the races there spoke the same language and wrote with the same script. When the island continent was finally destroyed, the survivors spread out north and east into Europe and through the Mediterranean, and west and south into the Americas and beyond. They brought the gift of writing with them. The original of these marks. I doubt the people who carved these stones knew the meaning of the words."

"Do you?" Poe asked.

"I do," Pfeifer said, then suddenly stood and pointed with his cane. "There! This is our destination."

The trail opened out into a perfectly circular island of dry earth, surrounded by a tall wall of trees and weeds. An enormous flat stone dominated the center of the circle. Twelve etched oblong stones lay flat on the ground, radiating from it as if pointing to numbers on a clock face.

"Thirteen stones," Poe muttered.

"And we have thirteen boxes," Tempest said.

11

Still, unmoving, completely invisible in the tall grasses and dipping trees, Virginia Dare watched Poe and Tempest unload the boxes from the wagon. Pfeifer had taken up a position on the largest stone in the center of the circle and shouted instructions. The two men ignored him.

Virginia had grown up in the wilds. She had been born over two hundred and forty years ago, and had spent most of that time in and around the rich forests of North America and Canada. She knew the sights and sounds, the scents and tastes of the landscape.

And right now, she knew something was terribly wrong with this place.

Everything about it was off. There was no sound. No birds sang, no animals called, no insects buzzed. It smelled of death and decay, when it should have been bursting with rich, loamy life. And the taste from the water droplets that coated her lips was not of fresh rot, but of something long dead and putrid.

Virginia had no idea what the stones were, but she knew they were not natural. Growing up, she'd come across similar columns. The forests of the East Coast were littered with stones etched with Native American pictographs, Viking runes, and Celtic Ogham. Even as a young girl, she had known that there were those which could not be so easily identified, which hinted at an even older history. Later, when she became immortal, her master had told her the true history of the world and about the survivors of the legendary lost island of Danu Talis who had carried learning out into the world and left behind their knowledge carved in stone.

She'd been moving through the tall grasses, running parallel to Pfeifer, when he'd explained about the writing. She knew he was wrong about that also. She squinted at the stone directly in front of her, tracing the white lines, the curls and grooves carved into it. Her eyes followed a waving line into a circle and were drawn into an inner circle. She felt her stomach lurch as a wave of nausea rolled over her. Squeezing her eyes shut, she forced herself to look away. She was beginning to think that the stones might not even be from this world.

Dropping to all fours, Virginia moved silently through the grasses, getting as close as she dared. She didn't think Pfeifer would do anything before all the coffins were out of the wagon, but she wanted to be as close as possible when he made his move. She imagined that move would come when the last coffin had been laid out on the thirteenth slab.

Virginia watched as the two men moved each box onto the circle of carved stones. The coffins were slightly smaller than the blocks. As they were laid down, gritty tendrils of earth leaked from the boxes onto the stone. Virginia distinctly caught the scent of roses, but it was not the heady scent of a new rose, it was the cloying stench of a dead flower in putrid water. In the fading light, she saw the stones momentarily brighten, and the leaking black soil turned to white ash. The woman nodded; there was power in this ancient place. Probably three of the four elemental magics: earth, water, and air also. All it lacked was the magic of fire. It was no surprise that Pfeifer wanted to bring the coffins here.

Poe and Tempest hauled the last of the boxes out of the wagon. Pfeifer had been quite insistent that this box be laid on the center stone. Although this box looked a little smaller than the others, it was clearly the heaviest, and she could see Poe, especially, struggling with the weight. One edge slipped from his grasp as they were maneuvering it over the flat stone, leaving a trail of ragged splinters in the palm of his hand. A corner struck the stone and cracked against it, the sound like a gunshot. Pfeifer raged in German and two other languages. However, with Tempest's help, Poe regained control, and together the two men lowered the last box onto the stone. The stone visibly pulsed with a long, slow heartbeat, and suddenly the air was filled with the crisp tang of burning wood. She squinted: the bottom of the crude box had grown a score of scorch marks.

Pfeifer strode around the perimeter, examining the placement of the boxes, tapping each one with his walking stick. He came so close to Virginia's hiding place that he almost stepped on her. He wanted the box at the nine o'clock position straightened and the box in the two o'clock position to be completely reversed.

Finally satisfied, he checked the time on an enormous gold pocket watch and Virginia saw him turn and glance toward the heavens. She followed his gaze but could not see anything. Only Venus had appeared; no other stars were visible yet.

"You should go now," he said to the two exhausted men. He was walking counterclockwise around the coffins on the white stones, stopping occasionally to trace the glyphs with his stick.

"I do not think that is a good idea," Tempest said. "Much and all as we'd like to leave, we'd be traveling in full night. Mr. Poe would have to walk ahead of the horses with a lamp to light our way. Progress would be painfully slow. And a single misstep could take us off the road into the water."

"You cannot stay here."

"We'll stay out of your way . . . ," Poe began.

"I insist," Pfeifer snapped.

"You can insist as much as you like," Tempest said, keeping his voice calm and reasonable. "We're not heading out into the swamp at night. It's a death sentence."

"So is staying here."

Virginia saw Poe's hand disappear into his coat and reappear with the gun in his hand. "That's sounds remarkably like a threat."

"A warning. A friendly warning. Go before it is too late."

"It is already too late," Tempest said firmly. "We're not going into the swamp at night. It is too dangerous. We're safer here."

"Oh, I can assure you that you are not."

12

Pfeifer pulled the scarf down from around his face, revealing his ghastly white flesh, thin black lips, and rotten teeth. His skin was ashen, mottled tissue drawn so tightly over his face that it resembled a skull. Standing in front of the center stone, he tapped on it three times with his cane. "I knew you would not leave," he said. "But I gave you a choice. And you choose to stay. So what happens next is entirely your own making."

Poe moved to the right, the big pistol in his hand, while Tempest stepped off to the left. He was armed with a short-bladed navy cutlass.

"This is not of our choosing," Poe snapped. "You planned all this. You know that no sensible man would cross the swamp at night. You may have offered us a choice, but you've fixed the odds in your favor." He raised the pistol in both hands and pointed it at Pfeifer. "We are staying here for the night. We'll head out at first light." He tried to keep his voice steady, but it cracked at the end.

"I gave you a choice," Pfeifer muttered, almost to himself. "You choose to stay. So I bear no responsibility for what happens next. Your choice. Your choice. Your choice." He lifted his walking stick and started to unscrew the silver head. "Humans are so predictable."

Poe and Tempest expected to see a sword blade emerge from the black cane. But Pfeifer surprised them by shaking out a long black tube. Pulling the scarf from around his black-bruised neck, he used it to clean the tube before bringing it to his lips and blowing into it. A single shimmering note emerged, pure and clean, indescribably beautiful, rising and falling like a sigh.

And in the gathering gloom, the thirteen stones shivered white light in time with the note.

Pfeifer's black-nailed fingers moved over the flute and he blew a series of whispering notes, each one sounding like an urgent, breathy voice, full of promises and secrets.

Poe pulled back the hammer on the gun. "Stop," he tried to say, but his tongue felt too large in his mouth, and his lips were dry.

Pfeifer played again, a complicated sequence of short, sharp notes, insistent, questioning. The thirteen stones pulsed responses in time with the music.

"Stop." Poe's voice cracked.

Tempest tried to step toward the captain, but it was as if the air around him had thickened. He tried to raise the cutlass, but the short sword now weighed a ton.

"You should have left," Pfeifer said. "But I am so pleased that you did not. It saves me going in search of a meal for our guests." He looked around. "Six horses, two humani.

It should be enough." He played another note. The gun fell from Poe's suddenly nerveless hands, and Tempest's cutlass dropped to the ground, almost impaling his foot. "Before there was language, there was music," Pfeifer said. "And that music came from the stars." He spun the flute in his fingers, twirling it like a baton. It sighed and moaned of its own accord. "And the music of the heavens is the most powerful of all."

As he was speaking the gloomy sky abruptly brightened. To the north and east, specks of light, like tiny stars, blinked into existence.

Pfeifer turned and pointed into the sky with the flute. "Shooting stars. Every year, they come to us from the same spot in the heavens, deep in the constellation of Leo. And every thirty-three years, they are abundant. Tonight, they will be spectacular."

Above their heads, dozens turned to hundreds and then thousands of speckles of fire in the night. Meteors. In the atmosphere, some exploded into firework cascades; others streaked across the night sky in long trails of light.

"Most are simple rocks," Pfeifer shouted, accent thick and guttural. "But not all. Some are more, much more: scattered among the burning stones are gifts from the gods. Fire from heaven, carrying with it the spark of life itself. Fire destroys, but it also creates."

Pfeifer played again, a wild, shrieking tune that turned painful and drove Poe and Pfeifer to their knees. The notes quickly rose above human hearing but still vibrated in the air. The tethered horses whickered and whinnied, desperately trying to get away.

The sky was now afire with the meteor shower. Huge washes of light and color turned night to day. Stones roared out of the night, splashing into the swamp in muddy explosions of stinking steam. A trio of smaller meteors no larger than pebbles punched deep into the ground, scattering incandescent beads everywhere.

Pfeifer danced in time to the music, a manic caper, his coat flapping open to reveal that he wore a bizarre multicolored vest beneath.

"He's drawing them in!" Poe screamed above the screeching music. "Calling down the fire from heaven!"

As Pfeifer played, more and more of the meteors crashed into Hockomock Swamp. Some blazed white-hot, matching the color of the thirteen slabs of stone, which throbbed in a rhythmic heartbeat. A hailstorm of flaming motes blew over the clearing, scattering across the wooden coffins. One by one the boxes started to smolder. A second wash of burning dust settled across the coffins. Dry wood leaked white smoke before suddenly blazing alight, and one by one, the circle of coffins burst into flames. Only the center box remained untouched.

Pfeifer stopped playing as a slender chunk of meteorite roared overhead, detonating into hundreds of colored speckles. They fell in a fiery rainbow over the clearing and onto the untouched wooden box, where they settled in a circular jewel-like pattern, like a huge eye. Gradually the cinders died, making it look as if the eye closed. When the last light disappeared, the white slab beneath stopped beating and the box erupted into a geyser of fire.

And a burning figure stepped out of the flames.

Standing on the pulsing stone, wrapped in smoke, sheathed in cinders, the figure raised its arms to the star-streaked heavens. Shapes moved in the burning coffins, coming to their feet, and twelve figures stepped out of the burning boxes.

13

Letter from Edgar Allan Poe to Dr. John Dee

December 1833

There is still so much that I do not know about that night.

Even now, with the advantage of time and reflection, I find it difficult to shape into words what occurred in that accursed place.

I recall looking to my left and found Tempest on the ground. In the unnatural light from the meteor shower, I could see that he was bleeding from his ears and nose, and that his entire face appeared to be covered with a shining red mask. When I rubbed at my own face, my fingers came away bloody. I realized then that I could not hear clearly. There were sounds, but they were muffled and distant, like voices in another room. All I could hear was the thump-thump-thump of my own tell-tale heart.

*I knew we were in desperate trouble. I knew
we would probably not survive the night.*

*And in that moment all I felt was regret.
Regret not for what I had done and the many
stupid mistakes of my life, but for all the things I
had not yet done. I wanted to be a poet, a writer,
a journalist. I had such stories to tell . . . but then,
I guessed I would never get to tell them. I was sure
that I would die there, in the Hockomock Swamp;
my body would never be found and no one would
ever remember the name of Edgar Allan Poe.
A selfish thought, I know, but the prospect of
imminent death focuses the mind.*

*I rose to my knees. If I was going to die, then
I would try to do so standing on my feet. I saw
Tempest stirring and crawled over to help him
stand. Keeping one another upright, our faces
bloody masks, we turned to look at the thirteen
creatures Pfeifer and the fire from heaven had
brought to life.*

*Vampires: I knew the stories, but these were
nothing like the elegant creatures of legend.
I doubted they had ever even been human.
Looking at them, I knew that here was an old
race, something from the dawn of time. Here
was something which had hunted man. Foul
creatures which had died and now, through some*

combination of eldritch magic, Pfeifer's piping, and the arcane fire of the meteors, had come back to life.

The fire had burned away their hair, leaving them looking like mole rats with huge domed skulls. Their skin was the color of dead fish, and their jaws and cheeks recalled the angles of a rat or a bat. Their nostrils were slits, their eyes were yellow, the color of a bruised lemon, and their mouths were filled with far too many needle-sharp teeth.

The twelve monsters faced the one in the center. He was similar to them, though slightly smaller in stature, and his features were slightly less bestial.

The vampires bowed to him.

Throwing back his arms, scattering sparks and cinders, the creature looked to the star-streaked heavens and howled. At first it was nothing more than noise, a beast screaming in pain and rage, but then I thought I recognized a single sound—a word—repeated again and again. And then all the other creatures took up the word, until it throbbed in the air, filling the night with a cacophony of horrific noise. It was the most terrifying sound I have ever heard. A part of me, a deep primal core, reacted to it, and I knew

without a shadow of a doubt that our ancestors
had known that sound in ages past.

Sturm.

With a shock, I realized I understood that
sound, that word. Was it the monster's name, or
his title or a battle cry, or perhaps it was nothing
more than a noise which my brain interpreted and
overlaid with meaning: Sturm. The German word
for storm.

A whistle cut through the noise, and the
thirteen creatures fell silent.

Pfeifer stepped out of the shadows and took
his place beside the central monster. Black-nailed
fingers danced across the flute, and I realized he
was communicating with them.

And then, as one, thirteen heads turned
to look at Tempest and me. Thirteen mouths
opened, revealing black tongues and needle
teeth. Pfeifer pointed and the creatures launched
themselves at us.

I am not ashamed to say that I closed my eyes.

14

And when I opened them again I was still alive.

Tempest had suggested that Miss Dare was not entirely human. I'd scoffed at him. Today, I knew what he meant.

She stood between us and the charging monsters, a tiny figure in brown buckskins. She dangled what I first thought was a blowpipe, a slender tube etched with curling patterns. When she brought it to her lips, I realized that she too had a flute. She blew into it, and no doubt because of the damage to my ears, I heard nothing. But I felt it, a deep tremble that vibrated up through the soles of my feet into my bones.

The vampires' charge slowed.

I saw Pfeifer blow on his own flute, felt the pain of the sound through my skull, and the creatures lurched forward again, as if they were pushed toward us.

Virginia Dare waited and I saw her fingers dance across her flute. Then she sank into a straight-backed, cross-legged position directly in front of me.

The ratlike vampires descended on us, stinking of smoke and decay, of rotting flesh, old blood, and crushed flowers.

And suddenly the night came alive with monsters.

A ragged thunderbird swooped out of the meteor-filled sky, dug scimitar claws into a one-eyed vampire, lifted it out over the swamp, and dropped it . . . into the maw of an enormous black snake which surged out of the water.

Beasts flowed past me, neither dogs nor wolves, but something in between. Behind them padded a trio of enormous black panthers. Dog and cat swarmed over the creatures in a snarl of fur and teeth. I tried to close my eyes against the carnage, but I could not.

A huge, hairy, bearlike beast, seven feet tall, with glowing red eyes, draped in weeds, rose out of the swamp. Clutching a fallen branch like a club, it batted at the nearest vampire, sending it sailing into the water, where others of the beast's kind pounced on the twisted body, dragging it down beneath the oily surface.

Thick-bodied snakes coiled out of the underbrush, wrapping around the creatures, pulling them to the ground and dragging them away.

And in the middle of all the chaos sat Miss Dare, fingers moving on the flute. I was fearful of Pfeifer, frightened by the ratlike vampire, but in truth, I was terrified by Miss Dare.

What power did she possess to call forth the creatures of the night? Pfeifer had drawn down the fire from heaven and used it to animate thirteen undead vampires. Dare had commanded legions of darkness. Was she any different from Pfeifer?

I saw twelve of the vampires fall to the Hockomock monsters. Sturm alone escaped. He raced past me, almost close enough to touch, pursued by two black panthers and one of the bearlike creatures. No doubt they hunted him to his doom in the swamp.

And then, as quickly as it had begun, it was done. The Hockomock monsters and Pfeifer's vampire were gone, leaving Tempest and myself, Virginia Dare and Pfeifer.

Tens of thousands of shooting stars splashed across the skies, bringing the night to dancing life. The shadows turned Pfeifer's face into a skull, painted his eyes red and his teeth black.

I watched him bring the flute to his lips. Deafened as I was, I still could not hear the sounds. But I felt them: knives of pain slicing into my bones, pressing against my eyes, stabbing into my lungs.

Virginia stood, blowing her own flute. The pain vanished immediately. She advanced on Pfeifer, still playing. And as she moved, the earth beneath her feet sprouted fresh green grass.

Pfeifer's cheeks were full, puffed out as he blew savagely into his flute. The white stone in the center of the circle suddenly cracked, splitting right down the middle.

Virginia started to move clockwise around the circle, still playing. The etched glyphs glowed briefly silver as she passed.

Pfeifer blew again. Another two stones directly in front of him developed spiderwebs of cracks, and when he blew again, the stones crumbled to pebbles.

I watched Virginia Dare as she completed her circle of the stones. Those which remained intact were now flickering in time to her unheard music, the symbols throbbing, leaving dancing afterimages on my eyes. I watched Virginia's face: her eyes were red in the starlight, and she looked at Pfeifer with an expression of loathing. There was something almost inhuman about her in that moment.

She stepped into the circle, standing toe-to-toe with Pfeifer. Her fingers danced across her instrument almost too fast for the eye to follow. In contrast, his movements were clumsy. Her hair shifted, the buckskin fringes on her clothes blew back, and I could feel the energies crawl across my skin like insects, while every hair on my hair stood upright.

Pfeifer suddenly lurched and staggered.

He removed the flute from his mouth and looked down. The ground he was standing on had turned to mud.

Virginia slowly walked around him, counterclockwise, the wooden flute pressed to her lips.

Pfeifer sank, and for a moment, I thought he had fallen to his knees. When I looked closer, I discovered that he had sunk almost up to his thighs in the sticky earth.

And I had no doubt that this was Virginia Dare's work. She was turning the ground to liquid to swallow him up. I saw her lips moving and knew she was talking. I wondered what she had to say to him.

She had moved around behind him, so she did not see his hand sneak into his coat. He pulled it out and there was a flash of silver metal: a six-shot pepperbox pistol.

Perhaps I shouted; I do not know. I threw myself to the ground, rolled, scooped up my own fallen pistol, and fired.

The recoil almost broke my wrist. When the plume of black smoke cleared, Pfeifer had vanished and the ground where he'd been standing was a bubbling morass of viscous mud. I watched Virginia nudge Pfeifer's pistol into the muck, where it disappeared without a sound. She took a longer moment looking at his fallen flute, then suddenly stamped on it, snapping it in two, and kicked both pieces into the mud.

She looked at me and smiled and, in that moment, became human again.

15

"I am delighted to see you are fully recovered, Mr. Poe."

"Thanks to you."

Virginia Dare and Edgar Allan Poe were sitting on either side of a blazing fire in Dare's drawing room. November had given way to December, and Boston was eerily silent, coated with a thick mantle of snow.

Virginia was dressed as she had been when Poe had first seen her: in a man's morning suit. He was wearing the same clothes he'd worn when he'd come to see her three weeks previously, and for a single instant, he found himself wondering if perhaps the entire adventure had been nothing more than a fever dream. Only the scrapes and bruises on his hands and an incessant ringing in his ears suggested it had been real.

"And Monsieur Tempest?" she asked.

"In more or less good health. He still cannot hear out of one ear and is prone to bouts of dizziness. He sends his regards and thanks you—as do I—for your most generous payment. He said he will come and see you as soon as he can walk in a straight line."

"He is a good man," she said. "I am sure I will have some work for him."

"I've spent a lot of time with him over the past few weeks," Poe said. "I am thinking I will write a story about him. Might even name the character in his honor."

"I do hope I will not appear in your stories, Mr. Poe?" Although the question was asked with a smile, there was no doubt it was a warning.

"I will never use your name," Poe promised, then leaned forward. "Thank you for seeing me on such short notice. I came to ask you about . . . about that night."

"You were there," she said. "You saw what happened."

"But what happened? Bits I know are real . . . but there are other parts I am not so sure about. I know, for example, that the shooting stars were real."

Virginia nodded. "They were real. I read that at one point there were seventy-two thousand meteors per hour falling to the earth."

"Not all were magical, though, were they?"

"Nothing more than space dust. Rocks. Chunks of ice. But a handful were remarkable. Even I am not sure how or why they were different. They were clearly imbued with some ancient energy or life force. I have written to Dr. Dee, and he is intrigued enough to look into the matter for me. If there is an answer, then he will find it."

"And the vampires? They looked like no vampire I have ever read about."

"These are not the pretty ones. These were Nosophoros of the Nosferatu clan. An old race, which rose after the fall of Danu Talis."

"Are they dead?"

"The Hockomock creatures destroyed all but the leader. He fled into the swamp. He may very well be dead—again—but if not, he'll turn up sooner or later and come to my attention. He'll not escape."

"And those swamp monsters?"

"As I suspected, the Hockomock Swamp is at the nexus of a handful of ley lines. Creatures and beings from a dozen nearby Shadowrealms shift between worlds. They came when I called them; you saw that they have as much use for the blood drinkers as we do."

"Riding into that place, I thought Hockomock Swamp would be our doom. It was our savior. You were our savior."

"As you were mine, Mr. Poe. I saw what you did."

Poe's cheeks flushed. "Tempest tells me I missed."

"You did. But it startled Pfeifer and allowed me to complete my mission."

"And your mission was killing him."

"I swore an oath I would put him in the ground. And I did."

"This Pfeifer—did you know him, Miss Dare?"

"I'd never met him, but I have long known of him."

"When I saw you both had flutes, I thought there might be a connection."

"Similar magic," Dare admitted. "But put to different uses."

"Who was he?"

"A monster," Dare answered. "Perhaps even worse than the vampires. They have little control over their appetites. They view humans as cattle and food. Pfeifer was different. Once he was human, but the power of the flute corrupted him. Over five hundred years ago, in 1284, he used his flute to enchant one hundred and thirty children, draw them away from their homes and families, and lock them up in a nearby hillside. None of the children were ever seen again."

Poe frowned. There was something familiar about the story.

Virginia Dare nodded. "You know the tale. The town he kidnapped the children from was called Hamelin. The locals called Pfeifer the Pied Piper."

16

Letter from Virginia Dare to Dr. John Dee, encoded in the Angelic script.

24th day of December 1833

Dear John,

We both know the real truth about Christmas, so I will not insult you by wishing you a merry anything. In truth, I am about to ruin whatever holiday cheer you may have.

Two days ago, Poe came to me with reports of blood-drained cows and a mysterious sleeping sickness infecting people in and around Hockomock Swamp. I sent a raven south to the swamp and spent the day lying in my bed, watching through its eyes. (Raven sight really is the most nauseating work; you must come up with an alternative.)

The hole I buried Pfeifer in was exposed. There is no sign of a body. I know he was dead when I put him in the ground, and there was no way he could have crawled out by himself. And he was buried too deep for any beast to have dug him up.

You know I have no gift for foresight, but instinct and intuition tell me that Sturm has dug up the Pied Piper and brought him back to life.

Your (concerned) friend,
Virginia Dare

NICHOLAS
AND THE KRAMPUS

1945

My dearest Virginia,

Wishing you a belated Happy Christmas and the
very best for the coming year.

Apparently, the holiday of December 1945
is already being called the Greatest Christmas
Celebration. And why not? The war is over, there
is the promise of lasting peace, and the troops
are coming home. A couple of months ago, the
US military started a program called Operation
Magic Carpet, designed to get as many of their
eight million service men and women home
in time for Christmas. Over twenty thousand
now return every day, and more are on the way.
Everyone wants to help the war heroes reach
their homes, no matter where they are, and I have
heard stories of ordinary people driving the men

and women hundreds of miles just to reunite them with their families. The roads out of every port city are experiencing the worst traffic jams in living memory.

What a time to be alive!

I am over two hundred years older than you, and even though we have lived so long and seen so much, the last few years have been difficult. All of us—human and nonhuman alike—did our bit to bring this terrible war to a conclusion. Scathach's stories could fill volumes, and Joan and Saint-Germain were instrumental in the liberation of Paris. We have not heard from Aoife since the Battle of Stalingrad, but Scathach assures me that her sister is alive. Will Shakespeare has promised to write about his experiences with Palamedes in MI6 during the Blitz, but I doubt he will do it. He will claim that his reticence has to do with the Official Secrets Act, but in truth, I think he has writer's block. Palamedes tells me that Will has been working on Love Labor's Won for centuries.

I heard whispers about a Miss Dare in the Pacific and guessed they referred to you, and I have it on good authority that you were in Tibet during the Nazi expedition there in 1939. Next time we meet, we will share stories.

I am sorry Nicholas and I missed you in Nevada. We had to leave in rather a hurry, as you can imagine, and I know that the army and the FBI are still looking for us. I am not too concerned; we change identities as easily as other people change clothes.

I trust you are well and fully recovered from your adventure in the Grand Canyon. I am so glad you took my advice and brought Billy with you. All I can add is a warning to stay away from archaeologists: they are too much trouble! (Or perhaps it is just the archaeologists you associate with.)

Since your little run-in with the Rattenfänger, I know you like to keep up with the latest mythological immigrants to your land. Toward the middle and end of the nineteenth century, the nonhumans could mingle unnoticed with the waves of immigrants and slip into the country. Now I am afraid that the war in Europe has displaced those immortals and the were-clans who choose to remain on their native soil. I understand it is the same in the Far East. With their homelands in ruins, the immortals have been forced to travel farther afield. It was inevitable that some would come to America. No doubt they believed that with so many distracted by the war, their efforts would go unnoticed.

They were wrong, of course.

Over the centuries, I have come to know most

of the protectors of humanity, those of you who stand against the Dark. What would the humans say, do you think, if they knew that a legion of immortal humans, Next Generation, and a few Elders protected them against the ever-present danger of the return of the Dark Elders or the Earthlords?

One of the truths Nicholas and I have discovered—and one you know all too well—is that at the heart of every legend, there is a grain of truth.

Well, this Christmas, December 25, 1945, three legends came to New York.

One of them was Nicholas—and for once, I am not talking about my husband. The others were Frau Perchta and her companion, the loathsome Krampus.

Perenelle Flamel
1 January 1946
Hell's Kitchen
New York, New York

PS: Rather than send you a Christmas card, I thought the following pages from my diary might be of interest! (Use the da Vinci cipher to decode them.)

1

Monday, 24 December 1945
Christmas Eve

And there it was again!

An odd odor on the chilly air, something distinctly alien to New York streets. I had caught a hint of it earlier, when I stepped off the subway train in the Herald Square station. A musky odor, completely out of place among the scents of hot metal, smoke, and a mass of heaving—and often unwashed—humanity.

The same instinct that has kept me alive for centuries sounded an alarm in the back of my mind.

It might have been nothing—some natural scent I'd not encountered before. Perhaps someone in the crowd was carrying a food I'd never experienced. It was Christmas Eve—the first Christmas since the end of the war—and a madness had gripped the people. Soldiers, sailors, and airmen were coming home. Everyone was out looking for whatever meat and vegetables they could find for their Christmas Day feast. Looking around, I could see a dozen nationalities in the crowd. Was one of them carrying some unusual herbs or spices?

I allowed the crowds to push me along toward the stairs that led up to Herald Square.

I had spent the morning working with the ladies in the Salvation Army, wrapping donated presents for servicemen and servicewomen recuperating in the local hospitals who would not make it home to spend Christmas with their families. I was dressed in a plain blue two-piece utility suit with an A-line skirt, my distinctive white-streaked hair tucked up under a hat of the same color. It had been snowing on and off over the past week, and I was wearing my heavy gray wool wraparound coat, which I'd made from old blankets. As I slipped in alongside a group of similarly dressed women, I tugged the belt open and allowed the coat to hang loose, giving myself easy access to the secret pocket I'd sewn into the coat's satin lining.

The women pushed up the stairs and I kept pace with them, being careful not to touch anyone. Halfway up, I caught just the faintest hint of the odor again: it was definitely a musk, and it triggered a memory. I had smelled this before, and even without turning my head, I knew it was coming from behind me. I was being followed.

At the top of the stairs, I turned left in Herald Square toward Gimbel's, the huge department store. The streets were crowded, and Gimbel's windows were bright with Christmas gifts, toys, and decorations. The pavement beneath the red awnings was heaving with people staring through the glass, with more queued to get into the store. I stopped before a window filled with the latest kitchen gadgets. I focused on a $2.95 Pyrex coffee percolator, which made six cups of coffee, and allowed my eyes to adjust.

Using the glass as a mirror, I quickly scanned the crowd behind me. After half a millennia of running, I knew what to look for.

Ah, there you are.

I found the tail almost immediately. A surprisingly tall woman was standing on the opposite side of the street. She had a vaguely military bearing and was wearing trousers beneath a double-breasted wool trench coat. She had her hands stuffed deep in the slit pockets, and I noted that, like mine, her belt hung loose. It was hard to make out her features—she was wearing a Homburg hat with a net that came down over her eyes. While everyone else on the street was watching the crowd or staring into the windows, her eyes were fixed on me.

I looked into Gimbel's window again, weighing my options. I had no idea who the woman was; Nicholas and I have made many enemies over the course of our lives. We have lived long enough to see allies become enemies, and in the preceding few years, we had worked for—and then against—the British and the Americans. We had successfully prevented German scientists from developing the atomic bomb, and for the past eighteen months we had been trying to sabotage the development of the American atomic bomb. We'd failed, of course. We were there, in Alamogordo, when the first bomb was detonated. We were both terrified that the explosion would rip a hole in the fabric of space and create an opening to a Shadowrealm. Thankfully, it didn't, but our desperation had made us sloppy, and the American military became suspicious. We managed to get out just before they came for us.

The wartime intelligence service, the OSS, had only recently been dissolved, but I wondered if the woman was one of their agents. If she was, then it was highly unlikely that she was working alone, which probably meant that I had at least one more watcher.

I moved on to the next window: a complete kitchen, showing all the latest mod cons and linoleum patterns.

In the glass, I watched the woman across the street shift to keep me in sight. So she was definitely following me; it was not my imagination. The musky odor which had first alerted me was stronger now. It must be coming from the woman. That immediately suggested she was nonhuman . . . and that opened up a world of possibilities, none of which were pleasant.

Closing my eyes, I focused on the scents surrounding me, identifying and then eliminating wet clothes and unwashed humani, as well as the parcels they carried: freshly baked bread and stale fish, overripe fruit and raw meat. Homemade perfumes and tobacco mingled with horse manure, hot metal, and oil from horses, cars, and belching trucks crowding the street.

When I had put a name to all the smells, I was left with not one, not two, but three distinctive and unnatural signatures swirling on the New York air. They did not belong in the city: these were animal odors, combining to form a rich forest musk.

I was jostled by the crowd and opened my eyes in time to notice a second woman at the end of the street. She was as tall as the first woman, and dressed in an almost identical costume. But I had smelled three odors. . . .

Looking up, I suddenly saw a tall, hatchet-faced woman bearing down on me. For a single instant her face flickered, planes and angles shifting, revealing something bestial, a hint of fur and slablike teeth.

I knew then that these were not humani spies—these were shape-changers.

2

Ignoring the lines—and the disapproving shouts—I pushed my way into Gimbel's.

The huge department store was heaving with people, and the noise was incredible, a cacophony of voices in a dozen languages, along with the pinging of cash registers. I knew Gimbel's well—it was one of my favorite places, though Nicholas hated it. The store was vast, filling twenty-seven acres, and had everything—including a restaurant and a bank—and I was counting on the fact that my pursuers would not know its countless entrances and exits. I could cut straight through the store and out onto the opposite side of the square. I needed to get to Nicholas and let him know that we were being hunted by one of the Torc clans. I was unsure of which one: wolf, dog, and boar immediately came to mind. The Torc were usually neutral, but some hired themselves out as trackers and hunters. The real question was: Who was employing them?

I deliberately did not look behind me, but I used every reflective surface I passed to see if I was being followed. I could no longer smell the creatures' musk. The stink of massed

356

humani, plus Gimbel's vast array of goods, filled the cavern-
ous interior of the store with a thick fog of odors.

I took an elevator to the third floor, got out, and stepped
into the next elevator going down. I deliberately moved
through the perfume department, allowing the cloying scents
to attach themselves to my clothing, disguising my own
scent. In the candy department, I lingered before a display of
freshly made chocolates. The air was thick with the aromas
of sugar and cocoa.

I knew I could take the elevator to the underground
passageway that led to Penn Station, but I was sure this hunting pack would have someone stationed below. I wondered
how long they had been following me and where they had
picked up on my scent. I would worry about that later. Right
now I needed to get to Nicholas. Then we'd need to make a
decision. Should we stay and fight, or should we run? We still
had not really unpacked since we'd escaped from New Mex-
ico, so it would only take us ten or fifteen minutes to shove
everything into a bag and get on the road again. But to be
honest, I was tired of running. I was going to suggest to my
husband that we grab one of the were-creatures and find out
who was employing them. We could make a decision then.

I headed back downstairs, confident that the thick stew of
Gimbel's scents would completely disguise my own unique
signature.

I was guessing that my pursuers would be watching the
entrances. But Gimbel's had a vast number of doors, leading
out to Herald Square and also to the subway station. They

could not be watching all of them, and I had only smelled three scents.

Doubling back the way I had come in, I pushed against the crowd and stepped out into Herald Square through the same door I'd come in thirty minutes earlier. The blast of chill December air cleared my sinuses, and in the same instant, I caught the musky odor and was aware of movement on either side of me. Iron-hard grips locked onto my elbows and practically lifted me off the ground.

Without saying a word, the two tall women half dragged, half carried me across Broadway into the warren of side streets behind West Thirty-Fifth, before finally turning into a narrow, filth-piled alleyway, where the third were-creature was waiting for us. This was the hatchet-faced woman I had seen earlier. When she looked at me, she deliberately allowed a partial transformation to flicker across her face, revealing huge eyes and a soft nose, flat fur, and blunt teeth. For the briefest of moments, there were hints of antlers on either side of her skull.

I knew what she and her companions were then: Torc Fianna. Were-deer. The rarest and most dangerous of the were-clans.

3

"Did you think you could run from us, Madame Perenelle?"

There was a hint of Eastern Europe to her accent, or perhaps even farther north, Sweden or Russia.

The two creatures on either side released me, dropping me staggering to the ground. I glanced at them. I doubted they were related, but they looked alike enough to be sisters. Now that I knew what they were, I could see the inhuman look in their eyes and cheeks. The last time I had encountered the Torc Fianna, they had been in the service of the Elder Artemis, and that had not ended well.

"Did you think you were going to lose us amongst the stench of humani in their temple to commerce?"

"The thought had crossed my mind," I answered, and moved toward the speaker, putting as much distance as I could between myself and the two figures flanking me.

"We have your scent now, Madame Perenelle. You cannot disguise it with perfumes or chocolates. The humani possess a mere five million sense receptors; deer have two hundred ninety-seven million. We could track you across the world."

Now that I was close, I could tell that the woman stood at least six feet tall. Her hair was cropped close to her skull, emphasizing her huge brown eyes. Her musk was undeniable: the rich odor of a deer. She was dressed like her two companions, in trousers and a double-breasted coat, but she was leaning both hands on a thick walking stick, which I was sure she did not need.

"You are Torc Fianna," I said.

"You know us."

"I have encountered your race before," I answered. "I am not your enemy."

"We have heard of you, Perenelle Flamel, and of your husband, the Alchemyst, Nicholas."

I took another step forward. It was clear that the creature was struggling to hold her human shape. Fur was appearing and disappearing on her cheeks, and I watched the bones in her hands thicken, welding her fingers into a hoof as she tried to clutch the walking stick. She had clearly spent a long time in this human form. Most of the were can transform only for short periods, the timing usually triggered by phases of the moon. The last full moon had been on the eighteenth, and the next would not occur until the seventeenth of January; the fact that the Torc Fianna were holding their human forms between full-moon phases was testament to their incredible strength of will.

"Well, you have found me. What do you want?" I moved slightly to one side, allowing my coat to gape open. In the secret pocket sewn into the lining, I carried a silver-handled whip. The thong was woven together from snakes pulled from the Medusa's hair.

"You will come with us," the Torc Fianna leader said.

"I do not think so," I said.

"This is not a request." The were-deer bared her teeth in what she probably thought was a human smile. She raised her stick and pointed behind me. "And if you touch the whip in your pocket, my sisters will drive arrows into your thighs. Not fatal, but very painful, I can assure you."

I glanced at the two Torc Fianna behind me. They were both holding elegant crossbow pistols, aimed at my legs.

"Do you think you can get to your whip before my sisters dart you?"

None of the Torc clans I had encountered used modern firearms. Most preferred the traditional weapons of swords and spears. The Torc Arzh Gell, the were-bears, used axes and war hammers. The Torc Fianna, however, were archers, and their skill with bow and crossbow was legendary. I raised my hands, signaling a truce.

The senior were-deer stepped closer, enveloping me in her rich odor. "We know you are a skilled sorceress, Madame Flamel. I am sure you could unleash myriad spells, but you should know that we already have your husband, and if you wish to see him again, you will come with us."

I worked hard to keep my face expressionless, but

something must have shown in my eyes, because the Torc Fianna took a step back. "He is unharmed," she said hastily.

"He had better be. If you are lying to me, there is no place in this world, or on any Shadowrealm, where you can hide," I promised her. "Now. Take me to Nicholas."

4

Not another word was spoken as we moved across New York City.

The short-haired woman walked on my right side, while her two companions took up the rear. My mind was whirling in confusion, but I was not fearful. I was born in the year 1320, and one of the lessons I learned early is that humans spent a lot of time worrying about things that might never happen. I was confident that I could escape these three easily enough. I was the seventh daughter of a seventh daughter, and my natural powers had been honed by centuries of training and study with some of the most powerful immortals and Elders, including Circe and Medea. I knew some Babylonian spells that could turn these creatures to grains of sand, and a particularly nasty Nubian incantation designed to reduce them to assorted liquids. I had my whip in my coat pocket, and I was confident I could pull it out and strike all three were-deer before they could react. A single touch would turn them to stone. All that prevented me from acting was knowing that they had snatched Nicholas. Once I knew he was safe and unharmed, I would allow them to experience the powers of the Sorceress. What really troubled me was the question of who had employed the Torc Fianna to track and find us, and then go to the trouble of kidnapping us in broad daylight. We had enemies aplenty, but most of them would have been happy to see us dead. I briefly wondered if it might be John Dee again. The English Magician was still in search of the Codex, the extraordinary compendium of knowledge that included the spell that kept us alive. But Dee was not subtle; he had burned cities to the ground, unleashed powers that caused earthquakes and set volcanoes to erupt. I doubted he would come after us with Torc Fianna; he'd use something cruder, like Golems.

We kept away from busy thoroughfares, moving north-ward, heading toward the docks. Streets started to get nar-rower, buildings poorer, cobbles and pavement more broken. New York was a relatively new city that, like most cities, had its share of slums. Slowly but surely, they were being cleared, but I knew where we were going: the area known as Hell's Kitchen, one of the poorest and roughest parts of the me-tropolis.

There were no brightly lit shops, and the people had no time to linger. Half a dozen blocks away, the streets were bright with Christmas, but here, there were few signs that the holiday was upon us. Most of the people hurrying past were wearing mismatched bundles of clothes. The accents had changed also: outside Gimbel's, they'd been mostly English, but now they were Irish, German, and Italian, and while the

Irish spoke accented English, the Germans and Italians used their native tongues.

We turned down an alleyway that looked like it had not changed in two hundred years. Slimy walls speckled with tattered flyers pressed close together, and gutters were heaped with stinking rubbish. Rats, some as big as cats, perched on discarded boxes and watched us.

We must have made for a strange sight as we moved through the alleys and crossed open courtyards: four well-dressed women, walking in grim silence. I was sure we were being watched; no doubt people took us for members of the Salvation Army or one of the hundreds of other church groups who worked in the tenements.

What little daylight remained quickly faded to gray gloom. Huge snowflakes spiraled down, but rather than disguising the dirt and squalor, the soft whiteness only served to emphasize it. I resolved that when—no, if—Nicholas and I concluded this adventure, we would return to Hell's Kitchen and use some of our vast wealth to improve conditions here.

We turned into an alley so narrow we were forced to march in single file. I caught a peculiar mixture of scents—unwashed humani, tobacco, oil, boiled cabbage—just before two men stepped into the alley's opening. Wearing ill-fitting bowler hats, stained overalls, jeans, jackets, and battered army boots, they looked like they worked the docks. And they were carrying chopped-down baseball bats.

They were both big men, but it was the smaller of the two

who stepped forward and stretched out his right hand, holding his bat. "Ladies, ladies, ladies. This is a dangerous part of the city for those like yourselves to be wandering so late in the day. . . ."

The Torc Fianna in front of me did not even slow down. The walking stick she carried flashed out, catching the bat and snapping it in two. Both pieces ricocheted off a wall and bounced back onto the startled man. Then she jabbed with the blunt end of the stick. It caught the man in the center of the chest, propelling him back into his companion. They both went down in an untidy tangle of limbs. The Torc Fianna simply walked right over them. The big one reached out to catch my leg as I passed, but one of the were-deer behind me stomped on his wrist. I might have heard bone snap.

Another alleyway brought us to a dead end. A mountain of filth was piled high against the rear wall, and I could see strands of barbed wire and sparkling shards of glass set on the top. Looking over my shoulder, I realized that the two Torc Fianna who had been following me had retreated to the mouth of the alleyway and taken up position on either side. As I watched, one flickered in and out of her human-deer aspect.

I turned back just as the senior Torc Fianna tapped on the wall with her metal-tipped stick. The movements were lightning quick, the musical plinking clearly a code. And even though I'd been expecting it, I was startled when the outline of an arched doorway appeared in the wall.

The moment the door solidified into metal-riveted

decorated wood, it was opened by an elderly woman dressed in the black bonnet and long black dress of the previous century. Her face had collapsed in on itself and was such a mass of wrinkles that it was impossible to discern an expression. It took me a moment before I realized that her dramatically hooked nose was made of metal. Her eyes were a vivid sky-blue. They stared at me with such intensity that I actually felt my aura flare, and wisps of white smoke curled off my fingertips.

I looked over the woman's shoulder and saw there was a second door behind her. Carved from a rich golden wood, it was arched and decorated with incredibly detailed twisting holly and mistletoe.

"You are the Sorceress, Perenelle Delamere."

It was a statement rather than a question, and the voice did not match the body; it belonged to a young girl. She spoke the ancient Breton dialect of my youth. I did not bother to answer. Clearly this was no human, and I did not think she was an immortal, either. Who, then? An Elder, probably, and one I had not encountered before.

In my experience, the reclusive ones are those you definitely do not wish to meet.

The woman stood back. "Enter freely and of your own will."

I did not cross the threshold. "You know me, you know my name." I started in Breton, slipped into French, and finished in English. "There is power in knowing a person's name. Will you share yours with me?"

"You will not know me by my original name."

"I might." I thought I detected something like amusement in the woman's childlike voice.

"I have many names. Once, when the humani were young and I had power and worshipers, I was called Berchta."

I shook my head. She was right: I had no idea who she was.

The old woman giggled in her little-girl voice. "Now I am known as Frau Perchta."

I knew who she was then, and felt the cold wash of fear slide into the pit of my stomach. I was in serious trouble! The old woman looked at me with her bright blue eyes, and then, from deep within her long black dress, she produced a thick scroll of paper and allowed it to unfurl. "Are you on my naughty list, I wonder . . . ?"

5

"Will you bring Madame Perenelle in? Don't leave her freezing on the doorstep." A deep male voice came from behind the second door. "And stop teasing her, Holle."

The old woman grimaced—or it might have been a smile—and respooled her paper. It was covered in what looked like runes. "I will check this later."

I bowed to the old woman and stepped over the threshold. Immediately, the three Torc Fianna darted into the hallway, and Frau Perchta closed the door, leaving us in a thick darkness.

Then the ornate second door opened, flooding the small dark hall with bright light. I squeezed my eyes shut, but too late: tears flowed down my face, and I was momentarily blind.

Feather-soft fingers closed around my left hand, tugging me forward, and I moved from cold to warmth.

I blinked and blinked again, but the world ahead of me was a shimmering mess of liquid colors. I heard the muted crackle of fire and smelled the rich pine of logs. The comforting aroma of freshly baked bread made my stomach rumble.

I knew what had happened: we'd stepped through a ley-gate into a Shadowrealm. But I knew the location of all the North American leygates. And the nearest New York gate was on Bedloe's Island, which held the Statue of Liberty; certainly not here, deep in Hell's Kitchen. Yet over the centuries, Nicholas and I had encountered a handful of Elders—and Marethyu—who had the ability to create their own gates.

A shadow moved before my watering eyes, and I smelled that rich mint I had first breathed nearly six hundred years ago: my husband, Nicholas. And then his arms were around me, his breath soft against my ear. "I'm fine," he said, answering the question I was about to ask. "But I'm not sure we're safe. Something is off here." He dabbed at my eyelids with a handkerchief that smelled of motor oil.

I opened my eyes.

I have lived a long time, and have traveled the length and breadth of this world. I have walked some of the myriad Otherworlds that border our Earth and have seen wonders and terrors in equal measure. So since I had encountered Torc Fianna and Frau Perchta in this one day, I'd been expecting something spectacular.

I was disappointed. The place was surprisingly ordinary.

I had stepped through from New York's bitterly cold Hell's Kitchen into a brightly lit, almost uncomfortably warm log cabin. The place was huge. The wooden floor was stained and warped with age, and there was a high arched ceiling, spanned by exposed beams. Directly ahead of me, a log fire blazed in an enormous grate. The wall to my left was filled with leather-bound books of all sizes, while the mismatched shelves covering the right-hand wall were filled to overflowing with snow globes.

A fir tree grew directly out of the floor in one corner of the room. The tip of every outstretched branch held a thin, lighted candle. I wondered if it was an illusion, because I could see no strands of dripping wax.

Standing in front of the fire was a small dark-skinned man, wearing what looked like a monk's brown robe, belted with a white cord.

Nicholas caught my hand and led me forward. "Come and meet our host," he said in archaic French. He always slipped into that dialect when he was nervous or excited.

I was aware of movement beside me and turned in time to see Frau Perchta shimmer into black smoke, which swirled into grayness before finally coalescing into a gaseous egg shape. A slender, pale-skinned, white-haired girl stepped out of the smoke. When she turned to look at me, I saw that her eyes were still bright blue. Whereas before, she had been dressed all in black, now she was in a short white shift dress, which revealed that her left thigh was thickly covered in white feathers and the leg below was coal-black and stick-thin, with webbed feet, like a swan's.

While I had been looking at Frau Perchta, the three Torc Fianna had shrugged off their human form and taken on their magnificent deer aspects, complete with branching antlers.

"Come, Madame Perenelle. Stand here and warm yourself." The dark-skinned man darted forward and ushered us toward the blazing fire. "You must be freezing. New York is so cold at this time of year." I caught the hint of an accent—Greek, perhaps?

Nicholas helped me out of my coat, and I saw his hand feel the coil of the whip in the inner pocket. He draped the coat over the back of a chair and came to stand beside me, in front of the fire.

The small man shifted nervously from foot to foot as he looked at each of us in turn. "I know your husband will have nothing—I have already asked—but surely you, madame, will have something warming to drink after your long walk. Hot chocolate, perhaps? Mulled wine? I have the most delicious cinnamon, and my cloves are fresh from the Maluku Islands this very morning."

"Hot chocolate would be lovely," I responded.

"Oh, an excellent choice. I had some Criollo delivered only yesterday. It is the rarest of all the chocolate varieties, and my personal favorite. Though I have cut down of late." He patted a flat stomach and hurried off.

I watched him as he moved away. There was an almost childlike nervous energy about him. He was constantly moving, adding wood to the fire—even though it didn't need any—adjusting random books on one side of the room and then darting over to run short, stubby fingers over the snow globes. As he touched them, the snowflakes within came to swirling life. The door at the far end of the room opened as he approached, and where there had been a dark corridor I could now see a vast workspace, bright with copper piping and metal vats.

I glanced sidelong at Nicholas, but he shook his head almost imperceptibly. We had been together long enough that I knew to ask no questions.

"I saw a wonderful coffee maker in a window at Gimbel's today," I said, making casual conversation as we took in our surroundings. "Makes six cups at one time."

"How much was it?" Nicholas asked.

"Two ninety-five."

"So expensive! I can buy a cup of coffee for twenty cents," he said.

"You don't drink coffee anymore," I reminded him.

The small man reappeared with a carved wooden goblet filled to the brim with luscious chocolate, and I got my first real look at him. He was a little shorter than me, with the deep olive skin of one from the Mediterranean countries. His thin hair was twisted in a mess of tight curls, and his eyes were the same color as the chocolate. His nose had been broken at least once, so it bent to one side.

"I know what you're thinking," he said as he unwrapped a cinnamon stick from a twist of paper and allowed it to sink into the thick chocolate.

"And what is that?" I asked, wrapping both hands around the goblet and breathing deeply. The scent of chocolate and cinnamon—and was that a hint of chili?—was mouthwatering.

"You are wondering if I am who you think I am?"

"I do wonder. But you do not look like"—I paused, unwilling to insult him—"what I imagined you might look like."

He grinned, revealing a mouthful of perfectly white teeth. "Well, it's complicated. I was born in the year 270 in the town of Patara in what is now known as Turkey but was then part of the sprawling Roman Empire. I became a priest and then a bishop and finally a saint. By then, of course, I had also become immortal. You know what that's like. Stories spring up around you. Sadly, you've no control over them—even when they ruin your reputation and are completely untrue."

Frau Perchta slid up beside the small man and gently kicked him with her swan's leg. "Ignore him," she said, her girl's voice no longer eerie, as it matched her appearance. "He loves celebrity. Besides, he's created most of the stories himself."

"Well, not the new ones," he said indignantly. "They've got nothing to do with me."

"So what do I call you?" I asked.

"My name is Nicholas of Myra. You can ignore the 'saint' bit."

I glanced at my husband. "Two Nicholases. That's going to be confusing. Do you mind if I call you Nick?"

"Just don't called him Santa Claus," Frau Perchta said with a cheeky grin. "He hates that!"

6

Four Torc Fianna in their human form carried in a large circular table and set it down in the middle of the floor. The surface was etched with a series of interlocking Celtic knotwork designs that shifted when you looked at them, forming new patterns. It was both hypnotic and unsettling. One of the Torc Fianna, a delicate-looking woman who moved with the same deadly grace I'd seen in Scathach, arranged half a dozen snow globes in a circle on the table. Two of the weredeer carried over one of the largest globes I'd ever seen, easily the size of a human head, and set it down in the center of the polished wood. The white flecks within twisted and whirled, obscuring whatever lay inside. Finally, the Torc Fianna arranged four high-backed wooden chairs around the table.

"Please, sit," Nick said to us, indicating the chairs closest to us.

Neither Nicholas nor I moved. "You owe us an explanation," the Alchemyst said. "Although technically, your Torc Fianna did not kidnap me—they implied that my wife was already in your hands."

"And they told me that they'd already taken Nicholas," I added. "So we were coerced."

Nick shrugged his broad shoulders. "You must forgive the Torc Fianna. They are warriors beyond measure, but not too bright sometimes. They take instructions rather literally."

"How did a Christian saint end up with the deadliest of the Torc clans?" Nicholas asked.

"It's a long story."

"Tell us the short version," I suggested.

Nick sighed. "Before I became immortal, I did a favor for the Elder, Saulė."

"We've met her," Nicholas said shortly. "She nearly killed us."

"She nearly killed *me*," I reminded him. "You, she liked!"

"She was not always so short-tempered," Nick said. "But I would not take any payment from her. So she gifted me with her sleigh and her Torc Fianna bodyguards, who pulled it. There are eight . . ." He lowered his voice and glanced toward the door. "I can't get rid of them. They are oathbound to me for eternity."

Frau Perchta, who seemed to be called Holle when she was in her young girl form, snorted. "Ignore him. He loves to ride that sleigh across the night sky."

Nick looked vaguely embarrassed. "It is rather wonderful," he admitted. "You must come out with me some evening."

I bit my lip and said nothing. Over the course of my long life, I have done many wonderful, extraordinary, exciting, and stupid things. But I've never imagined riding through the heavens in Santa's sleigh.

"So before San . . . before your legend of the reindeer and the sleigh, Saulė rode the heavens in a similar sleigh?" I asked.

Holle barked a quick laugh. "Before Saulė, the sky belonged to Tanngrisnir and Tanngnjóstr, the goats who pulled Thor's chariot across the sky; Freyja's celestial chariot was pulled by cats; and before Nick was given Saulė's sleigh, I commanded the skies in a sleigh of my own, pulled by eight Perchten."

"Must have been a very crowded sky," Nicholas remarked.

"In the days following the sinking of Danu Talis, the world was indeed a place of wonders," Holle said. "And terrors," she added, blinking away the sudden tears in her blue eyes.

I looked at Nick. "You still haven't told us what brings you to New York or what you want with us."

Nick gestured to the four chairs set around the table. "Sit, please. And I will tell you all I know." He pulled back one of the chairs. "Madame Perenelle, please?"

We remained standing.

Nick sighed. "I once did a favor for a hook-handed man. I am sure you know of him: Marethyu. It starts with him."

Nicholas and I looked at each other, and then, without a word, we took our seats at the table. Centuries ago, Marethyu, the hook-handed man, sold us the Codex and started us on this long immortal journey. He appeared occasionally to ask for a favor, something he was either unwilling or unable to do himself. Though, to be honest, I don't think there is anything he could not do. If Marethyu trusted Nick, then we knew we could trust Nick also.

Holle took the seat directly opposite me, while Nick sat facing my husband.

Reaching across the table, Nick picked up a tiny snow globe. Glittering speckles of sand swirled within. "Marethyu gave this to me and said that if I was ever in trouble, I could use it to call upon him." He pushed the globe toward us and we looked into it. The sand settled to reveal a sickle-like hook spinning in a circle. "Yesterday, I used it for the first time, and I spoke to the man known as Death."

"And what did the hook-handed man tell you?" Nicholas asked.

"Surely the better question is why you chose to contact the hook-handed man in the first place," I said. I waved around the room. "Clearly you are not without power."

Nicholas smiled at me. "That *is* a better question." He raised his thin eyebrows and looked at the round-faced man.

Nick sighed. "For centuries I have been trailed by a monster, a creature born of chaos and old night. I thought I'd lost it in Europe decades ago, but yesterday I learned that it is en route to this New World. My past has caught up with me," he said dramatically. "I contacted Marethyu to ask for his advice. He told me you were both in New York and that I should seek you out. He said, 'Find the Alchemyst and the Sorceress; only they have the peculiar combination of powers that will help you.'"

Nicholas and I exchanged a look.

"You still haven't told us why you contacted Marethyu . . . ," my husband said.

Nick rubbed his hands together and sighed again. "Well, it's complicated. . . ."

"Everything is complicated with you," Holle snapped. "This, however, is not." She looked from Nicholas to me. "The Krampus has come to New York to kill—"

"And eat," Nick interrupted. "Don't forget that. Eat like a piece of gingerbread."

"The Krampus has come to New York to kill and eat Santa Claus."

"Don't call me Santa Claus."

"Kris Kringle, then."

"Hate that."

"Sinter Klass."

"Hate that even more!" he muttered.

7

"I have no idea what a Krampus is," Nicholas said.

But I did. The goat monsters were common to all the Celtic lands, including Brittany, where I had grown up.

Nick pushed another snow globe across the table. My husband picked it up and shook it. Glittering black sand swirled and spun to reveal a monster.

"The Krampus," Nick said. "Or a version of it, at least."

Within the small glass globe, the creature moved and turned, almost as if it were real. Tall, with the muscular body of a man, the Krampus had a huge goat's head, with thick horns curling on either side of its head. Beneath leather and metal armor, it was completely covered in shaggy, dirty-white fur, and its eyes were bloodred. But through the matted coat, there was almost the outline of a human skull. A thick chain was wrapped around its waist and trailed on the ground behind it.

"It is Torc Gabhar? A were-goat?" Nicholas asked.

"I have dealt with the Torc Gabhar many times," Holle said. "This is not a creature of the were."

"This is something older, far older," Nick said. "I have often wondered if it was one of the fabled Earthlords."

Nicholas and I shook our heads. "Earthlords are serpentine," I said. "This definitely has the look of a goat about it."

"And those are not the teeth of a goat," Nicholas said, tilting the globe so that I could see into the creature's mouth: it was filled with a double row of needle-pointed teeth. "Guessing it's not an herbivore either."

"It has a taste for humans," Nick said softly.

"Humans in general or special humans?" Nicholas wondered.

"There was a time when the Krampus was not too fussy. But in the past few centuries, I understand it has developed a taste for immortal humans. Now it will eat nothing else. It considers them a delicacy."

"It will think its entire Christmas dinner has come at once if it sees the three of us," I said. "Nicholas will be the starter, you the main course, and I the dessert, of course."

Nicholas pushed back from the table. In his plain blue suit, rumpled shirt, and stained tie, he looked like an accountant, but even Leonardo da Vinci admitted that Nicholas Flamel was a genius. Without looking at me, my husband said, "So you expect us to help you—what? Fight the Krampus? Why?"

Nick looked confused. "Marethyu said I should talk to you. He said only you have the peculiar combination of powers to help me. I'm not sure what he means," he added. "You know the hook-handed man. He can be a bit cryptic sometimes."

The small man tilted his head to one side and smiled sadly. "Before the war, the Krampus had busily devoured his way through a dozen European immortals. This war, and the previous one, have complicated matters."

"I would have thought the chaos of war might have helped conceal its crimes," Nicholas said.

"On the contrary. Individuals and communities are so much more suspicious now. The Krampus, like many of us, lives in the shadows. European society is shattered, entire communities scattered, and when it reforms, it will be very different indeed. It would be impossible for the Krampus to remain invisible. Also, the Krampus's preferred meal, the immortal human, has moved on. Most of the immortals chose to fight in the war, for one side or another. Many gave their lives in the ultimate sacrifice. Those European immortals who survived are seeking anonymity in America. I knew it was only a matter of time before the Krampus made his way across the Atlantic. And now that he has reached these shores, I have no doubt that once he has finished with me, he will start to munch his way through those immortals he finds here."

I looked at Nicholas and nodded. We could not allow the Krampus to roam freely across the Americas. We had too many immortal friends here.

I looked across the table at Holle. "Before we come to any agreement, however, we need to know who we are fighting alongside. I know a little about the legends of Saint Nicholas, and something about Frau Perchta. Is it not unusual to find you together?"

"Once, perhaps," Nick said with a grin, "but no more. We have joined forces. We are two halves of a whole. I reward the good, whereas Holle punishes the wrongdoers. For centuries, separately, we roamed this world and the Shadowrealms, protecting the innocent and punishing wrongdoers. Now we do it together."

"Why don't we hear more about you?" I asked Holle. "Santa Claus is everywhere."

She jerked her thumb at Nick. "I prefer the shadows, but this one, well, he is his own best publicist. Have you seen the latest images he's come up with—the red suit, the white hair and beard, the sack bulging with gifts?"

"Hey, that had nothing to do with me," Nick protested.

Holle continued to stare at him, until he finally relented. "Well, maybe just a little."

"And the poem," she persisted.

"Which one?"

"The one with the reindeer names. Dasher, Cupid, Comet . . ."

"*Shhh.* For goodness' sake, keep your voice down. Don't let the Torc Fianna hear. That was not my doing!"

The three of us stared at him.

"Well, maybe just a little. Look, I might have put the idea in a couple of writers' heads at the same time, but I definitely did not give either of them the names of the reindeer."

"Dunder and Blixem . . . ," Holle said.

"I changed those names. . . ."

"To Donder and Blitzen."

Nicholas rapped on the table with his knuckles, silencing the squabbling pair. "Quick question: Have we any idea where the Krampus is right now?"

"Moving across Europe. Later tonight it will arrive on Bedloe's Island, stepping through the leygate in the tunnels beneath the Statue of Liberty."

"He will not be alone," Frau Perchta said. "We've learned that he is bringing the Turon with him. And while the Krampus prefers immortals, the Turon love the taste of human flesh. If they get off the island, they will level this city."

"So we have to stop him on the island," Nick said.

Nicholas raised a finger. "And the Turon. What are they?"

Nick tapped the largest of the snow globes in the center of the table. The smoke within swirled and cleared to reveal a heaving mass of beasts. They looked like a cross between a bull and a man, with huge pointed horns jutting from their heads. Their jaws hung loose, revealing ragged teeth and lolling black tongues. And then, one by one, the Turon stopped moving, before turning to look directly at us. They surged forward, pressing themselves against the glass, peering out, and for a heart-stopping moment, I imagined they were trapped within, pushing to break out.

"They are on a distant Shadowrealm," Nick said quickly. "We are looking at them through a slab of ice. They should not be able to see us. . . ."

"The big one is definitely looking at me," Nicholas muttered.

"Perhaps they see shadows moving on the ice." Nick touched the globe, and the image faded.

"How many will answer the Krampus's call?" I wondered.

"Eight."

"Eight Turon, eight Torc Fianna," I said, and looked at Holle. "And you had eight Perchten to pull your sleigh."

"Eight is the magic number," she said.

"And if I were to ask you when the Krampus will arrive with his eight friends," Nicholas said, "you would tell me . . ."

"Tonight," Nick said. "At midnight, when Christmas Eve becomes Christmas Day."

8

Nick and Holle left to round up the Torc Fianna and arm themselves, leaving us alone in the huge wooden room. We wandered around, saying little, aware that there might be eavesdroppers. Without Nick in the room, the Shadowrealm no longer seemed so solid. Occasionally the walls would thin and flicker, revealing what looked like an ordinary warehouse outside. The tree growing out of the floor was no longer as green or as vibrant as it had been, and most of the candles—which I'd initially thought were a terrible fire risk—had gone out.

"Not a true Shadowrealm, I think," Nicholas said finally. "More of a simulation. A powerful one, though—it takes extraordinary skill to keep something like this together."

"Not all fake. The hot chocolate tasted real."

"Probably was. Table is real also, as are these." He stopped before the shelves of snow globes.

There were thousands, of all shapes and sizes. Most were filled with white speckles to simulate snow, but others had red, black, gray, or brown particles. The scenes within the globes were fantastically detailed, and those containing characters—human or monster—were extraordinarily realistic. A scrawl of indecipherable words was etched onto a brass plate at the base of each globe.

"I feel I know some of these places," Nicholas muttered.

I ran my finger over the text. "Looks like Ogham, or Runic. Frau Perchta has a list covered in similar writing."

"The naughty list?" Nicholas asked with a smile. "Were you on it?"

"We didn't find out. If we don't come up with a plan to defeat the Krampus, the next list we're going to be on is a menu." I realized Nicholas was not listening to me. He was staring intently at one particular globe. I followed his gaze. Within the globe, a city of crystal towers perched on a spit of land. Shifting sunlight turned each of the towers into refracting rainbows. "That's the Lyonesse Shadowrealm," I said.

Nicholas smiled. He pointed to another globe: a golden city encircling an enormous pit in the ground, surrounded by sand dunes and desert. "And that looks like the Ophir Shadowrealm, built around the fabled gold mine."

I looked along the shelves. "Here are Tir Tairngaire and Tir na nÓg together. This looks like Asgard, and this is definitely Lyonesse." I squinted into the Lyonesse globe. I could actually see tiny flea-sized people moving on the golden streets.

Another shelf held a series of globes showing places around the earth: the Eiffel Tower, the Taj Mahal, the recently opened Golden Gate Bridge with Alcatraz Island in the background. The Tower of London sat alongside the Colosseum.

The top shelf held a dozen empty globes. Nicholas picked

one up and turned it over in his hands. "These are leygates," Nicholas said finally, unable to contain the excitement in his voice. "This is how Nick can be all over the world at the same time on a single night. Miniaturized portable leygates," he said in an awed whisper. "He can hop from world to world, place to place, in a heartbeat, be everywhere simultaneously." He stopped.

"And the empty globes?"

"For when he discovers a new Shadowrealm." Nicholas held up the globe. "He can capture its . . ." He paused, struggling to find the word.

"Address," I suggested.

"I was going to say essence, but yes, address will do. Then he can add the location to his list of places to visit."

"But if he's that powerful . . . why does he need us?" I said, then answered the question myself. "Because he did not create these."

Nicholas held up the empty globe. "These are ancient beyond reckoning."

"So Nick's powers are limited. Which is why he needs us."

Nicholas blinked at me, his almost colorless eyes taking on a gold tinge from the surrounding wood. "Madame Perenelle. You are a genius."

"So you keep telling me."

He caught me in his arms and hugged me close, his mouth close to my ear. "And can your genius shed any light on our present predicament?" he breathed.

"I'm wondering whether we're allies . . . or bait."

9

It may sound rather wonderful and dramatic in poetry and song, but dashing through the snow on a sleigh pulled by eight enormous reindeer is anything but wonderful. Dramatic, yes; spectacular, of course. But no one tells you that those reindeer smell!

Nicholas and I were huddled in the back of the sleigh, behind Nick and Holle, who'd transformed back into her Frau Perchta aspect. Nick was dressed in an all-black version of the red suit we'd come to associate him with, while Frau Perchta was wearing what looked like a collection of tattered rags, which flew around her like flapping wings.

Nicholas and I were unrecognizable, wrapped up like enormous mummies, in furs and blankets, with gloves, boots, and hats. And I was still freezing. Even my eyeballs were cold. Usually, I'd bring up my body temperature with my aura, but we were afraid that any flaring aura might alert the Krampus.

Also, the sleigh ride was terrifying!

I've ridden nathair and peist, elephants, several ill-tempered camels, and even a thunderbird, and I have never been more frightened than I was in that sleigh. At first I thought Nick was showing off, or, more likely, he was simply a bad driver unable to control the Torc Fianna. When we set off from the flat roof of a nearby warehouse, we immediately plunged three floors before the Torc Fianna's special powers kicked in and they found traction in the thin air. We careered around Hell's Kitchen, clipping chimney tops with the edge of the sleigh while reindeer hooves scattered tiles onto the deserted streets below. We flew dangerously low, weaving between buildings so close together that the sides scraped the edges of the sleigh, scattering a rainbow of sparks behind us.

It was only when I caught glimpses of wide-eyed children watching us from bedroom windows, or stunned adults on the streets below dodging falling slates, that I realized Nick was doing this deliberately. He wanted to be seen. It was Christmas Eve, and he wanted people to know that Father Christmas was abroad. Perhaps, as Frau Perchta had suggested, he was publicity hungry, but I also saw the immediate blossoming of joy and wonder in the eyes of children and adults alike. And in that moment, I liked him just a little bit more.

New York spread below us in a glittering dusting of light and smoke. It had snowed on and off throughout the day, giving the city an almost cardboard-cutout appearance. Cities from the air are the most magical of places—you can see their twists and curls, the sweep of roads and stretches of boulevards. London is a scattered mystery from the air; the black line of the Seine cuts through Paris, emphasizing the straight lines of the boulevards and the confusion of narrow side streets; Rome is a wonderful jigsaw; Hong Kong is a glittering jewel. New York is different. The straight lines make it look like a child's drawing of what a city should look like . . . until you get to the big rectangle of Central Park cut out of the middle, which looks like someone erased the center of the drawing.

It was quiet now, that special Christmas Eve silence. The bars and restaurants had emptied, and the chill and snow had driven almost everyone indoors. I saw a few poor homeless souls on the streets. Most slouched along, wrapped in rags, head down, but a couple looked up and watched in wonder the sight of a sleigh pulled by reindeer flying over the rooftops. I hoped the image would remind them that there was magic in the world and that if Santa was real—and reindeer really could fly—then everything was possible.

We rose through thick, wintry clouds made bitter from the smoke of countless fires, and then, suddenly, we were above them, and a light from the half-moon thickened the clouds to a brilliant silver carpet. Water droplets became silver beads for a single moment, before Nick dipped us back into the snow-filled clouds again. When we burst out, we were over Jersey City, with Ellis Island directly ahead of us and Liberty rising on her plinth on the island beyond.

Nick took us low over the red roofs of Ellis Island, which was still a prisoner of war camp and hospital. As we neared Bedloe's Island, we dropped even lower, until the Torc Fianna's hooves were actually splashing across the surface of the waves. Lady Liberty was ahead to our left, standing tall on her eleven-pointed base. Nicholas had been friends with Bartholdi, who had designed the statue and whom I'd never liked, and the interior metal frame had been created by Gustav Eiffel, whom I'd liked and Nicholas hadn't.

Almost as if he knew I was thinking about him, my husband leaned closer. "When this is all through, we will take the ferry over and climb to the top. There is supposed to be an incredible view from the windows in the crown."

"We still haven't climbed the Eiffel Tower," I reminded him.

"We should make a list," he muttered.

And then the sleigh swooped in and the runners scraped loudly on the hard pavement an instant before the clattering rattle of thirty-two hooves struck sparks from the ground.

Nick swiveled around, cheeks bright red with the bitter air, and grinned. "Just in time," he said. "Happy Christmas!"

Over the icy waters of the bay, we heard the bells of New York ring in Christmas Day.

10

Tuesday, 25 December 1945
Christmas Day

When the bells faded away, everything fell unnaturally silent; even the lapping of the waves sounded muted and distant. Although it had snowed over the city, none of it had stuck here, and the rocks radiated a bone-freezing chill.

Nick hopped out of the sleigh and extended a hand to help me alight. He was grinning from ear to ear.

"You seem pleased for someone about to meet the Krampus," I remarked.

"Hard to feel down on Christmas Day," he said. "Besides, I have the famous Alchemyst, Nicholas Flamel, and the legendary Sorceress, Perenelle Delamere, with me."

"What about me?" Frau Perchta demanded in her little-girl voice. "I am not an immortal human, but I am an Elder, older than most civilizations."

"And I am grateful to have you here," Nick said hastily. "Between the four of us, we should be able to defeat the Krampus and save this country from horror."

Frau Perchta grimaced and then slipped away into the

night, ragged clothes swirling around her. "I will check around the other side of the statue. The bells should have awakened the Krampus."

Nicholas helped me out of most of the heavy, confining clothing. I kept the hat but had to lose the gloves. I've never been able to properly work a hand spell wearing gloves.

Half of the Torc Fianna morphed back into their human form. The four women were now wearing leather and chain-mail armor, and from the big sack on the back of the sleigh they pulled out an impossible number of swords, spears, bows, and crossbows. Without saying a word, they split into four teams of one woman and one deer and disappeared into the night, leaving Nick, Nicholas, and me alone at the sleigh.

"This is not how I intended to spend my Christmas Eve," I said, blowing into my cupped hands.

"Nor I," Nick said. "I have visits to make."

"Well, we'll try to defeat the monsters and get you on your way as quickly as possible," Nicholas said sarcastically. "A plan might be useful," he added.

Nick turned to look at Lady Liberty. "Frau Perchta tells me that the Krampus started moving across Europe a couple of days ago, jumping from leygate to leygate, from the Black Forest to Rennes-le-Château, on to Carnac, through Stone-henge into Newgrange, then across to Mystery Hill in New Hampshire. We believe he arrived in New York yesterday or Sunday. Liberty's plinth was built on the ruins of Fort Wood, and there is a warren of disused tunnels below. He's some-where down there, close to the leygate."

"Might be better to tackle him in the tunnels than allow him up onto open ground," Nicholas said.

"I did suggest that to Frau Perchta. She reminded me that the Krampus is a creature of tunnels and caves. He can see in total darkness."

"In the tunnels his size will be a disadvantage, though," Nicholas said. "We'd be able to control him." He glanced at me, and I nodded. Something did not add up.

"Agreed," Nick said, peeling off his gloves and shoving them in his pockets. "I had the same thought."

"And what did Frau Perchta say?" I asked.

"She said that we would only be able to come at the Krampus one at a time. Whereas out here, in the open, we can tackle him from all sides."

"And what about the Turon?" Nicholas asked. "Are they with him?"

"We're not sure yet."

"I think I would rather fight one Krampus in a tunnel than a Krampus and eight bull-men in the open," Nicholas said.

"We lose the advantage of the Torc Fianna in the tunnel," Nick said.

"And I am guessing Frau Perchta told you this?" I said.

Nick looked at me curiously. "She did."

I looked over at my husband and, even in the dim light, saw him nod.

Nick looked at each of us in turn. "What's wrong?"

"Run or fight?" Nicholas asked me.

"I'm chilled through to my bones, I'm feeling nauseous

from the sleigh ride, and the caffeine in the hot chocolate has given me a headache," I said. "We stand and fight. If the Krampus has jumped through a dozen leygates in the past few days, maybe he'll still be confused and disoriented."

"And we might just have the advantage of surprise," Nicholas said.

Nick was looking hopelessly confused. "What's wrong?"

"Frau Perchta has betrayed you. You haven't come here to kill the Krampus," Nicholas said.

"You've been lured here so the Krampus and Frau Perchta can kill you," I said.

11

"Call the Torc Fianna back," Nicholas said. "We'll fight here."

"No." I pointed toward the plinth. "Over there, on the other side of the plinth. This way." I wanted to put the bulk of the statue and the plinth between us and the city so that whatever happened would be invisible from New York. "Meet us on the east side of the statue."

"I've no idea where east is," Nick said. "The Torc Fianna navigate; I just hold the reins."

"East is the direction the statue is facing," I told him.

Nick darted off to find the Torc Fianna.

"We'll get our backs against a wall," I said to Nicholas. "Liberty is built on a plinth in the shape of an eleven-pointed star."

"A hendecagram."

"Show-off."

Nicholas grinned. "I was always better at math than you."

"And yet you still manage to get your formulas wrong. How many laboratories have you burned down?"

"I get confused between grams and ounces."

We turned a sharp-edged corner and stopped. The hendecagram shape meant that a long wall and a short one sloped inward to a point. "There." I pointed to a black metal door set into the wall.

Nicholas hurried after me. "You're sure Frau Perchta is behind this plot?" he asked.

"Something she said earlier stuck with me. Do you recall when she was talking about flying in her own sleigh . . ."

"Pulled by eight reindeer."

"No, not deer," I reminded him. "She said they were Perchten."

"I assumed Perchten were deer."

Digging into my pocket, I lifted out the small snow globe showing the image of the Krampus. From a second pocket, I lifted out a second globe. It showed a crude wooden sleigh sailing over what had once been a postcard-pretty village. Now every second building was on fire. I held my hand steady and allowed the flakes of artificial snow to fall. "What do you see?"

Nicholas leaned forward to squint at the tiny sleigh. "Frau Perchta," he said. And then he stopped. "Those are not deer pulling her sleigh." He took the first globe from my hand and held it up to compare the two. "The Perchten are astonishingly similar to the Krampus."

"Same tribe," I answered. "Now look at the Krampus again. Notice anything odd?"

Nicholas smiled at me. "You mean aside from the whole goat-monster oddness in general?"

"His foot," I said.

He tilted the snow globe again, squinting in the half-light. "Oh. He has one cloven hoof . . . and one human foot."

"And Frau Perchta, or Holle, or Berchta, or whatever name she chooses, has one human foot and one swan's leg."

"Coincidence?" Nicholas suggested. "A lot of the Elders have animal aspects to them."

"You know we don't believe in coincidences."

We both stopped, nostrils flaring. The salty, slightly sour air was fouled by something bestial. It was similar to the deer musk I'd smelled earlier, but this was stronger, so much more powerful. "Like a cowshed on a farm," Nicholas murmured.

"A very dirty cowshed," I said.

12

Led by Nick, the Torc Fianna appeared first.

They were all bloodied and battered, with two of the women leaning heavily against those still in their deer aspect.

"Ambushed," Nick snapped. "They didn't get a close look at what attacked them." He helped one of the women sit back against the stone wall. There was a long gash across her forehead, and she was flickering between her human and deer forms. Nick tore the furry end off of his sleeve and rubbed her face. "Take on your true aspect, rest, recover."

"We are bound to protect you . . . ," she muttered.

"And you cannot protect me if you are dead," he said gently. "Rest now. Heal yourself."

The woman closed her eyes, and immediately the transformation shivered her back into her deer form. The beast tucked into a protective curl and closed her eyes.

The leader of the Torc Fianna limped over. This was the hatchet-faced woman I'd encountered on the street only a few hours earlier. It seemed like a lifetime. "We were setting up around the entrance to the underground when thick black smoke poured out and enveloped us. It smelled of burnt wood and tar, and sickened us. That's when they attacked."

"And you didn't see any of them?"

"They fought like cowards, striking from behind," she said bitterly. "They stank of goat and bull, rotting meat and things long dead." She shook her head. "We have failed you."

Nick rested his hand on her arm. "You have not. We have been betrayed by Frau Perchta."

The Torc Fianna's eyes widened. "I warned you about her."

"You did. I should have listened to you."

"What did you not like about Frau Perchta?" Nicholas asked.

The Torc Fianna leader shook her head. "We've encountered Frau Perchta over the centuries, but only in passing. She specializes in punishment, whereas Saint Nicholas chooses to reward. About a century ago, she started appearing more and more regularly. Then she suggested she and Nicholas should join forces, remind people about the old ways."

"You told me not to trust her," Nick said.

"Before my mistress Saulė put us in your service, I had ridden with her for a millennia. I knew she distrusted Frau Perchta, whom we called Berchta. She belonged to those Elders who believe that humani are little better than a snack, to be enjoyed raw or lightly toasted."

Nick sighed. "I like to see the best in people."

"How many of you can still fight?" I asked.

The Torc Fianna leader looked around. Four of them had returned to their deer forms and slept off their injuries. "Four," she said.

The farmyard stench grew stronger, and I felt my already delicate stomach lurch. A thick black fog swirled around the edge of the wall and billowed toward us. Shaking my fingers loose, I allowed a little of my ice-white aura to gather in the palm of my hand. Rolling it into a ball, I tossed it at the black fog.

The smoking white ball touched the black cloud, turning it solid. It fell to the ground, shattering into what looked like black soot.

"They're coming," Nicholas said.

"They're here," the sharp-faced woman said.

The four Torc Fianna in their human form took up positions before us, spears and bows ready. They would not be taken so easily this time.

I stood to the right of my husband, and we pushed Nick behind us so that his back was against the metal door.

Frau Perchta appeared first, ragged clothing billowing around her like flapping bat's wings.

She rounded the corner to my left, followed by eight of the ugliest goatlike creatures I have ever seen: the Perchten. These were no were-creatures, I realized. There is a certain natural beauty to the were, both in their human and animal forms; they have a grace and dignity. But not these creatures: shaggy, matted fur clung in patches to diseased-looking flesh. They were all horned, though some of the horns were chipped and broken, and their jaws hung slack. Armed with axes and hook-topped spears, they spread out in a line on either side of Frau Perchta.

"Are they dead?" Nicholas muttered. "Dead and re-animated?"

"Constructed creatures, I think. Abominations. Made, not born."

Foul air swirled and the earth trembled, and then the monster appeared around the side of the wall.

The Krampus was huge. Covered in filthy black fur, it towered ten or twelve feet tall, with two enormous horns adding to its height. The long goat's face was traced with the white lines of old scars; its eyes pulsed red and black in a slow rhythm, and a long black tongue lolled out of its mouth. While its right front leg ended in a cloven hoof, its left was a misshapen human foot. As it moved, it clattered and clanged, and I realized that human bones were woven into its unkempt fur. Wrapped around its waist was a long, thick chain, which dragged on the ground behind it.

"Ugly," Nicholas murmured. "I can see the resemblance to the Perchten."

Behind the Krampus, eight more creatures appeared. Tall, bulky, with massive shoulders and sharply curled horns, they had bulls' heads set on human torsos. "Torc Tarbh," Nicholas said. "The Turon are were-bulls."

"They were, once," I agreed. "But no longer. Look at their eyes."

Nicholas squinted and then gasped in horror. "They haven't got any." He took a step forward, and I grabbed his sleeve. "I think they're dead."

"Dead, but kept alive and moving by some foul sorcery. How is your math now?"

"Eight Turon, eight Perchten, plus Frau Perchta and the Krampus. That's eighteen, by my count."

"And we have four Torc Fianna, one immortal human, one Alchemyst, and a Sorceress."

Nicholas grimaced. "The odds are not in our favor."

I reached into my coat and pulled out my whip. The long thong hissed like a serpent as it curled onto the cold ground.

Frau Perchta stepped forward, and the Krampus lumbered up behind her. He pulled at the chain around his waist, gathering it up, starting to spin the loose end. The old woman pointed a black-nailed finger at Nick. "Two hundred years ago, I told you that Christmas belonged to me. But you would not listen. You said Christmas should be a time of happiness and joy. . . ." She almost spat the words. "I reminded you that December belonged to the darkness and that we, the creatures of the shadow, were its rightful rulers."

Nick pushed between Nicholas and me. "This is a time of celebration. Midwinter has come, and now the world turns toward longer days and toward the light!" he yelled back to her.

Frau Perchta limped forward, and the Krampus followed her. Behind them, the sixteen monsters shuffled into place, enclosing us in a half circle.

"You insisted on creating your own legend, promoting yourself, imprinting yourself on people's memories and consciousness. Once we ruled Midwinter; now no one remembers us. Well, tonight, that changes. This time next year, the entire world will know our names and worship us. Tonight we kill Santa Claus and return December to its rightful owners."

13

A spear bit into the grass not two feet in front of us. Two of the Torc Fianna fired their bows, and the nearest Perchten and Turon were hit with long feathered arrows. It had no effect on them.

"Killing the dead has always been tricky," Nicholas muttered.

"We can take out the monsters, I think. One of the elemental magics: fire, perhaps?" I suggested.

"They are dead. They will be upon us before the fire can consume them," Nicholas said. "And we're up against at least one Elder. I have no idea what the Krampus is."

Nick leaned forward and put his hands on our shoulders. "I am desperately sorry I involved you in this." He sounded genuinely upset. "I didn't even know you were in New York until the hook-handed man told me."

I looked at Nicholas at precisely the same moment he looked at me. "Why did Marethyu embroil us in this misadventure?" Nicholas wondered. "There must have been others in the city he could have called upon."

"He specifically told me to find you," Nick said. "Even

gave me your address. Find the Alchemyst, Nicholas Flamel, and the Sorceress, Perenelle."

Frau Perchta and the Krampus edged ever closer. "It is unfortunate that you two are here!" she called, her little-girl voice cracking with excitement. "Well, unfortunate for you. A tasty snack for us."

"Marethyu never does anything without a reason," I reminded Nick.

"Tonight you too will die beneath this silly metal statue. You'll not die in vain; we will have an early Christmas feast."

We both looked up. "Liberty Enlightening the World," Nicholas muttered. "A copper statue."

And I heard it then. That sound I had come to know and love. The excitement in my husband's voice when he'd discovered something exciting. He turned to me, colorless eyes tinted vaguely green in the reflection from the statue. "Madame Perenelle, I am in need of your aura."

Without hesitation I put my hand in his and allowed my ice-white aura to blossom around my body.

"Do you think your parlor tricks will have any effect on us?" Frau Perchta shouted. "We have killed Elders, and Next Generation, Earthlords, Ancients, and Archons have fallen before us. And humani: we have devoured them through the generations."

My entire hand turned into a dove-white glove, and then the smoke wrapped around Nicholas's flesh, curling along his wrist to disappear up his sleeve. It steamed out of his collar and drifted across his face, turning his eyes white.

Another spear bit into the ground before us, closer this time.

The Krampus stepped forward, spinning its chain, and snapped it out. It ripped away a chunk of earth not three feet in front of us.

Nicholas raised his left hand and pointed toward Frau Perchta and the Krampus. His index finger drew a perfect circle in the air. At the bottom of the circle he traced a cross. The symbol hung shivering in the air, outlined in traces of my white aura, now tinged with the green of his.

"Copper," Nicholas Flamel said. "Soft, malleable, ductile copper. One of the Seven Metals of Antiquity. And the first metal used by alchemists." He turned to look at me, eyes, nostrils, and mouth smoking with my aura. "I will need everything you have."

"Always."

I was vaguely aware that Frau Perchta and the Krampus were advancing, aware that the Torc Fianna were returning fire, but with no effect. The Krampus's chain cracked out, catching one of the warrior women, slamming her back into the wall.

"Do you remember the night we bought the Codex?" Nicholas asked me.

"I will never forget it." I could feel my strength seeping away as Nicholas absorbed my aura. I was struggling to stand.

Suddenly Nick stepped between us, wrapping an arm around each of us, holding us tightly together.

"Remember Francis Bacon," Nicholas said dreamily, "and his mechanical man . . . ?"

"Talon," I whispered. Bacon had come for us in Paris and set his stinking, talking metal creation on us. Talon, unfortunately, had encountered Scathach and ended up in the Seine, minus his head.

"You know I spent a long time studying how he brought that metal man alive."

Nicholas jerked his left arm up, fingers wide. Green light, the same color as the copper sheets that covered the statue, flowed from his hand. Five thin strands shot up, thickening as they rose, then whipping around the base of the statue, glowing brighter, spinning faster as they rose higher and higher.

Suddenly Liberty's torch blazed to life, and light strobed across the bay.

"Are you calling for help?" Frau Perchta cackled. "No one is going to see your light. No one is coming to your aid tonight."

The Krampus pushed past Frau Perchta and advanced on Nicholas, chain buzzing in a lethal whine. The beast's mouth opened, strands of sticky saliva dripping onto its fur as it licked its lips. When the chain was a spinning blur, he would snap it forward—

Like a huge hammer, Lady Liberty's torch drove the Krampus straight into the ground.

Perhaps there was noise—metal grinding, copper screeching—but I heard nothing. I saw the statue crouch on her stone plinth and use her torch as a baton, sweeping aside the Turon and Perchten, sending them cascading out to sea.

I watched the Krampus clamber out of the torn earth and stagger to its feet. It lashed out at the statue with its chain, which scored a long gouge in the soft copper. Liberty opened her left arm and dropped the tabula ansata, burying him beneath it. Even though I heard nothing, I felt the entire island shake with the detonation.

Frau Perchta looked on in horror. She was flickering between her two aspects, almost too quickly to see.

I saw Nick's lips shape her name as he spoke. "Holle . . ."

She stopped, the right side of her body young and unblemished, the left side withered and ancient.

"Holle," Nick said. "This is for you." He tossed something small and round toward her. Almost unconsciously, she reached out and caught it. It was a snow globe. The snow within started to swirl and then exploded from the globe, spiraling madly around the creature before flowing back into the globe. I didn't need to look: I knew Frau Perchta was now trapped in the glass sphere.

I fell away from Nicholas, and one of the Torc Fianna caught me before I hit the ground. Slipping in and out of consciousness, I watched as Liberty almost delicately picked up the tabula ansata and settled it back in the crook of her arm. With the last of Nicholas's aura buzzing green about her, she climbed back onto the plinth and settled into position. Her light blazed green and white before fading to darkness.

Nick caught my husband as he fell to his knees and helped him over to lie beside me.

"Happy Christmas," Nicholas whispered.

"I haven't gotten you a present yet," I told him.

"That coffeepot sounded nice. Six cups, you say?"

"You don't drink coffee."

"I could start again."

14

Two days later, we awoke in a hotel in Vero Beach, Florida, with no idea how we'd gotten there.

The room was filled to overflowing with brightly wrapped Christmas presents, including one of every item in the Pyrex kitchen range. Luckily, they all came with receipts, so we could return them.

In a wooden box, we found a snow globe. It showed a wood-paneled room, with a tree growing out of the corner and a fire flickering in the grate. There was a note written in a looping childish curl: *If you ever need help, just shake.* It was signed *Santa Claus.*

BILLY THE KID AND THE VAMPYRES OF VEGAS

2005

I never wanted to be immortal.

Like just about everything else in my life, it happened without my asking. I didn't even know I'd changed until I fell off my horse and rolled halfway down a mountainside. That fall broke just about every bone in my body. I could hear them snapping all the way down. By rights that fall should have killed me—but I got up and walked away.

I knew then I was different. Really different.

It wasn't until much later that I discovered what I had become: ageless. I wasn't too upset about it at first. Then I discovered that being immortal comes with some serious enemies, and only a few of them are human.

But sometimes your friends are even more dangerous than your enemies.

From Notes & Scraps
Being the Private Journal of William H. Bonney

Commonly known as Billy the Kid
(Undated, possibly September 2005)

1

"Billy, let me be very clear," said the white-bearded Elder Quetzalcoatl. "You do not open the jar."

The young man in the faded Route 66 T-shirt and weathered blue jeans nodded. Hooking his thumbs in his belt, fingertips resting on the ornate buckle, he leaned over and looked at the beautifully decorated earthenware vessel in the center of the table. Its wide mouth was sealed with what looked like black wax etched with sticklike writing.

"Don't open the jar," Billy repeated quietly to himself, then asked, "Why—what's in it?"

Quetzalcoatl remained expressionless. "You do not want to know."

"I do, actually." Billy the Kid looked at the slender figure with the hawk nose and solid black eyes standing across from him. "If you want me to deliver this, the least you can do is tell me what's in it."

A look of irritation flashed across the copper-skinned Elder's face. His long serpent's tail, bright with scales and feathers, swished beneath the hem of his white cotton robe and rasped back and forth over the floor.

Billy reached out to poke the jar with a calloused finger. But before he could touch it, a spark crackled from one of the ornate decorations ringing its surface. Billy leapt back, shaking out his suddenly numb fingers. He stuck his thumb in his mouth and sucked. "That hurts."

"I told you not to touch it."

"You told me not to *open* it," Billy corrected the Elder. Quetzalcoatl's black eyes fixed on Billy. The American immortal shrugged. " 'Don't open,' you said, not 'don't touch.' "

"Do not touch," Quetzalcoatl snapped.

Billy grinned. "Then how am I going to carry it?"

The Elder's mouth opened and his black tongue flickered through razor-sharp teeth. "Your smart mouth is going to get you killed one day."

"Maybe," Billy said. "But only when I'm no longer of any use to you."

Quetzalcoatl leaned toward the Kid, wisps of his beard brushing the jar, which gave off tiny blue-green sparks. "Do you know how many humani servants I have?"

"No." Billy's cold blue eyes stared, unwavering, into the Elder's face. "How many?"

Swirls of oily color moved across the surface of Quetzalcoatl's black eyes. Then he leaned back and his mouth opened in what might have passed for a smile. "Maybe I *should* let you open it," he said. He tapped the jar with his black-nailed index finger. "This is a pithos."

"I thought it was a jar," Billy said. He looked back at the table. The jar was about four feet tall, with a wide mouth above a bulging body narrowing to a circular base. The body of the artifact had been etched with horizontal lines of ancient script and spiral decorations resembling waves.

"A pithos *is* a jar. Didn't you learn anything in school?"

Billy shook his head. "We spent a lot of time on the road when I was young; there wasn't much time for schooling, and I went to work when my ma died. I was fourteen. Anything I've learned I taught myself."

Quetzalcoatl shook his head. "I sometimes wonder why I made you immortal."

"Because I saved your life," Billy reminded him with a grin. He held up his forefinger and thumb. "If I remember correctly, you were *this* close to ending your ten thousand years upon this earth."

Quetzalcoatl spun away and moved across the low-ceilinged room. Late-afternoon sunlight washed in through the large open windows, and the air smelled of exotic spices. "Just remember, Billy, I can take away your immortality just as easily as I granted it."

Billy the Kid bit back his response and folded his arms across his chest. He'd never asked for immortality, but he'd come to enjoy his extended life span and knew that if he was careful he could live for another one or two or even three hundred years. He'd heard stories of European immortals who had lived for more than half a millennium. His friend Black Hawk had told him that he'd once met an immortal human who was reputed to be one thousand years old. Billy wasn't sure he believed that; Black Hawk was a hundred

417

years older than Billy, and delighted in telling him the most outlandish stories.

Quetzalcoatl returned to the table with a thick brown canvas sack. He shook the sack open and a handful of gnarled brown beans rattled out. "Hold this," he commanded. Billy held the sack, coughing as the dry bitterness of cacao wafted up from the interior. Quetzalcoatl was addicted to chocolate and had the finest beans shipped in from all across South America every month. Lifting the pithos, the Elder carefully placed it in the sack and tied the neck with a strip of leather.

"I want you to take it to this address in Chinatown. Hand it over to the person there. I will call her as soon as you leave and tell her you are bringing it. She's expecting it. And, Billy," Quetzalcoatl added with a ragged grin. "Do not talk to her. Don't try to be smart or funny or clever. Just give her the pithos and walk away. Make sure you put it into her hands. And then forget you've ever met her."

"Trying to scare me?" Billy raised an eyebrow.

"Trying to warn you."

"Well, I don't scare easy." Billy the Kid lifted the bag. It was surprisingly heavy. "You're sounding a little nervous there," he teased the Elder. "Who is this woman?"

"No humani woman. This is the warrior's warrior, sometimes called the Daemon Slayer or the King Maker. This is Scathach the Shadow, and she is deadly beyond reckoning."

2

"See you next week. Keep practicing." The slender red-haired young woman with the shocking green eyes bowed as the last of her students left the dojo, then locked the door and turned back to the broad room. The artificial smile she always used when dealing with humans faded and her features turned sharp, almost cruel. She looked about seventeen, but Scathach had been born in the dark days after the fall of Danu Talis ten thousand years earlier. She had spent more than two and half thousand of those years on the Earth Shadowrealm. She had never been entirely comfortable among the humani; bitter experience had taught her not to get too close to them. She was always happiest when she was alone. And she had been alone for most of her long life.

Humming a tune that had been popular in the Egyptian court of Tutankhamen, Scathach opened a narrow cupboard and pulled out a broom, its head wrapped in a yellow cloth. Starting at the back of the room, she began to sweep the floor in long, rhythmic strokes.

The martial arts dojo was plain and unadorned, painted in shades of white and cream with black mats scattered across the gleaming wooden floor. Long beams of late-afternoon sunlight slanted in through the high windows, trapping spiraling dust motes in the slightly stale air. Four evenings a week Scathach taught karate classes, and every Friday morning she held a free self-defense workshop for women. Twice a week she instructed a handful of special students in the ancient Indian art of Kalarippayattu, the oldest martial art in the world. None of her students realized that their teacher had been one of the originators of the ancient fighting system, which had inspired the Chinese and then the Japanese martial arts.

"I'd better go out and buy some food later," she decided as she swept. Scathach was vampire. She had no need for food but had long ago realized that in order to blend in with the humani world, she needed to do what they did. In the ancient past too many of her clan had betrayed themselves through either stupidity or arrogance. And the most common mistake was being seen as not requiring everyday necessities like food—fruit, milk, tea. She'd made sure most of the shopkeepers in her neighborhood knew her. She even faked poor Mandarin or Cantonese to speak to them. She knew both languages perfectly but thought it would make her less conspicuous if she seemed to struggle.

When she'd finished sweeping, Scathach stepped into the tiny office at the back of the dojo. Like the rest of the space, it was plain to the point of austerity: it contained only a simple wooden desk with a battered kitchen chair behind it, facing the door. There were no martial arts certificates on the walls—no one ever questioned her skills—but one wall was adorned with antique weapons from around the world: swords and scythes, axes, spears, nunchaku and sai, khanda and claymores. All of them were nicked and battered from centuries of use in countless fights across a hundred Shadow-realms.

The cordless telephone and answering machine on the corner of the desk were the only modern devices in the room. The answering machine was blinking, a red 2 flashing on and off.

A flicker of surprise shifted across Scathach's normally expressionless face. She rarely received any calls on this phone. The number was not only private, even the telephone company didn't have it in their records. Any calls were routed through a dozen switching points and bounced across two continents and one satellite, making the number untraceable. Scathach could count on the fingers of one hand the people who knew how to reach her here. It had been a year—no, fourteen months—since the last call, and that had been someone selling life insurance.

Scathach shook her head slightly. This could only be trouble. And trouble meant she would have to move. She sighed. She really loved San Francisco; she'd hoped she'd be able to stay here for another decade at least before her unchanging appearance would force her to relocate to avoid suspicion. She could return in a century or so when everyone who had known her would be dead—but she didn't want to leave quite yet.

She pressed Play. "You have two new messages."

"I understand you have been seeking a certain pithos." The voice was an arrogant rasp, speaking in a language that had not been used on the American continent in millennia. "I am in a position to give it to you."

"Of course you are," Scathach whispered with a smile. Quetzalcoatl had phoned her deliberately, allowing her to see that he knew where she lived. She had recently discovered— quite by accident—that the snake-tailed Elder had the artifact in his collection of antiquities. During the past few weeks, she had visited a dozen of his agents and let them know she wanted it. She knew the message would get to Quetzalcoatl sooner rather than later, and knew that he would contact her. The Elder known as the Feathered Serpent would gladly give up the pithos to keep her from rampaging through his Shadowrealm in search of it. Scathach was likely to leave his world a smoking ruin.

"Although the pithos is of great personal value to me, I would like to present it to you as a token of my goodwill."

Goodwill! Scathach was surprised Quetzalcoatl even knew how to pronounce the word. Her lips curled in a cruel smile. He was giving her the jar because he was afraid of her.

The answering machine tape hissed for a minute and then there was a coughing sound and Scathach realized that Quetzalcoatl was attempting a laugh. "I have no wish to make an enemy of you. I was a good friend to your parents. Indeed, I believe we may even be related by blood on your mother's side. We are not that different, you and I."

"You have no idea just how different we are," Scathach murmured into the pause that followed.

"My representative will call upon you later today. He is an immortal humani and knows of your nature. He can be a little arrogant, but I would be grateful if you did not kill him. He is useful to me."

There was a click and then the message stopped.

"Well, that was easy." Scathach grinned. She'd been quite prepared to invade the Elder's Shadowrealm in search of the famous pithos. She pressed the Play button again to listen to the second call.

"A long time ago, you told me that if I was ever in any trouble I could call upon you."

Scathach's breath caught in her throat. It was a voice she had not heard in a long time, a youthful man's voice with just a trace of an accent. A man she *knew* to be dead.

"But when I called, you did not come, and I paid a terrible price. You failed me once. Scathach, I am in trouble now. Deep trouble. I need you, Shadow. There are vampyres in Las Vegas, and they are hunting me. I'm staying at—"

Before he finished his sentence the call was cut off.

3

Billy had driven around the block twice looking for a place to park and eventually decided that he was not leaving his precious Thunderbird at a parking meter. He found a garage on Vallejo Street and parked his bright red convertible as far away from any of the other cars as possible. Two weeks earlier someone had bumped into his door with a shopping cart, leaving a long, thin scar in the paint. It had taken him an entire day to buff out the scratch and another to repaint the door.

Wrapping his left hand in the leather cord around the sack's mouth, Billy hefted the heavy bag holding the pithos over his shoulder and set off down Vallejo Street toward Stockton. Although he had lived in and around San Francisco for the better part of a century, he'd never spent a lot of time exploring the city itself. Narrow streets and crowds made him nervous. He preferred the open countryside.

He walked past two youths leaning against a wall—one unnaturally skinny, the other muscular—and saw how their eyes drifted across him and settled on the bag. They exchanged a look. Billy knew their type: he'd ridden horseback

424

alongside them once and fought against them for the rest of his life. "Don't even think about it, boys," he said lightly as he strode past. "You do not want to mess with me today. Or any day." There was something about the expression on his face and the look in his eyes that made both young men step back and turn to hurry away. Billy grinned. All bullies were cowards.

The immortal turned onto Stockton Street, then left onto Broadway, walked past the Sam Wong Hotel and turned right into a cramped back street. He knew he was close. He consulted the address on the sweat-stained scrap of paper in the palm of his hand. He was in a narrow alleyway barely wide enough for one car. The buildings on either side were so high they blocked out the sun, leaving the alley in gloomy shadow. Metal bins, stinking with rotting food and buzzing with flies, lined one wall. Billy took care to breathe only through his mouth. He had no idea who this Scathach person was, but he didn't think much of where she lived. Quetzalcoatl had called her the King Maker and the Daemon Slayer and had said she was a Shadow, whatever that meant. A shadow of her former self? Billy was guessing she was a dumpy old bag lady who probably kept cats. Dozens of cats. He shifted the sack from one shoulder to the other and once again wondered what exactly it contained. It looked like a Greek wine jar, but he was almost certain there was no wine in it. He'd shaken it when he'd put it in the back of his car, then pressed his ear against the rough cacao-scented cloth. For the merest instant he could have sworn he'd heard voices coming from inside the jar. Maybe it was full of Nirumbee—Little People. If so, he was in no hurry to open it. Fifty years earlier, in Montana, he'd rescued Virginia Dare from some of the little horned monsters and they'd both barely escaped with their immortal lives.

Billy rounded a pile of trash and found himself facing a building at the end of the alleyway. There were no windows, and the only door was behind a narrow-slatted metal grille. As he got closer he saw a simple plastic sign next to the door. KARATE CLASSES. SELF-DEFENSE. QUALIFIED INSTRUCTOR.

He stopped and checked the address again. It was correct. He turned slowly, making sure he wasn't being followed, and then pressed a small white bell under the sign. His acute hearing picked up the rattle of what sounded like wind chimes. He checked the alleyway, the habits that had kept him alive for so long making him look behind him once more.

Billy was turning back to the door, finger outstretched to press the bell again, when he realized that the door had opened and a young woman with spiky red hair was glaring at him. He stepped away and smiled to hide his discomfort; he hadn't even heard the door open.

"Hi. I've got a parcel for a Mrs. Skatog."

"Scathach," the young woman corrected him, reaching for the sack.

Billy took a step back and shook his head. "I can only give it to Mrs. Scathach herself."

"I'm Scathach," the woman snapped, green eyes flashing.

"And how do I know that?" Billy asked. "You can't be too careful these days."

"You are the servant of Quetzalcoatl, the Feathered Serpent," she snarled. Her nostrils flared. "You stink of his foul odor." And then her mouth opened to reveal vampire teeth. "I am the Shadow."

"Yes, ma'am . . . ," Billy said. He thrust the bag toward the young woman hastily. He didn't want anything to do with those teeth. As she reached out to take it, a phone started ringing from somewhere deep inside the building.

Scathach turned without a word and disappeared, leaving Billy holding the bag.

4

Scathach had no idea who the young man was. An immortal, certainly, and judging by his appearance, he'd been granted immortality when he was still quite young; he looked like he was in his late teens or early twenties. Handsome, too, with startling blue eyes. His two front teeth were a little prominent, and he deliberately kept his mouth shut to hide them. His red-pepper scent was layered with Quetzalcoatl's serpent odor.

Scathach flew across the polished wooden floor and snatched up the phone on the third ring. "Hello?"

"Do you remember my voice?"

In her long life, Scathach the Shadow had faced down monsters and challenged terrors. She had ridden across nightmare landscapes and fought creatures that should never have existed. There was little that frightened her. Yet the sound of this voice set her legs shaking. She sat down heavily in the chair.

"It's been a long time," she whispered. Scathach was overtaken by a wave of swirling memories, and all the good ones were washed away by bitterness. "I thought you were dead."

"Almost."

"I looked for you," she said, her voice quavering.

"Not hard enough," the man said, a touch of sadness in his voice. "I came back, Scathach. I came back in search of you. I looked everywhere, but I could never find you."

"Where are you now?" she said quickly. "I'll come to you."

"I'm in trouble. Terrible trouble. I'm in Las Vegas. The town is run by vampyres and cucubuths. And they're hunting me. Scathach, I need you. You won't fail me again, will you?"

There was a sudden shout, which turned to a crackle on the line . . . and then silence.

"Hello? . . . Hello? . . . Hello?" Scathach called, slowly standing.

She heard a click, followed by a dial tone.

And for the first time in many years, the Shadow buried her face in her hands and wept bloodred tears.

5

Billy the Kid stood awkwardly in the doorway, the sack in one hand, his boots in the other, and looked at Scathach. Blood—thick and bright red—seeped between her fingers.

"Are you all right?"

The creature that looked up at him was no longer human. Her pale skin had tightened across her cheekbones and chin, and her eyes—completely red now—had sunk into her skull. The flesh had drawn back from her jaws, revealing the savage vampire teeth Billy had glimpsed earlier, and her hair had stiffened into needlelike quills.

Billy bit down hard on the inside of his cheek to keep his face expressionless; he'd never shown fear in his life. He held up his boots. "I hope you don't mind. I invited myself in. I didn't want to leave the pithos on the steps. And I took my boots off. I know you martial arts types don't like people walking across your floors in their street shoes." He looked down at his threadbare and mismatched socks. "If I'd known, I would have worn better socks. My ma always did tell me to wear clean underwear and decent socks when I went out. . . ." His voice trailed away as the creature behind the desk rose to her feet. She turned and started lifting weapons off the wall and piling them on the table.

"Look, this might not be the best time," Billy continued. "I'll just leave this here and head out. I've got some—"

"What's your name?" the Shadow asked.

"William Bonney . . . well, Billy. Everyone calls me Billy."

"I'm Scathach. Don't ever call me Scatty." She turned to Billy again. Her face had smoothed out, the vampire features hidden. As he watched, the solid redness in her eyes swirled away, revealing grass-green irises. She rubbed at the streaks of dried blood on her cheeks. "Do you have a car, Billy?"

"Sure do. A 1960 Thunderbird, Monte Carlo. That's the Second Generation model with a 430-cubic-inch 350-horsepower V8—"

"You're going to do me a favor, Billy," Scathach interrupted.

"I am?"

"You are. And your Elder Master will be thrilled that I'll now be indebted to you and thus to him. He knows I'm the sort of person who takes favors very seriously and remembers each one. Someday you will need a favor from me and I will repay you."

"I'm sort of big on favors myself," Billy said with a shy smile. "That's the way I was brought up. What can I do for you, ma'am?"

"For a start, you will never call me ma'am again."

"Yes, ma'am. Sorry, ma—sorry, Miss Scathach."

"Just Scathach. Do you have plans for the rest of the day?"

"Not really."

"Good. I need you to drive me to Vegas."

"Vegas!" Billy looked nostalgic for a moment. "I haven't been there in more than a hundred years. I used to stay at the Old Adobe Hotel, and I think I might have been in jail there once or twice."

Scathach stared at him, saying nothing.

Billy shrugged. "It was a long time ago. And I was innocent. I think. . . . Or at least that time I was innocent. I take it we're not going to Vegas for the shows."

"A . . . a . . ." She hesitated, looking for the right word. "A *friend* of mine is in trouble."

"What sort of trouble?"

"Vampyre trouble," Scathach said, gathering up the weapons and shoving them into a sports bag. "I'm going to get dressed. Take the pithos and put it back in the car—we're bringing it with us."

"Vampyres," Billy muttered. "I hate vampyres. Nasty, toothy, clawy . . ."

The Shadow stopped. "I am a vampire," she said, showing him her teeth.

Billy picked up the pithos. "I'll get the car."

6

"I'm driving Miss Scathach to Las Vegas." Billy spoke into a Bluetooth headset. He handed his passenger the cell phone and transferred the call from the earpiece to the handset. "He wants to talk to you. He sounds upset," he added with a grin.

"Is there a problem?" Scathach snapped. The sun was low in the sky, and she pulled a pair of mirrored aviator shades off her head and slipped them over her eyes. The lenses reflected the white facade of the Embarcadero.

Quetzalcoatl started to speak, but Scathach cut him off. "Something came up and I needed transportation. No, I still haven't learned to drive, but no doubt you know that. I suppose I should be honored that you've obviously kept tabs on me over the centuries. Just as I've kept them on you," she added. The Shadow glanced at the young American immortal. She knew he could not speak the ancient language of Danu Talis, but she was careful to keep her tone neutral so he couldn't pick up the nuances of her speech. "Your servant arrived just when I needed him." She turned to Billy and reverted to English. "How long will it take to get to Vegas?" Traffic along the Embarcadero was at a standstill.

He shrugged. "Once we get out of the city, it should be fairly easy. At this time of night, with me driving, I'd say eight, maybe nine hours."

"Do you sleep?" she asked.

"Not much anymore. Naps every few days."

Scathach turned back to the phone. "If he drops me on the Strip and turns around, he should be back in San Francisco by midmorning tomorrow. I'll make my own way home," she continued in English, before slipping back into the language of Danu Talis. "I hope this is not too much of an inconvenience for you, but I am sure you have many other servants."

"None like Billy the Kid," Quetzalcoatl said. "Try not to damage him."

Scathach hung up and passed the phone back to Billy. "He likes you," she said.

Billy laughed delightedly. "That old monster. He doesn't like anyone. I'm not even sure he likes himself."

Scathach shifted in the seat to get a better look at her driver. "So you're the famous Billy the Kid. I thought you'd be taller."

"I'm five eight," he answered, then paused. "You know, people used to say that all the time. But I haven't heard it in a while."

"Why not?"

"They're all dead." Billy smiled. "The curse of immortality, eh?"

Scathach nodded and turned away, looking out across San

Francisco Bay as Billy swung right, then circled left onto the Bay Bridge.

"I know you're not human, so I'm guessing you're an Elder, like Quetzalcoatl?"

"Next Generation," Scathach said shortly.

"What's the difference?" Billy asked.

"I was born after the fall of Danu Talis. Quetzalcoatl was born on the island."

"So you've lived a long time. You know what it's like to be immortal, to see everyone around you age and die. How do you deal with that?"

"You need to ask your master," Scathach snapped.

"He doesn't tell me anything."

Scathach remained silent for a few moments. "I've seen many humans face immortality, and they never get used to it. You'll learn to accept it. You'll learn never to make a close association with a mortal human." She turned to look at Billy. "You'll never take a mortal wife, or have a mortal girlfriend. You'll learn to artificially age yourself. You'll dress differently, add gray to your hair, grow a beard, and then move on. You'll never live too long in any one place. You'll spend the rest of your life on the run, looking over your shoulders."

"I did that when I was human," Billy said. "I'm well used to it."

"You're young. Enjoy it while you can. In another hundred years, two hundred, five hundred, a thousand, you will see things differently."

"You're just a bundle of laughs," Billy muttered. "I was enjoying being immortal."

"Billy, I have lived on this world—and others—for ten thousand years. I have watched the very Earth reshape itself. I have seen empires rise and fall." Her voice turned lost and lonely, and Billy caught the hint of what he recognized as an Irish accent, not unlike his mother's. "I have watched the death of nations; I have seen entire tribes vanish into myth and great civilizations fade to dust. I have seen so many friends die . . . and do you know the true curse of immortality?"

Billy the Kid shook his head. "Not sure I want to know now. . . ."

"The curse is that you remember every single face." Her expression became hard, lips disappearing into a thin line. "Ultimately, that's what will drive you mad."

"You remember all the faces?"

"All of them," she breathed.

"But you're not mad," he said lightly.

Scathach peered at him over the top of her aviator glasses. "How do you know?"

7

Quetzalcoatl sat in a room surrounded by the remnants of a lost empire, holding a cell phone in his hand. It was a slender rectangle of glass, metal, and liquid crystal, the very latest in high-tech gadgets, and yet incredibly crude when compared to the technology of his youth.

Every day Quetzalcoatl mourned the loss of his world. Once he had been worshipped as a god—now he was almost forgotten, remembered in a twisted collection of stories and folk songs that barely hinted at his true nature. But his time would come again. He had ruled the humani in the past; he would rule them once more. Even now, plans were in place to return the Elders to the earth. Within two years, three at the most, the humani would be nothing more than slaves again. There were, however, a few inconveniences—certain Elders and Next Generation and a few immortal humani—who would stand with the humans and fight. They had to be removed, but carefully, discreetly, quietly. Scathach presented a particular problem. There was no point in sending assassins after her: she had survived innumerable attempts on her life.

And then she invariably went after the would-be assassin's employer.

Quetzalcoatl had been authorized to try a much more devious method of killing the Shadow.

He hit Send and watched a 702 area code number scroll across the screen. The call was picked up on the first ring. "She is on the way," Quetzalcoatl said.

"Alone?"

"She is being delivered by one of my servants, an immortal humani known as Billy the Kid." The Elder sighed. "She has told me she will send Billy back to me, but I know his nature: he will want to help her." Quetzalcoatl's thin lips twisted into a sneer. "So be aware that you may have two enemies."

"If he sides with her, he will die with her."

The Elder shrugged. "A pity. His loss would be an inconvenience. If you can spare him, I would be grateful."

"I have a pack of cucubuths I've been starving for the past week and a nest of vampyres—proper blood drinkers—that I have not permitted to feed for a month. Once I unleash them, there will be no escape for Scathach or her accomplice."

"I will not advise you to be careful, but let me offer a word of friendly caution: you have never dealt with anyone like the Shadow before," Quetzalcoatl said.

"Ah, but I have, Elder. You forget: Scathach trained me."

8

Billy was happiest when he was driving. It represented the ultimate freedom. He didn't remember learning how to ride; riding was just something he had always done. A huge body of myth had grown up about the special bond between cowboy and horse. In truth, Billy had never felt that connection with an animal, and had known few cowboys who did. You took care of your horse the same way you took care of a car. It got you from point A to point B faster than you could walk. But he did remember the precise moment he'd bought his first car. It had been—naturally—a Model T, and in 1916, it had cost him over seven hundred dollars, which was a fortune in those days. He'd driven Fords for the next forty years, until he bought the 1960 Thunderbird convertible. He'd instantly fallen in love with the car with the sweeping tailfins and had never bought another. In the past five decades he'd spent a fortune maintaining the Thunderbird, and he didn't regret a single cent. This car was his pride and joy. Sitting back, he pressed gently on the accelerator and the big V8 engine surged forward with a low bubbling growl.

"Careful," Scathach said, the first words she'd spoken in

over three hundred miles. "We don't want to get pulled over for speeding."

"I'm always careful." Billy smiled.

The red-haired woman straightened in the seat and pushed her sunglasses up onto her head. She looked around. The road on either side was lost in the night, only briefly illuminated as the headlights washed over road signs. "Where are we?"

"We've made good time. We've just gone through Barstow and turned onto Interstate 15. Maybe two and half hours to Vegas. We should arrive there with the dawn."

Scathach stretched, working her head up and down. Muscles popped. "You've been driving all night. How do you feel?"

"I'm fine. I love driving. One of these days I think I'd like to drive from one side of the country to the other, coast to coast."

Scathach nodded. "I went by train a long time ago," she offered. "I never really thanked you for this, did I? I know you didn't exactly volunteer."

"No, I didn't," he admitted, and grinned. "But I didn't think I was in a position to protest. I thought you were going to bite my head off. I didn't realize you were a vampire."

"I don't drink blood," she said with a smile, deliberately showing her teeth. The dashboard lit her face from below, turning it into a terrifying mask. "My clan, the vampires—vampire with an *i*—are vegetarians. There are others, vampyres with a *y*, who are blood drinkers."

"That's good to know. I thought you were all blood drinkers. How can I tell the clans apart?"

"You can't. The best advice I can give you is to stay away from all of them. We're bad news."

"Even you?" he teased.

"Especially me."

Billy grimaced. "So," he said, changing the subject. "Your friend who's in trouble. What are you going to do?"

"Rescue him."

"All on your own?"

"You really have no idea who I am, do you?"

The immortal shook his head. "Never heard of you before today."

"Well, let's hope you never find out."

"Look . . . ," Billy began slowly. He'd been thinking as they drove. "I'm not real comfortable with the idea of you facing off against a bunch of vampyres—with a *y*—on your own. Maybe I could hang around and back you up."

It took the Shadow a moment before she could answer. She threw back her head and laughed, the sound high and pure on the desert air. And then, as quickly as it had come, the laughter died. "Why, do you not think I'm up to it?"

Billy shook his head. "No, no, nothing like that. But there might be a lot of them, and besides, everyone needs a helping hand sometimes."

Scathach straightened and quickly reached down for the nunchaku on the floor by her feet. The chain connecting the two short lengths of wood rattled as she picked it up.

"Something wrong?" Billy glanced in the rearview mirror. They were the only car on the long, straight Interstate 15.

"We've got company," Scathach said quietly. She pointed off to her side of the road with the blunt end of the nunchaku.

For a moment, the immortal saw nothing, and then a dozen red and golden circles briefly flared before vanishing. "Coyotes?" he asked.

Scathach shook her head. "Too big. Wolves."

"There are no wolves in this part of California."

"Exactly."

He peered out into the night. "Where are they?"

"They're here."

The road curved slightly and the Thunderbird's headlights picked out four huge gray wolves sitting up ahead at the edge of the highway. As the lights washed over their snouts, their eyes glowed golden.

"I'm guessing these are not natural," Billy said quietly.

"What do you think?" Scathach asked. She leaned back so that Billy could look across her. The wolves were loping silently alongside the car, keeping pace with it.

Billy checked the speedometer. "We're doing seventy-five miles an hour. What kind of unnatural are they?"

"Cucubuths. Shape-changers. Abominations. They're the spawn of a vampire and one of the were-clans. Can you see their auras?"

Billy squinted into the night. Wisps of smoke curled off the running wolves. "Dirty gray?"

"In their human form, they will have tails, but their auras will always reveal them."

"Will they attack?"

"No. They're merely monitoring our progress."

"So we're expected."

"*I* am expected," she clarified.

"You said your friend was being held captive by vampyres."

"I did."

"So who told them you were coming?" Billy asked. "And coming down this road?"

The Shadow shook her head. The same thoughts had been running through her head.

"Sounds to me like you're riding into a trap," Billy murmured.

"It wouldn't be the first time." Scathach showed her vampire teeth. "And I'm still here."

9

The apartment took up the entire top floor of one of the newest towers in Las Vegas. The walls were entirely glass, offering a 360-degree vista of the city and the surrounding desert landscape. And while every room in the hotel and casino below had been decorated to the most particular specifications, the penthouse was unfinished. Snaking loops of wire curled from the metal ceiling joists, the supporting columns were bare metal, and the concrete floor was still covered in thick sheets of plastic. Workmen's tools were piled in one corner of the huge room, cans of paint and ladders in another.

The golden-haired young man in the impeccably tailored black suit was reflected in the dirty floor-to-ceiling windows. Opening a sliding door, he stepped out onto a broad curved balcony. Far below him, spread out in a glittering sweep of color, lay Las Vegas. He loved this view. There were taller buildings in Vegas, more spectacular hotels and casinos, but none of them had this view. The apartment had been chosen and designed to allow him to look out over the city he secretly ruled, but he'd stopped construction midway to completion.

Before it could be finished, there was something he needed to do. Someone he needed to kill.

Bitter memories soured his expression, making his beautiful face ugly and cruel. Maybe when the night was over, he would be able to call in the builders to complete work on the apartment. Stepping back inside, he looked around. He knew exactly how this room would be: pure white. White Italian marble would be laid on the floor, and tiny spotlights in the ceiling would outline the constellation Cygnus. In some Eastern and African cultures, white was the color of mourning. He would keep this room as a shrine to the memory of the woman he had once loved . . . before she betrayed him.

Suddenly, the dry, gritty air was touched with an indefinable musky scent and he felt a vibration. He adjusted his tie the instant before a shape stepped out of the shadows behind him.

"She's coming." The creature spoke in the ancient language of the Celts.

The young man turned and spread his arms wide. "Morrigan, Great Queen," he said in the same tongue. "It is good to see you."

Pale-skinned and dark-haired, the woman had a narrow, angular face, with prominent cheekbones and a pointed chin. Her eyes were hidden behind small black circular glasses. The Morrigan was dressed from head to foot in figure-hugging black leather. An ornate corset was studded with silver bolts and bars, giving it the appearance of a medieval breastplate, and her leather gloves had rectangular silver studs sewn onto the backs of the fingers. The gloves had no fingertips, which allowed the Elder's long black nails to show. She wore a heavy leather belt decorated with thirteen round shields, and draped over her shoulders was a shimmering cloak made entirely of ravens' feathers. The ancient Irish had called her the Crow Goddess. She was worshipped and feared throughout the Celtic lands as the Goddess of Death and Destruction.

The man caught her right hand and bowed over it, pressing his lips to her cold flesh. "Thank you for coming."

The Morrigan stood at the window and looked down over the city. Even in the early hours of the morning, it was a kaleidoscope of lights. "Are you sure you want to go through with this?"

The young man blinked in surprise. "I never thought I'd hear you say that."

"I've known the Shadow a lot longer than you. I have followed her down through the millennia in this world and the other Shadowrealms. She is fearless and deadly."

He turned to stand shoulder to shoulder with the Morrigan. "Ah, but we have a huge advantage." The Morrigan glanced sidelong at him, razor-thin eyebrows raised in a silent question. "We have the element of surprise," he continued. "Scathach believes she is coming here to rescue me." He laughed and his breath created a moist circle on the glass. Pulling a white handkerchief from his pocket, he ran it over the glass. The white cloth came away smeared with dirt, and he tossed it aside. "And in that moment of surprise lies her doom. I will have my revenge."

"Revenge is always a dangerous game," the Morrigan said quietly. She slid open a door and stepped out onto the balcony. A waft of sour, dry heat accompanied by a dull, buzzing rumble of traffic washed in from the city below. Then, climbing onto the rail, the Crow Goddess launched herself into the night, soaring high over the never-sleeping city.

Uninterested in the Morrigan's flight, the young man turned away from the window, slid a flat black phone from his shirt pocket, and hit a speed dial number. The phone was answered on the first ring. "She's coming," he announced. "Remember, the red-haired female is mine and mine alone. Any companions are yours." His smooth, handsome face turned bestial. "If she is harmed by anyone other than me, my vengeance will be terrible."

10

The lights of Vegas bloomed on the horizon, a glowing stain against the waning night.

"Decision time," Billy said. "Where are we going?"

"*We?*" Scathach asked.

"We. I've decided I'm going to hang around for a while. Just in case you need a hand."

"It is a very sweet offer," Scathach said, sounding genuinely moved. "But if you stay with me, you will end up dead. Everyone does. It's one of the reasons I don't have a companion."

"I'm not that easy to kill," Billy said. "Trust me, a lot of people have tried and failed. I'm still here and they're not."

"It's your decision. I can't be responsible for you," Scathach said, her voice turning cold.

"I wouldn't want you to be," Billy said. "I've been responsible for myself for my entire life. This is my decision."

"As you wish." The Shadow turned away and looked back outside at the cucubuths still keeping pace with the car.

" 'As you wish'?" Billy said. "That's it? No arguments?"

"Would you listen to me if I argued?"

"No."

"Would you obey me if I told you to leave me alone and head back to San Francisco?"

"No."

"Exactly, so what's the point in arguing?"

"There is none." Billy grinned. "I'm sticking right here. I have a feeling that hanging around with you might be fun."

Something like a smile curled Scathach's lips. "Fun. I don't believe anyone has ever said that to me before. You know something," she added, reaching for the nunchaku on the floor, "these cucubuths are really starting to irritate me!"

Without warning she leapt from the moving car.

Billy stood on the brakes, locking the tires. The heavy car fishtailed down the road, rubber screaming and smoking. By the time he came to a stop, Scathach had landed in the middle of the startled creatures. Instinctively, one lashed out at her, dagger-sharp curled talons hissing through the air toward her face. The Shadow moved her head a fraction and the claws missed her; then the heavy end of the nunchaku shot out to hit the creature between the eyes above its long wolf's snout. It fell without a sound. A second threw himself at her, transforming from a wolf into a man in midair. The nunchaku struck him down, and as he fell, Scathach caught him and flung him into another creature. They tumbled into the dirt together, yelping and barking like dogs. The Shadow's nunchaku whirled around her in a buzzing blur and then connected with both creatures' skulls. They crashed back into the dry undergrowth and lay still.

"You should not have done that," another of the monsters lisped, its tongue struggling to make sounds in a mouth never designed for human speech.

Scathach whirled. She was facing three huge cucubuths. They were caught halfway between their human and wolf forms: a wolf's head on a human body, animal claws on the end of muscular human arms. The biggest creature dangled a length of chain, while its two companions carried clubs.

"You cannot take all of us," the creature said.

Scathach laughed, her face rippling through a change that revealed the vampyre beneath the flesh. "Oh yes, I can."

Suddenly, the three creatures were lit up by approaching red lights. The Thunderbird appeared, engine howling as it backed toward them at high speed. Brakes screamed and the car rocked, sliding sideways, slamming into the three cucubuths. Two were catapulted off into the night, while the biggest was shoved straight toward the Shadow. Her nunchaku whirred and the creature stopped as if it had run into a wall. It folded to the ground at Scathach's feet.

Billy launched himself out of the car and darted around to examine the passenger side. The door was buckled and there was a deep indentation on the front wing. He pulled a handkerchief out of his back pocket and rubbed furiously at the longest of the scrapes.

"I don't think it's going to rub out," Scathach said gently. "That was a very brave thing you did. Great driving, too."

"Get in the car," Billy snapped. "We're going to Vegas. I've stripped inches of rubber off the tires, and do you know what a new door for one of these costs? Someone is going to pay for that."

11

Elvis—fat, white-suited Elvis—was standing on the sidewalk across the road from the Las Vegas Wedding Chapel of the Bells. Marilyn Monroe, wearing a badly fitting white dress, was leaning against him. Both looked as if they had been out all night. Marilyn was wearing a Just Married sign around her neck.

"That's the third Elvis we've seen so far," Billy said, grinning. "And always the jumpsuit-and-rhinestones Elvis. Say, you don't know if he was ever made immortal, do you?"

Scathach shook her head. "I have no idea. No, that's not true. I do know—because I sang with him once," she said absently, "and I would have known if he was immortal. So no, he wasn't."

Billy was so startled, he almost ran a red light at Sahara Avenue. "You sang with Elvis?" He turned in the seat to look at the red-haired girl. She had rested her elbow on the window and her chin was in her palm, long fingers touching the side of her face. She would never be called beautiful, Billy knew, and yet, in the kaleidoscopic wash of lights from the Las Vegas strip, she was striking.

"I was a backup singer. It was a long time ago."

Billy shook his head. "I had plans to see him in Indianapolis in '77, but something came up and I couldn't go. I've got all his albums on vinyl, though."

"I'm more of a Dean Martin fan myself."

"Don't tell me you sang with him, too," Billy said breathlessly.

"Twice," Scathach said. "Once in this very town, back in 1964."

They were almost opposite the Sahara Hotel when Scathach abruptly straightened. She'd spotted a figure sitting on the bench inside a bus shelter. "Pull in here," she said very quietly.

The figure stood and Billy squinted. "It's someone wearing a superhero cloak." He watched the warrior slide a long, narrow dagger out of its sheath and hold it flat against her arm. "I'm guessing it's not a superhero cloak." And then he saw who was standing by the side of the road. "Try not to do any more damage to the car," he muttered as he pulled into the Buses Only zone and stopped.

The Morrigan stepped out of the shadows of the bus shelter and examined the indentations in the car door. "Those cucubuths are tougher than they look," she said. As she spoke she opened her mouth in a smile, revealing sharp teeth.

"You were watching us," Scathach said.

The Morrigan pointed a black-nailed finger upward. "I was around. It's a shame about the damage. It should never have happened," she added. "But it's your own fault: you

453

should never have engaged the cucubuths. They were ordered to leave you alone." She leaned forward to look squarely into Billy's face. "Good evening, Billy."

"Evening, ma'am. Or should that be good morning?"

"I see you've met," Scathach said.

Billy nodded. "The Morrigan is an old friend of Quetzalcoatl—my master. She's come a-calling once or twice." Although he kept his face expressionless, he was unable to disguise the distaste in his voice.

"It is not too late for you to turn back, Billy. Siding with this"—the Morrigan paused, looking for the correct word—"this *creature* would be a mistake."

"That's what she said." Billy grinned. "And I didn't listen to her, either."

"And while the cucubuths are under instructions to leave the Shadow alone, the same protection does not extend to her companions."

Billy laughed. "I ain't afraid of no dogs."

"You should be," Scathach and the Morrigan said simultaneously.

"Since when did you two become my mother?"

The Morrigan glanced up and down the street, then folded her arms and leaned casually against the side of the car. She looked down at Scathach. "I seem to remember that you were told you would die in an exotic location." She deliberately spoke in English for Billy's benefit.

"I'm not sure Las Vegas counts as exotic," Scathach answered. "It only thinks it's exotic."

"You will die here, Shadow. Before the sun rises."

The red-haired girl shrugged. "So, I take it you know why I've come?"

"I do."

"Is it true, then? Is he here?"

The Morrigan blinked her black eyes and then she nodded. "He's here."

"A prisoner of the vampyres?"

"The blood drinkers are everywhere."

"And you—why are you here, Morrigan?"

"Oh, Scathach," the Crow Goddess said, reverting to the Irish language. "I was there at the very beginning, all those centuries ago. It is only fitting that I should be here at the end. I will give you a proper burial and sing the old songs over your corpse."

"I'd really prefer that you did not."

Scathach and the Morrigan eyed each other silently, and finally Billy cleared his throat. "Ladies," he asked, "are we going to sit here and chat all night?"

The Morrigan tossed a scrap of paper at Billy, who deftly caught it in his right hand.

"It's the address of an as-yet-unopened hotel and casino," the Morrigan snapped. "Drive around the back and into the garage." She smiled at Scathach, and a dark hunger flickered behind her eyes. "You will find what you are looking for on the top floor," she said in English, and then continued in the ancient language of Danu Talis. "I will come for your corpse after your defeat." She looked at Billy. "Take her there now . . . and if you value your immortal life, turn around and drive away."

"See you on the top floor," Billy said cheerfully.

The Crow Goddess glared at the immortal. "You won't even get past the lobby." She stepped back into the shadow of the bus shelter, and her form warped and changed. Billy pulled away from the curb as the huge crow took to the sky in a slow ascending spiral.

They drove down Las Vegas Boulevard toward the garish lights of the enormous hotels and casinos. After a few moments Billy broke the silence.

"So what's the plan?" he asked.

"I don't plan. Anyone in my way can either step aside or I will step over them."

"You're my type of girl," the immortal said admiringly.

Scathach laughed. "Oh, Billy. I'm a ten-thousand-year-old vampire. I am most definitely not your type of girl."

Billy's cheeks suddenly reddened. "I was talking about planning. I—I'm not that big on planning myself," he stammered. "I wasn't suggesting anything else. . . ."

"Stop talking now," the Shadow commanded with a grin.

12

Billy felt the familiar rush of excitement as he pulled the car into the empty parking lot beneath the unopened casino. Black Hawk had once told him that one of the great dangers of immortality was boredom. Immortals didn't need to be cautious or careful. Wounds would heal; bones would mend. As they aged, some immortals sought out more and more dangerous or challenging experiences simply to remember what it felt to be human again. Billy had laughed; he'd always been that way—he needed excitement. He loved this feeling, the buzz at the base of his stomach, the tightness across his chest, the tingling in his fingertips. It had been a long time since he'd experienced it so strongly.

He turned off the car and the couple sat in silence, listening to the engine tick softly. Finally, he shifted in the seat and looked at the Shadow. She seemed unconcerned. "How do you feel?" he asked.

"Fine," she said, surprised. "Why?"

"The Crow Goddess said you could die."

"When you've lived as long as I have, that isn't really a threat anymore. I've done just about everything I've ever wanted to do, and a lot that I haven't as well. I've lived a full life, with few regrets. This is a good day to die."

"Well, I don't fancy dying today, if you don't mind."

"Then you should drive on," the Shadow said matter-of-factly. "Stay here with me and there's a very real possibility that you will be killed. And probably eaten, too," she added, pushing open the car door and climbing out. She twisted her body from side to side, stretching. "Pop the trunk."

Billy climbed out and opened the trunk. The cloying tang of cacao beans wafted out. Scathach unwrapped the pithos and tossed the bag to the side. She ran her fingers over the jar and the curling text shifted and twisted under her touch. Then she brought the jar to her ear and shook it.

"I thought I heard voices inside," Billy said.

"You did."

"Little People?"

Scathach grinned. "No. Worse. Much worse." She returned the jar to the trunk. "I've got a feeling that Quetzalcoatl conveniently surrendering the jar and this call to Vegas may not be unconnected."

"How do you reckon that?"

"The Morrigan. You said you had seen her with the Feathered Serpent. . . ."

Billy nodded. "More than once."

"And she is inextricably entwined with the story of my . . . friend." Scathach returned the pithos to the trunk. "When this is over, perhaps I'll visit your Elder master."

"He wouldn't like that."

"No, he wouldn't."

"I'd probably have to fight you," Billy said.

"And I wouldn't like that," Scathach said.

"Me neither." Billy watched the Shadow unzip the bag of weapons she'd packed and begin to sort through the metal and wood. When he'd first seen her standing in the doorway of the dojo, he'd thought she looked like a girl, but now he realized he was looking at a warrior. Scathach was dressed in black combat trousers, a short-sleeved black T-shirt, and steel-toed combat boots. She strapped two short swords onto her back, with the hilts protruding over each shoulder, added a handful of shuriken—throwing stars—to a pouch on her belt, and attached a second nunchaku to her hip, making a matching set. She coiled what looked like a long black metal jump rope around her waist. Billy had never seen anything like it before.

"What is that?" he asked.

"Manrikigusari. A Japanese throwing chain."

"Man-ri-ki-gus-ari." Billy struggled to pronounce the word.

"It means 'the strength of a thousand men.'" In a flash, Scathach pulled the six-foot length of chain off her waist and sent it hissing through the air. It snapped around a concrete pillar, the two heavy heads at either end cracking into the cement, biting out huge chunks. "I can also use it as a whip," she said as she went to retrieve the chain. "I'm betting you have a pair of six-guns, maybe Colts, and probably a Winchester rifle." When she turned around, Billy the Kid was holding a simple black police baton with a side handle.

The Kid's face was a solemn mask. "I haven't touched a gun in a long time," he said quietly. "They never brought me anything but misery while I lived."

Scathach nodded at the baton. "A tonfa. You're full of surprises, Mr. Bonney." She wrapped the chain around her waist again. "Do you know how to use that?"

Billy flowed into a defensive pose, right hand outstretched, left hand clutching the baton by the protruding side handle, the black stick stretching the length of his forearm. "Oh, I know how to use it. My friend Black Hawk runs one of the biggest security firms in the Bay Area. I help him out when he's short-staffed. Concert security is the best; I get to see a lot of great shows for free. The Rolling Stones are coming to SBC Park in a couple of weeks for two shows," he added, excited. "I'll be at both of them."

"If you survive tonight."

"I'll survive," Billy said confidently.

"Full of surprises," Scathach repeated, shaking her head. She clapped him on the shoulder. "If—and it is a very big if—we both survive this, come and visit me at the dojo. Maybe I could train you to use a matched pair of tonfa," she added lightly.

"I'd like that," Billy said. Then his face fell. "But . . ."

"But?"

"I'm not sure Quetzalcoatl would. I don't think he likes you very much."

"So don't tell him. You're his servant, not his slave. And let me give you a piece of advice: never admit to anyone—Elder, Next Generation, or immortal human—that you know me. I've made a lot of enemies over the millennia."

"I can do that. Never met you. Never heard of you." He smiled.

They walked across the garage toward the escalators and stairs. "Would you have a problem being trained by a woman?" Scathach asked.

Billy laughed. "Oh, I've learned a lot from women. You should have met my Ma. Now, there was a fighter. . . ."

13

Unseen, deadly and eternally hungry, vampyres controlled Vegas.

The first vampyres arrived when gambling was legalized in the 1930s, quickly realizing that the town would attract countless transients and tourists. It was a city where the nights were as busy as the days, and within the constantly shifting population, the vampyres could remain invisible. Over the years, more and more of the blood-drinking clan, and their close kin, the cucubuths, had made their way to the city. Most worked in the hotels and casinos; others found employment in the spectacular shows; a few were police officers, working the night shift.

And for the first time in a millennium, they owed allegiance to a single figure who was not one of their own, neither vampyre nor cucubuth, but an immortal human. Setanta.

The young-looking man moved around the empty penthouse, checking the traps, making sure his cache of weapons were in their positions. He had changed out of his elegant black suit into an outfit that almost matched Scathach's: black trousers, black vest, and high-topped steel-toed combat boots. He had no doubt that the Shadow would reach this room. The cucubuths were good, the vampyres even better, but no one was as good as the Shadow.

Except him. She had trained him. He knew her secrets.

Setanta had spent a thousand years—ever since he had returned to the Earth Shadowrealm—looking for the Shadow. He'd come close on a few occasions, but she had always eluded him. There were rumors of a young red-haired girl on the fringes of every major world conflict. He had learned that she was in contact with the Flamels, but he'd never been tempted to go in search of them or to offer a reward for information about them. Everyone knew that John Dee was hunting the Alchemyst and his wife. And even Setanta, with his deadly cucubuth guards and vampyre allies, did not want to cross the dangerous Dr. John Dee. Everyone knew that Dee was quite, quite mad.

And then, entirely unexpectedly, he'd received a call from an Elder he'd never heard of before: Quetzalcoatl. Setanta was stunned that the Elder even knew who he was, but he was even more astonished when the gravel-voiced creature had revealed that he knew Scathach's whereabouts.

Setanta had traveled the world in search of the woman, and for the last few years, she'd been little more than five hundred miles away, in San Francisco.

Setanta had immediately put in place a plan for vengeance, a strategy to lure Scathach to Vegas and her doom. And Quetzalcoatl had been more than willing to help.

A flicker in the half-light made him turn. The huge crow-like creature perched on the railing of the balcony outside his window shifted into the Morrigan. She pulled open the sliding door and stepped inside. "They're here."

"So it begins." Setanta rubbed his calloused hands together. "So it ends. Finally," he breathed.

14

The elevator door pinged open and Billy the Kid stepped out into an empty glass-and-marble lobby. The air smelled of sawdust and fresh paint, and all the furniture was covered in thick plastic sheets.

Billy looked around, mouth agape, as awestruck as any tourist confronted with the gaudy excess of Las Vegas. There was gold everywhere: an enormous gold-plated fountain dominated the center of the lobby, all the supporting columns were painted with gold leaf, and a spectacularly complex fresco depicting a man he thought might be King Midas took up an entire wall. There were a dozen golden statues of armored women scattered around the room, each one complete with a golden sword or spear. Even the mirror-glossy marble floor was a warm golden color. "Very shiny," he murmured. He wondered if the gold was real, and then, remembering that this was Vegas, decided that it probably was.

Billy was striding across the floor when the first of the vampyres appeared. They were all women, pale-skinned, dark-eyed, pointy-toothed. He counted six of them, and he had a feeling that there was at least one more behind him, but he wasn't going to look. They were dressed in an assortment of clothes: smart suits and croupier's uniforms, store clerk's smocks—there was even one in an exotic fish-skin circus costume. Billy's first reaction was one of relief—none of them were armed—but then he looked at their hands and saw the length of their nails.

"I thought there would be more of you," he said lightly, stepping over to position himself with his back to a wall. Although he'd sworn off guns a lifetime ago, he quite liked the idea of having a gun now, something big and ugly with lots of barrels. He tightened his grip on the tonfa.

He could handle seven.

"Oh, but there are more," one of the creatures said. She was shorter than the others, a small but powerfully built woman wearing a blue security guard's uniform. Four more women and two men stepped out from behind the gold pillars.

"Thirteen." He thought he might be able to handle thirteen.

There was a commotion on the stairs and three hulking cucubuths in wolf form appeared. The biggest one licked its lips.

"Sixteen." Thirteen vampyres and three cucubuths . . . that might be a stretch. "Are you going to turn me into a vampyre?" Billy asked.

"We're not that type of vampyre," the creature answered. They all chuckled, the sound liquid and ugly.

"What sort are you?"

"The flesh-eating kind."

"I'll give you indigestion," Billy muttered.

"Where is the Shadow?" the vampyre demanded.

"She'll be right along," he said vaguely. "Any minute now."

"She will find us feasting on your bones!" the creature screamed, and launched herself at Billy, mouth gaping, teeth bared.

15

Scathach had decided to get to the penthouse from the outside. The building was only fifty stories high, and she guessed there would be vampyres on every floor and probably cucubuths in the stairwells. Fighting her way up from the inside would be tedious and exhausting; climbing was the safest way to the top. The facade was decorated with a vaguely Celtic motif—intricate swirls and waves, leaf-shaped patterns that almost resembled shamrocks, and etched lines that Scathach thought looked remarkably like Ogham, the ancient writing of Ireland, were carved into its surface.

She used the manrikigusari chain like a lasso, wrapping it around the railing of the first-floor balcony and hauling herself up. She scaled the building quickly, finding finger- and footholds in the decorations and patterns. Halfway up she glanced over her head: the sky had lightened and was beginning to fade to purple. It would soon be dawn and the sun would quickly rise, and then it would only be a matter of time before someone spotted her and called the police.

She pressed on. Clambering over a Celtic spiral, she lost her footing—steel-toed boots had never been intended for climbing—and she lashed out with the manrikigusari, snagging the balcony railings above her in the last instant before she lost her grip completely. The chain rattled and then caught, and Scathach swung gently against the side of the building, holding on with one hand. She pulled herself up the chain and dropped onto the balcony, then looked down. She'd climbed about twenty floors. Only another thirty to go.

The door from the balcony into the suite was open and Scathach slipped inside, tracking black boot prints across the white carpet. The entire suite was probably bigger than her dojo, she realized; the bed alone was about the same size as her entire apartment. And did anyone really need six huge televisions in their room? Pressing the side of her face against the door, she closed her eyes and listened. Below, far below, her acute hearing picked up the noise of a commotion, and she grinned. That meant that Billy was still alive and fighting. She liked him; he reminded her of Joan of Arc.

Focusing, she turned to the corridor outside. Nothing. She was guessing the guards on the lower floors had been called down to deal with the Kid. There would be guards on the upper floors, but she could cope with them.

Pulling open the door, she found herself staring into the jaws of a huge, hairy, yellow-eyed cucubuth. He was cleaning his claws with a dagger as long as her arm. "Ska-tog," he squeaked.

The Shadow's right hand shot forward and up, the heel of her palm catching the cucubuth under the jaw. His teeth clicked together and his head snapped back. The force of the

blow lifted the cucubuth's feet off the floor; he was unconscious before he hit the thick carpet. Scathach stepped over
the body, shaking her head. She must be losing it; she hadn't
even smelled the creature. And then she stopped and returned
to the beast and bent low, nostrils flaring. Scathach blinked in
surprise. A cucubuth who showered; now, there was a first.

16

"You wouldn't hit a woman, would you?" the vampyre snarled, landing on her feet directly in front of Billy the Kid.

He smiled. "You're right. I wouldn't." He whipped his wrist and the tonfa spun around on its short handle. He snapped it out and struck the creature on the side of the head. "You're not a woman."

They swarmed him then, hissing and snarling like cats, long nails clawing, razor-sharp teeth snapping at him. Billy was fast, always had been. Speed had kept him alive in the Old West, and the past century had only honed his skills. The tonfa blurred about him as he turned, the heavy polycarbonate baton striking and blocking, while his right hand punched, shoved, slapped, and chopped. He kept moving, moving, moving. One of the first lessons he'd learned from an old gunfighter was never to present a still target.

A dozen more vampyres swarmed into the building. There were so many of the vampyres that they got in each other's way in their eagerness to reach him. A male vampyre in hospital scrubs struck out at him. Billy ducked and the creature's talons scored long gouges in the wall over his head. He cracked the tonfa into the vampyre's kneecap and the creature fell to the ground, howling. He turned, and another leapt onto his back, nails tearing at his chest, teeth dangerously close to his throat. Billy reached behind him and rammed the handle of the black stick into its mouth and then lunged backward, slamming the creature into a wall. Two of the cucubuths lumbered toward him, shoving the vampyres aside. They were enormous beasts, with the bodies of wolves but the heads and hands of men. Billy rapped the tonfa on the skull of the nearer one. His weapon bounced away.

"You'll have to do better than that," the cucubuth growled.

Billy spun, gripped one of the ornate golden statues, and used all his weight to push it at the creature. The heavy stone likeness of a Greek goddess carrying a bow shivered on its pedestal and then toppled toward the cucubuth, which simply reached up and caught it in both hands. "You'll have to do better than that, too," the creature growled.

"Will this do?" Billy lifted a foot and stamped—hard—on the cucubuth's bare toes. The creature bellowed and released its grip on the statue, which thumped onto its head, knocking the beast to the floor.

The second monster leapt at him. Billy sidestepped at the last moment and the beast crashed headfirst into the gold mural of King Midas. The cucubuth staggered back, flakes of gold paint stuck to its forehead, and Billy swung his stick, connecting with the base of the cucubuth's skull.

The room was littered with groaning and injured vampyres. He had hurt more than a dozen, but there were at least twice that number remaining. And Billy was starting to tire. The creatures were strong and fast, and his shirt and jeans were in shreds from their nails. He was bleeding from a score of scrapes and cuts, and his tonfa was scored with deep claw marks. He wasn't sure how much longer he could last.

The vampyres circled Billy warily. He knew that if they all rushed him at once, it would be over. But the best form of defense, he'd been told, was offense. With a scream of defiance, he launched himself at the nearest vampyre, a huge man in a casino security officer's uniform. Billy swung the black tonfa up, but the creature blocked it with his own baton, twisted, and sent the immortal's weapon spinning from his hand. The vampyre wrapped a clawed hand around Billy's throat and squeezed, but the Kid brought both hands in a ringing clap over the creature's ears. It hissed and staggered back and Billy wrenched the vampyre's stick from its hands. "I'll take that. Thank you kindly. . . ."

But the remaining vampyres were on top of him now, catching him, holding him, tearing at him. He felt claws in his flesh, in his hair.

And then Billy the Kid went down.

17

Scathach stopped five floors below the penthouse. She had run up twenty-five flights of stairs and had encountered no one, but now she could smell the guards on the floors above. Vampyre. The metallic odor of old blood and rotten meat.

The Shadow padded silently down a corridor and chose a door at random. It was unlocked. The room it led into was even larger than the one below, and even more opulently decorated. As she crossed the floor, she counted eight television sets. Sliding open the patio door, she stepped out onto the balcony. The view across Las Vegas was spectacular. Although it was still night overhead, the sky to the east had turned salmon and mauve and she knew it was only minutes until sunrise. The lights on that side of the city had faded and turned tawdry. Ignoring the Do Not Stand On This Railing sign, she climbed up and balanced on the railing. Turning her back to the city, she reached up and found a handhold. It was only five floors to the penthouse.

She could hear vampyres and cucubuths moving restlessly on each of the next four floors, and she caught fragments of a dozen conversations in languages no longer spoken on the Earth Shadowrealm. The creatures were worried; some even sounded frightened. They knew the Shadow was coming. Scathach grinned, showing her own vampire teeth: it was nice to know that she still inspired fear in the blood drinkers.

Catching the rail of the final floor, she heaved herself up onto the penthouse balcony. She stood outside the glass door and peered in to assess the situation. In the center of the huge space was a wooden kitchen chair, and tied to the chair, facing the door, with his back to her, was the man she had come to rescue.

Scathach's instincts were to charge in and untie him, but over the centuries she had learned to temper her first reactions with caution. Tilting her head to one side, she closed her eyes and allowed her other senses to expand.

Blocking out the acrid, sickly smells of the city, the blood and copper of the vampyre, and the paint and plaster of the room, she smelled the man. It was an odor she had not smelled in millennia, strong and heady: honey and wet grass, a hint of sea salt, the muskiness of wet bog land, the tang of peat smoke.

Scathach breathed in deeply, indulging herself for the last time, remembering the man, remembering the time when she had been in love. She had been happy then.

There was only his scent. He was alone in the room. And that was wrong. If he was a prisoner—then where were his guards?

Scathach breathed deeply again, and there, right at the edge of her consciousness, was a second odor. Faint and bitter: the chalkiness of crushed eggshells, the musty ammonia of a fouled nest: the Morrigan. The Crow Goddess had been here.

All this had to be a trap.

Scathach turned and scanned the lightening skies, but there was no sign of the Morrigan. She unsheathed her two short swords, caught the edge of the door, flung it open and launched herself into the room. Rolling across the floor, she came up behind the figure tied to the chair and her left-hand sword flashed, slicing through the thick ropes in one smooth movement.

The man surged out of the chair and spun to face her.

And even though she knew who it was, Scathach felt as if she had been struck a hammer blow.

He was as she remembered him: short, broad-shouldered and narrow-waisted, with eyes the color of wet stone and fine golden hair hanging to his shoulders. He had been born with seven fingers on each hand.

"I knew you would come for me," he said in the language of ancient Ireland.

"Cuchulain," she breathed. The only man she had ever loved.

18

"I've gone back to my original name. I'm called Setanta." He rubbed his wrists, smiling broadly at her. "You've not changed in the slightest." His eyes sparkled. "Except for the hair. Short. I like it."

"The—the last time I saw you . . . ," Scathach stammered. "I was dead."

The Shadow nodded. Her lips moved before she could find the breath to say the words. "Dead. Aoife and I came for you, but the Morrigan was already carrying your body away."

"You should have come sooner," Setanta said quietly. He clasped his hands behind his back and stepped past her to look at the rising sun. A thin bar of amber was creeping across the ceiling. "I needed you, Shadow. But you were not there."

"We came . . . Aoife and I . . ." There were bloodred tears on her face now. "We put aside our differences and came for you."

"Do you know how long it took for me to die on that hillside?" His voice had changed; there was a streak of anger running through it. He walked slowly around the stricken

Shadow. "Behind me, my entire army lay ensorcelled and asleep, and before me lay the horde of the Witch Queen. I was left to stand alone against the Queen's army."

"And you got what you always wanted: that day you became a legend," Scathach said quietly. "The stories say that you tied yourself to a stone and that none of the Queen's army dared approach you until a raven landed on your shoulder. Only then did they know you were dead."

"I died because you were not there," Cuchulain whispered, walking close to Scathach, pointing an accusing finger. The anger was now almost palpable in every word. "You are as responsible as they are for my death." He was behind her now, and as he spoke, he lifted a huge broadsword from behind a pillar, gripped it in both hands and swung.

Lost in her grief, the Shadow smelled the metal only at the very last moment. She heard it part the air. Instinct sent her forward and down, and the razor-sharp blade took just the tips of her spiked hair. She rolled to her feet, bringing her swords up as Cuchulain attacked.

"I blame you, Shadow. You. You. You." He hacked and slashed, the ferocity of his attack driving her back across the room.

Scathach defended herself but made no move to attack.

Cuchulain slashed at her with the huge broadsword. "The Morrigan rescued me before I breathed my last and brought me to the Tir na nÓg Shadowrealm. The Elder Crom Cruach made me immortal, but in return I was bound to him for a millennium of servitude. A thousand years in the service of that monster. You have no idea of the things he made me do, and for every world I've destroyed, I blamed you." He swung again, the heavy blade striking sparks off Scathach's swords. "For every death I've caused, I cursed your name." He cut again, and the Shadow jerked her head back. She actually felt the whisper of air as the edge keened past her throat.

"Cuchulain," she breathed.

"Setanta!" he roared. "Cuchulain died on that Irish mountainside when you betrayed me."

A surge of anger roused Scathach. "I never betrayed you. Because of you, my sister and I haven't spoken in centuries. I loved you. I have always loved you. I still love you," she added in a raw whisper.

"I don't love you." He thrust with the sword. Scathach sidestepped and the blade punched straight through what was meant to be shatterproof glass. When he jerked the sword free, the entire window dissolved into glass pebbles.

Cuchulain pressed home his attack, hacking and cutting. He had been trained by the best—Scathach herself—and she struggled to parry and block. It was like fighting her mirror image. The force of the blows almost drove her to her knees, and the edges of her own swords were chipping and denting.

"I took you into my home, Cuchulain," Scathach said sadly. "I trained you to be the finest warrior in the known world. And I broke my own vow—never to fall in love with a human. I loved you, Cuchulain, with all my heart. There was nothing you couldn't do. Nothing you couldn't do. But you betrayed me and fell in love with my sister," she added bitterly, and her anger flowed through her sword. Suddenly she attacked in a blur of metal. Cuchulain's sword was ripped from his grasp and went clattering across the room.

Scathach sheathed her swords and turned to face the broken window, breathing in the crisp morning air. "The phone call was nothing more than a ruse to get me here, I take it?" she asked coolly.

"You're the one who taught me to bring my enemies to my ground, to fight them on my terms. I've been hunting you for a thousand years."

"I did teach you that." Gripping the window frame, the Shadow looked out over the wakening city. She could hear car horns now, and the first white contrails from the early-morning flights were visible in the skies over Nevada. "Did I ever mean anything to you?" she asked.

Setanta hesitated a fraction before responding. "Once, perhaps, when I was young and knew no better."

"And now?"

"Now you mean nothing to me," he said cruelly.

"I don't believe that," she said wistfully.

"It's true, Shadow. You failed me and I became an immortal slave to a monster. In time, I too became a monster, a master of blood drinkers and flesh eaters."

"You became what you were meant to be," Scathach murmured. "You fulfilled your destiny."

"And now it's time to fulfill yours—it is time to die, Shadow."

Scathach turned.

Setanta was standing in the center of the room, holding a spear as tall as he was. The head of the spear was a pyramid-shaped wedge of barbed and hooked metal. The shaft was a pale white bone. "Recognize this?" he asked.

"The Gáe Bolga," she whispered. The Death Spear. She hadn't seen the legendary weapon in millennia. Any wound from this weapon—no matter how minor—was fatal. "I gave that to you a long time ago." She turned back to the window as if unconcerned. "What will you do when you kill me, Cuchulain?"

"I am Setanta," he insisted. "There is a war coming, Shadow. The Elders will reclaim this Shadowrealm. I have been told to build a vampyre army, to create legions of cucubuths and hold them in readiness to unleash them on San Francisco and Los Angeles. When the war is over, I will control the entire West Coast of America."

"You could stand against them and fight with me," she suggested. "We've faced down monsters before."

"I prefer the winning side."

"Did you ever wonder why I loved you, Cuchulain?" Scathach asked.

"Everyone loved me," he said arrogantly.

"I loved you because I once saw in you the very best of the new human race. But that love blinded me to what you really were."

Setanta ignored her words. Drawing back his arm, he flung the Gáe Bolga. It screamed through the air. "Time to die."

"Time to die," Scathach echoed. Without looking around, she stepped to the side, caught the spear in midair, turned and flung it back at the young man.

Setanta managed a single horrified scream before the spear took him high in the chest. The weapon vibrated, the bone-white shaft shimmering with bands of color. Setanta's golden hair turned gray, then white. His smooth skin ran with wrinkles. "You said you loved me . . . ," he breathed.

The Shadow's face was a mask. "I loved Cuchulain, but you're Setanta." She clapped her hands sharply together and the man exploded into fine white powder. For a single moment, a cloud hung in the center of the room, a vaguely man-shaped outline in dust.

The door burst open and Billy the Kid appeared. The sudden draft of air sent the powder curling past Scathach, through the broken window and out into the morning air.

Billy was red-faced and gasping and his entire body was covered in filthy gray-black grit. "You okay?" he wheezed.

"Fine." She turned back to the window and watched the Crow Goddess swoop over the city, following the almost invisible twist of dust in the air.

"Did you find what you were looking for?"

Scathach crossed the floor and lifted the Gáe Bolga, tapping the head against her boot. "In a manner of speaking."

"And the person you came to rescue?"

"Set free," she said. She looked Billy up and down. "I am pleased that you survived."

"I'm rather pleased myself." Billy grinned. "The vampyres were so intent on fighting me, they forgot about the sun!" He brushed some of the filthy grit off his clothes. "You should have seen it. One moment they were getting set to eat me and the next it looked like an explosion in a flour factory!"

"And then you raced up here to rescue me," Scathach teased.

Beneath the gritty ash, Billy the Kid's cheeks flared crimson.

The Shadow squeezed his shoulder hard. "You remind me of someone I knew a long time ago."

19

"You never did tell me what's in the jar I delivered," Billy said as they pulled out of the garage.

Scathach nodded. "Yes. The jar. Have you ever heard of Pandora's Box?"

"Sure," the Kid answered, then jerked his thumb behind him toward the trunk of the car. "But that's a jar, not a box."

Scathach smiled, showing her vampire teeth. "Well, *pithos* was a bad translation. It doesn't mean 'box.' It means 'jar.'"

"So we just drove to Las Vegas with all the evils in the world in the trunk of my car?"

Scathach nodded happily. "I could hardly leave it at the dojo. Someone might have opened it."

Billy shook his head and let out a sigh. "All the evils of the world," he murmured. "Can I ask what you're going to do with them?"

"I was going to lock them away where they would never be found. . . ."

"But I'm guessing you've changed your mind," Billy said.

The Shadow smiled. She dropped her mirrored aviators

onto her face. "There's a Shadowrealm I'm going to release them into. It's the home of the Elder, Crom Cruach." She paused and added hesitantly, "You could tag along if you like. It'll be dangerous." She turned to look at him and peered over the top of her glasses. "It might even be fun."

Acknowledgments

Surrounding every writer is a support network of family and friends, fans and professionals, who contribute in so many ways, seen and unseen, to the finished work.

Beyond a shadow of a doubt, this book would not exist would the continued and continuous support of Beverly Horowitz and the endless patience of Krista Marino at Delacorte Press. The Flamels could ask for no better advocates. I am always grateful to Colleen Fellingham for her precision editing and extraordinary memory.

Barry Krost at BKM will be embarrassed to find himself here, but Mr Flamel's adventures started with him a long time ago. It is appropriate to include the Saturday crowd with him: John Deshane, Nat Segaloff, and Ed Tinney.

I am pleased that so many of the people I thanked at the end of the last book remain friends, with some new additions. So, in alphabetical order (so there is no fighting): Kelli Bixler, Dick Cook, Julie Blewett-Grant, Hannah Hill, Susan Jaffee, Alex Gogan, Lydia Gregovic, Patrick Kavanagh, O.R. Melling, Pat Neal and, of course, Melanie Rose.

I've forgotten someone. I know I have, and if it's you, then I do apologize!

BEGIN READING

THE SECRETS OF THE IMMORTAL NICHOLAS FLAMEL SERIES NOW

Turn the page to start the adventure!

I am legend.

Death has no claim over me, illness cannot touch me. Look at me now and it would be hard to put an age upon me, and yet I was born in the Year of Our Lord 1330, more than six hundred and seventy years ago.

I have been many things in my time: a physician and a cook, a bookseller and a soldier, a teacher of languages and chemistry, both an officer of the law and a thief.

But before all these I was an alchemyst. I was *the* Alchemyst.

I was acknowledged as the greatest Alchemyst of all, sought after by kings and princes, by emperors and even the Pope himself. I could turn ordinary metal into gold, I could change common stones into precious jewels. More than this: I discovered the secret of Life Eternal hidden deep in a book of ancient magic.

Now my wife, Perenelle, has been kidnapped and the book stolen.

Without the book, she and I will age. Within the full cycle of the moon, we will wither and die. And if we die, then the evil we have so long fought against will triumph. The Elder Race will reclaim this Earth again, and they will wipe humanity from the face of this planet.

But I will not go down without a fight.

For I am the immortal Nicholas Flamel.

From the Day Booke of Nicholas Flamel, Alchemyst
Writ this day, Thursday, 31st May, in
San Francisco, my adopted city

THURSDAY, 31st May

CHAPTER ONE

"*OK*—answer me this: why would anyone want to wear an overcoat in San Francisco in the middle of summer?" Sophie Newman pressed her fingers against the Bluetooth earpiece as she spoke.

On the other side of the continent, her fashion-conscious friend Elle inquired matter-of-factly, "What sort of coat?"

Wiping her hands on the cloth tucked into her apron strings, Sophie moved out from behind the counter of the empty coffee shop and stepped up to the window, watching men emerge from the car across the street. "Heavy black wool overcoats. They're even wearing black gloves and hats. And sunglasses." She pressed her face against the glass. "Even for this city, that's just a little *too* weird."

"Maybe they're undertakers?" Elle suggested, her voice popping and clicking on the cell phone. Sophie could hear something loud and dismal playing in the background—Lacrimosa maybe, or Amorphis. Elle had never quite got over her Goth phase.

"Maybe," Sophie answered, sounding unconvinced. She'd been chatting on the phone with her friend when, a few moments earlier, she'd spotted the unusual-looking car. It was long and sleek and looked as if it belonged in an old black-and-white movie. As it drove past the window, sunlight reflected off the blacked-out windows, briefly illuminating the interior of the coffee shop in warm yellow-gold light, blinding Sophie. Blinking away the black spots dancing before her eyes, she watched as the car turned at the bottom of the hill and slowly returned. Without signaling, it pulled over directly in front of The Small Book Shop, right across the street.

"Maybe they're Mafia," Elle suggested dramatically. "My dad knows someone in the Mafia. But he drives a Prius," she added.

"This is most definitely not a Prius," Sophie said, looking again at the car and the two large men standing on the street bundled up in their heavy overcoats, gloves and hats, their eyes hidden behind overlarge sunglasses.

"Maybe they're just cold," Elle suggested. "Doesn't it get cool in San Francisco?"

Sophie Newman glanced at the clock and thermometer on the wall over the counter behind her. "It's two-fifteen here . . . and eighty-one degrees," she said. "Trust me, they're not cold. They must be dying. Wait," she said, interrupting herself, "something's happening."

The rear door opened and another man, even larger than

the first two, climbed stiffly out of the car. As he closed the door, sunlight briefly touched his face and Sophie caught a glimpse of pale, unhealthy-looking gray-white skin. She adjusted the volume on the earpiece. "OK. You should see what just climbed out of the car. A huge guy with gray skin. Gray. That might explain it; maybe they have some type of skin condition."

"I saw a National Geographic documentary about people who can't go out in the sun . . . ," Elle began, but Sophie was no longer listening to her.

A fourth figure stepped out of the car.

He was a small, rather dapper-looking man, dressed in a neat charcoal-gray three-piece suit that looked vaguely old-fashioned but that she could tell had been tailor-made for him. His iron gray hair was pulled back from an angular face into a tight ponytail, while a neat triangular beard, mostly black but flecked with gray, concealed his mouth and chin. He moved away from the car and stepped under the striped awning that covered the trays of books outside the shop. When he picked up a brightly colored paperback and turned it over in his hands, Sophie noticed that he was wearing gray gloves. A pearl button at the wrist winked in the light.

"They're going into the bookshop," she said into her earpiece.

"Is Josh still working there?" Elle immediately asked.

Sophie ignored the sudden interest in her friend's voice. The fact that her best friend liked her twin brother was just a little too weird. "Yeah. I'm going to call him to see what's up. I'll call you right back." She hung up, pulled out the earpiece and absently rubbed her hot ear as she stared, fascinated, at the small man. There was something about him . . . something *odd*. Maybe he was a fashion designer, she thought, or a movie producer, or maybe he was an author—she'd noticed that some authors liked to dress up in peculiar outfits. She'd give him a few minutes to get into the shop, then she'd call her twin for a report.

Sophie was about to turn away when the gray man suddenly spun around and seemed to stare directly at her. As he stood under the awning, his face was in shadow, and yet for just the briefest instant, his eyes looked as if they were glowing.

Sophie knew—*just knew*—that there was no possible way for the small gray man to see her: she was standing on the opposite side of the street behind a pane of glass that was bright with reflected early-afternoon sunlight. She would be invisible in the gloom behind the glass.

And yet . . .

And yet in that single moment when their eyes met, Sophie felt the tiny hairs on the back of her hands and along her forearms tingle and felt a puff of cold air touch the back of her neck. She rolled her shoulders, turning her head slightly from side to side, strands of her long blond hair curling across her cheek. The contact lasted only a second before the small man looked away, but Sophie got the impression that he had looked directly at her.

In the instant before the gray man and his three overdressed companions disappeared into the bookshop, Sophie decided that she did not like him.

✧   ✧   ✧

Peppermint.

And rotten eggs.

"That is just vile." Josh Newman stood in the center of the bookstore's cellar and breathed deeply. Where *were* those smells coming from? He looked around at the shelves stacked high with books and wondered if something had crawled in behind them and died. What else would account for such a foul stink? The tiny cramped cellar always smelled dry and musty, the air heavy with the odors of parched curling paper, mingled with the richer aroma of old leather bindings and dusty cobwebs. He loved the smell; he always thought it was warm and comforting, like the scents of cinnamon and spices that he associated with Christmas.

Peppermint.

Sharp and clean, the smell cut through the close cellar atmosphere. It was the odor of new toothpaste or those herbal teas his sister served in the coffee shop across the street. It sliced though the heavier smells of leather and paper, and was so strong that it made his sinuses tingle; he felt as if he was going to sneeze at any moment. He quickly pulled out his iPod earbuds. Sneezing with headphones on was not a good idea: made your ears pop.

Eggs.

Foul and stinking—he recognized the sulfurous odor of rotten eggs. It blanketed the clear odor of mint . . . and it was disgusting. He could feel the stench coating his tongue and lips, and his scalp began to itch as if something were crawling through it. Josh ran his fingers through his shaggy blond hair and shuddered. The drains must be backing up.

Leaving the earbuds dangling over his shoulders, he checked the book list in his hand, then looked at the shelves again: *The Complete Works of Charles Dickens,* twenty-seven volumes, red leather binding. Now where was he going to find that?

Josh had been working in the bookshop for nearly two months and still didn't have the faintest idea where anything was. There was no filing system . . . or rather, there *was* a system, but it was known only to Nick and Perry Fleming, the owners of The Small Book Shop. Nick or his wife could put their hands on any book in either the shop upstairs or the cellar in a matter of minutes.

A wave of peppermint, immediately followed by rotten eggs, filled the air again; Josh coughed and felt his eyes water. This was impossible! Stuffing the book list into one pocket of his jeans and the headphones into the other, he maneuvered his way through the piled books and stacks of boxes, heading for the stairs. He couldn't spend another minute down there with the smell. He rubbed the heels of his palms against his eyes, which were now stinging furiously. Grabbing the stair rail, he pulled himself up. He needed a breath of fresh air or he was going to throw up—but, strangely, the closer he came to the top of the stairs, the stronger the odors became.

He popped his head out of the cellar door and looked around.

And in that instant, Josh Newman realized that the world would never be the same again.

About the Author

An authority on mythology and folklore, Michael Scott is one of Ireland's most successful authors. A master of fantasy, science fiction, horror, and folklore, he was hailed by the *Irish Times* as "the King of Fantasy in these isles." Look for the six books in his *New York Times* bestselling The Secrets of the Immortal Nicholas Flamel series: *The Alchemyst, The Magician, The Sorceress, The Necromancer, The Warlock,* and *The Enchantress.*

dillonscott.com